Praise for the Texas Red River Mysteries

Gold Dust
The Seventh Texas Red River Mystery

"Richly enjoyable...reads like a stranger-than-strange collaboration between Lee Child, handling the assault on the CIA with baleful directness, and Steven F. Havill, genially reporting on the regulars back home."

—*Kirkus Reviews*

"It's a pleasure to watch [Constable Ned Parker and Texas Ranger Tom Bell] deal with orneriness as well as just plain evil. Readers nostalgic for this period will find plenty to like."

—*Publishers Weekly*

"Reading the seventh Red River Mystery is like coming home after a vacation: we're reuniting with old friends and returning to a comfortable place. Wortham's writing style is easygoing, relying on natural-sounding dialogue and vivid descriptions to give us the feeling that this story could well have taken place. Another fine entry in a mystery series that deserves more attention."

—*Booklist*

Unraveled
The Sixth Texas Red River Mystery

"This superbly drawn sixth entry in the series features captivating characters and an authentic Texas twang."

—*Library Journal*

"Not only does Wortham write exceptionally well, but he somehow manages to infuse *Unraveled* with a Southern gothic feel that would make even William Faulkner proud... A hidden gem of a book that reads like Craig Johnson's Longmire mysteries on steroids."

—*Providence Journal*

Dark Places
The Fifth Texas Red River Mystery

"Readers will cheer for and ache with the good folks, and secondary characters hold their own... The novel's short chapters fit both the fast pace and the deftly spare actions and details... the rhythm of Wortham's writing, transporting us back in time, soon takes hold and is well worth the reader's efforts."

—*Historical Novel Society*

Vengeance is Mine
The Fourth Texas Red River Mystery

"Very entertaining... This is a fully self-contained story, and it's a real corker."

—*Booklist*, Starred Review

The Right Side of Wrong
The Third Texas Red River Mystery

"A sleeper that deserves wider attention."

—*New York Times*

"Wortham's third entry in his addictive Texas procedural series set in the 1960s is a deceptively meandering tale of family and country life bookended by a dramatic opening and conclusion. C. J. Box fans would like this title."

—*Library Journal*, Starred Review

Burrows
The Second Texas Red River Mystery

"Wortham's outstanding sequel to *The Rock Hole* (2011)... combines the gonzo sensibility of Joe R. Lansdale and the elegiac mood of *To Kill a Mockingbird* to strike just the right balance between childhood innocence and adult horror."

—*Publishers Weekly*, Starred Review

"The cinematic characters have substance and a pulse. They walk off the page and talk Texas."

—*Dallas Morning News*

The Rock Hole
The First Texas Red River Mystery

One of the 12 best novels of 2011—*Kirkus Reviews*

"An accomplished first novel about life and murder in a small Texas town... Wortham tells a story of grace under pressure...a fast and furious climax, written to the hilt, harrowing in its unpredictability. There's a lot of good stuff in this unpretentious gem. Don't miss it."

—*Kirkus Reviews*

LAYING BONES

LAYING BONES

A TEXAS RED RIVER MYSTERY

REAVIS Z. WORTHAM

Poisoned Pen
PRESS

Published by Poisoned Pen Press, an imprint of Sourcebooks
P.O. Box 4410, Naperville, Illinois 60567-4410
(630) 961-3900
sourcebooks.com

Library of Congress Cataloging-in-Publication Data

Names: Wortham, Reavis Z., author.
Title: Laying bones / Reavis Z. Wortham.
Description: Naperville, Illinois : Poisoned Pen Press, an imprint of
   Sourcebooks, [2021]
Identifiers: LCCN 2020018080 (print) Subjects:
GSAFD: Mystery fiction. | Suspense fiction.
Classification: LCC PS3623.O777 L39 2021 (print) | DDC 813/.6--dc23
LC record available at https://lccn.loc.gov/2020018080

Printed and bound in the United States of America.
SB 10 9 8 7 6 5 4 3 2 1

This one is for my first cousin, Roger Wade Armstrong (November 28, 1957–January 22, 2020), a lifelong friend, hunting and fishing partner, and the inspiration for Pepper in the Texas Red River Mystery series. It was Roger who gave me the idea for this novel, and I'm deeply sorry he never saw it. Hoss, your passing left a huge hole in our lives, and I miss your voice and that distinctive laugh.

"Yesterday's gone on down the river and you can't get it back."

–LARRY MCMURTRY, LONESOME DOVE

FOREWORD

This is a work of fiction inspired by a tragedy that occurred in Lamar County back in 1964. I took what I recalled as a child, mixed it with a few geographical possibilities, and wove this tale that I hope entertains, but is in no way an explanation or supposition for what happened that night. I use R. B.'s real name to honor my dad's cousin and best friend. They shared adventures both in the river bottoms of their youth, and as part of the U.S. military's occupation of Japan. Boy, there were some stories that came out of that experience.

Most of us think the Red River is the true border between much of Texas and Oklahoma, but if you carefully examine a detailed map, you'll find the river has shifted through the decades, leaving slivers of orphan land in both states. To my knowledge, no one has ever tried to build on what usually amounts to sandbars, but as usual, I wondered "what if" and let the story take me away.

Chapter One

I rode against the passenger door in the front seat of my cousin's midnight blue 1964 Comet, watching the headlights cut through the cold darkness. Curtis was five years older than me, with brown hair that swept down above one eye and curled over his collar. His girlfriend, Sheila, sat right up against him and, despite her dress, rode with her left foot tucked under her right thigh. Her poufy blond beehive doo had so much Aqua Net in it, I was afraid she'd knock Curtis out if she turned her head too fast.

He didn't seem to mind that a knee was against the big steering wheel half the time, because Curtis drove with his hand resting inside the crook of her bare-nekked leg. Uncle Cody told me there was a big difference between naked and nekked.

Naked is when you're doing something you're supposed to, like taking a bath or jumping in the Rock Hole for a swim. Nekked is when you're doing something you're not supposed to, like Curtis with his hand cupping her thigh. Sheila was also what Miss Becky called blessed, which meant she had a set of ta-tas on her like I'd never seen on a young girl before. She wore her dresses cut low, and I tried not to look at the tops of her snow-white boobs in the dashboard lights.

My near twin cousin, Pepper, snuggled up with Mark in the back seat, making me the fifth wheel once again. I started to get in the back with them when we left the show, but Pepper jumped in after him and locked the doors. "Ride up there in the front with them."

"But there's more room for the three of us in the back. You're dang near gonna sit in his lap anyway."

"Yeah, but we want to be *alone* back here."

Mark had a strange look on his face, half grin, half embarrassed. I didn't want to argue there on the street in front of the Plaza Theater, so I rode home up front.

We'd been to Chisum that Friday night to see *Hellfighters*, John Wayne's new movie. Just out of the blue that afternoon, Curtis called to see if the three of us wanted to go to the show with him. I knew good and well he didn't invite us out of the goodness of his heart. It was his way of getting his new girlfriend into Uncle Ned's sights, hoping he and Miss Becky would approve. For some reason he needed them to say they liked Sheila.

There wasn't much chance of that because she was a little on the wild side. She sure wasn't hard to look at, but there was something about that gal that just wasn't right. She seemed plastic somehow, all painted up with too much makeup, lipstick, and nail polish. I could tell Pepper liked what she saw, though, because she'd started to paint her own chewed-off fingernails, and even her toes.

Now, Pepper had no intention of being a girly-girl. She's always been a rough-as-a-cob tomboy hippie and dressed like one from the time she was big enough to walk, but she'd been paying more and more attention to her looks. She'd wear makeup if she could get away with it, but Miss Becky'd have a rigor if anyone brought it up.

Instead, Pepper made do with feathers in her hair, one given to her by an Indian boy in New Mexico. She'd also talked about getting her ears pierced, but that was another round with both her mama, Aunt Ida Belle, and Miss Becky.

We chased our headlights through the dark and passed a fresh-killed armadillo on the shoulder. Curtis laughed. "Did y'all know ever third armadillo is born full-growed and dead on the side of the road? I heard 'em called rats on the half shell."

He laughed, and it took me a minute to realize what he'd said was a joke.

Sheila turned up the volume on the radio. "Born to be Wild" by Steppenwolf roared out of the metal dash's one speaker. Pepper grabbed the back seat and leaned forward. "I *love* that song! Turn it up and pull over! Pull over!"

Caught up in her excitement, Curtis whipped onto the two-lane's shoulder, and Pepper jumped out in the cold air. "Turn it up!" She ran around into the headlights and started dancing like she had ants in her pants.

"Ain't she something?" Mark slid out and joined her.

Curtis cranked his window down so they could hear the music, and Sheila turned it up even louder. Mark and Pepper danced like lunatics in the icy north wind while cars passed, honking their horns in fun. I stayed right where I was and adjusted the heater vent to keep warm. There was no way I was going to get out and dance on the side of the highway in the wintertime, and maybe get run over to be a Top-on-a-half-shell.

"Come on!" Curtis popped his door open and grabbed Sheila's hand, dragging her out under the steering wheel. A car swerved to miss 'em, tires squalling. The driver honked loud and long. Neither of those dopes paid him any attention, and, before you knew it, they were dancing in the headlights too. I kept an eye through the rear glass, hoping the passing cars wouldn't hit them or the Comet.

The song ended and they all jumped back in the car with cold radiating off their clothes. Doors slammed and Curtis stomped the foot-feed, throwing rocks from under the back tires. "That was a *blast*. Hey, now I'm in the mood for some fun. Let's swing across to Juarez, and I'll get some beer before I take y'all home." He glanced across Sheila's good-sized blessings at me. "Whadda ya say?"

Juarez was the name of the cluster of mean, cinderblock honky-tonks lining the two-lane on the Oklahoma side of the Red River. Seven joints were on the east side for easy access from Texas patrons. The roughest club of all was two miles farther north. Originally a poor man's version of a rural country club, the TV Lounge had fallen onto hard times.

The only one not frequented by white patrons was a sad little joint called Patsy's, a gathering place for local blacks who weren't allowed to mix with anyone else, not even the Indians. Choctaws, Cherokees, and a few Chickasaw Indians had their own joint in the rough country ten miles to the west of Grant, but no Oklahoma lawman would go there on a bet. Fights, cuttings, and more than a few killings were handled by the Tribal Police, even though there was no true "reservation" in that area.

"Why don't you take us home first?" I didn't like the idea of waiting in the Comet. I'd heard stories about fights and killings over there in dirt lots and didn't want any part of it, even though it was likely that Curtis would swing into the Sportsman for his beer.

Uncle Cody'd owned it for a good long while, but he finally sold the club before Christmas because he was sheriff of Lamar County. It was a stick in Grandpa's eye that Uncle Cody even *owned* a beer joint in the first place, although he called himself a silent partner in the business, but Grandpa still wasn't over his mad.

Pepper piped up in the back seat. "Sounds like a deal to me, as long as you let *me* have a sip."

The top of her dress pulled tight and straining the buttons, Sheila hung an elbow over the back of the seat. "Honey, you're not old enough to drink."

I tried not to look at the eighteen-year-old coming out of both the top and bottom of her clothes, with bare legs glowing and the possibility of her blessings popping out like dough from a busted can of biscuits. Instead, I stared straight ahead, listening to the bite of Pepper's voice.

"Neither are you, Sheila Cunningham, but I bet it won't slow you down none. I just want one sip. I like that first bitter taste in my mouth."

I sat there studying on when Pepper might have tasted beer when Curtis turned east onto the last county road before we crossed the river bridge into Oklahoma. The eastbound two-lane led us into deeper darkness, and we drove downriver. Curtis mashed the dimmer switch with his foot and in the brighter beam we got a wider view of pastures and trees lining both sides of the road.

Hereford cows watched us pass from behind sagging bobwire fences. I'd never been on that side of Highway 271 and there wasn't a dern thing that looked familiar. "Where are we going?"

"To a new place I heard about." Curtis slowed, and I realized he was looking for a turnoff.

"All the joints are on the Oklahoma side of the river, dummy."

He glanced up at Pepper in the rearview mirror and I wished he'd keep his eyes on the road. I'd heard about a feller who rolled his car off in a ditch over in Red River County and was pinned in his car for three days before anyone found him. He said he had nothing to eat but a box of Luden's cough drops, and I didn't want to die with that artificial cherry taste in my mouth.

Curtis tapped his brakes a couple of times and saw what he was looking for. "There. That's the turnoff." A single reflector on a bodark fence post was what he'd been looking for.

It was nothing but a bobwire gap, like every other gate in the county. I hated those cheap, aggravatin' gates. I had to wrestle them out of the way whenever Grandpa Ned went to feed in the mornings. But this time, instead of being wired up tight against the gatepost like ours, it was thrown loose in the dead grass inside the pasture.

My heart beat ninety to nothing. We were heading through absolute darkness, down a pasture road leading to a glow on the river that felt dangerous as a rattlesnake. Mark didn't like it any better'n I did.

He leaned forward in the seat. "Curtis, you trying to find a bootlegger? We don't want to be messin' with nobody like that."

"Naw, and what you don't know is that we won't be in Texas no more in about a minute."

"What?" Pepper popped up. "There ain't no bridges up in here."

"You're right about that. But folks think the river is the border all the way to Louisiana, and the truth is that the Oklahoma line sometimes cuts off the river and through some of these pastures, just like the one we're in. The river twisted out of its banks back in sixty-four, and left a little sliver of Oklahoma *south* of the river. Up there in a couple of hundred yards, we cross out of Texas. Their stupid laws in this county don't apply here."

The dirt lane threaded through a thick stand of trees growing up on a fencerow and into a second pasture. Straight ahead was a single pole light over a building hanging halfway out over the river, thirteen feet down below.

A blue-and-yellow neon sign looking like a star in a George Jetson cartoon glowed high overhead. It read "Starlite," and

I couldn't help but like it, because lines radiated out from the words, reminding me of Miss Becky's atomic plates with blue stars.

It was funny. George Jones singing "The Honky Tonk Downstairs" came on at the exact same time. My head swam for a moment and I was afraid my Poisoned Gift was going to wake up.

Sometimes I get this feeling of déjà vu, and then my head goes to spinning and I have to lay down if I can. Usually when that happens, I'm out for only a couple of seconds before waking up feeling like I'd rested for days. Other times the feeling is stronger, and I have visions.

Moonlight sparkled off the Red River behind the joint. Our headlights reflected off dozens of cars parked in ragged lines. The building wasn't like the dirty, toady joints I was used to seeing on the highway. The paint on the exterior was so fresh it looked wet. The word "cultured" popped into my mind, though in my opinion, the only culture we had in Lamar County was linen napkins at Reeve's Family Restaurant in Chisum.

Mark whistled low and long. "This place is brand new."

"You bet." Curtis's voice was full of importance. "This is the new, happenin' place. It's only been open a couple of months." He left the engine running. "I'll be right back. Y'all stay in here while I'm gone, and lock the doors."

Sheila slapped the lock button when he got out and adjusted the radio dial to clear the static out of the song. I got a glimpse in the crowded bar when Curtis went inside. I was nervous as a cat in a doghouse in that parking lot and like to have jumped out of my skin when Pepper's arm pointed over my shoulder toward the front windshield.

"There's Uncle Neal. What's he doing here?"

Neal Box, the owner of our little country store in Center

Springs, was threading his way through the cars and trucks with his skinny wife, Clarice. They both looked out of place, because the only time I ever saw them was in their store, or at funerals, but it was obvious they knew where they were going. Instead of going in the front, they followed a long wooden porch wrapping around the building and over the river. He knocked on a door near the back and it opened in a spill of light and a cloud of blue smoke.

Mark's voice came from the back. "He likes to shoot dice."

He had my attention. "Uncle Neal don't gamble."

"Sure does. Miss Clarice always goes with him to make sure he don't lose all their money. She just watches and drinks beer, but they used to go over to the Texoma Club when I was living over there with my aunt and her sorry-assed husband."

I had to study on that one for a minute. A brief image of her sipping beer through a paper straw popped into my head. "How do you know that?"

"Everybody knows on *that* side of the river. They just don't talk about it in Center Springs. I'll wager even Miss Becky knows, though she won't never say nothin' about it."

Cold air again flooded inside when Pepper yanked the door handle. "I gotta see this."

"Don't." Sheila whipped around and grabbed at her arm with a look of sheer terror on her face. I saw who she was at that moment. Instead of a woman under all that makeup, her little girl's expression told me the plastic I'd noticed was just a shell. She was a kid who wanted to be an adult.

Pepper didn't give a hoot'n hell, though. In many ways, she was older and tougher than Sheila. She yanked her arm free. "I want to see what's going on in there."

Mark slid out behind her, his long black hair flowing like water to his shoulders. Because he was Choctaw, he was the only boy in our school with hair like that, though for the life of me I'll never know why everyone tolerated it with him and nobody else. "I'll show you but stay in the shadows. We don't want anybody to see us."

Mark was always afraid that he'd do something to mess up his new life living with us. We were brothers and buddies, and I knew the fear he carried, but he was crazy about Pepper for reasons I couldn't begin to understand and followed her everywhere like a little puppy dog.

He took her hand, casting a wide arc outside of the glow from the neon sign and the light from fixtures set on the wraparound porch's walls.

All of a sudden, I found myself following them, though I don't remember getting out. It was one of those moments that change your life, and instinct told me something was going to happen.

We passed two dozen parked cars with frosted windshields that glittered like diamonds in the honky- tonk's lights. One car with fogged windows was running, white smoke coming from the tailpipe. Inside I could see the glow of the radio in the dash, and muffled music. As we passed, a small woman's hand in the back seat pressed against the glass, leaving a wet smear that ran with water. I caught a clear glimpse of a blond head, low against the door. Her face tilted upward, and I looked at her at the same time the Starlite sign briefly lit a young man's face. For a moment my eyes met theirs before I looked away.

They laughed, and, embarrassed by what I'd seen, I hurried to catch up with the others. The club's front door opened, and two men came outside, followed by Buck Owens's voice singing that he had a tiger by the tail. They must've had one heck of a jukebox in there for the music to be so loud. The song cut off quick when the door closed behind them.

A brand-new 1969 Ford Galaxie was parked at the corner of the building. I caught up with Mark and Pepper behind the gold-colored sedan just as the side door opened again. It must have been hot inside, because a man in khakis and rolled-up shirtsleeves stood there, fanning the door to get some air.

It reminded me of when we had to go to the storm cellar. The women and kids always lined the bench seats along both sides of the hole in the ground that smelled like raw earth. The men sat on the wooden steps, opening and closing the door both for ventilation from the coal oil lamps that gave us light, and to keep an eye on the storm itself.

I figured they needed air in the same way, because enough smoke boiled out of that side door that it looked like the honky-tonk was on fire.

Bigger than I thought, the room built out over the steep riverbank took up the back quarter of the building. Despite the cold, a handful of young people sat in the shadows on the back railing, their feet hanging out over the water far below. One of them glanced around and I recognized Gus Davis in the light. Even though he was a senior, he didn't come to school very much. Beside him with his arm around Gus's shoulder was a kid I didn't know.

I wondered what Gus got out of hanging around out back, but one of the others sitting on the railing tilted a bottle, and I realized they were likely close to the same age and had talked someone into buying them beer.

Inside, cigarette smoke hung low over a long, strange-looking table lit by a colorful billiard light. A crowd of men gathered around and there was a lot of jostling for a minute before everyone leaned forward. The crowd hollered and they backed away.

Boxes and crates were stacked head-high against the walls,

but even though it looked like a storeroom, the folks in there were having a high old time, laughing and yelling. Rough tables and chairs were full of people with drinks in front of them.

More happy yelling came through the door in a wave, along with a couple of groans. In the far corner Miss Clarice sat at a tall table with another woman who was poured into a candy-apple-red dress. They were surrounded by cases of beer and boxes with labels of W.L. Weller, Jim Beam, and J&B Scotch.

Two men, one in khakis and the other wearing slacks, stepped back from the table. Heads together, they talked. The one wearing slacks nodded and split and spoke to the man holding the door open. Both of them looked back toward the long table, and Slacks smoothed his slick-backed hair as he stepped outside to light a cigarette.

He had a big nose, undershot chin, and ears like the open doors on a Buick. The word *Italian* filled my mind, along with a flash like light glinting off polished metal. It was my Poisoned Gift, but it only lasted a second and was gone.

"Hot damn!" A familiar voice drifted out the door, and one of the men at the table stepped back. Cousin R. B. Parker laughed and slapped a blond man on the shoulder. R. B.'s hand was full of bills and he whooped. "I'm hot tonight! Shut that damned door before these dice cool off."

The last thing I saw before the door closed were those two men exchanging glances and then Slacks slapped the Italian in khakis on the shoulder and they slipped back inside.

"We just looked into hell." Pepper's words were startling.

Mark took her hand. "We've seen enough, too. Let's go."

We followed the same route back to the car, and Curtis was already behind the wheel and mad as an old wet hen. "I told y'all to stay in here. You kids don't have no business running around in these parking lots."

"I told them to stay, but they wouldn't listen." Sheila's expression was dark, and I knew she was scared.

Pepper flipped him the bird and got inside. "Chill, pill. You weren't too worried about bringing kids here in the first place, so screw you."

Doors slammed, and I kicked a six-pack of beer sitting in the floorboard. Curtis started the engine and pulled out of the lot. "Damn. I don't know what woulda happened if y'all'd got caught or hurt. Don't never do nothing like that again. Sheila, crack me one of them beers and let's get out of here."

The joint's front door opened just as Curtis shifted into gear. A crowd of men boiled outside, following two rawboned guys who looked like they were so mad they could spit nails.

One had a jean jacket on and wore a felt hat. The other'n was bareheaded and in his shirtsleeves. Hat stopped and Bare Head planted a foot and whirled around, throwing a roundhouse fist that looked to be as slow as molasses.

It must have been faster than it looked because Bare Head's fist nearly took Hat's head off his shoulders. I'd have gone down like a poleaxed steer, but he just rocked back. They tangled like two cur dogs as the crowd of onlookers closed in and blocked everything from sight.

As if he saw such a thing every day, Curtis steered away from the fight, and Sheila used a church key to lever two holes in the top of a Schlitz. She handed it to Curtis, and he took a swallow before holding it over his shoulder. "Here you go, Pepper. Have that sip."

It was quiet in the back seat for a long beat. "I've changed my mind."

"Suit yourself." Sheila was back up against him again when Curtis steered us back across the pasture. He drove faster than when we came in, and before I knew it, turned right on the county road. He dug in his shirt pocket and held up a hand-rolled cigarette with the ends twisted tight "Look what else I got. There's two more in there to go with it."

Sheila leaned forward to see in the dim light and laughed. "Looks like we're gonna get *high* tonight! Y'all sure you don't want to go with us?"

I glanced across Pepper to see Mark shaking his head on the other side. "None of us smoke grass."

"Suit yourself," Sheila repeated. "It'll be *our* party."

Ten minutes later, the three of us kids got out at our house, and the porch light came on.

Grandpa's car was gone, which meant he was off doing constable work. Miss Becky opened the screen door, standing there in her long nightgown with the dark kitchen behind her.

Curtis backed out and waved through his open window. "Night, Miss Becky!"

We were already on the porch when he pulled down the gravel drive. She waved thanks to Curtis and held the screen open. "How was your picture show?"

Pepper answered. "John Wayne's always good."

I stopped for a moment and looked up at the bright stars above. A streak of light passed to the east and winked out as a shooting star burned up.

"Well, y'all get in here and out of that cold." Miss Becky closed the door behind us as Curtis pulled back out onto the highway. "I swear, I don't know how he can drive with that little gal settin' right under him."

Chapter Two

Fourteen-year-olds get a lot more freedom in the country than the city. Back then, it was nothing to see one of us driving a truck down the highway or a tractor in the field. I was lucky I didn't have to work the fields every weekend, but a lot of my friends were already putting in enough time to make full hands. Me and Mark were spoiled, for sure. Neither Miss Becky or Grandpa expected us to work all day when we weren't in school. Grandpa said that would come soon enough.

We had a lot of other freedoms, too. Raised on BB guns, it wasn't much of a step to using real rifles and shotguns. Grandpa and Uncle Cody made sure me and Mark knew the guns could kill, and they took us out hunting every chance they got. It wasn't long before we could take the .22 or the little .410 shotgun down to the pool to shoot frogs and snakes.

Once they taught us to handle guns and we got a little older, nobody said a word when we picked up a shotgun and really went huntin', or fishing for that matter. They were always happy to see quail, dove, or geese on the table, or fish in the summertime.

Quail season was still open, and when Saturday morning

came around, we were both up early to hunt. Pepper spent the night with us and slept on the couch, but you couldn't drag her out of the sheets that early with a team of matched mules. We left her with her head covered by a quilt to block out the light.

I had Grandpa's Browning 12-gauge, and Mark carried the old Remington pump that always stood behind the door. Being a lawman and all, Grandpa kept the shotguns loaded with double-ought buck, but we switched the paper shells out for brush load #8s.

A light frost covered the ground as we stepped off the porch and down the hill to a line of trees across the highway from the house. My breath fogged in the air, and the canvas coat full of shells hung warm and toasty over my shoulders. Spiderwebs laced with ice crystals sparkled in the early sun. Soft loam underfoot was springy once our shoes broke through the thin crust.

My Brittany spaniel, Hootie, worked the fencerows that frosty morning. Loping along the edge of the field, he paused, staring down the long slope leading to the Center Springs branch.

"Nope. We're not going that way today." I waved my arm like Grandpa and Uncle Cody when they're hunting with him. "Hie on that way."

Hootie didn't want to go east. Uncle Cody and Aunt Norma Faye lived only half a mile from where we were standing, and there was always something to eat there for him. I read his mind. "Nope."

Mark paused, thinking. "You know, I bet Aunt Norma Faye'll fry us up an egg or two if we go over there. I'm kinda hungry."

"You ate three biscuits with pear preserves already."

"They were yesterday's, and besides, my stomach's growling already."

"Let's make a loop first, then we can eat."

"You love to hunt more'n any other kid I know."

We made our way from the house and down to a faint cut through the pastures and under sagging bobwire fences. After the war, the state built a new two-lane hogback highway to pass around the other side of the hill our house sat on, and the road lined by old-growth trees was fenced off and forgotten.

We followed Hootie, who seemed more interested in sniffing dirt clods than finding birds. He led us to the two-lane bridge over Sanders Creek, a mile from the house. Overhead, black wings circled the sky above bare limbs reaching upward like tortured arms and hands.

Mark pointed at a fresh set of tire tracks through the grass. His voice was full of worry. "Somebody's drove off in here." The gurgling water drew us down the steep slope and we held on to tall, dead grass and brush to keep our footing. Pushing ahead, Mark forced his way through a tangle of briars and stopped at the sight of an upside-down '47 Chevrolet pickup on the far side of the creek bed.

They hadn't been letting much water out of the Lake Lamar dam and the creek was low, with only a little muddy water trickling around logs, mud bumps, and half-buried limbs. From there it was dry up to the highwater mark just below the grass.

The top of the roof was under only two or three inches of water meandering through the open driver's window and out the other. It had washed out a little hole on the downstream side that was the source of the gurgling sound.

I studied the wreck. "Didn't nobody call Grandpa last night."

"Nobody knows but us, or there'd be a crowd here already." Mark pointed across to the other bank and the tall bitterweeds and Johnson grass pushed down by the truck. "He went off over there. If you weren't paying any attention when you drove by, you'd miss it, or think those tracks were old. I don't believe you can even see it from the road, to tell the truth."

A long liquid rainbow flowed from the gas tank near the driver's door. The slight breeze shifted, bringing the thick, familiar smell of raw gasoline. Hootie loped down the bank, leaving footprints in the mud, and splashed through the shallow water to the truck. He worked himself around to the driver's door and whined. I was rooted to the ground, because there was something not right.

Mark figured it out quick. "He's still in there."

"What?"

"The driver. There ain't no tracks or footprints in the mud on that side, nor on this one either. Hootie smells him."

I didn't want to think of something like that. The truck looked familiar, but upside down, I couldn't place it. "Unless somebody stole the truck and then shoved it off the bank."

"Maybe." Digging his heels into the frosty ground, Mark took a couple of steps farther down. "All I see are tire tracks. See the front bumper nosed into the mud where the bank drops off sharp over there? That's what flipped the truck upside down."

"He might still be alive if he's in there."

"He'll be drunker'n Cooter Jones if he is."

We unloaded our shotguns and put the shells in our shooting vests, then picked our way down the steep bank. The flat creek bed wasn't as boggy as it looked, until we got to the middle. The soft mud nearly sucked the shoes off our feet and *would* have if we hadn't tied them on tight that morning. There was no way to go any farther after that. We turned around and crawled back up the bank.

A pickup passed on the bridge without slowing. I was only halfway to the top, but I hollered and waved one arm. The driver didn't hear me and was almost up to our house by the time we reached the top. Leaving muddy tracks on the concrete, we crossed to the other end of the bridge. I kept hoping somebody else would come by, but it was too early in the morning and folks had other business elsewhere.

We leaned our shotguns against the steel guardrails. The bank was even steeper on that side of the bridge, and my feet went out from under me halfway down. I landed hard enough on my butt to bite my tongue and bring tears to my eyes. Mark grabbed one of the saplings and lost his footing too. It held and he didn't land as hard.

"Part of the roof's crushed." Mark reached the truck, placed his feet where the ground looked the driest, and knelt down to look through the shattered windshield. "I can't see through the windshield. I smell whiskey, though. It was probably some drunk driving home from Juarez."

I went around to the other side of the pickup to a spit of land higher than the rest of the streambed. Grandpa would have called it a drop-off, and that's where the fish hang out when the water's high. It was firm enough for me to walk out to the passenger window that was rolled down, so I didn't have any broken glass to see through.

My breath caught when I knelt on one knee. I saw an arm and a pale hand. "Mark! There's somebody in here after all."

I gave up on trying to stay on the driest spots and stepped closer into the cold water that immediately filled my shoes. The hand was far enough inside that I had to drop down on both knees to reach in and pluck at the man's khaki sleeve. "Hey, mister. Are you all right? Wake up."

His arm was limp as a dishrag when I pulled it, the hand waxy white. "Mister, can you hear me?"

I knelt until my chest was almost touching the trickle and looked inside. Half of my cousin R. B.'s buttermilk-colored face was in the water. The one filmed-over eye above the waterline told me he was dead.

Chapter Three

Ike Reader's pickup rocketed up Ned's drive, throwing gravel into the pasture when he turned sharp to stop beside the porch steps. Already concerned when he saw the truck speeding up to the house, Ned's mouth went dry when he saw Top and Mark in the cab with the jerky little farmer. Hootie rode in the bed, head over the side and nose flaring to take the wind.

The International slid the last two feet when he slammed the brakes, and Ike was talking the minute his door popped open. "Ned, got some bad news for you."

The old constable slammed the screen door open, pulling a jacket on over his overalls. He was down the porch and reaching for the passenger door's handle as Ike came around the front fender. Knowing the boys had been out hunting, Ned was afraid they'd shot one another, or someone else.

The kids were white as sheets when he got a good look at their faces. "You boys all right? You hurt?"

Miss Becky hurried onto the porch, a cup towel she'd been using to dry dishes ready in hand to help if they were bleeding. Top was the first out, his muddy shoe missing the running board. He almost fell before Ned caught his arm. The asthmatic fourteen-year-old had to catch his breath before he could answer in a wheeze. "R. B.'s dead."

"That's what I was a-tellin' you." Ike stopped in front of the truck, talking louder than necessary. "The boys say it's R. B., drowned down by the creek bridge."

Miss Becky threw her hands in the air and recoiled, her shocked expression blurring the familiarity of her features. For a moment, she looked like a stranger. "Naw he ain't. Y'all don't know that!"

Ned's stomach sank at the news. R. B. Parker was his nephew, the son of his youngest brother Joe. It took a few seconds for the news to soak in as Ned absorbed the boys' pants and boots, wet and muddy from the knees down. "Who told you that?"

"Nobody told us." Top took a deep breath. "I saw him."

Mark nodded. "We found him in the creek."

"That's what they say, Ned." Ike's hands flapped as if they had a mind of their own. "They come runnin' up out from under the creek bridge and waved me down, scared plumb to death. I was headed to Powderly for some…"

"Sweet Jesus!" Miss Becky held on to the porch post for support. "Top, are you sure? Maybe it was somebody that looks like R. B."

"He's right." Mark ran the fingers of one hand through his hair. "It's him."

"That's how come y'all are wet and muddy. You went down in the creek to see?"

"Yessir. We both seen Mr. R. B." Mark still hadn't gotten used to calling other family members uncle or aunt, or even cousin.

"He fall in or something?" Ned couldn't wrap his mind around the fact that R. B. had drowned in the middle of winter.

Holding a quilt around her shoulders and face puffy from sleep, Pepper appeared behind Miss Becky. She met Mark's gaze and pulled it tighter. An entirely silent conversation passed between them.

Top pointed east toward the bridge, as if the pickup was only a few feet away. "He was coming this way and his truck missed the bridge."

"You sure he's dead?"

As if he was responsible and full of guilt, Top lowered his eyes and nodded. "Yessir, far's I could tell."

"Mama, y'all stay here." Ned rushed inside to pick up his hat, badge, and pistol, throwing orders over his shoulder. "Call over to Cody's and see if he's still at the house this morning. I'll call it in on the radio." Everyone was standing in the same place when he came back outside, as if waiting for more instructions. "Ike, you can come if you want to."

"I'll foller you and use the truck to block the road."

"All right then." Not slowing, Ned dropped into the Plymouth's seat and stuck the key into the ignition. The big Fury's engine barely caught before he slammed the gearshift into reverse and spun the tires. Lined up with the driveway, he slapped it into gear and hit the gas, at the same time keying the Motorola's handset. "Cody. John. Either one of y'all in the car?"

Deputy John Washington's deep voice came back a moment later. "Sho' am. What's the matter, Mr. Ned?"

"My boys say there's a bad wreck down on the Sanders Creek Bridge. I'm on the way over there right now."

"Be there soon's I can."

The big engine roared and his tires squalled as Ned hit the highway. Less than two minutes later, he crossed the bridge and pulled off on the shoulder. Driving slower, Ike drove another fifty yards to the top of the hill and blocked the lane.

Below, Ned hurried across the two lanes of highway and saw where the boys had kicked through the grass and saplings, following the tire tracks. He paused at the sight of the truck's undercarriage pointed skyward. From that angle and position, it could have been any one of a hundred pickups from the area, but he recognized the Chevrolet's horizontal five-bar grille.

It was difficult for an old man with a potbelly to get down to the creek bed. Like the boys, he used the saplings to lower himself over the edge. Once down, he paused in the reek of gasoline to work out the kids' footprints.

It was R. B.'s truck, all right. He'd never been one to coddle a vehicle, and the old pickup wore very little of the original gray paint. Two sets of footprints that obviously belonged to the boys divided and trailed around the overturned Chevrolet where they stopped at the unopened doors.

Satisfied, he circled the truck, struggling through the mud and frigid water that filled his brogans. Placing his knee exactly where one of the boys had knelt, Ned leaned over and peered through the window. R. B. was twisted in an unnatural way, with his legs hanging over the upside-down steering wheel, and his chest flat against the roof. Head at a sharp angle, his cheek rested in the cold water.

"My God." Already recognizing the waxy color of R. B.'s skin, Ned still reached into the car and laid his fingers against his nephew's cold cheek.

Slamming doors on the highway told him someone else had arrived. Using the truck's overturned running boards to pull himself up, he rose to find Deputy Washington towering over the saplings at the top of the bank. "Who is it, Mr. Ned? Are they hurt bad?"

"It's R. B." Ned's voice broke, and he had to stop and regain control. "My brother's boy. He's dead."

"Aw naw." The big man's shoulders slumped. "You sure?"

"It's him." Ned swallowed and nodded, fighting the hitch in his chest. "He's cold."

The sound of tires and slamming car doors on the highway above told him a crowd was quickly gathering. Cody in jeans and an untucked sheriff's department shirt came racing over the edge, nearly losing his hat in the process. "Is it R. B.!!!???" He didn't stop to wait for an answer. R. B. had been one of his best friends for years, and they'd shared time in Vietnam.

He grabbed John's big arm to steady himself, then jumped over the bank, landing hard on the crackling mud. "You're just standing there!" He dropped to his knees with a splash, a sob catching in his throat. "R. B.! Can you hear me? He'll be all right. He's tough. He's made it through worse. Ned, help me get him out!"

With surprising strength, the old constable took Cody's upper arm. Age and experience steadied his voice. He'd pushed past the first rush of grief, knowing they'd have time to deal with it later. Cody needed him now. "He's gone, son. I saw his eyes. Now, no matter he's family, we got to do this the right way."

"But it's *R. B.*! He's layin' in that cold water."

"Yep, and he's been there a good long while. You're the sheriff, so get ahold of yourself. Those boys up there can't see you like this. We got to figure this out. John?" Ned scanned the creekbank behind them, but John was gone.

The big deputy's bass voice came over the bridge railing. "I got it, Mr. Ned. I done called for a wrecker and an ambulance." There was a long pause. "And the justice of the peace."

Ned licked his suddenly dry lips. They'd need him to pronounce R. B. dead before they could do anything else.

Chapter Four

We cleaned up and changed out of our muddy clothes, but Miss Becky wouldn't let us go back down to the bridge. I tried arguing with her, even using my advanced age of fourteen years, but it didn't do any good. A survivor of the Great Depression, and of death, she'd seen a lot of troubles over the years wouldn't be swayed.

The phone was ringing off the hook, and she finally shooed us back outside. "I got people to talk to, so y'all get out from underfoot. Stay close to the house or I'll cut a switch. Y'all ain't too big for me to tan your hides."

Pepper could talk the horns of a billy goat, but she gave up, too, and we went outside.

"I have an idea." I crossed the sandy yard to the smokehouse and came back outside with a splintered old wooden ladder.

Mark helped me lean it against the back side of the unpainted smokehouse and we climbed up on the roof. Pepper didn't say anything about my idea, and that was unusual for her. It also showed how sad she was. She crawled up there with us and we perched on the ridgeline with her in the middle, feeling the sun-warmed asphalt shingles through our jeans.

Below was the mile-long, arrow-straight Creek Bridge Stretch, where kids raced late at night when Grandpa was away from the house. Cars in miniature lined both sides of the two-lane. They had the highway shut down for the most part, but every now and then a vehicle crept past at walking speed.

Since R. B. was kinfolk, a steady stream of cars and trucks came up the drive behind us. Relatives and friends alike went inside to either console Miss Becky or came by out of pure-dee nosiness. Wails floated through the kitchen's screen door each time a new woman arrived.

Pepper glanced behind us over the smokehouse's ridgeline at a small knot of farmers parked on our gravel drive. They circled the bed of a pickup, talking across loose hay, baling wire, and empty feed sacks. She started to take the transistor radio out of her back pocket but changed her mind and shifted closer to Mark. "I hate this place."

He barely turned his head. "You always say that about Center Springs when things get bad."

"That's about every other damned day. What's with this uncool world?"

Gravel popped under tires, and I turned to see another car pull up. Uncle Jack and Aunt Bertha went inside without seeing us on the roof. I slid down the roof's back side until the ridgeline was just above my head, hiding us from those in the front yard. Mark saw what I was doing and slid down, too. Pepper followed just to be close to him. We lay quietly with our backs on the slope.

Though we were a mile away, I had a clear view of the tiny figures bringing up R. B.'s body covered with a sheet. Some men loaded him on a stretcher, slid it into the back of the funeral home ambulance, and left.

Mr. Tom Bell's 1955 Ford truck passed the house. It

disappeared for a second behind a line of trees under our hill and drove slowly up to the traffic jam. He parked beside Grandpa's red Plymouth.

Mr. Tom was living on the second floor of Uncle James and Aunt Ida Belle's house. He paid rent and worked hard to make it better than it was before he moved in. We all wondered where he got his money, because he didn't have a job that we could see. Besides, he was too old to work.

Pepper shaded her eyes against the morning sun. "When did Mr. Tom get a new truck?"

I shrugged. "Beats me."

The wiry old retired Texas Ranger stood out from the rest of the men down there in his jeans, black coat, and black hat. I was sure he'd figure things out right quick. After a minute, he disappeared down into the creek.

Pepper sighed. "I love that old man."

Mark nodded. "We all do, but y'all know we're gonna lose him sometime. He's about as old as dirt."

Tears welled in Pepper's eyes. "I wish you hadn't-a said that. Not today."

My stomach hitched. "Me neither."

We were about to climb off the roof when a wrecker backed up to the end of the bridge. I knew they were running a cable down the creekbank, so we stayed to watch. After a while, R. B.'s wrecked pickup finally appeared.

Pepper shifted again, close enough to Mark that their shoulders touched. "This place is full of death and misery."

"People have accidents all the time." Mark sat up and rested his chin on his knees. "I sure am sorry it's R. B., though."

It was several minutes before she spoke again. "Do we tell Grandpa where we saw him last night?"

A shiver of fear ran down my back and I sat up in alarm. "We'd get Curtis in trouble, and us too. What we saw won't help a bit." Crossing my arms over my knees, I rested my chin on my forearms. "They'll figure out soon enough he was over in Juarez. It caught up with him this time, coming home drunk."

We were silent.

Mark's voice was deeper, as if he'd aged ten years. "That kind of thing always catches up to you."

For the umpteenth time that day, tires crunched up the gravel drive. I twisted around and stretched up across the rough shingles so just my eyes were over the ridgeline. I'd seen the driver up at the store only a couple of days earlier. "That's the new Baptist preacher, ain't it?"

Pepper rolled onto her stomach to peek over the ridge. "Yeah. I saw him the first time he preached last Sunday. He was there with his wife. They say they have twins, but they didn't come with 'em. Something about staying with their grandparents over in Saginaw until the parsonage was ready for 'em to move in."

"What's the preacher's name?"

"You're not gonna believe this. Colt McClellan."

Mark and I answered in stereo. "Cool."

Hootie loped up to the car as the other three doors on the old Chevrolet Impala opened. Mr. Colt's wife got out. Her dark hair was curled and sprayed into place like a helmet. It was the kids who caught our attention.

The most beautiful girl I'd ever seen stepped out of the back passenger side and leaned over to rub Hootie's ears. She looked to be about three years older than me, and her long blond hair was parted in the middle and pulled back behind both ears. The left side dropped loose, and she used a finger to thread it back.

I knew that face. I'd seen her in the back seat of that fogged car in the Starlite's parking lot the night before.

A group of men were gathered on Grandpa's porch, talking. One of them was Mr. Dell Reed, a member of the Baptist congregation. He shook Mr. Colt's hand when he came around, patted the wife on the shoulder, and greeted the girl, who flashed a dimpled smile that hurt my heart. I had to take out my asthma puffer and squeeze some of the mist into my lungs.

Pepper noticed and rolled her eyes. "Oh, for cryin' in a bucket! Don't go ape over that girl. Her name's Blu, and she's so far out of your league, she's in outer space."

"How do you know her name?" Mark cocked his head.

"'Cause they're so cool! Like I said, the daddy is Colt, and the twins are Jett and Blu. I haven't seen him yet, but I bet he's as cute as her."

"Those are the craziest names I've ever heard." I threw another glance over the ridgeline. "Colt, Jett, and Blu. What's their mama's name?"

She stifled a laugh. "Mildred. A plain name for a plain woman."

A boy finally stepped out of the back seat, and Pepper's breath caught at the sight of Blu's twin. Also in jeans, he had the same straw-colored hair down below his light blue collar. Jett looked like a clothes model in the Sears catalogue. My head spun when I realized he'd been at the Starlite too, on the back deck with his arm over my schoolmate Gus's shoulders.

"I swear. That's the purdiest boy I believe I've ever seen." Pepper licked her lips. "How plain old Mildred popped out two kids that good-looking's a mystery to *me*."

She was done with the roof and crabbed down to the ladder.

I started to follow but caught something from the corner of my eye. When I looked back toward the creek bridge, my Poisoned Gift exploded in color.

Day suddenly turned to night, and I froze, half-conscious

enough to know that I was about to fall off the roof, but still wrapped in a world that didn't exist for everybody else.

A sick-green glow rose to the east, growing brighter and silhouetting of the tops of the trees on a starry, moonlit night. A star rose, sending streaks of colored light shooting in all directions. Half a second later, a hot beam shot into the air with sparks rising to catch on impossible currents and scatter against the stars.

As suddenly as it began, it was over, and I was lying on the ground with Mark and Pepper leaning over me.

"Smooth move, Ex-lax. You scared the pee-waddlin' out of me." Pepper's voice cut through the fog in my head. "I've never seen nobody fall off a ladder that way. It's a wonder you didn't kill yourself."

I licked my lips, surprised at how dry my mouth was. "Hey, don't have a cow."

"You'll be all right. You didn't land that hard." Mark's eyes bored into mine, and he spoke so quietly only I could hear. "You have another vision?"

My chest tightened and I fought the tears that suddenly burned my eyes. Before I could answer, a busload of people came around behind the smokehouse, including Miss Becky, the new preacher's family, and the men from the porch.

"My lands. It sounded like somebody fell off the roof." Miss Becky saw the ladder leaning against the smokehouse. "Top. Was it you?"

Pepper laughed. "Thought he could fly like Superman, but he flies like a lead duck instead."

Everybody was looking at me except for Jett, who couldn't take his eyes off Pepper. I sat up, weak as a kitten and feeling like an idiot. Blu slipped to the side so she could see better.

The twins were standing close together in front of their

parents, watching me lying there like some interesting bug. Pepper was right, Jett was *wayyy* too good looking for a boy, but Blu gave me a feeling I'd never experienced before.

Looking back, however, I wish we'd never set eyes on Blu and Jett McClellan.

Chapter Five

The business of being the Lamar County Sheriff settled Cody's emotions, and he was able to process the accident site. Ned Parker, Deputy Washington, Tom Bell, Deputy Anna Sloan, and Justice of the Peace Buck Johnson gathered on the creekbank. It was his job to pronounce the victim dead before the body could be moved.

Cody settled the tooled gun belt on his hips and hooked both thumbs into his front jean pockets. "Looks like he was coming back from Juarez and either went to sleep behind the wheel or was too drunk to steer." His voice was soft and full of pain.

No one ventured a guess, and it was obvious that they remained silent because R. B. was family. Buck thumbed open the long blade on his Old Timer folding knife and cut a hunk of Days Work chewing tobacco off the plug. He tucked the chunk into one cheek. "Looks to me like he's been down there three, maybe four hours."

"Could have been more, or less." Tom Bell's soft voice demanded attention. "It was cold last night, and that water's like ice. The coroner'll know for sure."

Ned rubbed his face. "Don't make no difference. Dead's dead, and all because of them damn beer joints."

"We don't know that." Cody glanced up to see the crowd milling and talking on the concrete strip. "He might have just gone to sleep or run off the road to miss a deer."

"There weren't no skid marks up top, was there, John?"

Nearly mythical in size, Big John crossed his huge forearms and shook his head. "Nossir. I looked. There's only clean ruts where the truck went off the shoulder and down the bank."

"I don't want to turn this into a suspicious accident." Cody absently patted his shirt pocket, looking for the cigarettes that hadn't been there for months. He sighed when he found nothing but a nickel pack of Juicy Fruit gum. He peeled a stick and folded it into his mouth. "After what happened with the mayor and his secretary over on the dam, here while back, we don't need folks talking this up. Right now, it's a single-car accident and that's all." Chewing slowly, he glanced across the distance to Ned's house. "I'm surprised you didn't hear it go in last night."

Ned shook his head. "The windows were down, and besides, I might not've been here. I got a call a little after three from Donald Ray Turner over in Caviness. Said he thought somebody was breaking into his store. I went out there, but me and him didn't see nothin." He dropped his eyes, shaking his head. "I didn't think there was anybody out there and shoulda told him so."

Cody reached out and rubbed the old constable's shoulder, feeling the soft blue material of his shirt that Miss Becky had washed and ironed for years. "You know how light Miss Becky sleeps. If she didn't hear it, you wouldn't have neither, not the way *you* snore."

Cody's way was to make jokes. Just like in 'Nam, the weak joke seemed to lighten the mood. Shoulders lifted and squared, and it looked to him like everyone took a deep breath, as if they'd been holding it while they waited for the car to reach the top.

"We'll get this figured out." Cody met each of his deputies' eyes and nodded at Tom Bell. "Let's wait for the autopsy." He stopped at the finality of the word and wet his lips. "Then we'll go from there. I'm gonna bet we find out that he drowned. That'd be my guess."

Nods all around showed everyone agreed with him, all except for Ned.

"It might be a while." Ned absently waved a hand.

Anna spoke up for the first time, clearly puzzled by the unusual procedure. The only female deputy in Lamar County, she had a different way of looking at things. "You're treating this as a crime scene, Ned?"

"He's family. I want this done right." He turned to Cody. "After I go tell Joe that his boy's gone, I'm calling the sheriff over in Hugo to let him know I'm crossing the river to talk to some folks in Juarez. I intend to find out where he was drinking and get to the bottom of this."

"The bottom of what?" Tom Bell frowned, deepening the horizontal wrinkles in his already corrugated forehead.

"I've been picking that boy up and taking him to jail since he came back from Vietnam. No matter how much he had to drink, R. B. never got where he couldn't handle hisself." Ned met Tom Bell's gaze. "R. B. was the best drunk driver in the county, and I don't believe he run off in here on his own."

Chapter Six

Still shaking from the trauma of telling Joe Parker that his boy was dead, Ned pulled into Neal Box's bottle-cap-paved parking lot at noon. Pickups were parked haphazardly between the country store and the domino hall. The oil road peeling off the highway at an angle divided those two structures from Oak Peterson's store.

All three buildings clumped together, and taking up less than a hundred linear yards, made up the tiny Northeast Texas community of Center Springs that was once a bustling cotton town at the turn of the twentieth century. By 1969, it was a dismal shadow of itself.

Clusters of farmers were scattered among the cars, most talking about the accident. Still wearing his barn coat, even though it had warmed up to a tolerable level in the sunshine, Ned waved at the nearest group and climbed the steps to Neal's store. The usual members of the Spit and Whittle Club were gathered in the sunshine at the edge of the shade. The Wilson brothers, Floyd Cass, and half a dozen others loafed on the porch. Mack Vick, a local cowboy, sat on his horse with his right leg hooked over the saddle's horn, rolling a smoke.

Floyd threw up a bony hand. "Ned, I'm sorry. Didn't come over to the house when I heard. Figured you had enough on your hands with all them people in the house and yard."

Face impassive, Ned nodded. "Thanks y'all. It's hard times." Addressing everyone at the same time eliminated the need for each of the others to speak.

In their ever-present hip waders rolled down like bell-bottom pants, Ty Cobb Wilson and his brother Jimmy Foxx rested on the much-whittled porch railing with their backs to the parking lot. The hook-nosed, scraggly-haired men were sharpening their pocketknives on small hand stones they kept in their pockets.

"Well, the wife's makin' up food to bring." Floyd's fingers fluttered in the air. "I'll be by with it directly."

Taking food for the grieving family was a tradition reaching back for generations. The food represented life for the living and showed that those bringing it cared for family members dealing with the shock of loss.

The RC Cola screen door protector rattled when Ned opened it. The scarred door behind it swung open with a creak. Dry warmth from the Dearborn heater enveloped him and Ned realized that no matter how much the weak sunshine had warmed the outside, it was still winter.

Neal looked up from his figures on the pad lying on the counter. Most everyone in the community bought "on the tab" and paid up at the end of each month or when they finally had the money. He paused, pencil in hand. "Ned."

"Howdy Neal."

"I'm sorry about R. B."

"Me too. Becky needs some flour and sugar. She tends to bake when things are bad."

"Already pulled it, and some baking powder." Neal pointed to a pasteboard box on the worn counter. "I know how she is."

"You know us pretty good."

"Since we's kids."

Ned paused, looking around the store containing everything from horse tack to dry goods to feed stacked against the back wall. Oak-framed glass cases held patent medicines, candy, and even playing cards. Coolers full of block cheese, unsliced baloney, eggs, bacon, and whole hams hummed quietly. It was a throwback, the last of a dying breed of stores that had served rural communities since the first settlers crossed into the Texas frontier.

Hands in the pockets of his overalls, Ned seemed lost. The door opened behind him to admit Wallace Jones, another local farmer. They exchanged nods, and Jones went to the back and returned with two sacks of chicken feed on one shoulder.

"You want to put this on my tab, Neal?"

"Sure 'nuff."

Jones's soft eyes rose. "Ned, R. B. was a good man."

Ned held the door, receiving a soft pat on the arm by way of thanks. He closed it and stepped over to the counter. "Neal, you go across the river ever now'n then…"

The store owner stood and reached into the meat and cheese cooler. As if studying a complicated question, he unwrapped a ham and put it on the slicer and turned it on. When the circular blade reached speed, he cut a slice and handed it to Ned. "I do."

It was quiet in the store. The men's voice outside were low and muffled. Ned took a bite. "R. B. went over there right smart, didn't he?"

Neal cut another slice for himself. "Yep."

"Which one of them clubs did he like?"

"It wasn't the Sportsman, if that's what you're thinking."

Ned's eyes softened, as if that was the answer he needed. "Which one, then?"

"Well, he liked the Red River, and the Texoma."

"You seen him over there lately?"

"Not lately." Neal took a bite and chewed, thinking.

"Which one was his favorite?"

"Hell, Ned. I don't know which one he *favored*. You know how it is when any of us go over to Juarez. Half the Baptists who see Baptists over there don't never talk to one another, because if you don't talk about it, it didn't happen."

Neal cut another slice. "Furthermore'n all that, half the time when a man goes across the river, it ain't to visit with folks from Center Springs or Chisum. It's to go drink and maybe dance, or…listen to music."

Ned started to speak, and Neal cut him off.

"A lot of these boys cross the river to kill the demons." He jerked a thumb at the men outside on the porch. "Take Wallace, there. I've seen him sit over in the corner of the Texoma Club and drink until he can cry about all the Germans he killed in the war. Ol' Les Crane drinks to forget about what he saw on them islands across the water. Clark Means, Herbert Hutchins, and Dabbs Taylor huddle up in the Circle Inn and talk about Korea. None of them can talk to their wives about it, nor any of us who didn't go in the service."

"Well, some go for other reasons."

"Yeah, I know what you're talking about, and I imagine that'll be the TV Lounge. Even though it's the roughest damn joint in Oklahoma, men have been going there to bird-dog women since Eve woke up beside Adam."

"Ain't none of them places fit for decent people."

Neal frowned and ran fingers through his curly white hair. "Well now, no need to be like that, Ned. You know, some folks don't think drinkin' and dancin' are a sin. Hell, I know one feller who goes over there just to smoke in peace because his wife gives him the devil about it when he lights up at home, and you know good and well them over at the Assembly of God think even a glass of wine's a sin."

"Well, them places sparks a lot of troubles."

Neal frowned and cut a dozen thick slices of ham that nobody had ordered. "Troubles can come from anywhere."

"This time it took R. B." Ned felt emotions rise in his chest and he turned his head until he was back under control.

Neal ripped a strip of white butcher paper off the roll and smoothed it on the counter. "We all know R. B. was full of the devil and has been since he was a kid. You remember the time when he wasn't about eight, he told Old R. M. Ainsley to kiss his ass when he said R. B. looked like a girl and needed a haircut, right out there in front of the domino hall?"

They chuckled at the memory of the tousled boy planting both hands on his hips and giving Ainsley a dressing down.

Ned shook his head. "Yeah, and his daddy should have whipped his ass for it."

"Whippin's never made a bit of difference to that boy. He'd just look you in the eye and say it didn't hurt. He'd fight a buzz saw, and I believe that's what got him through the war and back home."

"And now he's gone, because he was drinking."

"Is that what y'all think?"

"As far as I can tell right now."

Ned finished his slice of ham. "Who'd he drink with over there?"

Neal folded the paper around the meat, tore off a piece of masking tape, and sealed the package. "Most near anybody who'd sit down with him."

"Women?"

Neal huffed. "Of course. There's a few water moccasins who

hang out over there. He drinks…drank with all of them. Ever now'n then some old gal with a few ticks on her would show up from the Kiamiche."

They chuckled at the description of the backwoods Okies.

"I've seen him, and half the single men here in Center Springs…and a few married fellers…lined up to dance with gals who drove in from Dallas."

"Any particular names you can come up with? I need to get to the bottom of this."

"Now you know I ain't gonna be calling names."

"I'm just trying to find out who I can talk to."

"Then go on over there after dark and look around, but if I's you, I'd take Tom Bell with me. And don't go to thinking Cody's Sportsman caused all this. He used to be there quite a bit, but not lately, not since he sold out and they took to gambl—" Neal stopped abruptly and dropped the slices into the cardboard box with the other items he was sending to Miss Becky. He rounded the counter and picked up a loaf of Ideal Bread. "This is for y'all to make some sandwiches. I don't know much else to do."

"Much obliged." Ned picked up the box, studying on their conversation. There was something about the way Neal clipped off his answer that bothered him, but he couldn't put a finger on what it was.

Neal came around and held the door for Ned. He nodded goodbye to the loafers on the porch and put the box in the back seat of his red 1965 Plymouth Fury.

The Motorola bolted to the floorboard hump crackled. "Ned?"

He lifted the mike from the bracket on the dash. "Go ahead, Cody."

"I need you out here on 271. There's been a bad wreck.

Somebody run head-on into a hearse carrying Farley Scarborough's boy Del to his funeral. It's a mess."

"On my way." Ned had never liked Del Scarborough, who'd recently lost his life in Vietnam. Sorry as the day is long and mean as his old man Farley, Del had been arrested more times than he went to school, and Ned was glad when the draft got him.

But he never wanted the boy to pay the way he did.

Chapter Seven

Traffic on Highway 271 was a tangled mess, for those coming from Chisum ten miles to the south, and southbound vehicles lined up back across the Red River. A Pontiac GTO bearing Oklahoma tags had failed to yield to the hearse turning left, and slammed into the right front fender, spinning the big black Ford a full one hundred eighty degrees. The car containing Farley Scarborough and his weeping wife was positioned to get a perfect view of Del's casket exploding through the hearse's back doors on impact as if shot by a cannon.

Cody and John Washington were already there, trying to calm Del's hysterical mother and several other family members who were doing their best to organize a vigilante party and string the drunk Okie from a nearby highline post.

Ned killed his engine and approached the smashed front end of the hearse. The passenger window was shattered, and the funeral director whose head had almost gone through the glass was lying still under a stained ranch coat that most likely came from behind a pickup seat. The driver sat on the ground not far away, holding his neck and moaning.

Ned knelt beside him for a moment. "Clarence, you hurt bad?"

"My neck's killing me, but I ain't as bad as old Harvey laying there."

"Yep. At least you're breathing. Hang on, I hear the ambulance coming right now."

Clarence started to nod and winced. "I doubt my neck'll ever be the same. I seen people with whiplash walk through the rest of their lives with their heads tilted. I sure don't like the idea of seeing the world sideways 'til I die."

"Don't get to worrying just yet."

A Texas highway patrol officer pulled up close to the hearse at the same time Sheriff's Deputy Anna Sloan arrived. Ned recognized the state trooper. "Howdy, Billy Ray." He pointed at Clarence. "Would you stay right 'chere with him until they get him on the ambulance?"

"Sure, Ned."

The old constable stood, knees cracking. Anna immediately waved oncoming traffic to the side. A man slowed and leaned out. "What happened here?"

Anna leaned forward. "They're taking the last person who asked me that question to the hospital."

The man withdrew into the car like a turtle pulling into his shell. He sped away, and Anna kept waving others into the one lane getting by.

Ned saw Cody and John standing between the Pontiac and a group of angry men led by Farley Scarborough. The driver was still stretched across the front bench seat, his face smashed by the steering wheel. Most of his nose seemed to be torn off and the man was completely unconscious. "Piece of My Heart" by Janis Joplin still blared from the one speaker in the dash.

Scarborough was livid, and the worst side of the fireplug of a man's bad side was out there for all to see. "Cody! Y'all turn around and deal with this traffic and let me and my boys handle this son of a bitch."

Deputy Washington was silent, but the fire in his eyes meant business. Cody was doing his best to keep Farley from dragging the unconscious drunk from the car. White-faced from everything else he'd seen that day, Cody kept his voice calm.

"You know we can't do that, Farley. I see you're mad, but you can't do things like that these days."

"Look at my wife! Look at my boy over there. This ain't right. Del died for his country, and here this drunk Indian son of a bitch has done this to us."

"We don't know he's an Indian, and what difference does that make?"

"We shoulda killed more of them sonsabitches when we had the chance. Wiped 'em all out instead of letting them live high on the hog over yonder in the territory. Then we wouldn't have this mess."

Cody raised an eyebrow. "High on the hog?"

Though Cody tried to maintain his composure, Ned had no reason to restrain himself. He was too old, tired, sad, and worried, and furthermore and all that, Miss Becky was full-blood Choctaw.

Ned was through talking. The old lawman seemed thirty years younger when he bulled around Cody and John and grabbed Farley Scarborough by the black tie knotted around his neck. He jerked hard and the tie suddenly became a noose. Shocked by Ned's actions, Farley stumbled to within inches of the furious constable as the crowd of men faded away as fast as a school of fish flaring from a predator.

Ned held on to the tie as Farley's thick, wrinkled neck and face reddened. "Is this what you want? Is it? You want to lynch that man? How does this *feel*?"

Farley's eyes bugged out as he fought the constricting ligature. Ned's fist was so tight against his Adams apple that he couldn't speak.

"We don't need this right now, Farley! You're just making matters worse. Your boy's dead, my nephew's dead, and what we oughta be doing is dealing with our loss! Instead, you're out here acting the fool while your poor wife's over there cryin' her eyes out. Man-up, goddamn it, or I'll haul your ass to jail myself!"

Cody's calm voice cut through Ned's fury. "Uh, you might want to loosen that grip a little bit there, Ned. Old Farley's about as red as an apple right now, and we only have the one ambulance here."

Lips white with fury, Ned released his hold and stepped back. Farley stumbled away, fighting for breath. "Besides, I don't like you one little bit, so get over there with Coretta and settle your ass down." He stepped away and pointed a finger at the wrecked Pontiac. "And somebody turn that shit off!"

Traffic moved slow enough that Anna did everyone a favor by leaning into the Pontiac to flick the radio off. She took the keys from the ignition and dropped them into her pocket.

———

An Oklahoma state trooper crossed the bridge and steered around the tangle of traffic. The young officer joined the Texas officials and raised his eyebrows at the standoff. "Howdy, Cody. Anything I can do?"

"Hey, Bill. Sure is." He waved a hand toward the cluster of men milling around the wrecked cars. "Shoot the first one of these guys that touches that drunk man in the car there. We aren't having any lynching here today."

"Sure will. What happened?"

Ned pointed east. "That four-door there came across the highway from over yonder and slammed into the hearse." He pointed eastward to the dirt road that paralleled the river. "He's drunk as Cooter Brown."

The officer studied the scene. "I'd expect a drunk to be coming from my side of the Red."

Cody sighed and patted his pocket, looking for a toothpick. He finally located one that had been chewed more than once. He stuck the pulped, splintered end into the corner of his mouth and almost patted his pockets once again from habit to look for a lighter. "He was coming from that new club on this side of the river."

Most people assume the Red River is the dividing line between Texas and what some of the older folks still called The Territories, but the river is a wide, muddy snake that twists and turns of its own accord when enough rain falls to take it out of its banks. The 1964 flood caused the Red to squirm hard enough to cut a fresh channel that looped half a mile to the north, leaving a small section of Oklahoma land on the "Texas" side of the river.

Now the argument about who would patrol that orphan area was growing in intensity. Oklahoma said it wasn't theirs, since it was south of the river, and they had no intention of using Texas roads to patrol a business so far from everything else.

Texas insisted that the Starlite, and all the troubles it would bring, was Oklahoma's responsibility. Lamar County had washed its hands of the whole thing, leaving that small patch as a no-man's-land.

The Oklahoma trooper studied the wrecked hearse and sighed. "Our sheriff said to stay away from that place. It's y'all's problem."

"And our hands are tied on this side for the time being."

Seeing even more people gather around the crumpled cars, Cody broke off the conversation and waved them away. "You men, get back to your vehicles and stay there."

———

The trooper stepped away to direct traffic near where Deputy Washington stood to the side with those involved in the wreck, taking notes on the bent and creased spiral-bound pad from his back pocket.

Breathing hard and bleeding off adrenaline, Ned stuffed both hands into his pockets and turned his back on Farley and his family, who moved several cars back down the funeral procession.

Overwhelmed with grief and anger, he stared at a rusting Fina sign above the dirty white filling station not far away. There was so much death and drama swirling around that he couldn't think straight. It had been that way for several years, and he wondered how so much could be happening at one time in their small rural town.

More cars stacked up. Cody and John loaded the handcuffed and still unconscious drunk into the back of another ambulance only minutes after Anna waved it through. Feet planted solidly on the pavement, Ned watched the vehicle pull away, lights flashing.

The hearse's driver seemed better. Still holding his neck, Clarence came over to Cody and whispered in his ear. The sheriff listened, his head cocked toward the shorter man. Eyes narrowed, the sheriff waved for Deputy Washington to follow and they disappeared behind the hearse.

Rooted in place, Ned watched them. There wasn't much to do at that point, and he still felt twisted inside. The best thing for him right then was to keep shut of everybody until his temper cooled. Surveying the traffic jam, he swiveled to watch Deputy Anna Sloan direct traffic.

Footsteps stopped behind him. "Mr. Ned."

He recognized the deep voice without turning around. "Yeah, John."

"You might want to come take a look at Del."

"I've seen dead people."

"I know, but this is different."

Hands still in his pockets, Ned followed the big deputy. The once-polished oak casket wasn't fit for firewood. For the first time, Ned saw the figure in a black body bag. Bent almost double, it was lying halfway out onto the pavement, held in place only by the casket's securely latched bottom half.

He stopped beside the body. "Well, I never figured I'd have to deal with this sorry son of a bitch again."

John tilted his hat back. "See anything else?"

Explosions of white powder coated the body bag and the pavement. Not knowing for sure how bodies were shipped from overseas, Ned mistook what he was seeing. "You talking about all that lime? I figger they use it to keep the smell down."

"It ain't lime."

"What is it then?"

"I believe it's cocaine."

"Well, hell."

Chapter Eight

Grandpa and Miss Becky needed to get Mark and me out of the house for a while with all that was going on, and she jumped at the idea when Aunt Ida Belle suggested we come stay with them for a night or two. Adding us to their mix filled their house, since Mr. Tom Bell lived upstairs in the old two-story.

I was looking forward to it, because we hadn't stayed there since he'd moved in. There were three rooms upstairs. One big one at the head of the stairs served as his living area, with a bedroom on either end. He had a little hot plate up there to make coffee.

Mr. Tom told us boys to take the east bedroom, which was over the downstairs living room. Mr. Tom slept directly above the dining room. Even though there wasn't a stove on the second floor, the nights weren't very cold because all the warm air from downstairs rose to make comfortable sleeping.

We especially liked that room because a big oak grew outside the window. That Saturday night we waited until everyone was asleep before we climbed out onto a sliver of roof overhanging the side porch, grabbed a limb, and worked our way down to the ground.

Our breath was thick vapor in the moonlight. Pepper was

already there, looking fit to be tied. Her room on the ground floor gave her easier access to the outside. "What took y'all so long? I've been freezing my ass off out here."

Instead of answering, Mark gave her a big hug and a kiss that like to have turned my stomach. I faked a gag. "Y'all do that somewhere else."

She gave me a glare. "We would, but you're always around."

"Hey, I can't help it. I don't have anybody else to hang around with, but we need to get away from the house before you tear me a new one. Uncle James'll wear us all out if we wake him up and he finds us outside."

The moon was bright as a new nickel as they took off hand in hand. I buttoned my coat and followed them down the dirt drive. We didn't talk again until we stepped onto the oil road. "Where to now?"

She grinned, her teeth white in the moonlight. "We're meeting Blu and Jett McClellan behind the Baptist church."

I didn't like the idea worth a flip, even though I really wanted to see Blu. Mark glanced down the road. "Why?"

There was something in Pepper's voice that didn't ring true. "I thought it would be fun. It's ass-chilling cold, and where else are we gonna go?"

She was right. I was already freezing to death. "We could have stayed in bed where it was nice and warm. I can use some sleep."

"Sleep when you're dead." She led the way down the oil road lined with tall dark trees. Something was up because a dozen cars were parked in Oak Peterson's lot, and there was no reason for them to be there at that hour.

We stopped in the shadows of the trees growing along a bob-wire fence. I pointed at a glow from lights *behind* the store, realizing it was coming from flashlights. "Do you recognize any of them cars?"

Mark whispered a couple of seconds later. "Yep, one or two."

Pepper's answer was cut off by the hiss of tires on pavement. A glow brightened as a car came closer. The lights behind the store went out. We waited in the cold until the car coming from the Lake Lamar dam reached the stop sign, continuing on in what we called a California Roll. Without coming to a full stop, it turned left and disappeared over the hill toward Forest Chapel.

The flashlight flicked back on. Someone laughed and voices reached us.

Mark took our heads in both hands and pulled the three of us together so he could whisper. "They can't see here in the dark very good after looking into those lights. Let's sneak a little closer, but if anything happens, y'all run back to the house, and I'll lead 'em off."

My heart beat as loud as a bass drum. The shadows under the trees were thick, and pretty soon we could hear several male voices.

"What do you think they're doing?" I wanted to skin out of there and get back in the house. I was freezing my fanny off, and something wasn't right about men hiding in the dark behind a store.

A deep voice sounded familiar, but I couldn't put my finger on who it was. "Bill's the shooter."

The distinctive rattle of dice came to us. "Teneha, Timpson, Bobo, and Blair, gimme a seven and see if I care!"

"What does that mean?" I whispered.

Mark surprised me with an answer. "I've heard it before. It's a conductor's call on the Texas Railroad back during the war. Those are towns somewhere out of Houston, and they say it for good luck. They're shootin' craps."

An explosion of laughter told us something unexpected had happened. "Well, you got your seven, big boy!"

Pepper punched Mark in the shoulder. "I guess it's not lucky after all, smart guy."

I leaned into Mark. "Let's get outta here."

In their excitement, a beam of light lifted off the game and swept across the woods behind the store. I held my breath until it returned to the ground.

"I'm freezing to death." That voice was familiar, and I realized it was one of my much older cousins. "I can't believe we're shootin' out here tonight. I'd rather go over to the Starlite."

Another voice joined in, but I couldn't put a face to that one. "Hell, no. I'm not going again after what happened the last time."

"You don't know for sure what happened."

"I know R. B.'s dead, and that's enough for me. Nobody wins over there."

"Neal won a lot of money the other night."

"Yeah, but he's one of the lucky ones. I think them fellers at the Starlite let a few folks win to keep ever'body all wound up about playing. Nobody would come in if everyone lost all the time."

Someone snorted. "That's why they call it gambling, which is what we ain't doing right now if you don't throw them damn dice."

"I'm just sayin', when you win there, you win big."

"Yeah, but when you lose…"

"They're putting a roulette wheel in soon, I heard. I'd just as soon sit back there and play poker."

"Them cards is marked."

"You don't know that, neither."

"I'm a helluva card player, and I only won a couple of dollars the last time I was there. The house took most of it."

"You were playing blackjack. The house always wins, dummy."

"Well, that new coroner's boy from Chisum took home a sackful of money one night."

"Where'd you hear that from?"

"His daddy told Eli Windbush, who told Eugene Seay, who heard it from somebody else."

The group grunted and laughed. "Hearsay."

The first voice came out loud and frustrated. "Just shoot the damn dice! Gus, you kids get your asses out of here. I don't need any more bad luck."

I watched Gus Davis leave, head down with his hands in his pockets. It sure was strange to see him again after last night. He walked away toward his house about a mile away. Another shadow stood. Gus disappeared into the darkness as Mark tugged my arm at the sound of a car coming from the direction of Grandpa's house. The flashlights flicked off and the men waited in the darkness.

Headlights threw a fan of light down the highway and the bobwire fences lining both sides. The car slowed as it reached the stores. We waited, expecting it to either turn left toward the dam, or continue to the west. Instead, its speed dropped even more.

From where we crouched, we saw the high beams switch on, throwing the cars in Oak's parking lot into bright relief. The sedan pulled off the road and the driver stopped, leaving the engine running and the lights on.

The cluster of men went as still as rabbits. I figured they were waiting to see if it was someone else coming to shoot dice, or just a curious farmer wondering what was going on. A second later, the beam of a red light popped on and danced over the parked cars, one by one, as if trying to identify who they belonged to.

An even colder chill than the weather went down the back of my neck, and I knew for sure who it was. I knew that light.

Grandpa! Someone must have called the house about cars at the store at eleven on a Saturday night. We could see him sitting behind the wheel. Unlike the men shooting dice, our eyes were accustomed to the darkness and not the bright yellow from their flashlights.

He didn't come around to our side where we were hiding in the trees. Instead, he eased the car forward until he could see the huddle of men behind Oak's frame store.

"You men! This is Ned Parker, and I recognize ever' car here in front of this store and know who's drivin' 'em. Y'all come around here with your hands where I can see 'em. I'll shoot any one of you sonsabitches that run, and you can't get away, because Deputy John Washington's coming down the road. We got y'all between us."

He stepped out of the Plymouth, but all we could see was the beam of his flashlight sweeping over the sheepish men who filed around into the open. One, though, a slender shadow, leaped from the game and slipped through the shadows, nearly running into Mark, who grabbed an arm and yanked him to a stop.

Mark's voice hissed. "Be still. He'll see you moving."

Grandpa's beam swept from one white face to another, and it was everything I could do not to laugh when one of the dice players sighed deep. "Howdy, Uncle Ned."

Nearly every one of them was kinfolk.

"Let's get out of here." The second surprise was the slender person who'd accidentally joined us in the brush. It was Jett McClellan.

Chapter Nine

While Grandpa tore our kinfolk a new one, the four of us faded back into the shadows and slipped down the oil road. I was terrified that he would see us in the moonlight. By then our breath was like smoke from a steam engine. What I wanted to do was climb back up that oak tree and get into a warm bed, but Pepper had other ideas.

"We can't go back to the house right now. He'll either hear us or see us cross the road."

Jett pointed. "Let's go hide out in that barn. Who does it belong to?"

Pepper headed that direction. "Old Man Carter. He's the richest guy in Center Springs."

"That's not saying much." Jett's voice was sharp.

I felt my face flush at the comment but didn't say anything.

She led the way like she had a purpose. "We need to get in out of this wind. I'm liable to freeze to death if we don't."

Jett didn't look that cold. He followed, hands in his pockets, almost strolling along like he was shopping at the Big Town Shopping Mall over in Dallas. Since Grandpa was behind Oak Peterson's store, he couldn't see us cross the highway one at a time like running quail.

There was excitement in Pepper's voice, and she jabbered along a mile a minute, once she figured we were out of earshot. "I bet you've never been in a barn at night, since you're from the city. It's a great place to hang out and smoke a toonie."

I never did like it when she wanted to smoke in the barn behind their house, or up at the barn not a hundred yards from Miss Becky's kitchen. There was too much hay that could go up in a heartbeat, and that would cost us a lot of hide from our backsides.

Her comment piqued Jett's interest. "You have any smokes?"

Pepper shook her head. "Not tonight, but I get a couple of loosies every now and then."

Mark and I hung back, keeping an eye open around us. I didn't want Grandpa or Uncle James to come roaring up at us out of the dark. I'm not sure how Pepper didn't trip over something and fall, because she kept turning around to look at Jett.

Surrounded by big burr oak trees, Mr. D. N. Carter's white gabled barn was like one you'd see on a calendar. It was probably a hundred years old and sat on a slight hill not far from the cotton gin.

The big doors were closed, but around the side was a half-open stall door that opened into an empty corral. Pepper climbed the boards and was halfway across the pen by the time Jett flowed over the top like an oiled shadow, making it look effortless.

I was beginning to dislike him.

In seconds, we were inside, and I shivered. It was about ten degrees warmer and smelled like cow shit, dust, and alfalfa. There was enough moonlight peeking between the board walls to see down the great hall running the length of the barn. A ladder led to the loft, and Pepper shinnied up the rungs like a monkey. The rest of us followed and found her sitting on an alfalfa bale beside the loft door. She pushed it halfway open, letting in a thick draft and even more cold light.

"See? This is perfect."

Jett dropped onto the hay beside her. Mark hesitated, then pulled another bale from the stack against the wall and dropped it across from them. I sat down beside him, waiting to see what would happen next.

He simply rested both elbows on his knees and looked out into the night. It was quiet for a few minutes and the air was thick with tension.

I couldn't take it anymore. "Where's Blu?"

Jett snorted. "You have a thing for my sister, little buddy?"

"I don't have a *thing,* and I'm not your little buddy. I just wondered where she is. Pepper said both of y'all were gonna be here."

Ignoring my pushback, Jett dug a Zippo out of his pocket. "Even though we're twins, we don't do *everything* together. She's probably out somewhere getting her ashes hauled." He waited for the reaction we didn't give him. "I'm gonna burn one. Anyone else want a hit?"

What in the world did he mean? I shook my head. "I have asthma. I don't smoke cigarettes."

He held up a twisted cylinder that was bright white in the silver light coming through the loft door. "This isn't just a cigarette. It's a joint."

Mark shook his head. "I don't do grass. It makes you *stupid.*"

I caught the emphasis and knew what he was saying, but Jett snapped his lighter, firing up the weed. He took a deep drag and clicked the lid closed with his thumb. My heart almost stopped, thinking that the flame high in the open door was as bright as a lighthouse. All we needed was for it to catch someone's eye, and we'd all be in trouble. He blew out a cloud of smoke and inhaled again, holding it in. He offered it to Mark.

His face blank, Mark held up a hand. "Said no."

The bright red cherry floated across the space and came close to me. I leaned back and shook my head. "No thanks. It's illegal."

"There's a lot of things against the law." He laughed. "Like shooting dice, driving over the speed limit, underage drinking... trespassing."

The glowing red ember floated to Pepper. Not looking at us, she took it. The cherry glowed even brighter. She held her breath and in the pale moonlight her face was ghost white, as if she were scared to death. She let it out. "This is so cool!"

My fear of being discovered amped up when she dug the transistor radio from her back pocket and flicked it on. "Sunshine of Your Love" came on at the level I expected Gabriel's Horn to sound.

I reached for it. "Turn that *down*! Grandpa has ears like a bat." I poked a finger in the direction of the store. "He's right over there not a hundred and fifty yards away. He'll hear you, or old man Carter's dog'll be here barking at us."

She jerked the little radio away. "Chill, pill." She lowered the volume and laid the radio beside her on the hay.

The music played, and Pepper took another lungful and passed the joint over to Jett. I felt like an idiot sitting there in that strange barn, watching them smoke dope. The truth was, I had no idea what to do. I didn't want to look like a coward and leave, and there was nothing I could say to make them stop.

A quick glance at the moonlit side of Mark's face told me he felt the same way. His expression was stone calm, but his jaw was set. The eye I could see was fixed on Jett, but there was no fire in it. He was simply watching. Absorbing. It reminded me of a snake watching a mouse with dark patience.

The joint made its way back to Pepper. While she was taking another drag, Jett reached down and plucked a long straw from the floor. Sticking it in his mouth, he leaned in across the little space between us. "So, what do you hayseeds do for excitement in this little burg, *Mark*?"

Hearing his name called that way, I jerked, half expecting Mark to pop up from our hay bale and bust him in the nose, but instead he tilted his head like a dog looking at a new pan. "We find plenty to do."

"Yeah, such as?"

"Play basketball up at the gym, hunt, fish. Go camping."

"Dude. You just blew my *mind*."

"It's probably the *dope*."

Jett snorted and took the joint back from Pepper. "Don't Bogart that joint, girl." It was half-gone already. He laughed and started singing "Don't Bogart Me," a song I'd never heard before.

Pepper joined in, and where she'd learned the lyrics, I don't know. Their country version sounded surreal against the rock and roll music coming from her radio.

Heart in my throat, I patted the air with both hands. "Y'all cool it! Somebody's gonna *hear* you."

Jett laughed like a loon and took the stem from his mouth. "You worry too much, Zippy."

Pepper laughed in a way I'd never heard before. "Zippy. Lippy. Lippy Zippy! That sounds so groovy the way you say it. Hey, you. Zip your lip!"

My face reddened from embarrassment, and I was again glad we were in the dark. She always got my goat like that, no matter how I tried to ignore it. I hated nicknames, even though Top is short for my full name, Terrence Orrin Parker. Others stick to you like pine sap, and you can't get them off your whole life, no matter how hard you scrubbed or what you did to change what people call you.

I knew that for a fact, because people called my daddy Red.

And then there were names some of the local farmers had like Perchmouth, Possum, Catfish, Littlejohn, Tink, Nig, Shorty, and Runt. I didn't want anything like that hanging around my neck.

Jett took the hay stem from his mouth, snapped his lighter again, and lit it. The dry hay caught, and I watched him tilt it so that the tiny flicker climbed the stem. "You bumpkins need to loosen up."

Still seated, Mark wet his thumb and index finger and snuffed the flame. "Don't be so stupid."

Jett shot to his feet. "Who you calling stupid, Geronimo?"

"I didn't *call* you anything." Mark rose slowly. His voice was flat and sharp. "Pepper, turn that down or off. I don't intend to get caught out here tonight."

Startled by such a direct order, she reached for the radio at the same time Jett shoved Mark's shoulder. He must have been ready for it, because Mark went with it, letting his body relax and go back at the same time he popped Jett in the chest with an open palm. Surprised, Jett stumbled and fell backward over the bale Pepper was still sitting on.

He was up in a second, fists clenched. Pepper snapped off the radio and stepped between them. "Cool it! You two're killing a good buzz."

Jett waited for a moment, and when Mark didn't attack, lowered his fists. "You're not worth it."

"Heard that before."

I was done. "Come on. Let's go. I 'magine Grandpa's gone, and I'm freezing to death."

Pepper pushed between them. "Fine. Let's split. There's no way I can maintain a high with this vibe!" She stomped through the loose hay and backed down the ladder. Jett stood where he was, arms crossed and watching as Mark and I followed.

We were at the stable door when he came down. Instead of following us back out the little side door, he opened one of the two big doors in front and strolled out like he owned the place. He was headed toward the parsonage down the highway by himself.

Without talking, we cut through the woods. Fifteen minutes later, Mark and I were up the tree and back inside, settled in our warm beds.

My eyes had barely closed before Mr. Tom woke me up, hollering from his room. "James! Ida Belle! Y'all get up and call the fire department! Carter's barn's on fire!"

Chapter Ten

Ned shook his head at the sight of his nephews and cousins lined up against the back of Oak Peterson's store in the beam of his flashlight. They ranged in age from twenty to thirty. His voice dripped disgust. "Now ain't this something?"

"Aw, Uncle Ned." Ron Parker adjusted his coat and buttoned it tighter. He wore a snap-brim Bailey hat tilted down low over one eye. "We ain't doing nothin' but shootin' dice."

"I believe it's illegal, ain't it?"

"Well."

"It is. Who's holdin' the money?"

Somehow the designated spokesman for the group, Ron pulled a wad of bills from his coat pocket. Ned took the cash like it was nothing more than notepaper and stuffed it into his own coat. "Do I need to ask any of y'all if you're armed?"

"'Course not." Kenneth Armstrong shrugged down deeper into his coat. A cigarette between his lips, each exhalation was smoke and vapor. "Why would any of us have a gun? We wouldn't hurt you no-how. All we have are pocketknives. You want to see 'em?"

"Naw, pocketknives are just tools. Everybody has one." Ned

directed the light from one to the other. "I could take all y'all to jail, but I just don't feel like it tonight."

They men visibly relaxed. Ron grinned. "I knew you wouldn't do that, Uncle Ned?"

"Well, that don't mean y'all get off, neither. Here's what we're gonna do. Tomorrow morning, bright and early, I'm gonna finish my breakfast and step out on the porch and I'd better see every one of y'all standing in the yard."

Kenneth scowled. "But tomorrow's a Sunday."

"Yeah, it is. That means you won't be at church. Better double your tithe next week to make up for it."

"What are we gonna do?" Kenneth's question was nothing but a nervous reaction. They'd been caught shooting dice before, in that exact same place, and all knew the constable's way of dealing with young folks who flirted around the edges of trouble but hadn't yet fallen in with truly bad crowd.

Ned flicked his hand up and down the two-lane highway. "The county hasn't been doing its job, and the sides of the road are growed up, and they didn't get it cut before wintertime. Y'all bring some tools to cut the grass, and some 'toesacks for the trash. We're gonna tidy the road from Arthur City all the way to Forest Chapel."

"Aw, Uncle Ned, not again." Curtis Parker rubbed his cheek. "Even with all of us, that's likely to take all day, and most of the next."

"Or you can meet me in the morning, just like I said, and we'll drive to the courthouse and Judge Rains'll set your fine for gambling and trespassing."

"Trespassing?"

"Yeah, this store don't belong to none of you."

"That'll cost two days' wages if we don't show up for work." Kenneth's hands flapped like wounded birds.

"Maybe one day, if y'all work hard."

To a man, they studied their feet, thinking. Curtis Parker crossed his arms. "Maybe we can make a deal."

"You're not trying to bribe your old uncle, are you?"

"Nossir. What I mean, is if I know something about something, maybe I could tell you about it."

Ron's head snapped around. "Curtis!"

"Well, I just think he might need to know why we're shooting dice out here in the cold."

Ned reached out a hand. "That reminds me. The dice."

His nephew Bob Ray dug them from his pocket and passed them over. "They've probably cooled off anyways."

Ned put them in his pocket. "Now what something are you talking about, Curtis?"

"Well, everybody knows there's folks like to play cards and do a little gamblin' ever now and then over in Juarez."

"So?"

"So, things are changing over there across the river. I guess you know we used to play a little poker over at the Texoma Club, but there's this new place..."

Ron pushed off the wall and took two steps away from Curtis, as if to distance himself from what his cousin was about to say. "You know what you're doing?"

Curtis nodded. "I do. Ned, you know about the Starlite?"

The club was a sore spot between Ned, his nephew, Sheriff Cody Parker, and his longtime friend Judge O. C. Rains. For some reason he couldn't understand, O. C. wasn't in any hurry to shut the place down.

"Of course I do. That new honky-tonk stuck out on that little sliver of Oklahoma land."

"Yessir."

"What of it?"

"We'd be there right now, but it's a little rougher than most of us are used to, and I've lost my ass over there the last two times I went, so we decided to have a friendly little game here and out of the way of trouble."

"You ain't out of trouble, but the least you knotheads could do is shoot your dice in a barn somewhere."

"We see that now."

"You shoulda seen it before I got called out of bed tonight. You got anything else to tell me, other than they're gambling at the Starlite?"

Ron spun and Ned saw the rest of the men were staring hard at Curtis, who finally shrugged and shook his head. "Nossir."

"Then y'all get in them cars you parked right out in front in the open like y'all had good sense and get gone."

They lit out as fast as they could get in their cars. Using the Plymouth's dome light, Ned sat in the heater's warmth, licked the end of a pencil lead, and wrote the men's names on a Harold Hodges Insurance notepad. Being a constable paid little, and even office supplies had to come from somewhere other than his meager salary. Glad to work with local law enforcement, Hodges's company provided Ned with as many unlined notepads as he wanted.

Ned studied the names, grinning. They were good boys and, in more than one case, family men, and not up to any real meanness, but he had a job to do and that meant administering the law. He'd holler at Judge O. C. Rains first thing in the morning and explain what he was doing, just in case someone called in when they saw them cleaning the sides of the road like a Huntsville chain gang.

In Ned's opinion, chain gangs were the best punishment ever devised. A year on a road gang, three quarters of it in the hot Texas sun, cured ninety percent of convicts' meanness. Working from daylight to dark, with only short breaks for water and food, kept them from coming up with meanness for later, unlike what prisons were turning into.

He knew of only one man who served time on a chain gang and backslid into his old ways. That individual was mean as a snake when he was little and hadn't changed one whit since. He was back in the Walls Unit down in Huntsville, and Ned was the one who helped put him there.

The heater was blasting, and it was warm and comfortable in the sedan when a flicker in the side mirror caught his eye. Looking into the glass, he wasn't sure what he was seeing. Hanging one arm over the back of the seat, he turned and squinted through the rear window.

Flames licked out of D. N. Carter's hayloft.

"Dammit!" Ned jammed the car in reverse and whipped the wheel. The Plymouth's front end slewed around, and he shoved the transmission into gear. Spraying gravel, he shot across the highway and slid to a stop in Carter's drive, laying on the horn.

The porch light came on at the same time Ned snapped the handset off the bracket and squeezed the transmit button. "Dispatch! Who's there tonight?"

A gravelly voice came through the Motorola's speaker. "It's me, Ned. Bobby Lee."

"We got a problem here in Center Springs. Call the volunteer fire department and have Roger Armstrong get his men over to D. N. Carter's barn here in Center Springs. It's on fire."

Carter's head poked out the door. "What's wrong, Ned?"

Ned half-stepped from the car. "Get your britches on! Your barn's on fire!"

Dispatch squawked again. "What's the address?"

He keyed the radio as Carter disappeared from sight. "Ain't no address. Roger'll know where it is, like he knows where ever' other barn is in the county."

"I'm calling them now."

Neither of them looked toward Oak Peterson's store to see the figures of Jett McClellan and Gus Davis slipping around the corner to disappear into the store's rear shadows.

Chapter Eleven

The next morning after Mr. Carter's barn burned down, Grandpa came in from working his chain gang. Uncle James dropped us off at the house on his way to work in Chisum. Aunt Ida Belle was too upset over the fire for some reason to cook breakfast that morning, so we were hungry when we got there.

Miss Becky'd been in the kitchen since daylight, making breakfast for her kinfolk waiting in the yard. Though several of them had already eaten, she made everyone take biscuit-and-sausage sandwiches to hold them until noon.

Pepper didn't care that her mama didn't make breakfast, because she was too busy worrying about her weight, even though she didn't weigh much more'n a plate of biscuits. She had Tang and a piece of toast. I heard Mr. Tom Bell leave through the front door just as the sun peeked through the burr oak's bare limbs.

Me and Mark were finishing eggs, bacon, and gravy when the door slammed. Grandpa came in and passed so close I felt a chill come from the material of his coat. He glanced at us without saying anything, his mind somewhere else. Miss Becky was sitting at the telephone table in the living room, writing a note for him on another Harold Hodges pad.

Grandpa stopped in the doorway and grinned. "Them boys out there are working to beat the band, but it's colder'n a deep freeze. I believe I've broke 'em from shooting dice, at least up at the store again."

She'd just hung up the phone and barely paid attention to what he said. "Ned, that was Oak Peterson. He needs you up at his store. Somebody broke in last night."

"After the *fire*?" He looked back over his shoulder like we were the ones to blame.

"Said he didn't know when they got in."

"Well, it might have been before I got there, but them boys woulda said something if they knew, I reckon. What'd they take?"

"Odds and ends. Cigarettes, a box or two of those expensive cigars he keeps for Leon Epperson, I swanny, I don't think that man can go five minutes without one of them nasty things stuck in the corner of his mouth. Anyway, he had two watches he'd taken in trade. They got them too."

"They done it again. I told him he ought not be doing that."

We'd heard the older folks say they traded at one store or another, but that means they bought from them. I'd once asked Aunt Becky why they called it that, and she told me it came from the olden days when settlers and explorers traded beads, medallions, cutting tools like knives and tomahawks, sugar and coffee, and such with the Indians who made their way up to Center Springs. Trading goods for goods still happened, of course.

Miss Becky and quite a few of the farmers' wives in our community traded or sold butter and eggs to Oak and Uncle Neal up at their stores. One story that still made the rounds came from back during the Depression when Miss Emily Hatch once had a rat fall into her milk bucket and drown while she had it out to separate. She went ahead and churned her butter after she fished the body out, then went on and molded the butter. With the butter finished and wrapped in wax paper, she took it up to Uncle Neal's store and traded it to him for some baking goods.

For some reason, she told him what had happened after he handed her the money but ended with "What folks don't know won't hurt them." The next day, her husband, Mr. E. B. Hatch, came up to the store to buy a few supplies, and Uncle Neal convinced him to buy some butter, because Uncle Neal said it was the best he'd ever tasted.

He sold that rat butter right back to Mr. Hatch. He took it home and his wife cooked with it without knowing it was hers They were both long gone, but the story popped up every now and then.

I leaned toward Mark. "Why do you think Mr. Oak shouldn't take things in trade?"

"I believe Grandpa don't want him to start running a pawnshop here."

"What's that?"

He told me, and I remembered seeing one south of the tracks in Chisum. It sounded like a pretty seedy place to me, and I was glad Grandpa didn't want one in Center Springs.

Still wearing his hat, he turned from the living room. Miss Becky followed him into the kitchen with us. "I know the store's closed today, but I need a couple of things. I'm completely out of washing powder, and Top was coughing and wheezing last night. Ask Oak if you can get some cough syrup while you're there. I don't want to wait 'til tomorrow. You know how his lungs are."

"All right, then. You boys come go with me. You can help me feed the cows over in the Patrick patch." He mumbled to himself as we left the table like a couple of rockets, suddenly released from going to Sunday School. "Should have already done the feeding this morning instead of babysitting a bunch of criminals."

Grandpa didn't wait around very long if he took a notion to go somewhere, so we threw our coats on in record time. He was already climbing into his '48 Chevrolet pickup by the time we came outside.

Whoever got the window seat also had to get the gate. I never did like that job because they were those old floppy wire gaps that were harder'n hell to open and close, so I sat in the middle. Mark gave me a grin 'cause he knew my angle, and pulled a thin blue ribbon out of his pocket.

Grandpa twisted the key and the engine no more than caught before he shifted into reverse. Mark was still tying his hair back when we reached the end of the gravel drive and turned on the highway. I flicked the radio on, but it didn't even have time to warm up before we were at the store.

Grandpa coasted up to Oak's gas pump and shut the truck off. Cattycorner across the highway, smoke still rose from what was left of Mr. Carter's barn. "One of you boys get me about three dollars' worth of Regular, and not that Ethyl. The other'n come in with me for what Miss Becky wants."

Mark shouldered the door open. "I'll get the gas."

Any other time, I wanted to do it. I enjoyed turning the crank and watching the clear glass container on top of the gravity pump fill up. We didn't have very many times left to use the antique pump, because it was all around Center Springs that Mr. Oak was replacing them with those new kind where the numbers rolled to tell the price and gallons.

I followed Grandpa through the rusty screen door that rattled from the metal Ideal Bread and 7-Up signs screwed into the wood frame to prevent customers from pushing out the screen. Mr. Oak was behind his counter lit by two bare bulbs hanging from knob and tube wires running along the bare, dust-caked rafters overhead.

An old potbelly stove in the middle of the wooden floor kept the cold outside. Half a dozen unpainted cane-bottom chairs were scattered around the fire, left there by the last customers who pulled up close for the warmth, likely eating rat cheese and crackers, or roasted peanuts.

I stopped beside an oak and glass case full of candy. The wooden back of the case was busted where somebody had knocked it in to get at whatever was inside.

Mr. Oak wore the thickest glasses I've ever seen, and I always figured they did little to help him see. His right eye turned out, and whenever he had to see something, he held it only an inch or two from his good eye. Watching him tally someone's tab was a mystery, because his nose almost touched the paper.

He looked up from a pad in his hand. "Ned. They cleaned me out."

Grandpa stopped, hands in the pockets of his overalls. "Of what?"

"Why, anything that was worth money."

"Everything in here's worth money."

"Well, yeah. They got my cash box and two watches I'd traded for."

"How much were they worth?"

"Oh, twenty each, I reckon."

"How much was in your cash box?"

"Eight or nine dollars."

"You still using that cigar box?"

"Sure 'nough."

"I told you not to do that anymore, after the last time you were broke into. And I told you selling watches or anything else like that's gonna get you robbed again."

"I never figured they'd come back."

"They're not the same ones." Grandpa slid both hands into his pockets. "This time it's somebody new."

Mr. Oak slapped a giant cash register that took up an acre and a half of counter space. "This old girl quit on me right after the war. I don't want to spend any money having her fixed, or to buy a new one. My cash box works just fine. Hell, they'd steal the whole damn cash register if I had any money in it."

"Where'd they get in?"

"The back door. Kicked it in. They took two or three cartons of cigarettes, too."

"What brand?"

"Lucky Strikes mostly, and Pall Malls. Cigars too."

"What kind of watches were they?"

"One was a Timex, one of the good ones. The other'n was a gold Bulova. Blue face. Stole all my root beer barrels, too, and you know who has to have one every time he comes in."

Grandpa's eyes changed at the mention of the hard candy. "I do. Gus Davis."

"Yep."

"All right then. I'll let you know what I find out."

"You know who it was, don't you?"

"I have a suspicion of who it *might* be." Grandpa slid three dollars across the counter. "This is for the gas."

Mark was sitting in the middle of the truck seat when we came out. He gave me a grin and I slammed the door at the same time Grandpa started the engine and threw it into gear. "Where are we going?"

"To teach you boys something."

"What?"

"You'll see."

A couple of minutes later we followed the dirt Boneyard

Slash road as it wound around through the bottoms. I was lost as a goose when he turned on another dirt road, and then onto a two-track that led to an unpainted house set back in the woods.

Grandpa killed the engine in the yard and waited while a mangy yellow dog barked at us from the dirt yard. I had my eye on the dog that looked like it was starving, or sick. "Who lives here?"

"Some of your kinfolk."

That didn't tell me much. We had kinfolk scattered all through the county, and I didn't know half of them. "Which side?"

"Your daddy's."

A woman came out on the porch and hollered at the dog. "Shut up, Yeller! Ned, y'all get out."

"You boys stay in here." He got out and I rolled the window down to hear. A river of cold air poured in.

"Ruby, is Gus here?"

"Sure 'nough." Using a tissue, she wiped at a trickle of snuff drizzling down from the corner of her mouth and hollered back into the house. "Gus!"

He came outside, his face registering shock, and then fear. Shifting a bulge in one cheek that wasn't chewing tobacco, he stopped, half in and out of the screen door. "What?"

Grandpa put one foot on the porch step. "You know why I'm here."

Ruby Davis swung her head back and forth, trying to see them both at the same time. "Ned, what's going on?"

"Gus, you tell her."

He seemed to shrink about six inches. "I don't..."

"Yes, you do. Tell her about that watch you're wearing."

She whirled around as fast as a chicken on a junebug. "What about it?"

He started to spin a story, but then stopped and spat something onto the ground. It landed and bounced once. "Mr. Ned?"

"Tell her."

He sighed big. "Me and J. D. and Fred and Harry, we, uh, we uh, we..."

His mama stared a hole through him, judging the look on his face by what she knew about her own son. "You better start talkin' the truth, or I'm gonna tell your daddy and he'll get the truth out of you."

He studied his feet, then noticed me and Mark sitting in the truck. Here was Gus turning up again like a bad penny. My breath caught when our eyes met. I saw his expression harden, and I didn't like that look one little bit.

Mark rested his hand on my thigh, and I glanced over at him. His eyes were flat and cold. "Don't say a word."

Gus fidgeted a little, then dug at his ear. "I bought it up at the gas station in Arthur City."

He was talking about a tiny little station at the corner of Highway 271 and 197, the road that ran to Center Springs. The station was fairly new, with three glass sides that angled down from the roof and inward, giving it a sleek atomic appearance. The garage sat by itself a few feet away.

I'd been in there a time or two, and they had the usual stuff, plus fresh cookies in a glass jar, and some Texas souvenirs, since it was just across the river from Oklahoma.

Gus licked his lips and held up his arm to show the Bulova and leather band. "I had some money and saw this watch. I just wanted it."

His mama slapped the back of his head hard enough to rattle his brains. "You're a-lyin'. We barely got enough money to put beans on the table let alone wasting it on a watch."

He took the blow without a word, but the interior of the

truck grew ice cold because he never took his eyes off of me and Mark.

Gus was lying sure, and didn't buy that watch the night before, and Grandpa knew it. Held out his hand and Gus took the watch off and gave it to him. "You have any of them root beer barrels left?"

"Nawsir."

"Well, I won't be getting *them* back. Ruby, bring him up to the courthouse tomorrow morning. I won't cuff him now. Got too much to do today, but run him up there and let Cody do some paperwork on him. He won't be under arrest, but Judge O. C.'ll fine him for theft under five, that way he won't have no record, even though this here watch's worth more'n that. Gus, you better be there tomorrow, or the next time I come out here, I'll cuff you up and haul you to jail, you understand me?"

He nodded at the ground. "Yessir."

"Thanks, Ned. We'll be there." Miss Ruby yanked Gus by the collar and into the house. "Or what's left of him after his daddy gets finished wearing his ass out with a belt."

Gus watched us as he stumbled up the porch steps. I knew for sure it was him sitting on the back deck of the Starlite the night R. B. died, drinking beer with Jett McClellan. If he took a notion to tell Mr. O. C., or Uncle Cody that we'd been there that night just to make it easier on himself, then our gooses were cooked.

Chapter Twelve

Odell Chatworthy leaned over the workbench in his shop, listening to country music and wondering why anyone who didn't know anything about generators would have tried to fix this one. A local farmer took it off a '62 Ford and tried to change the bushings, doing more damage than the initial drop in voltage.

He was about to give up on it and call the farmer and tell him he needed a new generator. That would save Odell two hours' worth of work and give the man a generator he could count on.

A figure came through the small, grimy office and into the shop. "Sure is cold out there."

Not one for casual conversation, Odell squinted at the man and resumed his task. "That's because it's wintertime."

The guy in a bulky coat and worn felt hat grunted a laugh. "Then it'll be hot, and we'll be complaining about that."

"How can I help you?"

"Need you to take a look under my hood. My generator light came on and there's a grinding squeak under there."

"Those idiot lights worry everyone. Can you leave it?"

"No. It's the only car I got."

Odell sighed. The young man looked familiar, but he couldn't place him right off. There was something, though, and it gave him a sick feeling for a brief moment. "It out front?"

"Yep."

"Let me get my coat." Odell put down the screwdriver and pulled on a grease-stained jacket. "I was about to close up. You're lucky, I'd be gone if I wasn't waiting for Cy Hendershot to come pick up that truck out there. I ain't usually here on Sunday evenin's."

"Well, I sure appreciate it." The stranger followed him through a side door and into the frigid air.

A cattle trailer out front vibrated as a bull slammed against the side. "That's the Grim Reaper." Odell pointed at the trailer hitched onto the pickup he was talking about. "Been there since noon, and that old bull there's been bellering his head off. Probably thirsty."

Passing by, the stranger rapped a knuckle against the back gate. The bull slammed it with his forehead, making the man jump. Odell laughed. "Yeah, every time I passed, he butted that gate like he wanted to come out and eat me. Cy says he's a retired rodeo bull that he's putting out to pasture. If any of his calves have the disposition of this mean old bastard, they'll be dangerous by the time they get off the tit."

He pointed at the stranger's car parked right beside the trailer. "Pull the hood and start 'er up."

The man opened the door and dropped into the seat. The engine growled alive and he got out, leaving the door open. Odell frowned as the man came around. "It sounds just fine to me."

"Stick your head down there and listen. It ain't right."

Putting both hands on the frame, Odell leaned under the hood and turned so that his good ear could pick out what was wrong.

He caught sight of a crowbar swinging toward his head. The massive blow buckled both knees. Cy's left eye went black and the other that still focused registered the man's face that was suddenly familiar.

That damned dice game.

The second blow crushed his throat and Odell Chatworthy choked to death from a crushed larynx long before the Grim Reaper stomped his body into jelly in the back of the cattle trailer.

Chapter Thirteen

Buster Rawlins sat at the corner table to the left of the Starlite's red leather front door. Merle Haggard was singing some prisoner back home on the jukebox, the mournful song cutting through the thick scent of smoke and spilled beer. On Sunday night, there was no one else but the bartender and his employees.

Fidgeting in his chair, Rawlins tapped the tabletop with a forefinger. "I oughta kill all three of you dumb bastards."

Wooly gray hair slicked back with HA (Hair Arranger brand), white shirt, and plaid pants, he fiddled with the handle of a half-full mug of rodeo-cool beer. The dark bar was lit by neon signs advertising Miller High Life, Falstaff, Lone Star, and Schlitz.

Melvin LaFleur, Jess Plemens, and Ricky Toscani were familiar with Rawlins's sporadic rage, and none wanted to draw his attention to themselves. Filling the remaining chairs around the table, and desperate to avoid eye contact, they found other places to look.

"We don't want people to be watching this place!" The skinny, narrow-shouldered man swallowed half of the beer, then with his huge curved nose deep inside the thick mug, he drained the last few drops and slammed it on the table. Almost chinless, he scratched at three days' growth of whiskers on his neck. "I'm trying to run a nice *business* here, sell a little beer and some liquor under the table, let folks dance, and maybe a friendly little game out back.

"The Oklahoma sheriff's department don't want to drive the long way around to get here, and Texas law won't *touch* this little sliver of sand. This place is a gold mine and I don't need you *waterheads* messin' things up, especially now that we're moving nose candy."

Rawlins had a connection in California who was making great inroads in the drug scene. The unnamed sergeant stationed at Travis Air Force Base in California intercepted bodies destined for certain funeral homes manned by vetted clients and packed predetermined amounts of cocaine into the body bags.

The drug was quickly rising in popularity as musicians such as Johnny Cash and Bob Dylan recorded songs mentioning the white powder.

Sitting with his back to the barn, Melvin LaFleur absently rubbed at a rough, blue tattoo of a Mexican *chiquita* on his forearm. "What happened wasn't nothin' we ain't done before."

"Yeah, but I done told you we're gonna handle thissun different. We have a bird nest on the ground in this joint and I don't want it screwed up! This was exactly the kind of thing that drove us out of Louisiana." He turned the mug up again and realizing it was empty, held it up. "Johnny B.! Bring me another Blue Ribbon."

The weasel-faced bartender nodded and reached into the cooler and popped the top of a bottle.

Melvin LaFleur quit rubbing his tattoo and leaned back in the chair. He'd been with Rawlins through the Louisiana years and ramrodded their place in Bail, a small rural community south of Natchitoches. There they ran a little club back in the woods until a series of suspicious deaths caught the attention of the local sheriff who got to sniffing around enough for Rawlins to realize the payoffs to the deputy assigned to that part of the parish wasn't providing the promised protection.

It was time to get gone.

That's when Rawlins and LaFleur ran into a bootlegger named Doak Wheeler, who was running moonshine throughout Northeast and East Texas and looking to add Louisiana to his routes. While they were sampling his product one night down on the Cane River, Wheeler told him about Lamar County, just south of the Red River. According to the moonshiner, Lamar County was ripe for a forward-thinking businessman who was looking for just the right opportunity.

Staying one step in front of the Louisiana parish sheriff, Rawlins burned the backwoods club one night and they got gone.

Rawlins and his gang finally arrived in Chisum, Texas, and heard about Juarez, the cluster of honky-tonks across the river. It was in the TV Lounge one night when he learned about a spit of Oklahoma land south of the river.

Rawlins tilted the bottle and bubbles glugged upward. His prominent Adam's apple bounced up and down, seeming to almost hit the end of that nose that nearly curved over his mouth. "Tell me about that dice game on Friday night."

"Not much to tell. The guy wanted to leave with a pocket full of money." Digging at a cigarette burn on the table's surface with his thumbnail, LaFleur spoke with a slight Cajun accent. "Some of it our money. He started squalling when we said he had to stay a little longer to give everyone a chance to win it back."

Rawlins tapped the mug on the table. "So, in your opinion, rolling the son of a bitch wasn't an option."

"You told us the marks weren't to be touched on property."

"I said, don't get any blood on the floors. How did that translate to killing him, or anyone else for that matter?"

"He wouldn't *stay*." LaFleur lit the cigarette from the butt between his lips and switched them. Crushing the stub in a half-full ashtray, he inhaled a lungful of smoke and let it through his nose. "Dennis here told him to hang around through a couple more rolls, but some of the other shooters convinced the guy to leave."

"They knew one another."

Ricky Toscani spoke for the first time. It was as if he had information nothing of the others knew. "About half of 'em. There was a young man lived in Chisum. Heard him tell it to another'n. Then there were two Indians. Might have been brothers. The white-haired guy seemed to know everybody and told the mark that it was time to go. Said he'd won enough and not to push his luck. Said they'd never seen anyone win so much at dice and he should take his money and get gone. The rest listened to him like he was their grandpa, and he might have been. Hell, this is like back home down in Baton Rouge, ever'body's kin to ever'body else."

"What then?" Rawlins shook his head and drained half of the beer.

"We did everything we knew to hold him there, but he was done. Toscani here wanted to go cut his tires, you know, thinking he'd come back in and gamble a little more until he caught a ride home, but we didn't think that was a good idea."

"It was a better idea to kill him." Rawlins's sarcasm was whip-crack sharp.

"It wasn't none of *us* who did it. We roughed him up, but that's all. He was alive when we came back inside."

That comment came at the same time the song on the Wurlitzer ended. They sat in silence as the machinery selected another 45. The sounds were loud in the empty, smoky bar. The platter dropped and Jerry Lee Lewis began, "What's Made Milwaukee Famous." Rawlins listened as if they weren't having a conversation about murder.

"Jess, I want that song to play ever' half hour from now on. Ol' Jerry Lee must've written that one about us, and I want these people to be thinking about beer while they're here. Go to town and buy a couple of cases of the saltiest, cheapest peanuts you can find to make 'em thirsty."

"You got it." Jess Plemens took out a small pad and wrote the order down as if he might forget.

Buster Rawlins switched back to their previous conversation as if there hadn't been a break. "How much did he win?"

To a man all three dropped their eyes again. LaFleur bit his lip. "Nearly two thousand."

"Haven't had a winner like that in a long time. He must've been hot. Did any of y'all consider switching the dice on him?"

Plemens shrugged. "Darrel tried, but that guy was watching close. It seemed like he knew every trick in the book."

"Of course he did. I heard he was a vet! You know what those guys did while they were waiting troopships to kill Japs?" He didn't give them a chance to answer. "Let me tell you. They played cards and shot dice! That's what they did for *hours.* They shot *dice!*"

"Maybe *he* was using shaved dice, boss. Maybe *he* was cheating."

Rawlins shot Toscani a withering glare that almost glowed in the dim bar. "That don't make any difference now. I doubt he was cheating. He beat the house. Have you leaned on the rest of those who were in the game and saw what happened out in the parking lot?"

Plemens perked up. "Yessir. We've talked to them all, and they know better than to say anything."

"What'd you tell 'em?"

"That they weren't there in the first place, but if anyone talked out of school, it be them and us. Then I told 'em all they could drink for free until the end of the month."

"That's the smartest thing you've done yet. All right, keep an ear to the ground, and if you hear anyone talking about this, you deal with it right then."

"Yessir."

"We have too much at stake with this one, spent too much time setting things up. I don't want this to turn into another Natchitoches." He pronounced the town as *nak-a-dish* and waved a hand at the smoky bar. "We can't afford to light this one."

"Skip a Rope" was the next on the jukebox. Henson Cargill's song of immorality and social consciousness made Rawlins snort that the song was playing in his joint. "When's the next shipment?"

LaFleur thought for a moment. "Roth says tomorrow."

Toscani nodded.

"Under what name?"

Plemens chimed in. "Watley. Philip Watley."

Chapter Fourteen

Mark and I were sitting on a hay bale in Grandpa's pole barn before school Monday, looking out over the trail leading through the gate and up to the house. We'd helped him feed, and were waiting for him to come back from the house so he could take us to school.

Despite the chill, it was a good place to sit in the early morning sun slanting through the side. The fragrance of alfalfa, cow manure, and dust filled the air.

High clouds skudded across the gray sky, and a V of geese complained about the coming weather. Grandpa said a blue norther was on the way, and I hoped he was wrong. Cold weather would keep us inside, unless we could talk someone into taking us hunting.

Picking a dry sandbur from the hem of my jeans, I flicked it out into the dead grass. "All this trouble is making me nervous."

Mark settled down into his coat. "You worry too much."

"Well, I have a lot to worry about."

"Such as?"

"We were at the Starlite the night R. B. died, and that Gus Davis guy saw us there. Then the next thing you know, we were in a hay barn that burned down an hour later."

"Just don't say anything."

"I don't intend to, but dang it, I'm worried sick some of this is gonna get on us."

"The only thing Grandpa is going to care about is us being in Carter's barn before it caught fire. He'll blister our butts if he finds out."

The pit of my stomach dropped. "You know it was our fault. It was probably a butt that didn't go completely out."

"None of that was *your* fault, or mine."

"I was there."

"So was I, but it wasn't *us* that burned it down."

"Burned it down sounds intentional."

Mark turned his dark eyes toward me, then back to the house a hundred yards away. "I believe it was."

I studied on that comment for a minute. "Pepper wouldn't do something mean. You think it was Jett?"

"Yep. That boy's bad news. He was at the Starlite, and you know as well as I do he was shooting dice behind the store with the rest of 'em. Then the barn burns down while he's playing with fire. He was the last one down."

"Why would he do that?"

"No telling why anyone does wrong. I just wish Pepper would see what's behind his mask. I can't tell her. She won't listen. She's so crazy about that guy she'd think I was just trying to sour the deal."

"She's *your* girlfriend."

"I thought she was, but it's nothing official."

"He hasn't asked her."

"How do you know that?"

"Guys like that don't. The girls fall all over them, and they just soak it up until the next one comes along. They're like Dracula. They feed off whatever it is the girls give up, and then move on."

"What are you gonna do?"

He grinned. "What I been doing. Someday he'll be gone, and we'll be right back where we were."

"Yeah, except for the damage he causes."

"Pepper was already damaged."

"How?"

"You know about when she ran off to California."

"She only made it to Arizona."

"Yeah, but did she tell you what happened while she was gone?"

"She ran off. Grandpa and Uncle James had to get her back."

"The rest."

"What?"

"Then she never told."

"What?"

"I shouldn't say nothing, but it explains a lot about how she is."

"I still don't get it."

He scuffed through the hay with one foot until he reached dirt, then kept scratching the hole deeper and deeper while he studied on something. He looked past me and out the open front. "Maybe she needs to be the one tells you."

"If she hadn't told me by now, she won't. You know what makes her the way she is. Tell me and maybe I'll understand her."

"Well, the truth is, she *don't* know why she does anything, but she's gotten harder, sharper. She says and does things just to get a reaction most times."

"You're not telling me anything I don't already know."

Mark stopped scuffing. "Don't let on I told you."

"Cross my heart and hope to die."

"She was raped out there."

I was so shocked by the announcement, I could only stare at the little scar beside his nose. Eyes shining with embarrassment, Mark looked back at me. "You didn't know, did you?"

"No." My stomach fell and it took all of the energy out of me. "Now I wish you hadn't said."

"I know. It might help you figure her out, though."

"You think it will?"

"No."

We sat there in silence, watching a car pass down on the highway. I drew a deep breath. "You know we're gonna have to tell somebody what we saw out at that joint on Friday night. Grandpa's looking into R. B.'s death. He'll need to know."

"I knew you were going to do that."

I nodded. "I can't help it."

He kept looking past me and I finally figured out that he was staring at the empty corral half grown over with weeds. "What do you keep looking at?"

"The gate's open."

"So?"

"That kind of thing bothers me." He got up and walked out into the wind to close it. Watching Mark wire the gate in place, I wished I'd noticed and done it myself.

Chapter Fifteen

Without announcing himself, Constable Ned Parker walked into Tony Roth's office in the Sanitorium on Monday, barely noticing the County Coroner sign on the door. He was never much for knocking on administrative departments' doors. He felt he didn't need to since the sounds of clacking keys told him someone was inside and not on the phone or in a meeting.

Roth looked up from a report he was writing and paused with his fingers above the Underwood's black keys. He clamped down on the stem of a cold pipe and swiveled to face Ned across a cluttered desk. Although he was clean-shaven, his hair looked as if it hadn't seen a comb in a week. "You must be Ned Parker."

"I am. You Tony Roth?"

He removed the pipe and rested both elbows on a skinny bare spot on the desk. "At your service, I guess"

His hand stuck out, and Ned crossed in two fast strides. For a moment Roth almost pulled back until he realized the constable wanted to shake. He half rose, but the hand was there before he could straighten, and offered nothing but four fingers. Ned squeezed them and almost frowned. He never trusted a man who didn't know how to shake.

It was almost as if Roth wanted him to kiss that hand instead of shaking it, disgusting Ned. He turned loose and settled onto a soft, cushioned chair, leaving Roth still half-crouched at the desk, his limp wrist hanging in the air.

Ned removed his hat, holding it by the brim. He looked around for a hat rack, irritated there was no place to hang his Bailey, and surveyed the office located at the Sanatorium on West Washington Street. Soft chairs, framed oil landscapes, and a wooden bar cart full of glasses and cut-glass liquor bottles gave the room a more businesslike feel than one would expect in a medical facility.

The county coroner settled back after a pause, clearly uncomfortable. He adjusted the thin black tie around his neck and checked the cuffs of his rolled sleeves, waiting for the constable to speak.

"I haven't been in this office in years." Ned unconsciously worried at his hat brim. "Ol' Bill Callaghan had this room at one time."

"I'm afraid I don't know the name."

"You wouldn't. I won't be here a minute. I came by to get the autopsy report for R. B. Parker."

Roth glanced at the badge pinned over his shirt pocket. "I'm not sure I can release it without a court order."

"Won't need that. I'm next of kin."

"Oh, well, in that case, I'll have to see some sort of documentation to that effect."

"Don't have none. Look," Ned read the nameplate on the corner of Roth's desk, "Tony, we handle things a little different than where you come from."

"You know where I worked before?"

"Nope. But I got a good idy you came from the city, according to that tie and all the trimmings around here." He waved a finger around, finishing with a flick at the bar. "The truth is, I don't even need to take it with me. I just need a cause of death."

"I'm not through with the report, Constable, and I'll still need..."

"When will you have it done?"

"Maybe a month. I'm way behind..."

"Nope. That's too late. I need to wrap this up pretty quick."

Roth leaned back and laced his fingers. "I can't get it finished that fast, sorry."

"You're through with the body?" Like an attorney in the courtroom, Ned knew the answer before he asked the question.

"Yes."

"Then you know what killed him."

"Yes, but it won't be official until the report is filed."

"Who will you file it with?"

"Well, since it was an accident, it'll go to the sheriff's office. You can get it from him."

"Those usually go pretty fast, don't they? Just an outline of what happened."

"That's right."

"Sometimes that's only a phone call, 'cause there's nothing else to investigate."

On familiar ground, Roth reached into his desk drawer and withdrew a soft leather tobacco wallet. Using his forefinger in a familiar routine, he scraped cherry blend into the briarwood bowl of a well-cured pipe. "Right again."

"If it was suspicious, or a murder, the report goes to the sheriff and the county judge, and that takes longer."

Replacing the wallet, Roth scratched a gofer match alight and puffed at the pipe's stem. He dropped the matchbook on the desk, the side advertising the Dunes Hotel in Vegas. "You've done this before."

"I've been around a good long while. So, since you're about to call my kinfolk with the results, you can tell me now."

There was a slight pause between shaking out the match and puffing the pipe alight. Ned saw the hesitation and first signs of nervousness in the coroner.

"What kinfolk?"

"The sheriff, Cody Parker."

"I should have put two and two together."

"You should have, and R. B. was killed in my precinct, which gives me the right to see that report. So. What killed my nephew?"

Roth puffed twice and sighed through the sweet-smelling smoke. "He drowned."

"Any signs of suspicious bruises? Anything unusual?"

"No." Roth reached up to remove the pipe with fingers that weren't as steady as they were five minutes earlier. "It was a drowning."

"Truck went off in the creek and he drowned."

"It was classic. He was drunk. Probably passed out before the vehicle went off the road. I suspect his face was in the water and he could do nothing to save himself."

"When will that report be done?"

Roth inclined his head. "That's it I'm working on right now."

"This is your machine there?"

"It is, but there's procedure that I have to follow."

Ned saw how far the paper was rolled into the typewriter. "You're almost done. Finish it up. I'll wait."

"Like I said..."

"I'll wait."

Pipe stem clamped in his teeth, Roth swiveled back to the Underwood that was old when almost all of Chisum burned back in 1916. He tapped at the keys with two fingers, paused to collect his thoughts, and tapped a few more times. Not satisfied, he rolled the paper, struck over several words, and typed some more.

Ripping the report from the roller ten tense minutes later, he held it across the desk. "Here it is."

Ned took the sheet and read quickly. "There's a lot of strike-overs in this."

"I'm not a good typist."

"I can tell. Cause of death, drowning."

"That's what I told you."

"Needed to see it in writing." Ned folded the paper and stood. "Thanks."

"Hey, that's my only copy."

"There ain't much writing on here, and a lot of strikeovers. I bet the next one'll be better." Ned stood, looking down at the desk. A casino ashtray containing a book of paper matches rested beside a cold pipe. "The Dunes. You been there?"

Roth glanced down. "Yes I have. I've been to several casinos in Las Vegas."

"Them gofer matches ain't much use unless you're inside out of the wind."

"I like to collect matchbooks. I have them from all across the country, advertising everything from restaurants to hotels to bars." He slid back and opened the middle desk drawer. He pitched a handful on the desk. "This one's from the Stork Club in New York City, the 21 Club in New York, and this one is more local. The Adolphus Hotel in Dallas."

"Takes a lot of money to travel and gamble."

"Yes, it does. But if you'll permit me to say, there's a lot of money in dead people. In addition to serving as the county coroner, I hold part interest in several funeral homes in Dallas and California. Just bought into one here in Chisum."

"Um humm." Ned replaced his hat and turned toward the door. "I wouldn't take a lot of pride in dealing with other people's misery."

"If that's the way you look at it. Some people feel joy in knowing their relatives are now in Heaven, and we're taking care of the remains down here. It's all about life."

"And sudden death. Thanks for your help."

Roth leaned back, picked up the pipe, and bit the stem. "Hope that helps."

"It won't help R. B. Thanks for your trouble."

In the corridor, Ned closed the door and paused to read the autopsy report aloud. "R. B. died as a result of drowning while intoxicated. There were no unusual or suspicious bruises or marks on the body." He sighed. "Well, I reckon that'll do it."

A voice down the hall made him turn. "What'll do what, Ned?"

Recognizing the soft rasp, he looked up. "Howdy, Shorty."

The orderly nodded. Shorty Henderson knew Ned from a number of jobs he'd held throughout the years. He tended to work at a variety of jobs, usually for several months to a year or two before moving on to something else. "Sorry to hear about R. B."

"Thanks. Hard times. What're you doing here?"

"Lost my job over at B&W. Heard they were hiring here at the coroner's office. It's a lot less work than welding, and it's a helluva lot quieter, pushing dead people around. Whatcha got there in your hand?"

Before Ned could answer, a well-dressed young man in his twenties brushed past and walked into the coroner's office without knocking. Folks from small towns were raised to speak when they passed someone, but the man didn't even make eye contact.

Shaking his head at such rudeness, Ned glanced down at the paper in his hand as if he'd forgotten it was there. "I oughta yank that feller back out here and explain what manners are."

"Mr. Ned, he's Ray Roth, the coroner's son. Running for city council. Must have something on his mind, 'cause he's usually glad-handing everybody he comes across, 'cept for people like me, anyway."

"He's barely old enough to vote."

"He's been around for a good long while. His daddy's putting him in the right places so he can move up in politics. I heard that boy say one time that he intends to be governor someday, and then shoot for the presidency."

"Well, he better straighten up and treat everybody the same if he's gonna get very far in *this* town. He don't make it here, he won't make it down in Austin." He held up the sheet of paper. "Came by to get R. B.'s autopsy report."

"Figured you'd be by to pick it up. I'god, it's a damned shame what happened."

"It was his own damn fault."

"Well, you could say that, but we've all be in situations like that. It coulda happened to me a dozen times in the past. I've been in some rough places and run up against rougher men."

Ned frowned, wondering what Shorty was talking about. "Folks sometimes get on a bad road through their own actions."

Shorty nodded. "I kinda figured you'd get to diggin' around pretty quick."

"Why's that?"

"Well, it's your job, ain't it?"

"My job?"

"To investigate murder."

"Who's?"

"Why, R. B.'s, a-course."

Chapter Sixteen

I walked out of school with Mark to find the weather lowering and a dark line of clouds stacked up over the river. Grandpa would be there soon to pick us up, and I hoped he made it before the norther blew in, though it wouldn't be but a few minutes from the looks of that cloud. I zipped my coat and glanced around for Pepper.

Mark saw what I was doing and shook his head. "She's not riding home with us today."

"She's not going to walk home in *this*. That front'll be here before she can get home."

He looked as if he'd lost his best friend. "She's with Jett. She told me at lunch his mama was picking them both up. She's gonna study at his house after school."

I couldn't help but think that I wished Mrs. Mildred McClellan would offer me a ride to their house. I'd have given anything to sit in the back seat with Jett's twin sister, Blu.

Mark must have read my mind. "You stay away from her, too. She looks like an angel on earth, but those twins are two peas in a pod. There's something wrong with both of 'em."

"I've seen you looking at her in class."

"You can't help but *look* at her, and she has the prettiest eyes I've ever seen in my life, especially when she smiles. But you know as well as I do that the bloom on a bull nettle's pretty, but you better not touch it."

"She won't have anything to do with me anyway." I was still the shortest kid in my grade level and wasn't much taller than some of the eighth graders, and that included the girls.

"You're lucky, then."

Something in his voice made me look at Mark, who suddenly seemed uncomfortable. "She invited you to study with her too."

He nodded. "Yep, she did. But I told her no. I was Pepper's guy."

"But she's hanging out with Jett now."

"Complicated, ain't it?" He pointed. "There's Mr. Tom in his truck over there waving at us."

We crossed the dead grass in the schoolyard to the cracked asphalt drive. Mr. Tom grinned out the open driver's window. "You two hop in. Your granddaddy asked me to pick y'all up, so's you don't get caught by that norther comin' there. He's in town. I'll take you home." He looked past us. "Pepper coming?"

I rounded the front of the truck as Mark answered. "She caught a ride to Mrs. McClellan's house to study with Jett this afternoon."

He grinned, making his thick white mustache twitch. "Studying. With Jett."

Mark came around and slid into the seat. He slammed the door at the same time the norther hit like a sledgehammer. The truck rocked, and the air filled with flying leaves and dead grass. The kids in the yard screamed and ran around like chickens with their heads cut off. Some headed back inside the school, while a few of those who walked home took off at a dead run.

"Good Lord!" Mr. Tom shifted into gear and we took off.

He reset his black hat as if it was windy in the cab of that truck. "I ain't seen a good blue norther like this in years. It does my heart good. We didn't have 'em down in the Valley, at least not as strong. They kinda petered out before they got that far south."

The story I heard was Mr. Tom lived down there for years, rangering along the border until he showed up in Center Springs a few years earlier.

It was warm in the truck and I was glad to be inside. Texas blue northers hit hard and fast, sometimes dropping temperatures up to fifty or sixty degrees in less than an hour. This looked to be like one of those strong ones, the kind you want to watch while sitting in front of a fire somewhere.

"With Pepper hanging around with that boy, I figured one of y'all'd be interested in that sister of his." I was watching him as he cut his eyes across the cab, watching for our reactions from under his hat brim. "At least you, Top. Or Mark, maybe you feel like getting even with Pepper. Wouldn't surprise me none to see that."

I was surprised to see Mark grin. He shook his head in a weary adult way. "Aw, Mr. Tom, you know how it is. Girls are like hummingbirds, flitting around and looking pretty. She'll be back one of these days."

"Good Lord. How old are you, son? I've known grown men to cry like babies when their gals take a notion to look around."

He shook his head. "I'm not worried."

"You know what kind of boy Jett is, don't you?"

"Yessir. Saw it right off."

"That boy's trouble. He's gonna try everything he's big enough to."

I knew what he was warning about and felt my face blush. "Pepper's tough."

"Umm-humm. You think his sister's alike?"

"They have the same blood." Mark looked out the passenger window. "That's why I ain't studying with her."

The whole conversation had my head spinning as we left the school behind. Mr. Tom steered us down the road lined with bare trees. I watched the water tower grow larger.

"You're an old soul, Mark. That's for sure." Mr. Tom took his foot off the gas. "We're gonna pull in here at the store for a minute. I need to get some pipe tobacco, then I'll get y'all home."

Rusty bottle tops and red gravel crunched under the tires as he turned right and pulled between the domino hall and Neal Box's store. Smoke came from both chimneys, snatched away by the steady wind that didn't push us as hard between the buildings. The sky lowered and grew darker.

Mr. Tom jerked his truck door open and chilly air flooded in. "Y'all get out and come in and get you a bite. I figure you're hungry after studying hard all day. It's all on me."

We slid out as a V of Canada geese flew only yards overhead, calling steadily. The lot in front of the store was full of cars and trucks, hemmed in on one side by two cattle trailers parked parallel to each other and the highway.

Gray clouds covered the late winter sun. Holding his hat down with one hand, Mr. Tom moved pretty quick for an old man, and we were right behind as he hit the wooden steps fast and hard. No one was dumb enough to be on the porch, but several men were huddled around the stove in the middle of the cavernous store. It was the traditional gathering place for farmers and ranchers in cold weather, and brother, let me tell you, it was getting butt chilling out there pretty fast.

Only half an hour earlier, I heard one of the teachers tell another that it was about seventy degrees just before we got out of class, but I figured it was already close to freezing with no sign of stopping, and with darkness not far away, it was gonna be one of the coldest nights of the year.

Everyone around the stove looked up to see who was coming in. Uncle Neal behind the counter threw up a hand. "Y'all come on in here. Howdy, Mark. Uncle Top!"

From the time I was old enough to talk, I called him Uncle Neal, even though we weren't blood kin. When I was little, I thought everyone was related in Center Springs, and the truth was, most were in one way or another.

I knew almost everyone gathered around the old potbelly woodstove. The regulars were there, Ty Cobb and Jimmy Foxx Wilson. Mr. Floyd and Uncle Cliff were on cane-bottom chairs, their legs crossed at the knees. Bent over his old guitar, Uncle Cliff absently picked out a tune so soft you could barely hear it. He'd almost made it in Nashville back in the 1940s, but drinking led to nothing more than a two-room unpainted shack less than a mile from the store.

Two ranchers in barn coats and hats stood beside the fire, warming their hands. I figured they belonged to the trucks and trailers parked out front. A couple of strangers were in the aisles, picking up a few things.

Not wanting to draw any more attention to ourselves than necessary in front of the grown-ups, Mark and I waved and walked over to the cooler. Though it was cold outside, a Dr Pepper sounded pretty good right then. I had a quarter in my pocket and thought about buying a Baby Ruth to go along with it. That would be enough for Mark to get a candy bar, too, with Mr. Tom buying the drinks.

Ike Reader had his back to us and nearly twisted himself in two to see who'd walked in. They were talking about the weather. "Listen, listen. The weatherman at noon said this was gonna be the coldest norther in years."

Jimmy Foxx tucked both hands into the bulging pockets of his hunting coat. I figured they were full of shotgun shells, because one duck wing stuck out of Ty Cobb's game bag.

Ty Cobb grinned. "Huntin'll be slow for a day or so, then we'll have geese galore. Did y'all hear that bunch go over a minute ago?"

Mr. Tom shook hands around and walked over to a shelf packed with tobacco, both chewing and smoking. He jerked a thumb at the stove. "Neal, you're gonna have to feed this beast every hour for the next few days. Weatherman said this one was gonna be a booger. Snow's coming."

Uncle Neal grinned from behind the counter. "I hope to sell a lot of that wood stacked out there, too."

The ever-present blackened metal coffeepot stayed on top of the stove throughout the winter. Each spring, he threatened to pull out the woodstove and replace it with a propane heater, but the older men always managed to talk him out of it, enjoying the heat, camaraderie, and free coffee.

One of the strangers in a sleeveless sweater and slacks poured himself a cup of coffee and blew across the surface to cool it off. "I'd enjoy a little cream in here."

Neal shook his head. "All I got is sweet milk. Don't have any cream."

"This is pretty bitter." The man sipped again. "What's sweet milk?"

Eyebrows went up around the stove. Jimmy Foxx worked his chew into one cheek. "I don't believe I know you."

The man sniffed at the coffee. "From Dallas. Name's Leonard. On the way to spend a couple of days with my old grandmother. I don't get out here in the sticks very often, and then when I do, it's the coldest day in five years."

I fished a bottle of Dr Pepper from the cooler and turned to see the men's faces. They didn't look any too happy.

"Anyway," the city feller continued, "I always use cream in my coffee."

Ty Cobb tilted his head. "Even your *free* coffee."

Even *I* got the point, but Leonard didn't. He nodded as if they were all old acquaintances. "Even free coffee strong enough to stand up like Jell-O."

"Tell you what." Jimmy Foxx pointed at the door. "Old Earl here's hauling mama cows to the sale barn. Why'n't you go on out there and get you some cream directly from the cow?"

Mr. Tom turned at the suggestion, eyes twinkling. On his stool behind the counter, Uncle Neal straightened.

The stranger shook his head. "I can't believe I'd have to milk a cow just to lighten my coffee."

"Listen, listen." Ike Reader stood. "Since your grandmama's from the country, I reckon you know how to milk a cow, don't you?"

"Sure I do. You just grab one and squeeze." Leonard made a motion with his hand and it looked like he was playing Rock, Paper, Scissors all by himself.

The oldest rancher in a sweat-stained hat chimed in, eyes sparkling in fun. "Just climb over the top of the trailer and fill 'er up, if you want fresh milk. There's plenty of room in there. I don't have 'em packed that tight and they're used to being milked."

The bigmouthed city feller nodded, having talked himself into a situation he couldn't get out of. He thought for a second, and you could tell he needed to man up a little in front of everyone. "You have anything behind the counter to squirt the milk in?"

Uncle Neal spun on his stool and plucked a paper cup from the stack behind him. "Use this."

Squaring his shoulders, Leonard took it and disappeared

through the door. The men started to laugh, but Ike held up a finger. "Listen. Listen. Not yet. He'll hear you."

I looked over at Mr. Tom, who winked at me. "They're just funnin' a city feller. He brought it up."

Mark leaned in and whispered. "This is gonna be cool!"

The wind howled around the clapboard store. We listened but couldn't hear anything but the rattling metal signs nailed to the front and sides of the wooden building. Uncle Neal stood and adjusted the rags stuffed in the double-hung windows. He squinted outside.

Ike Reader looked worried. "You don't think he'll get hurt, do you?"

"Naw." The rancher shook his head and poured himself some coffee. "Those old mama cows are gentle as can be."

"Listen, not in a trailer, though."

"And not by a city feller, but I doubt he'll get in there with 'em." The rancher chuckled. "I 'magine he'll just get in his car and leave to keep from owning up to his brag."

The men were laughing up a storm when the door opened and Mack Vick came through, half-carrying the stranger, who looked like he'd been through a shredder. Shirt torn and covered in dirt and manure from head to one sockless foot, the stranger's eyes were turning black.

The room went silent at the sight of the mangled city dweller. Ike Reader jumped up from his chair and helped Mack sit him down. "Listen, listen. What happened?"

Mack tilted his hat back, revealing a white forehead. "You're gonna have to tell *me*. I pulled up in the truck at the same time this feller almost flew over the top of one of them trailers out there."

Ike shook the city feller's shoulder. "Listen, listen. You all right, buddy?"

"That thing almost killed me." He still had the paper cup wadded in one hand. "I thought she was gonna be a gentle old milk cow."

"They are." The rancher who'd suggested the prank frowned. "You're talking like there was just one in there."

"There was."

"You went to the wrong trailer, then. I told you go to the one full of cows."

"I saw that other trailer, and it didn't seem as crowded. I was afraid I'd get stepped on in there with all them other cattle."

The second grizzled rancher grinned. "The other'n was mine, son, and I ain't hauling milk cows."

Mr. Tom shook his head. "What's back there?"

"A retired old rodeo bull called the Grim Reaper."

The store filled with laughter, and Jimmy Foxx slapped his knee. "Just grab one and squeeze, huh? I believe you grabbed the wrong one this time."

The store was filled with laughter until Mack's face told them something was wrong. Neal held up a hand to quiet things down so they could hear what the cowboy had to say. "What is it, Mack?"

"You better call Ned. Odell Chatworthy's in that same trailer, too, and he's dead."

Mr. Tom stiffened, but it was Uncle Neal who went pale.

Chapter Seventeen

Ned climbed the courthouse steps after throwing a look at the line of black clouds out past Frenchie's Café on North Main, and well beyond the river. It was already cold enough to be uncomfortable, but when that cold front finally arrived, they were in for a bad spell of weather.

He stopped inside on the polished black and white penny tiles and unbuttoned his sport coat. Ned always wore slacks and a light-blue shirt when he went to town, his badge pinned just above the shirt pocket. His Sunday clothes were a little thin for the weather, and he wished he'd worn his overalls.

Across the foyer, Sheriff Cody Parker and Deputy Anna Sloan stepped off the elevator. Behind them, the new elevator operator waved and closed the doors.

Ned tilted his felt hat back. "I was coming to see you two."

A push of cold air from the brass doors and a deep voice that could only belong to Deputy John Washington caused him to turn around. "Howdy, Mr. Ned."

Anyone else might have jumped at the voice, but to Ned it was as familiar as Miss Becky's. "John. I was fixin' to call you."

"Good." Cody jerked a thumb upward. "John. Come go with us. Ned, where do you want to talk?"

"O. C.'s office?" Ned typically visited with the judge in his office.

Anna shook her head. "He's been in the jury room all day."

"Let's go up there, then." Ned led the way up the stairs, knees aching in protest, but riding the elevator wasn't the same now that Old Jules was gone. He heard the cables rattle through the old plaster walls as they ascended, and it made him think of the rattling bones of an old dry skeleton.

The jury room door was closed, but he twisted the knob without knocking and walked inside. Judge O. C. Rains glanced up from the stack of papers on the long, polished table in front of him. His bushy white eyebrows knitted in preparation to give someone an ass-chewing, but realizing it was Ned, he sighed deep and leaned back, his interest piqued when the old constable was followed by the sheriff and two deputies.

"You ever gonna learn to knock?"

"Not in public buildings." Ned knew just what to say to get the judge's goat, and always enjoyed sparring with him. "I'm a taxpayer just like the rest of 'em, and these doors belong to me too, but that don't matter none right now."

Cody and John Washington exchanged amused glances. Ned and O. C. were best friends and had been going at each other for decades.

Anna rolled her eyes at the tin ceiling and pulled out a chair, making a sound in the back of her throat. "*Guaaaa*. They're at it again."

Soon, four silver-belly hats joined the judge's black Stetson laying crown-down in the center of the oak conference table. They settled into the chairs, adjusting creaking gun belts and coats. The room smelled of old books, paper, and a slight touch of mildew.

In his ever-present black suit, Judge O. C. presided at the

head of the table, resting both palms on the file and paper-covered surface. "Well?"

Cody nodded at Ned. "Ned wanted to talk."

The old constable didn't wait. "We have a problem here."

Leaning back, O. C. laced his fingers across his belly. "Do tell."

Ned slid a folded sheet of paper across to the judge. "Read this first."

O. C. unfolded the paper and scanned the page. "Death Certificate, what there is of it. I believe this is the sorriest legal document I've ever seen. It needs to be notarized. It isn't signed, neither."

"No need." Sitting sideways to face the judge, Ned rested one elbow on the table. "It's all bullshit. I have information that I believe to be true disputing what's written there."

He told them all about the conversation with the coroner, then with Shorty Henderson out in the hall. The story went fast, for Ned wasn't one to embellish or bring out details that had no bearing on what he had to say.

"To tell you the truth, I think that feller Roth's hiding something, or at least don't know what he's doing. I'd hate to think we have a coroner who don't know shit from Shinola about figuring out how come a person died."

Cody whistled softly. "You believe Shorty?"

"I do. I've known that boy all his life. He ain't good at keeping a job, but I'god, he'll tell the truth ever' time he opens his mouth."

They paused when the windows rattled. A second gust hit even harder and the wind howled around the courthouse's pink granite eaves, the same granite used in the capital building down in Austin. Big John's eyes flicked to the windows. Even on the second floor, leaves and trash blew past the rippled glass panes.

O. C. laid the paper on the table and smoothed it with his hands. "So you think R. B. didn't drown."

"Not according to Shorty."

"Says here he did. Death by drowning. And how'n hell does Shorty know what Roth found?"

"Said he was eating his lunch outside of the autopsy room and heard Roth talking while he worked."

"Who eats so close to dead people?" Anna closed her eyes and shuddered.

Ned almost grinned. "Shorty, apparently. Look, I don't care where or what Shorty eats. What he heard was Roth talking, and then he went quiet. Shorty thought he was finished, so he waited a while and then went inside to move R. B. That Roth feller was gone all right, but he wasn't finished. Shorty said he must've got hungry and gone for lunch…"

"Eating again." Anna gasped when she realized she'd spoken out loud. "How can you stop an autopsy then go eat?"

Cody raised a finger, then nodded at Ned to go on.

Ned shrugged. "The point is that the room was empty and R. B. was laying there covered up with a sheet, but Roth's notes were on a clipboard and Shorty read 'em. He told me he read that there was no water in R. B.'s lungs. Not a drop. One of them notes said he'd been strangled, 'cause there was a bone in his neck broke. I know for a fact that when people are strangled, especially from behind, one of those little neck bones'll break most of the time."

O. C. picked up the death certificate again. He studied it for a second and passed it over to Cody. The Lamar County sheriff raised an eyebrow and slid it over to Deputy Sloan beside him. "This is a pretty skinny report."

The judge nodded. "Looks like he was just starting to fill it in, then got in a hurry. There's a lot of detail at first, then it just petered out."

"I hurried him up." Ned couldn't help but look out the

window at the dark, gray clouds. Light sleet rattled against the pane. He watched Anna slide the report down to John Washington, who dug a pair of glasses from his shirt pocket and perched them on his nose.

"Well." The judge rocked back and forth in the wooden desk chair. "Looks to me like he gave that to you just so's you'd get out of his hair. What do you think?"

"I think I smell a rat." Ned rubbed his bald head as he usually did when thinking. "And his name is Roth."

"Well, stay on it and let me know if you need anything from my office." Judge O. C. waited to see if anyone wanted to weigh in, but the sheriff and both of his deputies were deep in thought. "I'm gonna send someone over to get an official copy, and we'll see what that one looks like."

"There's something else, while we're all here. Two some-things, if y'all have time." Cody patted his uniform shirt pockets looking for the missing cigarettes.

The judge crossed his arms in an unconscious defensive gesture. "The cocaine in that casket? What'd you get with that warrant?"

"We went to Williams Funeral Home and found nothing. They only accept the closed and sealed casket when it's delivered from the military. They have all the paperwork that covers everything from when the body lands from overseas to when it shows up here in Chisum. The caskets have a seal on them, and you can tell when it's been tampered with."

"So, what are you doing?"

"There's not much to do, right now." Cody located a tooth-pick in his pocket and stuck it between his lips, talking around the tiny piece of wood as if it was a cigarette. "I called some folks I knew when I was in the Army, and they said they'd look into it. Other than that, we don't have much to go on. The family was pretty tore up over the wreck and the drugs. They just want to put their boy in the ground so he can rest."

Judge O. C. drew a deep breath. "You have a theory, though, don't you, Sheriff?"

Ned caught the inflection and waited to see what Cody would do.

"Sure do. John, Anna, and I've talked about it. We think someone intended to get the drugs after the funeral, probably pretty soon after everybody leaves and before they plant him."

"Good God. I never thought I'd see such a thing." Judge O. C. shook his head. "Why didn't they just take 'em out at the funeral home?"

"Well, you have to have someone working on the inside. Maybe they wanted to but couldn't get the casket open in time. But they might just figure the ground would already be tore up, so no one could tell anybody'd been at him. It's got me wondering if something like this is going on in other places. I've made some calls to other sheriff's departments in towns of this size and in Dallas and Houston. They see more boys come home in boxes than we do. Now it's a wait-and-see game."

Ned knew what was coming and was glad it was finally being addressed in front of O. C. "What's that second thing?"

"The Starlite Lounge." Cody adjusted his position in the seat as Ned and O. C. exchanged hot looks. Ned couldn't for the life of him figure out why O. C. didn't file the paperwork and give Cody permission to shut the honky-tonk down.

It didn't make sense, unless the judge was sympathetic to the fact that Cody once owned the Sportsman across the river, and even that didn't sound right. Ned wanted it closed. Right damn now. Judge O. C. Rains drug his feet, though, citing precedent and arguing that an Oklahoma judge dug in his own heels and pretty much told Texas that it had no jurisdiction on the orphaned land and said he'd file suit against the State if they attempted to interfere with the business.

Cody saw the look and frowned. "Judge, is there something here I need to know about? I don't like having an illegal joint operating in my county."

"But you ran one across the river!" Ned's voice crackled like a rifle report in the room. The Sportsman was a sore point reaching back to right after Cody returned from Vietnam.

Cody held up a hand. "Not the point, and besides, I'm out of the business. This is a dry county, and gambling's illegal. Hell, Ned, you gathered up half of our kinfolk the other night and put 'em on a road gang for the same thing."

A look from Judge Rains told Ned that he wasn't happy about the impromptu chain gang that cleaned up the sides of ten miles of Highway 197. Ned rubbed his head. "Saved us both a lot of paperwork, O. C."

"Humph. Well. Y'all leave that place alone, for now. I'm working some backroom deals to get that joint handled, but I don't need y'all over there right now, bollixing things up. Ned, you know the landowner allowed an easement to that club, so there's nothing..."

"Hell, folks're driving through his pasture ever' night without there being a *legal* business..."

O. C. shook his head. "...we're talking about another state's property. Texas law says you can't cut someone off from their own land. But that's not the point. If you drive across private property and into another state, you won't have jurisdiction."

"That little ribbon of land needs to be designated as Texas soil so we can go in and clean that nest of snakes out of there."

"I'god, Ned, you're talking about changing state lines and that ain't a-gonna happen. You don't know what a hornet's nest that is. I done told you I'm talking to the governor..." O. C.

didn't have time to dig any deeper into the argument. Someone rapped on the door, annoying both of the old lawmen to no end. The judge looked like a dog snapping at a fly. "What!"

Bernice Simpson cracked the door and stuck her blue-gray, heavily sprayed hair inside. Not even the salty judge rattled the veteran secretary. "Call for Ned and Cody."

They started to rise, but she shook her head. "I took the message. Said someone found the body of a man named Odell Chatworthy in a cattle trailer out there in Center Springs. Said a Texas Ranger, Tom Bell, figures it was supposed to look like the man was stomped by a bull, but he don't think it was an accident."

Ned felt his stomach fall. "That don't make no sense."

The judge nodded. "Thanks, Bernice."

His secretary withdrew as Anna frowned. "What doesn't make any sense?"

Ned leaned in, pulling his ear in thought. "Odell ain't no cowboy. He runs a generator service and lives just outside of town. Mostly generators for big rigs, eighteen-wheelers, but he does cars and trucks too. He makes good money, more'n most, but he blows a lot of it in the joints over in Juarez. He'd be a millionaire if he didn't gamble and drink most of it away. Cost him a wife and kids, but he still won't quit."

"So?"

"There's never a time when he'd be *in* a cattle trailer."

Chapter Eighteen

Bruce Jones was worrying himself to death over the dice game he was in the night R. B. Parker died. It had been weighing on his mind ever since, when he was working on the line at the soup company, when he came home and fed his cows, or when he was watching *I Dream of Jeannie*. It didn't matter. His love for shooting dice put him in the wrong place at the wrong time, and he wished he could snap his fingers and go back just far enough to drive across the river to the Sportsman for a drink, instead of the Starlite.

He always figured he'd have more money if it wasn't for gambling. It had cost him a family, and the house he'd built with his own two hands over the course of three years. Now he lived in a trailer parked on the only thing he had left, a remote thirty acres his late daddy left to him in the virtually nonexistent community of Elwood, forty miles west of Chisum.

Just home from his shift at the plant, Jones changed clothes and went out to feed his cows before the weather turned bad. Standing in the back of the truck, he put one knee against the side of a bale of hay and pulled on the nearest wire to yank it off. Reversing the bale, he did the same and the sections came loose. He pitched the squares out to the whiteface cattle gathered around his pickup.

From there he could see the yellow light coming from his trailer windows. It was one of those nights that the old place actually looked inviting. It was only an illusion, because once he came close, the rusty metal sides revealed all the dents from a thousand different reasons. The only good thing about the coming snow would be how everything would turn into a winter wonderland, making the empty trailer house look warm and comfortable.

An unfamiliar car pulled up into the yard, its headlights sweeping across the pasture and cutting through the dusk. He paused in breaking open another bale to see a man step out and look around. He disappeared for a moment, and Jones figured the stranger was likely knocking on the door. He'd find out soon enough that no one was home.

Wondering who was out on that rural county road so late in the evening, Jones finished throwing out the squares and ripped open a bag of nuggets. Climbing down from the truck bed, he walked through the cows, shaking out the high-protein feed, keeping one eye on the car that was still running.

Throwing the empty paper sack into the back, he slid beneath the wheel and pulled through the wire gap. Using a bodark cheater bar, he forced the gate tight against the post and drove into the yard. Despite the cold, the visitor was standing beside the car.

With a shock, he recognized him from the Starlite's dice game. "What are you doing here?" He stepped from the cab and slammed the door behind him.

"Why, I came to see you. I knocked, but no one answered."

"That's because there ain't nobody in there."

"Well, let's visit a minute." The man's eyes widened at the

sight of a fixed blade knife that suddenly appeared in Jones's hand. "Hey, I just came to talk."

"Get gone before I go to work with this blade. I don't want to talk to you."

"Okay." The man produced a snub-nosed .38 and shot Jones in the forehead.

Chapter Nineteen

At the same time Ned, O. C., and the others were gathered in the jury room, Lamar County Coroner Tony Roth was typing up a death certificate for Mrs. Essie Mae Lancaster, who'd died two days earlier of advanced age and complications from pneumonia. It was the easiest autopsy he'd performed all week, and he wouldn't have needed to do it, but she'd passed away with no one in attendance.

He took a sip of hot coffee from a thick mug on his desk when the door opened. Expecting his son, he almost spilled the coffee when two men stepped inside.

"Can I help you gentlemen?"

The man who came in first smiled and slumped down in a chair as if Roth'd invited him to sit. He spoke with a Cajun accent. "We need to talk."

Frowning, Roth glanced back and forth between the speaker and an Italian-looking fellow with oiled hair. "About what?"

"You don't know who we are, do you?"

Roth's spine prickled when he realized why the two strangers were in his office. "Look, I talked to Buster Rawlins and all this is settled."

The seated man twisted to look over his shoulder at the Italian. "Man says it's already handled."

"It ain't handled."

The seated man turned back around. "My friend Ricky don't believe 'dat."

Roth searched his memory and remembered that Buster Rawlins used two names to describe his associates, Melvin LaFleur and Ricky Toscani. He half-pointed toward the man with oiled hair. "You're Toscani."

"And he's my partner, Melvin LaFleur."

LaFleur grinned as if he was having a great time. "Now that we have all that straightened out, I need you to tell me why the law was here earlier."

"How do you know that?" Realizing it sounded as if he were being defensive, the coroner sat straighter, hoping to look tougher than he felt. "I don't have to tell you why he was here."

"Yes, you do." LaFleur dug under his coat and came out with a pack of Winstons. He lit one and laughed. "Winston tastes good, like a cigarette should."

Still standing beside a wooden four-drawer file cabinet, Toscani chuckled.

"You can't smoke in here." Roth wanted to establish dominance.

LaFleur leaned forward. "Don't get smart with me, buddy. I smell pipe smoke, so get off it. You better tell me why that law-man came in here earlier."

Roth folded at the man's tone. "He wanted R. B. Parker's death certificate."

"Did you give it to him?"

"Of course. He'd have gotten suspicious if I hadn't."

LaFleur smoked for several long seconds, staring hard at Roth. "Did he leave a card? A number for you to call?"

"No. He just took the certificate and left."

"What was on it? The cause of death?"

"Drowning due to intoxication."

"That's good. That's good, ain't it, Ricky?"

"That's good, all right."

LaFleur tapped his cigarette into the ashtray on Roth's desk. "Now, let's talk about that body that was supposed to get here today."

"Here?"

"No, the funeral home."

"Oh, fine then."

"We don't want to have anything happen like it did out on the highway. We're here to get what's inside now."

"I can't help you with anything going on in the funeral home. Even though I'm part owner in the place, I can't just waltz in there and have those people open up a casket so you can unload your…cargo."

"Do you have keys to the place?"

"Sure do, but they always have somebody inside for death calls."

Ricky Toscani frowned. "What?"

"Death calls. When someone passes away in the night, the funeral home has someone on staff to take the call and send a car out to pick up the body."

"So, when the car leaves, then there's only one person inside who answers the phone."

Roth nodded at LaFleur. "That's right."

"Well, then. We wait for that call this evening and you can let us in. That sounds pretty simple to me."

"I can't do that, but I've worked something out for you. I was gonna call Rawlins and tell him. See, I paid the gravediggers to bury it only a couple of feet deep, and not six feet down. They like it, because it's less work for a little extra money in their pockets. We all win, because that'll make it easy to go out after dark and dig him up." Roth leaned back and laced his fingers. "So you see? You can trust *me*."

LaFleur reached across the desk and stubbed his butt out in the ashtray. "Rawlins don't trust *nobody*, but we'll see how this works out. But if it don't, you can bet the next person we put in a shallow grave will be you."

Chapter Twenty

Mark didn't hold out like I thought. The cold front was a booger and the next thing we knew it brought a bad ice storm during the night. It started with black ice, and that's the most dangerous kind, a thin skin on top of the highway that's almost impossible to see. They called school off, but that didn't stop people from getting out, and that helped a little at first because the tires burned a lot of the ice off the roads, at least in long skinny lanes like roads in a pasture.

Mark called and asked Blu McClellan to come to the house and study. It wouldn't have been so bad, but Pepper was over at Jett's house with *him*, and left me with no one to hang out with. Blu's daddy brought her by on his way to visit a few shut-ins that were part of his congregation. He came inside for a few minutes and visited with Miss Becky in the kitchen. She fed him, of course, and Preacher Colt went on his way full of pie and hot coffee.

After he was gone, Blu and Mark stayed in the living room, because Miss Becky said it wasn't proper to have a girl in the bedroom, so that's where I holed up with a book. Outside was a freezer, with a heavy mist that showed me what it would be like inside a cloud. The droplets of ice collected on everything, weighing down tree limbs, power lines, and anything else that could droop. Long icicles grew from the eaves, and tall grasses in the pastures laid over.

Even though I concentrated on my reading, I could hear Mark and Blu in there, whispering and giggling. Every now and then Miss Becky would say something to them, just to show she was in the kitchen and listening.

"Blu, we have some bacon and biscuits left over from breakfast if you're hungry."

Her voice floated into the bedroom, and I had to quit reading for a minute. "No thanks, Miss Becky. I don't eat much between meals."

"That's why you're no bigger'n a minute. At least get a bite or two of this bacon, then."

"I will in a little while, if that's all right with you."

Miss Becky wasn't finished. "Mark, would you turn that television down and put on the radio? I'd like to hear the weather."

I knew good and well that she wasn't getting everything they were saying in there over the TV, and the radio always stayed at the same level. It'd be easier to hear their conversations.

Covered with a quilt in the chilly room and propped up in bed with pillows at my back, I lowered the book written by a guy named Walter Edmonds and glanced up. There was a little sliver between the door and the hall that gave me a skinny view of the couch where they were sitting. Blu shifted to her right and we saw each other. She gave me a slow wink that made my face flush. Mark's shoulder came into view, and she followed it back out of sight.

My whole body felt like it was full of electricity, and I kept running that wink through my mind, wondering what it meant. Was she saying hello? We'd already done that when her daddy brought her over. Was she up to something and thought I was in on it? Couldn't have been. We hadn't said more than a dozen words to each other since we met.

The side of her blond head reappeared and she used one finger to pull a strand behind her ear. Somehow, I smelled perfume and imagined it belonged to her. I shivered and couldn't decide if it was from the room's chill, or something else down deep inside.

Finally, I heard Grandpa come in, shaking ice water off his coat. Closing *Drums Along the Mohawk*, I went through the living room, trying not to make eye contact with Blu there on the couch with Mark. He gave me that grin that said he knew what he was doing and having fun doing it.

The kitchen air was thick and moist when I sat down at the table, full of the good smells of dinner on the stove. Miss Becky was stirring a pot of beans. "Where are you going next?"

Grandpa picked up a leftover piece of bacon from a saucer on the stove. "Not sure yet. I need to talk to that coroner again about Odell, but I don't want to drive all the way into town on these roads."

"Call him."

"I want to look that feller in the eye. Right now, I believe I'm going up to the store, to see if anyone's having troubles in this weather. After that, I don't know."

"Let Top go with you."

She didn't often give orders, and it surprised us both. He looked from her, to me, and back again. "He has company."

"*Mark* has company. Top's been in the bedroom reading all day."

"Why?"

"Ask him."

"Why you been in there? I figgered you'd be stretched out in front of that heater with Hootie."

I glanced through the door to see my dog asleep in front of the fire where he'd been all day and kept my voice low. "Didn't want to watch those two in there make goo-goo eyes at one another all day."

He frowned. "Well, get your coat and come on. Better put on a hat, too."

Quick as a wink I tugged on the billed sock cap I wore when we were hunting and shrugged into my coat. Grandpa was out the door and I followed. He took the truck, because the heater was already warmed up, so I slid in and slammed the door. The bed was full of hay to give the tires weight and better traction.

For a minute, I felt a sense of relief. I loved Mark, and was glad to have him living with us, but right then things were back to when it was just me and Grandpa. An old lawman with his sidekick, like in the movies, and I loved having that role.

The wipers barely kept the mist off the fogged windshield as we crept off the gravel drive and onto the slick highway. His big hands held the steering wheel harder than usual. "You have to move slow when the roads are slick like this. The light rear end of a pickup'll get out from under you in half a second."

He accelerated and shifted into second, taking his brogan off the foot-feed for a second to let the momentum catch up to the moving truck. When we didn't fishtail, he gave her a little more gas. "That hay's working back there."

I glanced out the side glass and saw a covey of quail scattered in the grass on the shoulder, feeding their way under a bobwire fence coated with ice.

He noticed. "They were there when I came by a little bit ago."

"How'd you know I saw those birds?"

"'Cause you perked up like a bird dog. We'll get Cody and go shoot a few once this weather breaks."

I loved bird hunting with them and secretly hoped Mark was

still tied up with Blu when the time came, so it would be just the three of us. For a moment, my ears grew hot with the embarrassment of wishing him away.

Again Grandpa seemed to read my thoughts as we drove at a walker's pace. "So tell me what's going on with Mark and that little gal back there. I probably know. She's cute as a little bug, but I thought him and Pepper were pretty tight."

"Pepper's mooning over Blu's brother, so he's took to calling her."

"Pepper's gonna learn a lesson if she ain't careful. Both of 'em if they're playing *that* old game." Grandpa cut his steely-blue eyes across the cab. "Well, him and Pepper's a complicated thing, not being real kin but in the family now."

"That's the same thing *he* said. Complicated."

We passed a rusting galvanized bucket turned upside down on a bodark fence post. It had been there ever since I could remember, and I'd always wondered who put it there and why no one had taken it off. "All this boy-girl stuff makes my head hurt."

"You were watching her too. I've seen you eyeing that little gal out in the schoolyard when I come to pick y'all up. You be careful with a preacher's daughter."

That one caught me off guard, and I had to study on it as we passed Uncle Henry's little frame house. Wood smoke rolled out of the chimney and immediately flowed down the tin roof and into the yard. Inside, I knew Aunt Mamie would have some baby chickens in a box by the fire, and if not that, it'd be piglets, or puppies, or kittens, or anything else not big enough to fend for itself in such weather.

Grandpa surprised me by pulling off in front of Oak Peterson's store. "Let's go in and see who's hanging around. I need to get the mail anyways."

The post office was in the back, secured by a half-wall and

bars, even in 1969. The old folks said it looked as it did back in the 1920s, when Center Springs was a thriving cotton town. Like Neal Box's store, there was a woodstove surrounded by chairs.

Even the gravel was slick, so we picked our way to the door and went inside. The warmth engulfed us, and I shivered at the feeling. Half a dozen men loafed around the stove and everyone raised a hand.

My Great-Uncle Hut, tall and gangly, was sitting in a chair turned backward, his arms over the back. "Hey Ned. Who's your sidekick there?"

"Aw, picked him up walking down the road. I think he said his name was Billy the Kid."

They knew who I was, and I knew all of them, some by sight. Henry Arney was what I called the Storm Cellar Man, from back when I was little. Two men I took to be Indians were kinda outside the circle, sitting side by side. Jimmy Lee Berry was there, in his ever-present overalls and cowboy hat.

Grandpa pointed. "Run back there and get the mail for me."

"Yessir."

"And don't rob nobody while you're back there."

Grinning wide at his kidding, and knowing I was to be seen but not heard, I waved and went to the back where Mrs. Betty Green had a bundle of mail and large manila envelopes for Grandpa. The big envelopes were law business from Austin.

Mail in hand, I drifted over to a wire rack full of comics that had been read so much they weren't worth buying. I picked one up and sat on a dusty wooden box close enough to the stove to feel the warmth.

Grandpa and those he knew'd been talking, but by the time I sat down, he stuck his hands in his pockets and nodded at the two strangers. "I don't know y'all."

I could tell they were both likely Choctaw, because that's

what we had the most of in our part of the country. They exchanged glances. One with a scar at the corner of his eye shrugged. "I don't know you, neither."

"Not surprised. I'm Ned Parker. Constable here in Precinct Three. I try to put a name to face with everyone who comes through."

Scar's buddy had a solid chin and hawk nose. Resting both elbows on his knees, he leaned forward and laced his fingers. "I ain't never seen a law in overalls. You're kinda old to be in that business, ain't you?"

"I'm old, and that's a fact. I got that way by being smart."

They watched him for a minute, then looked at the floor-boards anchored by square-head nails while he studied *them*. The other loafers quieted at the tension that became a physical presence in the suddenly too hot and steamy store. "Y'all living here now, or just passing through?"

"It's a free country." Scar's voice hardened.

"Never said it wasn't. Just making conversation." Grandpa's own voice had changed, and I felt like I was watching two strange dogs circling each other.

Hawk Nose licked his lips. "We're just passing through. We're on our way to…to a place we heard about."

"Where's that?"

"Oklahoma."

"That hadn't been much of a secret for a good long while. For work?"

It was Scar's turn. "To spend a little of the money we earned over in Monkstown."

"Ah, you're heading for the beer joints across the river."

Scar shrugged.

"I understand. Well, you boys make sure you don't come back across to this side after you've been drinking."

Hawk Nose started to say something, but he caught Scar's eye and stopped. They weren't too subtle about it if *I* could notice, and I know for a fact that Grandpa did, because he slipped both hands into his back pockets of his overalls. That move looked innocent enough, like a man relaxing in a friendly conversation, but I knew his right pocket contained a sap, and I saw the fingers on his left hand curl into the brass knuckles he always carried on the left side beside his billfold.

There was also his 32.20 Colt revolver always in his right front pocket.

I don't know what might have happened then, but the front door opened, and Mr. Tom Bell stepped inside, along with about a barn full of cold air that dropped the temperature around us. I swear, I never saw anything like that old retired Ranger in my life. Black hat, thick white mustache, and Wrangler jeans, he looked like a gunslinger.

He took in the men seated in front of Grandpa, me on my box beside the counter, and Mr. Oak behind his register. His right hand unbuttoned a hip-length waxed coat and pulled it back. I couldn't see from where I sat, but I knew good and well that old 1911 Colt .45 was riding on his hip.

"Ned. Sure is cold out there."

I believe he spoke so Grandpa would know who was standing behind him. I was right when he answered without turning. "You ain't a woofin'. That's what these boys and I were talking about, but I think two of 'em are leaving."

The Indians stood up, but Grandpa held out a hand. "Names? So's I'll know y'all the next time I see you."

Scar hesitated, but I could tell he was figuring the odds on pushing past those two old men, who looked to me as solid as oak trees. "I'm Isom Rainwater. He's Jincy Kettle."

"Good to know. Either of you boys ever heard of Silas Cornsilk?"

There was that look between them again. Grandpa went on as if talking to himself. "I heard about two fellers kinda matching your descriptions who hang around across the river with Cornsilk." Grandpa waited for a second. "He's one of your people, likes to gamble, as long as he's sober."

Hawk Nose bobbed his head. "I know him. Why?"

"Just wondering. Name came up the other day, and I haven't seen him in a while."

"Me neither. Probably laid up with some old gal till she takes all his money, then he'll turn up."

"He won't be the first." Grandpa stepped aside and they brushed past, giving Mr. Tom plenty of room on the way out. Another river of cold air came in as they stepped outside and were gone.

"Damn, Ned!" Uncle Hut stood up. "I thought that was gonna go sideways for a minute."

Mr. Tom stepped away from the door but watched through the window as the men drove away in an old truck held together with baling wire. It was only then that he pulled the waxed coat back over his Colt.

Grandpa'd been watching through the big windows, too. "I wasn't sure myself. What'd they have to say before I came in?"

"Nothin' much. They'd been by Neal's store and seemed surprised that he was closed. Said they were looking for him, then started asking a few questions about work, you know. Jobs."

I caught a motion out of the corner of my eye and saw Mr. Oak slipping a sawed-off double-barrel shotgun back under the counter. He looked up with that gotch eye of his and I heard Mr. Jimmy Lee suck in his breath.

"Good Lord, Oak. If you'd cut loose with that monster, we'd all caught part of that load."

"Aw, you'd-a got out of the way in time. I'd have to cock it first."

Mr. Tom pursed his lips and warmed his hands by the stove. Grandpa pulled a blue bandanna from his pocket and wiped his nose. I'd noticed that old men's noses watered when it got really cold.

Mr. Floyd leaned back and crossed his arms. "Are they wanted?"

Grandpa was done talking, too. He crooked a finger at me and patted Mr. Tom a thanks on the arm. "I'd-a taken them in if they were."

Chapter Twenty-One

The freezing rain was getting heavier as Deputy Anna Sloan turned off the road and onto the two-lane dirt track leading to the Starlite. Though it was early Tuesday afternoon, the sky was so dark and low, the bright neon sign reflected against the clouds.

Wearing brightly colored knit slacks and boots, she was there to take a look around. It hadn't been easy to convince Cody that she'd be all right by herself. Even though she was an experienced deputy, he was always overprotective to the point of straining their relationship.

Only an hour earlier they'd gone nose to nose in his office when she said she was going to the Starlite that evening to take a look around. "I just want to see what's going on in there."

He always said no at first when she came up with such ideas. "You don't need to go into a honky-tonk without your uniform."

"It'll cause problems if I do. I can't ask any questions, either, because it'll be official then."

"You don't need to be asking questions in the first place. No one can decide who that place belongs to, and Oklahoma may raise the devil if they find out you're in there."

"They don't care. I suspect they'll let us take care of whatever comes up, as long as they don't have to drive the long way around."

"You remember what happened down in Austin."

She grinned. "Yeah, I got a boyfriend out of the deal that I see about every two weeks."

"You know that's not what I meant. You almost got hurt."

"But I didn't. I'm just going in to see who's hanging around. I'll drink a beer and leave."

"Well, you're not going at night."

She raised an eyebrow. "Sheriff Parker, is that an official order or a suggestion between friends? You realize I have a life and can do what I want when I'm off duty."

He sighed and leaned back in his chair. Propping his boots on the desk, he grinned. "I guess that sounded like I was talking to Norma Faye, huh? It was between friends."

Norma Faye was his redheaded wife and also Anna's best friend. "Sure did, but since it's not an order, I won't take offense. Just to keep you from worrying, I'll go this afternoon, before the weather gets too bad."

"It's already bad. I wouldn't stay out long. They're calling for a second push of cold air and say the freezing rain'll turn to sleet, then snow."

"I hope it does snow. That's easier to drive on than ice. I've always liked watching it fall."

"Don't take the cruiser. Use your car, but call me before you leave your house, and again as soon as you get home." He paused. "*That* part's an order."

Once she'd won the argument, she had second thoughts at the mention of the deteriorating weather. "Maybe I need to stay in town and work the streets. There's going to be wrecks all over the county. This can wait a couple of days."

"No. I've called deputies in to be on duty while everyone's going home. Tomorrow's gonna be bad, and most folks won't get out. The highway patrol's put everyone on the streets this afternoon, too. You go check if you want to, and then come back and work the late shift until midnight if you feel bad about being gone."

"I won't be able to have that beer."

"Good point. You can work two shifts tomorrow."

"As punishment for arguing with you?"

He laughed. "John'll be out all day, too. Go dig around."

On the frozen pasture road, Anna wasn't as concerned with the ice. Keeping a constant slow speed helped maintain control as she drove through the gap in the trees, their limbs drooping with a heavy coating of ice, and came out in the bottoms. The long grass as far as she could see laid over under accumulating freezing drizzle. There were more cars parked out front than she expected. She swung around, ice crunching under the tires, and parked facing the trail, so she could get out quickly if she needed to.

The little snub-nosed .38 in the pocket of her thick sheepskin coat was reassuring as she opened the club's door and stepped inside. Despite the fresh, new spiffy neon sign high above the joint, there was nothing special about the interior. Beer signs on all four walls lit the bar. An equally bright Wurlitzer on the right-hand wall filled the smoky air with the honky-tonk music of Hank Williams.

A long, mahogany bar along the back was fully stocked, and six beer pulls anchored the center. Her eyebrow rose. Oklahoma joints legally served 3.2 beer and nothing else. Lamar County was dry, so liquor on display was the last thing she expected, and that fact alone told her the Starlite was different.

One door on the right led to the restrooms. She figured the

plain door on the left opened into an office or storeroom. It was an active bar for the weather. There were probably a dozen men scattered around the tables, but she was shocked at an equal number of women.

Some of the women sported beehive hairdos that looked fresh from the beauty shop. Even in the dim lights, she saw that every woman in there wore makeup, something unusual for the area. They were dressed in a mix of short dresses and polyester pantsuits. Conscious of how casual she looked, she wiped her palm across the top of her head and down the ponytail, stripping off the dampness.

A gum-popping waitress in an extremely low-cut top and tight-fitting shorts saw Anna pull out a chair at an empty table to the left of the entrance. She came around with a tray bearing an order pad. "What'll you have, hon?" She stopped when she got close, noticing Anna's damp hair. "Still falling out there, huh?"

"And getting harder." Anna took the thick coat off and hung it over the back of a chair. "I hate to get my hair wet."

"I know. I have to tie a scarf around my head on days like this, and it makes me feel like my mama. What're you having, hon?"

"Lone Star?"

"You got it."

She left to get the beer, and Anna took a seat, her back to the wall so she could maintain a good view of the room. She was barely in her seat when a skinny man with an abnormally long neck slid off his stool and came over. "Wanna dance?"

"Wow. That's fast." There was a neon Stroh's sign directly overhead, providing enough light to see his sickly barfly pallor. He wore thick horn-rim glasses that slid down on his nose. "I think I'll sit here and warm up for a little bit."

He pushed the glasses up with one finger, missing the deflection. "Oh, can I join you?"

She plucked a pack of Virginia Slims from her coat and held up a hand when he reached into his pocket for a lighter. "Have you heard the slogan for these cigarettes?"

"Uh, not that I remember."

She smiled to take out the sting. "You've come a long way, baby. I can light my own. I just need to be alone for a while."

"Oh, you one of them women's lib gals?"

"Not hardly." Out of character, she flicked him away with her fingers. He finally gave up and returned to his half-finished beer.

Lighting the cigarette, she shook out the gofer match and added her smoke to the thick cloud hanging in the air. The waitress came back with the bottle. "I see Larry's already hit on you."

"He was fast."

"He likes to think he is." She sat the bottle on the table. "My name's Mary Lou. You want to run a tab?"

Anna slid a five-dollar bill onto the table. "No. We'll just use this."

Mary Lou made change.

Anna pointed at dancers two-stepping to the music. "There's a lot of activity in here this time of the day."

"This ain't nothin'. The numbers are down because of the weather. It's usually packed."

"At *three*?"

"From ten to around four, then the girls head home to be there when their husbands get off the day shift at the soup plant. You wouldn't believe how many farmers' wives come in for an hour or so, neither."

Understanding made Anna grin. She dragged deeply on the cigarette. "I get it. Party while the boys are gone, then go home and cook supper."

"That's right. About an hour later is when the night shift goes in. Then the place really fills up with them and the gals who come out when the sun goes down. The nights are awful busy."

"For a Tuesday night?"

"Hon, folks like to rub bellies, no matter what day it is."

Hank Williams gave way to Lefty Frizzell on the jukebox at the same time two men entered and made their way to the bar. The couples on the dance floor stayed where they were and shifted into a waltz.

The bartender drifted over to take their orders. Everyone else seemed to be good on drinks for the moment. Mary Lou watched the newcomers. "Most of the girls in here lean toward dresses."

Knowing what she meant, Anna cursed herself for sticking out, the exact opposite of what she wanted. "I was. Had a little argument with my old man and needed to come in here for a beer. Didn't think pants would be a problem."

There was an instant bond. "I used to do the same thing, with my third husband. Arguing with him didn't do any good, so I'd just head over to the Sportsman for a couple of drinks. It always took the edge off."

"Don't sound like it did much good."

"You mean me working here?" She shrugged. "He wasn't much to look at, and one day he just disappeared. I went out by myself about a week later and when the owner of the club saw me there all alone, he came over and we got to talking. The next thing I knew, I was waiting tables at the Sportsman and happier than I'd been in years. He was a nice guy, and never even made a pass at me.

"But then he gets himself elected sheriff over there in Lamar County and wasn't around as much. He sold the bar, and that's when I came over here. These guys almost doubled my pay, and I get better tips, but I have to show a little more skin." She shrugged, bringing her arms in and pushing her breasts up. "The bigger the tits, the bigger the tips. What difference does it make? They're just boobs. You could do pretty well in here yourself."

Suddenly aware of her own breasts, Anna shook her head. She unconsciously checked to make sure her top was buttoned. "I spend most of my time trying to keep guys from looking at them."

Mary Lou laughed. "Honey, that's a lost cause." A couple on the opposite side of the club raised their nearly empty glasses. She waved back. "I'll come back by in a little while."

She left and Anna watched the dancers. It looked like every beer joint she'd ever been in. A man who needed a shave and a chin sat alone at table in the darkest corner of the club. She didn't want to stare, so she concentrated on her beer and cigarette.

A few minutes later, he rose, crossed to the bar, and went around behind. Check. Employee. Maybe the owner. He opened a register and fiddled with the money for a minute, then leaned on the bar and talked with one of the two men who'd just come in. Anna watched the action, and their hands. After a moment, a couple of furtive movements told her something was going on, but it was too dark and far away to see.

The man came back around, and the light from the Stroh's sign behind Anna lit his face, giving her a good look at the pockmarks on his cheeks. The record on the jukebox ended, and in the silence as the machinery changed disks, the front door opened and two more men entered.

They saw the chinless man with a large hooked nose going back to his table. One spoke with a Cajun accent. They joined in and settled around the table as the music returned with Ernest Tubb singing about walking the floor. This time the wooden dance floor filled.

Anna was the only woman not dancing, and more than one of the single male customers was looking in her direction. She quickly drained her bottle and held it up for Mary Lou, who'd been watching. A minute later she came by with another Lone Star on her tray, exchanging it for the empty.

"I'm gonna have to get you a stick. You better light another one real quick."

Anna was confused. "Huh?"

"A stick to fight these guys off. They all have their eyes on you, the ones who ain't already hooked up with someone. They see you light your own, they'll be one less reason to come over here and bother you."

"I'm pretty good at running them off." Anna blew smoke toward the ceiling. "I kinda like this place." She tilted her head to the right. "That the owner?"

"Yeah, but you need to stay away from that ugly bastard and all the rest of 'em." Mary Lou's voice was suddenly flat. "You're too sweet, and they ain't from around here."

"Sounds like one's from Louisiana."

"You have a good ear, but mind your business."

Two more customers came in from the cold, unbuttoned their coats, and made a beeline for the Cajun's table. He stood, caught Mary Lou's eye, and motioned with his fingers. She nodded and they went back out the front door, passing a new customer coming in.

May Lou remained beside Anna's table. "Melvin LaFleur and Ricky Toscani are the two who just came in over there with him. LaFleur's Cajun, too. The ugly guy who came around the bar a minute ago's Buster Rawlins. He owns the place, but don't ask me anything else. It ain't healthy for either one of us." Mary Lou relaxed. "And don't get too close to Rawlins. His breath's so bad it'd gag a buzzard off a tub of guts. Enjoy that beer."

She left to take the newcomer's order while Anna sipped her beer, hoping to look like a customer who intended to get drunk.

Chapter Twenty-Two

Top followed Ned out of Oak Peterson's store and into a sleet storm. Neal Box's car passed at the same time and turned in past the domino hall. He glanced down at the youngster. "I wonder if everything's all right. Get in the truck. We're going to run over there and see him for a minute."

Sleet rattled on the pickup's tin roof. The drive was so short that the radio didn't even have time to warm up, and chilly air blew out of the heater. Neal saw them pull up beside his car as he was unlocking the door. He waved and went inside.

Ned shifted into neutral. "You want to stay in here and wait?"

"Sure." Top adjusted the radio's dial, tuning into a rock and roll station. "I like hearing the sleet on the roof."

Ned set the parking brake. "I'll be back in a minute." The youngster looked back over his shoulder, and Ned patted his leg. "Don't worry. Those two are gone. They won't be back."

Top nodded, and Ned shouldered the stubborn door open. The store was chilly when he stepped inside, and Neal was rummaging behind the counter. "Ned, what're you doing out in this weather?"

"I was wondering the same thing. I thought you'd closed for the day."

"I had, but I remembered I'd forgot to bring the cash home when I locked up. Clarice wouldn't've slept a wink tonight with it here after they broke into Oak's store."

"Well, I was over at Oak's a few minutes ago and a couple of Choctaws come in asking about you. Oak said they came by here first."

Neal paused, then folded the bills and slipped them into his pocket. "What'd they want?"

"I don't have any idy." A Chisum newspaper lay on the counter, and Ned noticed the muzzle of a pistol sticking out. His eyebrow rose. "You'll have to ask *them.*"

"I will if they show back up. Did they give their names?" Neal licked his lips. "Not that knowing them would mean anything."

"Isom Rainwater and Jincy Kettle."

Neal's face went as pale as his white hair.

"They mean something to you, don't they?"

"Ned, I can't say."

"Yes, you can. I asked them about another Indian I've run into the last week or so. Took him to jail for driving drunk. Cornsilk. You know him too?"

"Yes." Neal's attention flicked to the icy parking lot, empty except for Ned's idling pickup. "Ned, I don't...well, I know the names from across the river."

"Umm-humm. Well, Cornsilk's been missin' since Friday night after he got out of jail." Neal couldn't take his eyes off the door and window, keeping an eye on the parking lot. Ned narrowed his own. "You oughta stay out of them places and save your money."

"You know we like to dance a little."

"You're gonna get in trouble one of these days, drinking and gambling."

Neal's eyes rose from the newspaper near his hand. "It's

across the river in Oklahoma. Not shooting dice over here like your kinfolk the other night."

Not rising to the bait, Ned picked up a pack of Juicy Fruit from a box beside the paper, moving the newspaper just enough to reveal more of the pistol's barrel. "Don't matter. Gambling's illegal." He laid a nickel on the counter.

Neal looked at the barrel, then the ceiling. "It's just a little harmless fun."

"Don't wall your eyes at me."

Neal chuckled, and Ned grinned.

"It's harmless until somebody loses or gets mad."

"Ned. I'm a grown man. Did you need something?"

"You don't usually keep a pistol on the counter or that much cash in your pocket. There's a lot of money in your hands, and I don't believe it's just a day's worth of business. Three quarters of what you do in a day is on tabs. That's hideout cash."

Neal's hands grew still.

"You didn't close because of the weather. The only time you lock that door is on Sunday. Money. A pistol. I believe you're getting ready to go somewhere. You going to tell me what's going on?"

"I just wasn't feeling too good this morning and this weather's keeping ever'body inside, so I locked up. There's nothing I can tell you, Ned."

"You would if you could?"

"I would if I could."

Ned nodded and put his hand on the door latch. "But you can't right now, can you?"

He didn't wait for an answer but stepped onto the porch and out into the falling weather and a frosty world turning white.

Chapter Twenty-Three

Pepper and Jett McClellan were in the parsonage's small living room, books open on the coffee table. Because both of her parents were gone, the books hadn't been touched in over an hour. They were the only things that hadn't been touched.

Heart beating fast and breathless, she pushed him away as a wave of sleet rattled against the window glass. She ran a finger across her bottom lip. "What time does your mama get home?"

"Dammit. Why'd you do that?"

"Cool it. Don't have a *cow*." She reached over and turned her transistor radio down. "Why are the damn commercials always louder than the music?" Adjusting her clothing, she stood. "I just don't want her to come walking in on us."

He laughed. "She wouldn't know what she was looking at anyway." Seeing Pepper's puzzled expression, he laughed. "By this time every day, her lemonade has her so laid back, she doesn't pay any attention to anything."

"She drinks? She's a *preacher's* wife."

He laughed. "That's *why* she drinks."

The laugh was infectious, and Pepper joined in. "I've heard

about preachers' kids, and now I know that's the truth, but I never thought about a grown woman doing that."

Jett smirked, and Pepper couldn't tell if it was because she'd found out about him, or if it was disrespect for his mother. "Hell, she's already found the bars. She'll slip over there until people figure out who she is, and then we'll have to move again in a few months."

Pepper went to the window and was surprised to see the yard was already white with sleet. "I can't believe they leave you alone for so long. That wouldn't happen with my people. Mama'd be through here a dozen times just to adjust the blinds if she was home, and she damn sure wouldn't leave me alone with a boy. Where's Blu?"

Jett smirked. "Probably somewhere doing what we were just doing, only she'd likely be further down the road."

Despite herself, Pepper blushed. "Well, we're through with *that* for the day."

"You're gonna leave me hanging here?"

"I need to go."

"Wait, I have something else we can do."

Suspicious, her eyes narrowed. "What's that?"

He disappeared for a minute in the back of the house and came back with a joint. "Let's burn this."

She drew back. Trying to act cool, she said the first thing that popped into her mind. "They'll smell it when they come in the house, dummy."

His eyes glittered. "Damn. I knew you were special. You want something with a little more punch."

"That's not what I meant. I'm not drinking today, either. I'm probably going over to my grandparents' house for the night, and Miss Becky can smell booze a mile away."

"I have something with a lot more kick. There's a couple

of black mollies back there, and if that don't toot your horn, I have something really special I've been saving. Got it in Dallas."

Pepper shook her head, but curious, she turned the radio down even though she loved the song "Jumpin' Jack Flash." "What's that?"

"Blotter acid."

"*Whoa!* Dude. Licking one of those'd be suicide for both of us right now. You can bet somebody's going to be coming home pretty soon in this weather."

A click caught her attention. "What was that?"

Jett laughed. "It's the phone. I didn't want anyone to call and interrupt us, so I took it off the hook."

A look of horror came over her face. "Are you on a party line?"

He shrugged. "Maybe. I really don't know what that is."

"You never had one where you come from?"

"No. We've always lived in the city. Why're you so uptight?"

"Because people can listen in. You were on the phone when I came in, weren't you?"

"Yeah, but I hit the disconnect button before I laid it down."

Pepper picked up the receiver and listened. Her eyes widened. "I don't know who's on this line, but I bet you got an earful, didn't you? Well, you better keep it to yourself."

Someone on the other end hung up.

Stomach tightening with fear, she flipped through her mental files and tried to remember what they'd said or if Jett had used her name at any point while she was there. She replaced the receiver and turned back toward Jett. Over his shoulder, her grandaddy's truck pulled into the drive. "See? Don't I know my family? There's my ride."

Jett turned to see where she was looking. "Ain't that the shits."

"You beat anything I ever saw. Where'd a preacher's kid come to talk and act like you do?"

"Out back of the church, while the old man's up there preaching."

Chapter Twenty-Four

Deputy Anna Sloan finished her second beer and sat in wonder at the number of people flowing into the Starlite, despite the weather. Several times she'd seen people go to the bar for drinks, then slip something into their pockets that wasn't change.

The dance floor was never empty, and she'd turned down three more invitations to join the party crowd. She'd gathered as much information as she could, sitting alone at the table. It was time to do something else.

Catching Mary Lou's attention, she held up one of the empties and received a nod of understanding. She rose. There'd been a steady stream of people flowing in and out of the far door at the end of the bar, obviously where the restrooms were located.

It was the other door that interested her. She rose, and when the bartender was looking the other way, opened it as if looking for the restroom. Just as she figured, it was a small office. Empty.

Another plain, unmarked door on the far wall called. Putting her ear to it, she listened. Voices came though. She turned the knob and peeked inside, hoping her alibi of looking for the restroom would hold up if someone was in there.

She found a whole different world in a room one quarter the

size of the bar in front. The usual beer signs lit walls stacked with cases of liquor and beer. It was the two card tables and a brand-new craps table in the middle that told her how the Starlite was different from the joints across the river.

That's what's been bothering me. There are more cars in the lot than people in the bar. The rest are already back here, gambling.

Only one of the card tables was in use. Concentrating on the games, none of the players noticed as she peeked inside. The quick look was enough. They were making bets as she closed the door and spun, hurrying back across the room. Taking a deep breath, she opened the door leading back into the honky-tonk proper and stepped through.

The only person who noticed was Mary Lou, who frowned for a moment, then pointed to the opposite end of the bar and the restrooms there. Anna waved thanks and went inside, coming out a few minutes later to find a fresh beer on her table, along with a heavyset man with Johnny Cash hair who grinned when she walked up.

"Bought you a beer."

"You paid Mary Lou?"

"Well, I was just joking. She took it out of what was on the table."

Anna picked up her heavy coat and shrugged into it as she left. "Hope you enjoy it."

Chapter Twenty-Five

Knuckles rapped against the driver's-side glass of Isom Rainwater's Chevrolet pickup parked out front of the TV Lounge. "Howdy boys."

Isom Rainwater and Jincy Kettle jerked as one, startled by the appearance of someone they'd rather not speak to. They'd driven to the TV to resupply for the night. Most of the clubs on the Oklahoma side served only 3.2 beer, but if you knew the right person behind the barn, regular 4.5 or 5 percent beer could be had, as well as liquor by the bottle, bypassing state stores that were already closed by ten in the evening. They'd finished a fifth of Old Crow between Center Springs and the honky-tonk and had just enough money for a case of Miller High Life and two packs of smokes.

Rainwater cranked the handle to lower the glass, being careful not to spill the open can in his hand. "What do you want?"

The man in a bulky winter coat and stained felt hat held up a bottle of Jack Daniel's. "I saw y'all out here and figured I'd be neighborly. I knew y'all were drinking Jack and Coke at the dice game the other night, thought you might need some antifreeze."

Rainwater and Kettle exchanged glances in the dim light

coming from the dashboard. Rainwater turned the radio down as Kettle swallowed, eyes on the bottle. "Well, we weren't at that game. Remember?"

"I do, but they said our alibi was meant for anytime the law asked." He shrugged and glanced over his shoulder at an idling Ford with smoke boiling from the tailpipe. "I figured we were all friends and wanted to let you know everything's all right."

"We didn't take none of that money."

The man laughed. "Never said you did. It isn't about that. I just wanted to refresh your memories so you don't let the cat out of the bag, if you know what I mean."

"We do."

Eyes on the bottle in the man's gloved hand, Rainwater licked his lips. "Say that bottle's for sharing?"

"Sure as hell is. Hang on a second." The man pulled off a glove with his teeth and drew a metal collapsible cup from his coat pocket. Snapping it open with practiced ease, he wrestled with the cap for a moment before pouring the cup half full. Extending the bottle, he grinned. "Here you go. I just need this one for the road."

Rainwater took the bottle by the neck and nodded his thanks.

"Here's the cap." The man held it out.

"Won't need it." Already half-drunk from the Old Crow, Rainwater laughed and tilted the bottle, taking two long swallows before passing it over to Kettle, who matched him, giggling in glee at their sudden good fortune. Sighing with satisfaction, Kettle chased the liquor with half the can of Miller.

The man in the hat laughed. "You two are something else."

"That we are."

"Well, y'all have fun tonight."

Rainwater saluted him with a can and watched as the man walked back to his car. "What was that all about?"

"He just wants to make sure we don't call anyone's name about that dice game."

Rainwater shifted into reverse. "Where to?"

"Anywhere but here. The sheriff pulls in and finds us drinking in this parking lot, we'll spend the night in jail."

"Again!"

Kettle laughed. "They have a paper out on me over here. Let's get back on the Texas side and drive around in the snow for a while. I love it like this, riding around all nice and warm and drinking good whiskey."

"Any free whiskey is *good* whiskey!"

"Don't I know that." Kettle tilted the bottle again as Rainwater pulled onto the highway.

At the same time they crossed the bridge into Texas, Rainwater's head spun. "Damn, that's good stuff. I'm already gettin' a buzz."

"Me too. Maybe we should have gotten something to eat."

"I would have back at the store, but that damned constable showed up."

"We still need to talk to old Neal Box." Kettle took another drink and chased it with the beer. "I wanted to warn him to stay away from the Starlite. I like that old man. You know, he's loaned me money to gamble with from time to time. I always paid him back, too."

"We can talk to him later. Pass me some more of that whiskey."

"It's going down pretty smooth, but it sure tastes sweeter than usual."

"That's because it's good whiskey, and not that rotgut we usually drink." Rainwater steered onto a county road. He took a pull from the bottle. "That's going straight to my head."

"You ain't talking clear."

"That's because I'm gettin' drunk. Crack me another one of them beers."

They followed the road around a bend and Rainwater suddenly felt the truck's rear end break on the ice. "Uh, oh." He overcorrected and the Chevrolet slid to the left, then the right. The next thing they knew, the truck was in the ditch.

"Whoo hoo!" Slurring his words, Kettle drained more of the Jack Daniel's. "That was fun."

"How'n hell we gonna get out of this ditch tonight?" Rainwater's eyes were half closed, his head leaning back against the seat.

"Who cares? It's warm in here, and we have plenty to drink. I'd just as soon drink in the quiet and watch the snow fall." Kettle poked Rainwater. "Hey, you awake?"

"Barely." Rainwater scarcely understood what came out of his friend's mouth. Neither of them had ever gotten so drunk so fast before. Through cracked eyes, he checked the fuel gauge. "Uh, oh. We should have filled up."

"Don't matter. We can walk back to the Starlite if we need to. It ain't that far."

Rainwater didn't hear him, because the lethal dose of antifreeze in his system knocked the man completely out. Kettle passed out soon afterward, and they were both dead two hours later. Not long after, the truck ran out of gas and snow piled up around the pickup that became their tomb.

Chapter Twenty-Six

The cold was sharp the next morning, reminding Ned of those winters when he was a kid. The kind of deep-freeze chill that immediately nipped a man's nose and cheeks and settled into his bones if he got still. Even with his coat and the longhandles under his overalls, he was chilled. Both feet in wool socks and brogans were ice cold by the time he came back into the house after feeding the cows and breaking the ice on the pool so they could drink. He'd thought about waking the boys up to help, but school was called off, and he let them enjoy a rare chance to sleep in on a weekday morning.

They'd be excited when they woke up, because more than three inches of snow was on the ground and still falling.

The radio announcer droned, and the kitchen windows ran with sweat from breakfast cooking on the stove. Miss Becky straightened from checking the scratch biscuits browning in the oven. "My lands, you're covered in ice."

"This'a bad one. I bet it got down close to zero last night. I haven't seen ice that thick since the thirties." He slipped out of his coat and hung it on a rack beside the door. Melting snow and water flew off his hat when he slapped it on top of the coat.

She poured a cup of coffee from a small pan simmering on the stove. "The radio says it's not gonna let up for the next several days. There's another front gonna be here this afternoon and another'n after that."

Ned glanced at the floor beside the stove. "Where's Hootie?"

She grinned. "I let him out and he came in and made a beeline straight for the boys' room. He's asleep under their bed."

"Dogs lived outside when we were kids."

"They died out there, too. Times are changing."

He took a sip and grimaced when the phone rang. Leaving the steaming mug, he rose and went into the living room to answer. The voice on the other end of the line was unfamiliar. "Constable Parker. This is Ryan Prescott. I live over here east of Slate Shoals, almost to Faulkner. Got some news for you."

"I bet it ain't good."

"Well, it ain't. I went to feed this morning and saw a Chevrolet pickup off in the ditch. Looks like it's been there since before the snow started falling. Anyway, there's two dead men inside."

"Dead how?"

"That I don't know. I wiped at the glass, but it was so iced over I couldn't see in. The door was froze shut, but when I finally broke it free, I saw 'em sittin' there in the seat. They was cold when I felt 'em. I drove straight here and called you."

"Where's here?"

"At my house out here on Route 2. Highway 906, then take 47400 to…"

"Hold on." Ned picked up a pencil to write down the directions. "Go ahead on."

———

Gray clouds hung low and snow was thick on the road and falling so fast the wipers on his Pontiac had trouble keeping up. There were few tire tracks in the fresh snow, Ned figured mostly from farmers forced into the cold to feed or chop holes in the ice for their livestock to drink.

Following the directions on the notepad, he drove through a world covered in soft white. There was little wind, and snow collected on the tops of bodark fence posts, the wires themselves, and bare limbs. Dead vegetation in the fencerows laid over with the accumulation getting deeper with every minute. Cedars in the pastures drooped with the weight.

It was a gray, monochromatic world.

Three pickups loaded with hay and sacks of feed idled in the middle of the county road when he arrived, tailpipes smoking in the frigid air. The drivers gathered in a cluster, hands buried deep in their coat pockets. Inside of one truck, a youngster near Top's age watched through the glass.

Leaving the engine running and the heater on high, Ned slid out and met the men stamping their feet to maintain circulation. A gangly man stuck out his hand. "I'm Ryan Prescott."

"I recognize you now." They shook. "Seen you up at the sale barn a time or two." Ned nodded at the others huddling in their coats.

"Yessir." Prescott nodded toward the car. "Other than when I first got here, nobody's been down there."

"Good." Ned studied the car, then checked the tailpipe. There was no melted snow or ice behind the sedan. "Engine was off?"

"Yessir."

Ned picked his way through the snow. Prescott's footprints were already filling in. Tall grass in the shallow ditch was the only thing that marred the surface on the opposite side. Since the driver's door had already been opened, Ned started there.

Despite the cold, the air reeked of whiskey. The driver leaned over the steering wheel, an empty fifth of Jack Daniel's in one hand. Ned knew who it was as soon as he saw the wide scar at the corner of the man's left eye.

"Howdy, Mr. Isom Rainwater." He looked past the body at the passenger covered in a coat, instead of wearing it. The man leaned against the other door, and Ned was glad he hadn't started there, because the corpse would have likely fallen out in his arms. The floorboard was full of beer cans. Another nearly empty fifth of Jack Daniel's Black Label lay on the dusty cloth seat between them. Some had leaked out onto the material and Kettle's pant leg, the puddles looking dark as blood. "Jincy Kettle."

The key was in the ignition. Ned gave it a twist and the needles jumped. The fuel gauge showed empty. "That explains that."

Leaving the door open, Ned returned to the men waiting on the shoulder. "Y'all stay up here."

Apparently the spokesman for the trio, Prescott pulled the collar of coat higher. "You know who they are?"

"I do. Both of 'em. A couple of old boys from Oklahoma."

"What killed 'em, you think?"

"Looks to me like they got drunk and froze to death when they ran out of gas."

———

Cody arrived in his sheriff's car, followed by Buck Johnson, the justice of the peace. Despite the storm, cars and farm trucks continued to arrive, drawn by the activity in the bar ditch and the telephone grapevine. Snow-covered men milled around the long snakes of car tracks winding around and through the haphazardly parked vehicles.

It didn't take Buck long to examine the bodies. He waved the ambulance drivers forward and rejoined the lawmen standing off from the rest of the crowd. "Looks like hypothermia to me."

Ned raised an eyebrow.

Buck worked on the ever-present chew tucked into his cheek. "Fancy word for people who die from exposure. Froze to death, but you can't tell how long because of the cold. Tony Roth'll have to make it official, but it looks to me like they were drunk and slid off in the ditch sometime during the night." He spat a brown stream into the pure-white fluff at his feet. "When they ran out of gas, they made the mistake of thinking whiskey would keep 'em warm. I've seen it before."

Cody nodded as the ambulance drivers worked to get the stiffened bodies out of the car and onto the stretchers. "It feels warm going down, but that's all."

"I could use a snort right now." Buck chuckled. "I'm gone, boys." Returning to his car, he made a careful three-point turn and disappeared back toward Arthur City, the snow quickly drawing a thick lace curtain closed behind the car.

Ned watched the taillights wink out and turned to Cody. "Come go with me."

"Where to?"

"We're going to the store."

"Which one?"

"Neal's."

———

The store was open, and the woodstove warmed only one person, Neal Box. He looked up when Ned walked in, shaking snow from the coats and hats. He built a smile that faded when the Lamar County sheriff walked in behind him.

Ned expected him to ask what was wrong, but Neal took another trail toward where they were going. "How can I help you boys this morning?"

"Neal, I've never had you ask me that question in my entire life." Ned pointed a finger at the day's paper laying on the counter and humped in the middle. "You're expecting trouble. I've known you since we were kids, and you never had a pistol on the counter from the time you opened your first store. It was always under the counter. I'd've expected you to ask us what's wrong. I saw it in your face."

"What's wrong?"

Ned leaned in. "Something's happened. We just left Isom Rainwater and Jincy Kettle."

Neal licked his lips. "What'd they have to say?"

"Not much." Turning his back on the two old friends, Cody walked over and warmed his hands over the stove. "They were both dead."

Ned saw the shock in Neal's eyes. "What from?"

"Froze to death last night."

Neal glanced out the window, likely not seeing the snow. "How?"

Ned snorted. "They got real still for too long."

Sensing Ned's temper was growing short, Cody turned and backed up to the stove, hands behind him. "From what we saw, they ran out of gas east of Slate Shoals and died of hypothermia. It looks like they tried to drink themselves warm, but it didn't work."

Shaking his head, Neal studied the paper in front of him. "I doubt that's what happened."

Relieved that he didn't have to push his old friend any harder, Ned relaxed. "Now you can tell me what you know."

Neal deflated, defeated. "I don't know where to start."

"Find a place."

"Well." He swallowed, fear evident on his lined face. "Now don't get mad, Ned. I should have told you up front, but I thought I was wrong."

"About what?"

"About R. B."

Ned went empty inside. "You need to quit circling the corral and get to it."

"I was with R. B. the night he died, shooting dice at the Starlite."

Ned's head whipped toward Cody, who held up a hand to stop the attack he knew was coming. "It's been hard enough for Neal to get started. Let him tell his story, and you can chew on me later when it's just us."

The door opened, halting conversation as big John Washington opened the door. "Mr. Neal. Mr. Ned. Howdy, Sheriff. Is it all right if I come in? The back door's locked."

Neal waved a hand. "John, you don't have to ask. You can always use the front door."

Cody looked at his deputy. "Something wrong? You looking for us?"

"Not 'specially. I's passing by on my way to the courthouse. Got up late this mornin', but Mr. Cody, I didn't get in last night 'til after three, working wrecks..."

"You don't have to explain to me. I know you were out till late."

"Yessir, well Rachel fixed me breakfast this mornin' and the kids wanted to play in the snow awhile, so I wrapped their shoes in bread sacks and watched 'em awhile 'fore I come in." Plastic bread sacks often served as cheap galoshes for families that couldn't afford anything more expensive. "Saw y'all's cars when I went by and thought there might be trouble. You been broke in, Mr. Neal?"

Cody grinned. "It's good. Neal was telling us something that you probably ought to hear, too. I'd have to tell you anyway." He threw that in last so Neal would know John would hear later, and there was no reason to stop talking now. "Go ahead on, Neal."

"Like I's sayin'. Me and Clarice went over to that new club Friday night to listen to some music and maybe dance."

"And drink."

"Ned!" Cody's voice was sharp. "Let's listen."

Big John's eyebrow rose, and he unbuttoned his coat, remaining beside the front door.

Eyes shining with embarrassment, Neal spoke to the counter. "I'd heard there might be some dice, too. You know, most of the other places over in Juarez have backed off that, because Cody's been running the Sportsman. But now that he's sold out, I think the TV Lounge is still letting guys play cards or shoot dice, but I don't like taking her to that place n'more."

The TV Lounge was so tough that when Merle Haggard played there one night, he said he'd never come back because it scared even him and his band, who were used to gun and knife clubs.

Cody crossed his arms. "Y'all remember I'm out of the club business, right?"

"Not as much as I'd like." Ned shook his head. "You shouldn't have been in it in the first place."

Neal didn't miss a beat. He'd heard that argument several times before. "So, when the Starlite opened, we went over there and liked it. Nice and clean inside, and the prices aren't too bad. It has a decent dance floor…"

"And?" Ned's impatience was showing.

He swallowed. "They serve liquor, and I learned they have a room in back where you can play cards or shoot some dice." He rushed through so's not to be interrupted. "And Ned, it's all right, 'cause they say it's on Oklahoma land, so we don't break Texas law when we're there."

Cody held up a hand. "We'll chew over that part later. Go on with your story."

"Well…" Neal swallowed again. "Like I said, we were there the night R. B. died, and he was winning. Winning big. I've never seen anybody with so much cash as that night. I couldn't win a throw, so I got out, but there was others who started riding his wave, and I swanny, the cash just kept coming.

"Those dice were hot that night, and he could do no wrong. It was after midnight when he finally started losing, and so he quit. Said he was done and gonna go out front and drink. The guys who own the club didn't like that one damn bit. They said he needed to play a while longer, that maybe the dice would heat back up again, but he said he wanted to drink and dance. There was a little gal out front he'd been talking to and he wanted a chance at her. He said he figured that when she saw that wad of money, she'd fall in love with him, for that night anyway.

"So he left, and those guys in there got to talking about how he might've been cheating. One of 'em was Cajun, and he was mad as a Jap. The longer they talked, the more they convinced themselves that R. B.'d been cheating. Three of 'em huddled up and got to talking, close enough that I could hear 'em planning to get their money back. I didn't have any business being there no more, so I cashed in and me'n Clarice left."

Ned's voice was full of venom. "And you just left R. B. to fend for himself."

Neal swallowed. "I'm paying for it. I can't get it out of my mind that they rolled R. B. in the parking lot, and that he must've fought back. Maybe they hurt him bad, and he tried to drive home, but ran off the road and drowned."

"So, if you think it was an accident, why're you worried?"

"Because Odell Chatworthy was in that game. Jincy and Kettle were there, too. That's why I have a pistol under this here paper."

Chapter Twenty-Seven

"Who else was at that dice game, Neal?"

Big John Washington backed up to the stove with Cody. Ned stayed where he was in front of Neal. Outside, the snow slacked off, falling at half the rate from an hour earlier.

Neal Box seemed more relaxed now that the story was out. "Them that I know, Silas Cornsilk, Me, Vaughn Cunningham, you know Rainwater and Kettle, Bruce Jones, Warren Christie, and Butch Walls. Them're the ones I know, but there was three others, and two Okies."

He started to add something else but stopped. "There were a couple of women whose names I can't recall."

"Can't?" Ned raised an eyebrow.

"Won't."

Cody wrote the names down on a pad he kept in his back pocket. "Have you ever seen those other three men before?"

"Yeah, two of 'em in other clubs. They've been to the Sportsman, Cody."

The sheriff winced, knowing Ned was shooting daggers with his eyes. "What'd they look like?"

"Nothing special. One has a sharp chin, black hair, fairly

brushy eyebrows, slender. The other 'n's stocky. Losing his hair. Has a tattoo of a girl on one arm. I think he might've been in the Navy. The girl's sitting on an anchor." Neal thought for a second. "They all lost a lot of money. Lots of it." He licked his lips. "One of 'em...well, never mind. They all lost their shirts."

John Washington took notes while Ned studied his old friend. He didn't like what he was seeing. "How many times you been there?"

"I don't keep count. Ned, I'm not a bad person. You know as well as I do that me and Clarice don't have nothin' but this store. I work six days a week. If I'm not sittin' behind this counter, I'm sittin' in front of the television. I don't have nothing else to do, so we drink a little beer and have some fun. That's all."

"Nobody says you've done anything wrong." Cody paused as the lights flickered. They went out for several seconds before coming back on again. They watched the single light bulb above the meat cooler, as if keeping an eye on it would tell them if the electricity would stay on. He continued when it steadied. "But that club's not where you want to be. Once Judge Rains cleans things up with the state, somebody's going to shut that place down, either me, or Oklahoma."

"I haven't been back."

"So you didn't think we needed to know any of that?"

"I didn't know what to think."

"But you're worried."

"You're mighty right I'm worried. Four of those men are dead now, starting with R. B., and I don't know why."

"They all look like accidents."

Ned shook his head. "They aren't, and now we know what we're dealing with."

Chapter Twenty-Eight

The second cold front arrived after noon, bringing another round of snow. From what I'd seen in my young life, winter storms usually dropped the temperature for a day or two. Sometimes snow or ice lasted only a few hours before warm weather came up from the gulf and melted everything away. A year earlier we woke up with five inches on the ground, but the sun came out that afternoon and it was warm enough to go outside in shirtsleeves.

This arctic front on top of us settled in to stay a while. The base of freezing rain, then sleet, cooled the ground enough for the first round of snow to stick.

Norma Faye, Uncle Cody's redheaded wife, was in the kitchen with Miss Becky. They'd been cooking all day, and the warm, rich smells of freshly baked bread filled the house. Pots bubbled on the stove, and they chattered like magpies, though every now and then their voices lowered when they didn't want us to hear.

That's when I knew they were talking about us kids.

I was wrapped up in a quilt on the couch, reading a book called *The Moon Tenders* by August Derleth.

Mark was on the phone with Pepper, talking low and quiet, but I knew they were arguing about her and Jett. I wasn't sure yet where he was with Blu, but it was as clear as the nose on my face that something was about to happen between all four of them.

Norma Faye chuckled at something Miss Becky said. "They're just wrestling with hormones."

I held my place with one finger and listened.

"Well, I'm not used to that. I swanny, I don't ever remember being that-a-way."

"Miss Becky, you're different from anybody I ever knew, but *I* sure remember. I kept the boys twisted up in knots and didn't know why." She paused. "Even when I was twenty and married Calvin. You know what kind of mistake that was, and I knew it when it happened. I'm just lucky Cody came along when he did."

It got quiet in there and I knew they were both thinking about what happened between her dead husband and Uncle Cody and Grandpa. Snow was falling hard when we heard cars pull up the drive. Hootie was asleep in front of the stove and barked once to let us know he was doing his job. I looked out the window to see Uncle Cody's sheriff's car leading the way with Grandpa following in his tire tracks. Mr. John Washington's marked car was behind them.

Miss Becky opened the wooden door as soon as they were on the porch. They stomped snow off their boots and shoes before coming in. Uncle Cody gave her a big hug and moved out of the way when Mr. John filled the doorframe. She almost disappeared in his huge arms.

I'm not sure, but I think Mark just hung up on Pepper when I went past and into the kitchen. He followed me, and the next thing you know we were all in the kitchen.

Country folks believe in food. Miss Becky turned toward the stove. "Y'all sit down. You hungry?"

Grandpa took his usual seat at the head of the table, his back to the sink. Uncle Cody always sat on his right, but Mr. John hesitated. I got to thinking, the last time he was in that kitchen was when he brought me and Pepper in the house after we'd been grabbed by a bad man.

Miss Becky saw Mr. John standing there and pointed at a seat. "You sit down there, John."

"Miss Becky, I'll stand…"

"I said sit down, hon."

He knew better than to argue and lowered his big frame onto an aluminum chair that looked to be too small. Me and Mark sat down with them and pretty soon the smell of hot coffee filled the air. Norma Faye ruffed my hair as she went by with a fresh coconut cake.

Grandpa drummed his fingers on the table. "So back to what Neal told us, what're you gonna do, *Sheriff*?"

That word sounded pretty hard, so I knew he had something on his mind. Uncle Cody frowned. "About what?"

"You know what I'm talking about."

Uncle Cody shot a look at me and Mark, then sighed. "Are we go'ng to talk about the Sportsman, or what's going on right now?"

Miss Becky sat a steaming cup in front of Grandpa and squeezed his shoulder. I'd felt that squeeze before, and it meant for me to be quiet. I figured it said the same thing to him.

Grandpa took a sip, then shook a few grains of salt into his coffee to cut the bitterness. "We have four men from a dice game who're dead. I think we go over there and close that joint down."

"It ain't legal, Ned. O. C. won't give us a warrant. He's play-ing a chess game with Oklahoma, and I think he's afraid if he makes the wrong move, it'll backfire on him. We're right back to that problem of who owns the land, but no matter what, since it's unincorporated, they think they can get away with anything. Maybe I can get them for selling liquor. That might be the best way to deal with it."

They grew silent as Miss Becky and Norma Faye sliced and served the cake. Mark and I were the last to get ours, but I didn't care. We were at the table with the men.

Another car pulled into the yard, and Miss Becky glanced out the kitchen window. "It's another sheriff's car."

Uncle Cody nodded. "It's Anna. She was checking something for me. I told her to come meet us here."

It didn't take her long to come inside out of the cold. Miss Becky held the door open for her. "Howdy, hon. I've heard about you. Come in here and sit down."

Mark rose. "You can have my place."

I wish I'd thought to give up my seat. Mark put his plate on top of the chest-type deep freeze and took another bite of cake. Not wanting to be the only kid at the table, I got up and stood beside him.

Miss Anna hugged Norma Faye and sat down, but didn't take off her hat, and I couldn't take my eyes off it. I'd never seen anyone sit at the dinner table with a hat on their head. Uncle waved with his fork. "Did you get that wreck out on Bonham Street straightened out?"

"Sure did. It wasn't bad. A car slid into another and they both wound up in the ditch. There's not much else. Nobody got hurt. It's snowing so hard most everybody else is staying inside right now."

"Good. We're talking about the Starlite."

"I figured that."

"What'd you find out?"

Her eyes flicked to Aunt Becky, then Norma Faye. "Well, I went in and looked around. Nobody knew who I was."

"Any trouble?"

"No. Had to brush a couple of guys off, but that's all."

Miss Becky's eyebrows rose and her mouth pursed as she listened.

Watching her, Uncle Cody's eyes sparkled at her sour expression. "Good. What'd you find out?"

"They have a craps table in the back, and two or three card tables. I think they go in a side door. They sell liquor and beer, and I imagine a lot of it. But it's what's coming across the counter that I couldn't figure out for sure. I believe they're moving drugs, but I didn't get a look at what they were passing. I doubt it's grass, so it's likely to be pills, cocaine, or maybe even heroin, but don't ask me to testify on it."

Grandpa put his fork down. "You sent her in there all alone?"

"I wasn't in uniform, Mr. Parker, and it was more my idea. I got in and out without a lot of attention. There's no one here who could have done that."

Miss Becky couldn't stand being quiet anymore. "Well, women ought not to be going in places like that."

Uncle Cody pushed back from the table. "We know a lot of women who go to clubs, but let's not get off on that. Now that we know for sure this place is crooked, we need to do something about it and these guys who're dying."

Miss Anna held up a hand when Norma Faye tried to give her a slice of cake. "Do you have any of that coffee left? It smells great."

"Sure do." She poured her a cup from a small saucepan.

"Well, we don't have any suspects in these deaths, so I'm not sure what to do." Ned sipped at the scalding coffee.

Uncle Cody patted his pockets for the cigarettes that still

weren't there. Realizing what he'd done, he held up his coffee cup for a refill instead. "I know a couple of those guys. I'll talk to them. We need to find out who that Chisum guy is."

"None of 'em were my people, I don't reckon." Mr. John's voice rumbled across the table. "I don't see what I can do right now."

"Ask around and see what your folks've heard." Uncle Cody blew across the surface of his cup. "Maybe there's talk. We don't know where the liquor or beer's coming from. There aren't any distributors who'll chance losing their licenses providing booze for that place. They must be buying it on the black market or stealing it. John, see if Sugar Bear knows anything; you probably need to stick your head in there pretty soon anyway."

"Sure will."

"No matter what, that place is still in business." Ned's voice was full of disgust.

"Maybe we can do something about that, Mr. Ned." Mr. John's voice rumbled again.

"How?"

"We may not know who's responsible for where the Starlite sits, but if we put a car out there on the road where they're turning off, maybe it'll change a few minds. What do you think, Sheriff?"

Uncle Cody grinned. "Shut off their water."

"Sure 'nuff. There's a few folks don't care who sees 'em turn off there, but quite a few don't want to be recognized. How 'bout we take turns watching who goes in and out?"

Grandpa liked the idea. He grinned across the table at me. "I bet we even have a few kinfolk that don't need to be there."

His words seemed directed at me, and my stomach clenched. I couldn't help but look at Mark. His eyes widened, and he barely shook his head.

Grandpa's voice cut sharp. He'd seen something between us he didn't like. "You boys know anything you need say?"

Mark spoke up. "Sure do." The kitchen went quiet and my stomach fell, but before I could say anything to get us in trouble, he grinned. "I'd like more cake!"

They laughed, but it seemed like Uncle Cody was watching us, too, and didn't seem to laugh as much as the others.

Chapter Twenty-Nine

The frozen air was still when the meeting at Ned's house broke up. It was so quiet on the porch he could hear the snowflakes land with a steady hiss. He watched the cars pull slowly onto the covered highway before coming back inside for his hat. "Mama, I'm going to town."

"It's bad out there. Why don't you wait until it quits?"

"The radio said that's liable to be three or four days from now. I'll be careful."

He glanced at the boys who were back at the table. There was something going on between those two, but he also knew there was trouble with them and the preacher's twins. Figuring it was teenage woes, he shook his head. "Y'all behave yourselves. We might have a talk when I get back."

Ned left, following the tire tracks in the snow. He crossed the creek bridge, glancing down at where R. B. had gone off only three days earlier. It seemed like a year ago.

The world was soft and quiet, buried under a steady accumulation of snow that covered the trees and the ice-shored creekbanks. Smooth humps and mounds signaled low grasses and brambles on the shoulder. While it wasn't as thick in the woods, dark splotches under the understory cedars broke up the smooth surfaces.

He wished he was walking through the woods with a shotgun, hunting rabbits, instead of trying to figure out what was going on with that damned club not ten miles away. Rabbit hunting along the edge of wooded pastures was one of his favorite memories from when he was young and alone with no troubles to weigh his mind. Back then he'd stop and wait for the rabbits to grow nervous and usually give in to panic, bounding away.

The same strategy should work to shake things loose over at that honky-tonk. His favorite way to gather information was to poke around then pause and wait to see what might happen. Rabbits grew nervous when a hunter stopped abruptly and waited. He hoped the same would happen with those responsible for R. B.'s death.

The other way to hunt rabbits was to trail them through the snow. The day after a snowfall was the best time, when they emerged to search for food. Then it was easy to follow them to their burrows or hiding places in the brambles.

The rabbit trails he was chasing weren't clear in his mind. They twisted every which-a-way, but none led back to where his prey was hiding. He was confident at least one of those paths led to the Starlite perched on that no-man's-land south of the river.

One way or another, they'd explode from cover when they were spooked enough.

Highway 271 was down to a single path through the snow. Only one car was in sight, heading north at a snail's pace. By the time he reached Powderly, the north wind picked up. Snowflakes fell at an angle as Ned accelerated enough for them to swirl in his slipstream. The Motorola in his floorboard crackled to life with an exchange about a car wreck in Chisum.

His habit of talking to himself arose. "Folks oughta stay home in this kind of weather."

Rabbits were back on his mind when he came upon a set of tracks crossing the two southbound lanes, across the medium on the turnaround, and then turning south.

Rabbit trails.

"I wonder how many are heading for that joint today?" Going with his instincts, he slowed and made a U-turn. "I ain't no use in town right now."

Steering carefully, he made his way back to Arthur City. Just as he suspected, more than one set of tracks turned onto the road running past the Starlite.

"People drinking in this weather. What'n hell are they thinking?"

The Pontiac's back end broke when he made the turn, despite his slow speed. Taking his foot off the accelerator, he allowed the sedan to stabilize, then followed the ruts through an open wire gap and toward the line of trees between the road and the club.

Knowing what he was doing would make Judge Rains mad if he found out, Ned couldn't help himself. He drove under bare limbs hanging low with the weight of accumulated snow and broke into a winter wonderland of smooth humps, bent and drooping cedars, and toward that building on the edge of the river. Despite the falling snow, a colorful glow thirty feet above the joint looked almost Christmassy.

Half a dozen dirty cars were parked haphazardly in the open. Two were completely covered in snow, and it was obvious they'd been there for hours. The rest were in various stages of collection, and in the gray light, it was almost impossible to determine their color, make, or model. A web of crisscrossing tire tracks carved the blanket covering the lot, evidence of several vehicles that had been there and gone.

"Long as I'm here."

He killed the engine and stepped out into the knee-high accumulation. The red, leather-covered door opened into darkness smelling of smoke and beer. He paused as warmth flowed over him, along with the Tammy Wynette's heartbroken voice. "Stand By Your Man" played as he paused for a minute for his eyes to adjust to the dim light, finally picking out three men scattered down the length of the bar. One leaned over and bummed a light from the barfly two stools away. The flickering lighter revealed two strangers.

The third turned to check out the newcomer, then returned to his beer.

Three men sat at a table in the front corner to his left. Everything else was in shadow or lit by neon signs. Still in his buttoned-up coat with his hat pulled down low, Ned hesitated, wondering what to do next. He didn't drink, so ordering a beer was out.

Feeling the bass bump of the music coming from the Wurlitzer, and wondering why it was so loud, he walked up to the end of the bar near the restrooms and pulled out a stool. The bartender with greasy hair drifted over. One strand fell over his forehead and almost in his eye. "What'll you have?"

"Coke."

"What kind?"

"Co-cola."

"You want whiskey with that?"

"No."

"We don't get many teetotalers in here."

"I bet not."

The bartender opened the cooler and popped the top off a bottle of Coca-Cola. Thumping it on the mahogany surface, he stuck a paper straw into the neck. "You looking for something else? A little action?"

The straw rose with the bubbles. Ned plucked it out and laid it on the bar. When it left a wet spot, he moved the straw over on top of a cardboard Schlitz coaster. "What kind of action?"

"Well, we don't have girls here, or that kind anyway. All the girls who come in to dance are gone for the time being. They'll be back after dark, if the weather clears. When we have more customers, there's a couple of games going on in the back."

Ned wondered why the man was so free to talk, and figured his age made the bartender comfortable. The action he referred to was prostitutes. Somewhat relieved there were no girls involved, Ned was more interested in the games. "Dice?"

"Sure." He inclined his head to the three men at the table. "You have to get Mr. Rawlins' permission first, when things get rolling back there. You look more like a card man yourself. They're more likely not to drink."

"How do y'all get away with that, what with the law and all?"

The bartender grinned wide. "Mr. Rawlins has all that taken care of. The law don't go in here. We're on a no-man's-land. Nobody knows who owns this little piece of dirt we're built on. Mr. Rawlins says they're all tangled up in the courts, so we do what we want."

"You have a lot of regulars playing out back?"

"Sure do. From all over. About half of 'em are farmers, but we get professionals in here, too."

"Professional gamblers?"

"Naw, people who work professional jobs. Businessmen, a dentist, folks who own car dealerships and stores. Like that."

Tammy's song ended and he glanced at the trio lined up along the bar. The bartender paused, wiping the bar while the jukebox's machinery clicked and Merle Haggard's "Mama Tried" filled the smoky air. Ned figured it was the perfect song for such a place and tiled his Coke, taking two long swallows.

The bartender picked up the used straw and dropped it somewhere out of sight. "The best nights are when some of the guys bring their wives and girls to shoot dice. Whoo wee! It gets loud back there then."

It had never occurred to Ned that women shot dice, and the bartender saw it on the old man's face. "The higher those guys bet, the louder the gals squeal, and, before you know it, there's tons of money on the table, 'cause they're urging them on. It's something else."

Women. Neal hadn't mentioned women, but Ned knew Clarice always went with him. Was Neal trying to keep her out of harm's way?

"Well, I'm here about a dice game. I hear tell there was a lot of money on the table Friday night."

The bartender immediately shut down. His eyes narrowed and he was finished. "I was off."

"I'd like to get in a game. Anything going on back there tonight?"

He shrugged. "Nope. Too much snow. You need anything else?"

Ned swallowed more of the Coke. "Naw. Not right now."

"That'll be four bits for the drink."

"For a Coke? That's more'n four times what I pay at the store."

"This ain't the store."

Ned dug two quarters out of his pocket and laid them on the counter. The bartender took the coins and glanced over Ned's shoulder. "Mr. Rawlins wants to see you."

Ned turned. The three men at the corner table were watching them. "He can come over here if he wants to talk to me."

"I'd go over there if I was you."

"You ain't me."

"Look, old man. Let me give you some advice. When that

fella over there who owns the place tells you to do something, then you do it."

"He owns it, does he?" Ned drained his bottle in two long swallows, feeling the carbonated burn all the way down, and put the empty on top of the now-damp coaster. "I'm too old for people to tell me what to do."

Done with the place, Ned turned for the door. Rawlins called out, "Hey, buddy. Come here for a second."

Ned kept walking but waved a friendly hand at the table. "Gotta go."

"I *said* come here." His voice snapped like a whip. The two men on either side stood, but Ned reached for the door handle and at the last minute, noticing a hand waving from the opposite dark corner. Thinking it was another one of Rawlins's men, Ned gave him a good look.

It was Tom Bell. Surprised to see him sitting there, Ned nodded in recognition and left.

No one followed him back out into the storm. Starting the Pontiac, he made a wide turn and drove back out. A cruiser was parked on the county road when he reached the open wire gap, and he saw it was John Washington, already doing what they'd talked about, presenting a presence to would-be customers.

He made the turn and waved.

John waved back.

Chapter Thirty

Buster Rawlins choked down a flush of irritation at the old man's refusal to come when he called. "You guys know who that was?"

Melvin LaFleur and Jess Plemens shook their heads. LaFleur crushed out his cigarette. "Just some old fart who likes sody water."

Plemens chuckled and checked the razor-sharp part in his hair with one fingertip. "One who should have learned his manners a long time ago. There's another old man over there in the corner. The weather must bring 'em out."

"I hope it brings in a busload today." Rawlins scowled. "We're gonna lose a lot of money if this damned snow keeps up."

"Radio says we might have another week of it. That's what I hate about running a joint this far north."

They laughed at the idea of being "up north" as opposed to being barely two hundred miles west from where their old club had been located.

Rawlins watched the other elderly man in the corner. In a black hat and clothing befitting an old cowboy, he'd been nursing a beer for the better part of an hour. He hated that kind of a customer, one who ordered one Lone Star and took up a chair for an hour or two. No one could make any money on people who just like to sip their beer.

The front door opened, and Rawlins thought it was the fat old man coming back. Instead, it was his man, Ricky Toscani. Knowing where they'd be, Toscani made an immediate left and joined them. "Two more down."

"Who?" Rawlins glanced over at the old cowboy to see if he heard. The man simply sat there with his back to the corner, apparently studying the bar.

Toscani pulled up closer to the table. "Those Indians, Rainwater and Kettle."

The man in black finished his Lone Star and rose. He was halfway to the door when Rawlins crooked his finger. "Got a question for you, old-timer."

He hesitated for a moment, smoothed his thick white mustache, and crossed the room. "Shoot."

"I haven't seen you in here before."

"That's a statement, not a question."

"Okay." Rawlins smirked. "I haven't seen you in here before. What's your name?"

The elderly man's face was in shadow under the brim of his hat, but when he raised his head, the lights from the beer sign illuminated piercing eyes that looked cold as the snow outside. "Tom Bell."

"Well, Mr. Bell. I hope you like the place."

"It's all right."

"I hope it's more than that. We're trying to build something here."

"Looks like every other beer joint I've ever been in."

Rawlins nodded and studied his craggy face, as if Tom Bell's statement was profound. Despite the old man's age, he looked like a classic tough-as-nails cowboy. Bell showed no expression, neither fear of friendliness, and Rawlins suddenly realized the man despised him.

Rawlins felt a flush of anger. His lips twitched, and he made a conscious effort to close his mouth to keep from revealing stained teeth that hadn't been brushed in days. Each morning when he looked in the mirror, he saw the exact opposite of the chiseled, attractive elderly man who'd never worried about his chin, his nose, or big ears that stuck out at right angles. It increased his hatred for the old man, who'd likely never had a woman turn from him in disgust. He needed, more than anything else in the world, to take every cent Tom Bell owned. "You look to be a man of means."

"Not really. I'm just living on a little retirement."

"Well, does it give you enough left over at the end of the month for a little fun?"

"What kind?"

"Oh, we offer a little more than most of the clubs around here. We have a few games out back when the weather's better than this. Girls, too, for them that are interested. Why don't you come back some other time?"

"I might do it. Thanks."

"I'll front you twenty dollars to get started. Just remind the bartender I told you that when you come in."

"I'll keep it in mind." Tom Bell turned to leave but was stopped by Rawlins's voice. "Hey. One more question. Do you know who that guy was who just left?"

"Why?"

"He's pretty disrespectful."

"That's your opinion. You don't want to prod an old bear like that. He's liable to turn around and bite you."

All four chuckled. Rawlins took a long swallow to finish his beer. "There's nothing scary about him."

"Suit yourself." Tom Bell looked at each one. "You'll learn about such men, if y'all live long enough."

He reached for the door handle when Rawlins's sharp voice cut through. "Hey, buddy! I'm not through talking to you. Get your ass back over here."

The music ended at that moment and the silence was as thick as the smoke drifting in the neon light. His hand on the door, head down, and face again partially in shadow, Tom Bell seemed intent on the latch.

"Buddy." Bell studied the name for a long beat, then shook his head. He turned toward the four men at the table and tilted his head like a puppy pondering some strange insect. "Mister, the way you said that's disrespectful back where I come from, so that's your one warning. Come to think of it, you'd better learn to watch your mouth, or the folks in this county'll bring you down off your high horse pretty quick."

The menace that radiated from the man in black was almost palpable. Instead of popping off again, Rawlins lowered one hand below the table. At the same time, his toadies stood, uncertain what was going to happen next.

The next record played a simple guitar lead.

Unafraid, Tom Bell took his hand off the latch and slid it under his coat near his right hip.

"You boys think. You've been drinking. You're not yourselves."

Rawlins licked his thin lips and the hand that was reaching for a pistol returned to his beer bottle. "Sit down boys, and let that customer go on home."

Keeping his eyes on all four, Tom Bell left, and they sat still, listening to Roy Acuff sing about a great speckled bird.

Chapter Thirty-One

Butch Walls opened his eyes and tried to focus in the dark, wondering where he was. He was moving, that's for sure. Cold. Folded up like a card table in a tiny dark space. Wait, he was in the trunk of a car!

How'd he get there?

Mind reeling, he couldn't remember, but fear rose in a tidal wave.

The car stopped. He tried to move, but his hands were tied behind his back. His feet were bound.

The trunk opened and filtered light poured in. Gray skies outlined the shape of a man wearing a hat. He leaned in, and the last thing Butch saw was the flash of a hammer swinging toward his head.

Pain filled his shattered skull as the hammer swung again, and Butch Walls's spirit rose over the cedar tops above the Sulphur River bottoms as the man reached into the trunk to lift out his limp body.

Chapter Thirty-Two

The coroner walked out of the examination room, drying his hands on a pure white hand towel, to find Sheriff Cody Parker half-sitting on his desk. "Sheriff. I'm surprised to see you out in this weather."

"Howdy." Cody held up a paper cup of coffee from the percolator sitting atop a chap bookcase under the window. "Pretty good coffee."

"That's one of the things I insist on." Tony Roth pitched the hand towel into a bin. "What can I do for you?"

"I came by to see about those two bodies that came in this morning, Rainwater and Kettle."

"They've only been here a few hours. I haven't completed my report yet."

"Don't need all the paperwork. Just the cause of death."

Roth selected a pipe from a holder and knocked out the dottle in an oversized glass ashtray. "Hypothermia."

"Both of 'em?"

"Of course."

"Any signs of foul play?"

"No."

"Wounds? Bruises? Scratches?"

Roth clamped the pipe stem in his teeth and rounded the desk. He picked up his tobacco wallet. "Like I said. No. One of them had a hangnail."

Cody grinned. "Okay. Tell me about Odell Chatworthy."

"Now that one's finished." He finished filling his pipe and plucked a sheet from the top of a pile. "You guys are working me hard here. Adding this many unusual fatalities to my everyday workload is gonna force me to request an assistant."

"No skin off my nose." Cody read the death certificate. "The city council's liable to squeal, though."

"That won't be a problem in the future. My son's running for a council seat, and he understands the things that are necessary to provide for a town of this size. He's going to make changes around here that will be good for us all."

Cody raised an eyebrow at the proclamation, all the while reading the form. "Death by extreme physical trauma."

"Read the attachment."

A page was stapled to the certificate. Cody flipped it over and read a long list of contusions, bruises, cuts, open wounds, and broken bones. He whistled. "I wish there was one more thing you could add here."

"What's that?"

"Why he was in the trailer with a rodeo bull in the first place."

"Good question."

"Anything suspicious?"

"Like what?"

"Ligature marks, blown capillaries in his eyes, restraint marks, the like."

"You been reading medical magazines?"

"No. I've had some experience with violent death."

"Well, I saw none here. He wasn't choked, so your capillary

idea is out. No signs of rope or handcuffs on his wrists. He wasn't strangled. It looks like a complete accident."

"Except for the part where a guy who owns a generator service had no reason to be in the cattle trailer with an irritable bull."

"I can't answer that question. I could examine the man's brain all night long, but there's no way to find out what was in his mind."

"Well, I have four mysterious deaths on my hands in less than a week."

"Yeah, and I have a room full of bodies that need examining. You know, I don't just handle cases like this. People die at home, in hospitals, and in real accidents. I imagine there'll be a couple more come in today from wrecks or falls on the ice. On top of that, I'm willing to bet your office is going to get calls about people dying at home, maybe from their electricity going out, or some dummy'll have a clogged chimney and die from carbon monoxide, or a house will catch fire from the fireplace. That's why I need help, and my boy will make sure that happens when he gets into office."

Wondering why Roth kept telling him about his boy's political aims, Cody sipped his coffee and started to answer when a knock came at the door.

Roth called out. "Come in."

Deputy Anna Sloan cracked the door and peeked inside. "Am I interrupting anything?"

Roth looked from her to Cody. "No. Are you with the sheriff here?"

She stepped inside and opened her coat in the warm office. "Yes, I am. Cody, we just got a call on the radio. I knew you were here, so I drove over."

"What's up?"

"A man named Silas Cornsilk called and wants to meet you at the office. He wants to talk to you."

"Ol' Silas finally popped up." Cody drained his cup. "What's he want to talk about?"

"That dice game."

He glanced down at the report in his hand. "Good timing."

Anna opened the door to leave, and a young, blond-haired man almost fell inside. He straightened, annoyed. Adjusting his tie, the man's eyes slipped off her face and traveled down her shirt. "You yanked the knob right out of my hand."

She blushed. "Sorry."

Roth's voice snapped across the office. "Ray! Here are some people you need to meet. The sheriff and Deputy Sloan."

Two beats later the man's eyes lit, and he extended his hand first to Anna, then Cody. "I'm sorry. I was preoccupied with a meeting with the mayor that I just left. I've been meaning to come by and introduce myself to you, Sheriff. Just got out of college and I'm back in Chisum."

Anna smiled. "Graduated midterm?"

"Yes, ma'am. Back home and ready to get started."

"Your daddy was just talking about you running for city council. Good luck with that." Cody noted his fresh haircut and smooth face. "You must have an affinity for politics. Hope the mayor treated you right."

"Yes, sir. I plan to run for city council, so I knew the two of us needed to sit down and talk about this town and what you need to run it the right way."

Roth spoke up. "Ray has high goals. He's not like these long-hairs who only want to have sit-ins and protests." The coroner's chest puffed out. "He has an ambitious *plan*."

Cody crossed his arms and leaned back. "Young people with goals. I like that."

"Yes, sir!" Ray Roth adjusted his dark, skinny tie. "City council here, then when I have some experience, I'm planning to run for state representative. From there, the governor's office, then the sky's the limit. Maybe president someday."

Cody grinned. "I meant what are you plans for Chisum?"

"Oh, we need to bring this small cotton town into the twentieth century. Chisum has potential and we should mine it to its fullest. With good leadership in the city council, the sky's the limit."

Talking points, and a repeat to boot. Another politician full of meaningless drivel. Cody nodded as if those words held deep meaning. "Well, good luck with all that."

Ray Roth shook his hand. "I'd love to have your support."

Anna opened the door. "I have to go. It was nice to meet both of you."

Ray turned loose of Cody's hand and stepped forward, taking hers in a long shake. He placed his other on top. "It was a pleasure to meet you, ma'am." With his attention on Anna's surprised face, he spoke to Cody. "Sheriff, I look forward to talking with you soon."

"My pleasure." Cody turned back to the coroner. "Thanks for the quick turnaround."

The young man's proud daddy nodded. "I hope there aren't any more."

"Me too."

Chapter Thirty-Three

Deputy John Washington waved at Ned as the constable left the Starlite and turned onto the county road. Parked facing west, he slid a lever on the dash to lower the heat, opened his short-waisted uniform jacket, and turned up the radio. Despite the weather, WBAP in Dallas still came through, but crackling with static.

"...meteorologist Carl Young here. Folks, it looks like we're in for some serious weather for the next several days, with temperatures at night down into single digits and barely getting out of the teens during the daylight hours. Fronts are stacked up between here and the Arctic, but at the same time a succession of lows moving across the country from California will bring even more snow to everyone from Wichita Falls to Shreveport and as far south as Waco and College Station. If I were you, I wouldn't go north anytime soon..."

John turned the radio down until the weather and news ended, waiting for music. He unwrapped a piece of Wrigley's Spearmint gum and dropped the foil wrapper into the ashtray. His radio came alive with a report of still another accident in Chisum. It was a lead-pipe cinch that he'd get a call about a wreck nearby, forcing him to leave his stakeout position.

The truth was that he really didn't need to be there right then. The snow had already choked down most of the Starlite's customers, but he wanted to get a good look at the traffic coming in and out. Besides, he'd have to wait somewhere until that call came in and right there was just as good as anywhere else. He figured the sight of a sheriff's car idling across the road might disinterest customers and make them think twice about turning in.

A snow-covered pickup containing two men came down the road, carefully following the ruts. They hadn't been traveling long. Some of the snow had blown off the roof, but most on the hood and fenders was thick with several hard inches. The driver instinctively braked and, likely noticing the sheriff's car on the shoulder, automatically signaled his intention to turn into the pasture. John chuckled at the sight of the blinking light. He doubted the driver used his indicator more than once or twice a year.

The truck turned through the gap and drove several yards before the brake lights flashed. The truck paused for several seconds, then continued, disappearing through the gap in the trees.

John glanced into the side mirror, registering the steady cloud of exhaust from his tailpipe. The passenger mirror revealed snow and the empty road behind. The weather report was over, so he adjusted the Motorola down to background noise and turned up the radio to hear Bobby Goldsboro sing "Honey."

Two songs later, a car approached from the Starlite. It, too, was covered with so much snow John couldn't make out the model or color. He decided that he was wasting his time. If anyone was out in that weather, they were determined to get a drink whether he was sitting there or not. The approaching car'd likely been there since daylight, so his presence wasn't discouraging. He sighed. He couldn't get good descriptions of the vehicles or their passengers through the frost-covered windshields anyway.

The four-door sedan slowed as it came through the gap in

the trees, as if studying the idling sheriff's car. Arm across the bench seat, John watched it reach the gate and pause for a second before turning right.

The windshield was partially covered by so much snow the passenger side wiper didn't work. The remaining wiper was doing little to clear the glass. The driver was only a foggy shape behind the wheel.

The window in the driver's door was blocked by a coating of ice, but the back glass was down.

It was dark in there. "Why in the world's he driving with the back glass down?"

The sedan made the full turn, parallel to John's car.

Movement in the back seat.

The back of his neck prickled, and John threw himself down in the seat as his front passenger window exploded with a flash of contained lighting. Glass, shrapnel, and cold filled the car as another shotgun blast took out the right front tire.

It boomed again, the third load slapping the front passenger door with that distinctive sound of lead punching sheet metal. One pellet punched through the door, burying deep into the top of John's right shoulder. He shouted with pain.

Unconsciously counting the three blasts, he rose and drew the .38 from his holster. Most country people were dove hunters who kept a plug in their shotguns, maxing their loads to three shells instead of the five most magazines were capable of handling. He was banking on them being good old country boys who didn't want to get crossways with the game warden, even though they obviously didn't mind shooting at sheriff's deputies.

The car couldn't speed away on the slick road, but it had already moved far enough ahead that John couldn't shoot through his shattered window. Any rounds he threw through his own windshield would likely be deflected.

Yanking at the handle of the door, he wriggled out from under the wheel and leveled the revolver to fire. The gun in his fist lined up for a second before his hand dropped, his wounded arm refusing to work.

"Dammit!"

Using his left hand as a brace, the big deputy held his damaged arm up and squeezed the trigger, but the round missed. By the time he thumb-cocked the hammer with his left hand and readjusted his weakening grip, the vehicle had disappeared into the falling snow.

Movement to the right caught his attention, and that same pickup from moments earlier reappeared, moving at a slow, steady rate of speed. Fully expecting another attack, he threw himself back inside, reaching for his shotgun. Again using his left hand, he rose and laid the barrel across the snowy roof and tucked the stock into his left shoulder. It felt awkward, almost alien to have it on the off side.

He flicked off the safety as flakes stung his eyes.

The pickup advanced and paused at the gate, blinker flashing. The driver apparently saw the shotgun's wide muzzle pointed at him, and the pattern of holes in the door. He accelerated too fast, and the back end whipped around, barely missing the cruiser's front fender.

Shifting his weight to keep the muzzle trained on the truck cab, John saw the vehicle was no immediate threat and relaxed. Hot blood welled from the shoulder wound and drenched the uniform shirt under his coat.

Still panicked, the driver whipped the opposite direction as he fought the wheel. The truck's engine whined and the rear end swung back again. It was several seconds before the pickup disappeared into the snow.

No one else was coming. Shaking with adrenaline, John

dropped back behind the wheel and used his good hand to pick up the Motorola's handset from its holder on the dash. "Dispatch! John Washington. Officer down! I've been shot!"

"Where are you John?"

"On the road out front of the Starlite."

Cody's voice came through. "We're on the way, John. Hang on."

"That's all I got to do right now."

Chapter Thirty-Four

Grandpa's little house was closing in on us by Wednesday morning, so Mark and I persuaded him to take us over to Pepper's. I needed to get out, but Mark wanted to check on her. I also think he wanted to either make sure Jett didn't come over, too, or at least be there if he did.

Though the clouds were still low and gray, it'd stopped snowing for the time being, but it looked like the North Pole. I wished all that snow had come earlier, to give us a white Christmas, but at least it got us out of class, and we heard it might be a whole week before classes took up again.

I was surprised to see both stores were open as we passed. I guess some of the Spit and Whittle Club needed to get out of the house as well. The black stovepipe sticking out of the domino hall's roof poured out a steady stream of smoke into the icy air.

Grandpa slowed the Pontiac to scan the cars and trucks scattered out front. He always liked to see who was up at the stores. It was still so cold that even the tracks were white. The lots were usually a muddy mess after a storm, but the cold was so deep it looked like ski areas I'd seen on television.

When we pulled up in front of Uncle James's house, his truck was gone, leaving a black, bare spot under one of the big red oaks. Aunt Ida Belle's car was gone, too. Jagged piles of snow bordered those areas where they'd broomed off the cars. I couldn't believe that my timid aunt was out driving in such weather, but something must have come up.

Remembering that Mr. Tom now lived upstairs, I twisted around to see his truck was gone from where he parked it beside the fence, leaving a third bare rectangle of dark, dead grass and leaves.

Mark frowned at the four sets of footprints leading from the front door. "I told you we should have called first, Top."

Grandpa rested one hand over the wheel, thinking. "Who'da thought the whole bunch would be gone?"

I sighed and sat back. "Can we at least stop back by the store for a banana flip or something?" I'd recently decided I loved those sugar-filled Hostess cakes with a glass of milk.

He started to answer when the Motorola came to life. "Ned?"

Recognizing Uncle Cody's voice, he picked up the handset. "Go ahead."

"Where are you?"

"Sitting here in front of James's house."

"Good. At least you could get out. Miss Becky phoned up here to the office and said Pastor McLellan called about something up at the Methodist cemetery. He was out this morning, checking on shut-ins, when he happened to glance over and see something he didn't like out there in the back part."

"What was it?"

"Well, I don't know for sure. He said he pulled up to the gate but couldn't get it open and drive the car through because of the snow. He's in dress shoes and a light coat for some reason in this weather. Anyway, he said it looks like a grave's been disturbed back there, but he didn't walk all the way out to look."

Grandpa cut his eyes over at us and sighed. "All right. I'll run by and see what he's talking about."

"You drive careful. We're getting a lot of wrecks here in town from people sliding into one another."

"Snow's deep enough out here for pretty fair traction. They just need to slow down."

"I'll tell them you said so."

Grandpa didn't get it, but me and Mark laughed. Grandpa frowned us quiet and keyed the mike. "How's John this morning?"

"You know we're on an open channel, don't you?"

"'Course I do."

There was a pause. "Call me when you get home, but he's fine."

Replacing the handset on the bracket, Grandpa shifted into gear and slowly drove back around toward the stores. "Looks like you two get to stay out for a little bit, after all. We'll stop at the store on the way back."

Making the hard turn onto Highway 197, we headed west, following ruts packed by the passage of several vehicles. It was a good thing, too, because skid marks showed where someone slid off into the ditch. Deep, wide tracks from a tractor told us how they got out. We went over a hill and the highway leveled, but zigzagged past peaceful-looking farms, barns, and a couple of cheap trailer houses. The rest was unmarked pastures for the most part with cattle trails winding through the fluff.

It would all be beautiful when the sun came out, but right then it was simply cold and gray.

The little cemetery behind the hundred-year-old Presbyterian church looked like something from a postcard or calendar as we passed. I enjoyed the ride and wished I'd brought my camera. Mark seemed to enjoy it too, but I could tell Pepper was on his mind.

When we came around the curve by the Methodist church, Grandpa slowed, squinting across the mounded headstones and toward a line of trees at the back of the cemetery. "There it is."

I looked but didn't see what he was talking about. He pulled around to the gate, stopping in the ruts made by the Baptist preacher who'd called in. "What're you looking at?"

He pointed. "Back there in the corner."

I still didn't see anything, but after a second, I made out a dark smudge in the distance. "What is that?"

"Looks like fresh dirt to me." He opened the door. "Y'all stay in here."

"We have our galoshes. I'd like to get out and see the snow."

He looked back inside, and I saw Mark raise an eyebrow. Grandpa nodded. "All right, but y'all walk where I step. I don't want any more tracks out there."

Zipping up our coats, we got out. The gate was frozen and drifted shut, so he worked his way down the bobwire fence surrounding the cemetery until he got to a loose top strand. He stepped over easy-greasy, but it was too tall for us. The gateposts were strong, though. We put our feet on the hinges, brushed off the snow, and climbed over.

Grandpa crooked a finger at us and swung wide of the preacher's tracks that went about forty yards down the bare ribbon of road used by hearses and mourners when they had funerals. The snow was almost knee-deep there, but I figured it'd be easier walking than winding around the headstones.

It was quite a ways back to the corner, but when we reached it, another set of tracks came from the snow-covered gravel road that ran down the west side of the cemetery.

"That's why we're coming in this way." Grandpa pointed toward the footprints. "It looks like two or three folks came through there. Mighta been last night, but I'd have to look."

"How'll you tell?"

"It quit snowing around midnight, and there hasn't been much wind, so they'll be clearer. If they came in before that, they'll be partially filled in."

Mark paced me, hands deep in his coat pockets. His breath fogged and we looked like fire-breathing dragons. The closer we came to the dark smudge, my gut tightened. Maybe I was picking up what Grandpa felt, or just the idea of fairly fresh dirt in a snow-covered cemetery weirded me out.

Grandpa stopped by Frank Hayslip's waist-high headstone and held out one hand. "Y'all stay here, now."

We did, and he picked his way forward to get a closer look. I didn't need to get any closer than I was. He studied the fresh-turned dirt, talking quietly to himself.

I couldn't stand it after a while. "What do you see?"

He didn't answer for a full five minutes. By that time, I figured he was ignoring me. The cold was getting to my feet and nose, and I was about to turn around and head back to the car when he started talking like I'd just asked the question.

"It looks like somebody dug something up. Scraped the snow back, piled up the dirt and when they got what they wanted, shoved it back with a little of the snow."

We saw it because of the color. Mark turned in a full circle. "When do you think they did it?"

"Sometime before it stopped snowing last night, I think. There's some fresh powder on top, but not much."

"What'd they come out and dig around in a cemetery in weather like this?"

"I have an idy, but there's something else that bothers me worse."

"What's that?"

"I believe I see a hand sticking out of the ground there, too."

Chapter Thirty-Five

Ned hung his hat on the rack beside the door in Cody's office and sat down on a chair. "Where's O. C.? I thought he was coming."

Cody had been working on the stacks of paper rising above his desk, making some headway. Deputy Anna Sloan pared the paperwork down while she'd been recuperating from a gunshot wound several months earlier, but no matter how hard Cody tried, the stacks remained the same height.

He picked up a mug of hot coffee and took a sip, amused at Ned's blunt entrance. "In his office. On the phone. Bernice stuck her head in a little while ago and says he's chewing somebody's ass down in Austin about the Starlite and where it sits."

"Good."

"He's been working pretty hard on shutting it down, you know. He wants to do it right, instead of getting into a long court battle. He's doing it this way to keep you from working yourself all up."

"He didn't say nothin.'"

"Didn't need to. He's doing his job and expecting you to do yours."

Anna came in, followed by Big John with his arm in a sling, a thick bandage on top of his right shoulder. Ned looked relieved. "They didn't keep you long."

Anna pointed to the only other chair. "Sit there."

"No, thanks," John shook his great head, "Miss Anna, I…"

"Sit. I'm not the one shot."

"It ain't that bad." Big John knew when he was whipped. He settled into the chair with a wince. "Ol' Doc said it wasn't deep. Number four buck, but it was pretty much slowed from going through the door. Hurts, though."

"I 'magine." Ned rubbed his bald head.

Cody sipped again from his stained mug, glancing outside. Wind from the new cold front whipped the snow against the window, piling it up on the sill. While signing papers and sorting them on his desk, his mind had worked on the incidents that were somehow connected. "What'd you find out happened at the cemetery?"

Resting both elbows on his knees, Ned laced his fingers. "Well, we got some men out there and started poking around. Bruce Jones is buried only a foot or so under the ground. Looks to me like somebody got in a hurry to plant him. Probably got cold."

Anna leaned against the oak filing cabinet. "So, somebody killed him and went out there and buried him in a cemetery? That really doesn't make any sense."

"It does, in a way. He was at that dice game the night R. B. was murdered. Got a list of the players from Neal Box."

"We don't have evidence that R. B. was murdered." Cody held up a cautioning hand. "So be careful what you say when other folks are around."

"All right then. The night R. B. *died*, but it's just us here. The fact remains that another player's dead, and for me everything points toward R. B. He was the priming cap for all this. There's a feller out there trying to tie up all the loose ends for something we can't figure out.

"I believe that Starlite's crooked and needs to be shut down. Anna, you said yourself they might be selling drugs across the bar. For all I know, R. B. might've been in on it and tried to get out, and they killed him."

Cody adjusted a pen and several pages in front of him, thinking. "Ned. We don't have any evidence for that, so let's not get sidetracked."

"Well, I don't believe they went out there to the cemetery just to bury Jones. That don't make no sense a-tall, especially with all this falling weather where we can see where they dug. Hell, if it was me, I'd just throw the body in the river. Nobody'd find it for a month, and by the time the water goes down, it'd be in Arkansas.

"After we got Jones out of there, one of the men helping us thought he felt something else under the ground. He was right. It was the casket, barely under the surface."

Cody studied the coffee mug in his hand. "What does that mean?"

"It means the box wasn't buried proper. Only a couple of feet down instead of a full six. It was cocked toward one end and down, like it was just dropped in there."

Anna frowned. "I still don't get it."

His chair creaked as Ned shifted his weight. "There's a couple of likelies I can think of. One is they dug up the casket from six feet down, and then dropped it back in and shoveled a little bit of dirt in over it."

Big John's voice rumbled. "Drugs, like in the casket with that boy, Del. Here's another suppose. What if somebody who don't have nothing to do with drugs or that dice game took Jones out there, killed him and used a fresh grave to cover him up? Might be nobody would have thought much about that turned-up dirt, only it quit snowing before it was all covered up good."

"Could be." Ned nodded.

"That's too much of a coincidence." Cody chewed his lip. "It's all a part of those dice game murders. We're going to have to believe that's what it is, and Jones is the latest victim."

Voicing opinions had developed into a system over the last several months allowing each of them to work their way through a scenario, sorting out their thoughts in the open.

Studying Ned with his elbows resting on his knees, Cody leaned back in his wooden chair. "It could be worse. That casket could have been buried barely under the surface at the outset. That means we're dealing with something even more extensive than a renegade honky-tonk. It could involve the funeral home and even more people. That's where I'm leaning right now."

Ned drew a deep breath, as if overwhelmed at the enormity of what they were dealing with. "We're waiting for a paper from O. C. so we can finish digging up the box. You know as well as I do that even though a grave's been disturbed, you can't exhume a body without the order. But I suspect we're gonna find there was drugs in it, just as John said, like with Del Scarborough's."

Cody drained his mug, scratching the back of his neck. He was surprised to find that he still missed the long hair that once hung over his collar. He wished for the days when he didn't have to wear a uniform shirt and let his hair grow and sleep late without the phone waking him up for some problem and...

"Mr. Ned." John's voice brought Cody back into the room. "You don't mind if I don't go out there for that part, even though it ain't far from my house."

"Naw. I need you working on your side of the tracks."

Cody raised an eyebrow. "Ned, I believe that's my job to tell a deputy where and how to work."

"Why'n't you tell him, then?"

He grinned. "Go work your side of the tracks, or wherever you want to."

Ned rubbed his head again. "We don't have time for that kind of foolishness in here."

"Right." Cody was back to business. "All this could indict Williams Funeral Home, and they've been in business for a hundred years without anything shady. So it means there might be some new folks who're crooked. *Intentionally* planting a casket in a shallow grave would be proof they were coming back, so all we have to do is find out who ran the backhoe. Anna, talk to them over there and dig around to see how many people've been buried here in Lamar County in the past few months, people from overseas, especially soldiers from Vietnam."

"You got it."

"John, you take it easy, but keep your ears open. This may not be all white folks doing this, or some of your people might've heard or seen something."

"Okie doke."

"Find out how long he was gone before they planted him. I need a handle on this whole mess, because the mayor's done called me half a dozen times on the phone, wanting information, and you can bet your boots that he'll be right in here as soon as the roads are clear. Ned, let me know as soon as you can what the coroner says about Jones's cause of death."

"We're giving that ol' boy a workout." Ned rose. "He's earning his money."

Anna stood and held out a hand to John, as if her hundred-pound frame could pull him upright. "Maybe the mayor'll convince the city council to hire him some help."

"Not hardly." Cody picked up his pen and went back to work. "But he's looking for his boy to do that. Y'all let me know what you find out."

As they filed out and the snow fell again, wind rose behind the newest front and the sheriff pondered what little they knew about the puzzle.

Chapter Thirty-Six

With the added weight of new snow, and the wind that howled across the river, power lines went down. Some fell when the poles snapped, others when limbs broke and took lines down. In more than one instance whole trees fell, sometimes taking out several poles in one long chain reaction.

The power flickered at the house that afternoon and the next thing we knew, the lights went out. "Well I swan." Miss Becky went from room to room, bringing oil lamps into the kitchen to make sure they all had kerosene.

Lucky for us, both the stove and space heaters ran on propane, and Miss Becky always made sure the tank out beside the smokehouse was full before Christmas. "This reminds me of when your granddaddy and I were young."

"The coal oil lamps?" Mark sat down beside me at the table to watch. "We didn't have electricity in half of the houses I've lived in."

"No, hon." She unscrewed the half-inch cap on the reservoir base of the lamp. Laying it aside, she inserted a funnel and trickled kerosene into it from a metal can. "I'm talking about this weather. It was just like this when I was a little girl, and well up through the Depression.

"Of course the houses weren't built this well, or at least the ones we lived in. Wind blew through cracks in the walls. We had to stuff rags around the windows and doors to keep out the drafts, and even that didn't help much."

Finished with that lamp, she filled another. "I'd like to hear the weather forecast. At least back then radios ran off batteries."

"I need to get a transistor radio like that little one Pepper has."

She shook her head at me. "No, hon. They were big batteries, like what's in your granddaddy's car. Sometimes they weren't quite as big, but they weighed right smart."

I watched her pick up a pair of scissors. "What are those for?"

She removed the clear globe and set it aside. "I need to trim the wick so it'll burn bright and even. When we were younger, storms like this came three or four times a year. People learned how to deal with the cold and snow. That's why your grand-daddy don't complain about it too much, and he can drive in the snow."

We watched her trim the wicks. "There." She lit one with a kitchen match and sat it in the middle of the table. It wasn't like electric lights, but that single lamp pushed back the gloom of the dark, gray day. "And there was light."

I knew that was from Genesis, and we were getting danger-ously close to a Bible lesson. "Hey, you wanna get out of here?"

Mark frowned at the window and the monochrome world outside. "I'm not going out there, unless we have to feed or get the eggs."

"That's not what I meant. We can ask Grandpa if he'll take us over to Pepper's…"

The phone jangled in the living room. "Hon, would you get that? I've got soot and coal oil all over my hands."

I picked up the receiver. "Hello?" A sharp click told me Mrs. Whiteside picked up on her end of the party line.

"Who's this?"

I didn't recognize the lady's voice. "Top Parker."

"You Ned's grandboy?"

"Yes ma'am."

"Is Ned there?"

"No ma'am"

"Is there anybody there I can talk to?"

"Miss Becky's here, but she has coal oil all over her hands. I can take a message."

"Well, I guess that'll be all right. Would you tell Ned that my husband's gone?"

"Gone where?"

"Honey, I mean he hasn't been home in a while and I'm worried about him. Now you tell Ned that he ain't run off on me. I don't mean that."

I had to think about that one for a second, then I realized she meant he hadn't left her for someone else. "I understand. I'll tell him. Who is this?"

"Oh. I guess I oughta tell you. I'm Roberta Walls. My husband's name is Butch, but Ned'll know that."

I picked up a yellow #2 pencil and wrote it down. "What's your phone number so he can call you back?"

"I don't have no phone. I'm calling from Neal Box's store. Ned knows where we live."

"Yes ma'am." She hung up, but I held the phone to my ear for a few seconds, then couldn't help myself. "Miss Whiteside, can you tell me how to spell Roberta?"

A sudden intake of breath told me she was there. The phone clicked on her end of the party line as she hung up. I went back into the kitchen at the same time the lights came back on.

Mark looked surprised. "That was like something Pepper'd do."

I grinned at what I took to be a compliment.

Chapter Thirty-Seven

The Starlite was devoid of customers by dark. The second cold front was so strong that no one wanted to be out, not even the barflies or alcoholics. The winds scoured the loose snow from the open spaces, driving it in deep drifts against the woods, fences, cedars, and man-made structures.

Buster Rawlins and his men, Melvin LaFleur, Jess Plemens, and Ricki Toscani, sat at their usual table while the wind howled around the club's eaves. The interior was warm, and almost homey to men who were used to such joints.

A handful of dimes were scattered on the table nearest the jukebox. This time Hank Williams sang "Hey, Good Lookin'" while the men absorbed a considerable amount of their own stock.

Rawlins frowned in the dim light. "What made you two decide to dig up the drugs in this weather?"

Plemens and Toscani were buzzed enough to answer Rawlins's question with the truth. Toscani used his thumbnail to peel the label off a Miller High Life. "Hell, Buster. It's been snowing so much, it was the perfect time to get 'em. The grave was still fresh, so we figured that it'd be a quick in and out. After the snow covered everything up, no one would know for a week. By then it'd melt and water the grave in and settle the dirt."

"So you did get it all."

"Every kilo." Plemens stubbed out his Kool. "Goddamn, it was cold. That's what we didn't figure on. The first two feet was hard digging, even though it was fresh turned. Froze. After that, we made good time, but wedging a casket out of the ground ain't easy. Next time we're just gonna bust through the lid without trying to take it out."

"Can't."

"Why not?"

"Because that steel just dents. You'd work harder with a chisel."

"Well, it was a bitch to pull that heavy bastard out. Anyway, the packages were at his feet just fine. This is working like a charm."

"It is right now, if we don't draw attention to the cemeteries or ourselves. From now on, we're unloading the caskets when they get to the funeral home instead of letting them bury them first. We made it too complicated and too risky. We'll figure a way in and out. Maybe one of y'all can get a job there. That'd make it easier."

"I saw highway patrol car when I came in earlier." Plemens lit another cigarette, changing the subject. "He was out on 271, but I think he was keeping an eye on who was headed in this direction. I imagine he was out there because of that incident with the deputy."

"It wasn't any of our doings." LaFleur ran fingertips through his oiled hair. "The ones who shot at that deputy was a couple of damned Okies from some place called Cloudy. They was drinking and don't like niggers. One was named Banks. I never heard the other name. I was sitting right over there at the bar when the Carver boys rolled in talking about seeing him sitting out there across the road when they turned off. The Okies hatched up that idea to shoot at him right here in front of me and took off. Hell, I thought it was the whiskey talking and they wouldn't do it." LaFleur paused. "Surprised the hell out of me."

"You should have stopped those dumbasses." Rawlins's eyes flashed. "That's the worst thing that could've happened. We don't need people looking at us any more'n they already are. To this point they've left us alone because it'd be more trouble than we're worth, but now I imagine we'll see more law around here."

They listened to the music for a minute.

"The only saving grace is that it happened out there on a county road and not on Fritz Haulett's property around us." Rawlins took a swallow of his Jax. "Haulett sent word that he wasn't any too happy that happened, neither."

Eyes drooping for all the beer, Toscani tilted his head in question. "Who?"

"Haulett." Rawlins pointed toward the wall. "The guy who owns the land between us and the highway. We've paid him an ass-load of money for that little trail through here, but he's getting worried that now the county'll start digging around." He grinned. "I believe that feller's had a little trouble with the law in the past."

Plemens raised an eyebrow. "Do I need to talk to him?"

"Not today. Go feed the music box. I want to hear some Lefty Frizzell. Hey, play that Buck Owens song about Oklahoma and the Red River." Rawlins laughed. "And trouble."

While Plemens punched numbers and letters into the jukebox, Toscani went behind the counter for more beer. They listened to "Sweet Rosie Jones" until Rawlins came to a decision. "We need to head off this problem with that shooting. Ricky, you know those two Okies that shot that deputy?"

"Know *of* 'em, and I have an idea where they live."

"Good. Find out what their names are and as soon as this storm blows through, call the sheriff's office. Tell 'em who you are, where you work, and who did the shooting. Use my name and tell 'em we're doing this to prove we don't want any trouble. That should smooth their feathers and get 'em off our backs."

"Admitting what happened's liable to bring 'em in here on the double."

"I don't think so. The shooting wasn't in here, it was out there on Texas land. They'll pick 'em up and we won't have no trouble from Oklahoma, neither." He laughed. "Hell, they won't drive over here in this weather just to growl at me. We're sittin' pretty."

Rawlins took another long swallow. "Now, where'd you put that shipment?"

LaFleur pointed at the door. "Most of it's in my trunk, buried out there under snow. I figured we'd leave it where it is until this weather breaks, and I'll take it to Dallas. The rest is in the back in one of those whiskey cases. We've measured out a good bit of it to sell."

"All right. As soon as it gets warm, let's get those games geared back up. We're losing money."

The men laughed as the cold north wind searched for a way into the building.

Chapter Thirty-Eight

Saturday morning was a repeat of the weather. Every time Mark and I went outside, we brought in ice and snow on our shoes that melted on her linoleum floor. We were driving Miss Becky crazy. "You two stay in or out. My lands, y'all need to get back in school so I can clean these floors."

"It's Saturday." Mark had an idea. "How about we go to Pepper's house?"

He was starting to sound like a broken record, but Miss Becky didn't mind us finding somewhere else to hang out. "I don't care where you go. Just get out from underfoot for a while."

Of course Mark just wanted to go check on Pepper, who was gone the last couple of times he called, but I didn't mind a bit. We took off on foot, kicking through the snow where it drifted deep with the wind.

Mr. Tom came along when we were halfway to the house and stopped in the middle of the lane. "Hop in, boys."

I climbed in the cab and Mark followed. Mr. Tom gave us a grin from under that big black hat he wore. "What're you two outlaws up to today?"

"We're going over to hang out with Pepper."

"I was heading back that way myself. Had to go to town this morning."

I twisted around to see several paper sacks full of groceries in the truck bed, along with several other boxes. "You sure bought a lot of stuff."

"Well, your Aunt Ida Belle feeds me, so I figured I'd buy her a bill of groceries to pay her back. I also needed a few other things."

Mark hung his arm out the window. That's Texas for you. One day it's so cold you can't get outside, and the next, you're driving around with the windows down. "Mr. Tom, if you're thinking about rebuilding another old house, I'd like to help. I'm thinking I want to be an architect someday, and I'd like the practice."

He looked surprised. "Well, the truth is I've been thinking the same thing." He shifted gears in the truck, but I don't know why, because we were driving so slow, he coulda kept it in granny low. "But I'm too old to do much building now. If I run across a place that needs work before I can move in, I'd have to hire a few strong young men to do the job."

"Count me in."

"Me too."

He nodded and grinned. "I probably need to get out somewhere on my own, anyway." He grinned over at us. "Them stairs are getting to my old knees."

Instead of driving directly to Uncle James's house, he pulled off on the oil road that ran past the Assembly of God church. "I have to make a stop or two, so you boys'll be good company."

"Where we going?"

"Stopping off at Miss Becky's church first. One of those sacks back there's for the preacher." He pulled into the gravel lot between the Assembly church and the preacher's house. "Mark, would you get that sack with the Ideal Bread on top and take it up there for me? I doubt there's been much in the collection plate the last week or so."

"Sure will." He hopped out and reached over the tailgate. After a second, he picked up a sack and climbed the porch. No one came when he knocked, so he sat it in front of the door and came back. "You want me to leave a note or anything?"

"Naw. Don't matter where it came from. They just need it."

Mark slammed the door. "Where to now?"

Mr. Tom shifted back into first and pulled back out on the road. "We're stopping at a house down in the bottoms, if we can get there."

"Whose?"

"Some folks who moved in that old shack down near Love Thicket. I don't know their name."

It was roaring hot in the cab, and I reached out to turn the heat down. Mr. Tom shook his head. "Won't do no good. It's stuck on high, and I can't get it to shut off. Mark, roll your glass down to cool us off a little."

He turned the crank and had the window down as we passed a barn with big snowdrifts up one side, then a run-down shack that was falling in. Dozens of weathered shacks scattered around the bottoms were a sad reminder of the Great Depression and hard times during the war. Some had already collapsed. Most were just empty buildings with gaping windows and doors that to me looked like empty eye and mouth holes in gray skulls.

Grandpa told me on more than one occasion that in the 1930s and early '40s, he had nearly a hundred kinfolk living within a two-mile square, all of 'em helping one another and scratching a living from the cotton and cornfields that covered the bottoms.

Now there was nothing but a few families struggling to survive on hardscrabble farms in the last houses that had never seen a coat of paint. We turned right onto an intersecting dirt road that would be a muddy mess when it finally warmed up.

Luckily, the house he was looking for wasn't much farther. Built on bodark blocks, it wasn't much more than four plank walls and a tin roof. Smoke rose from a pipe sticking out of the far wall.

He pulled in the yard and a friendly hound dog came roaring up from under the porch. At first he blocked our way, barking for all he was worth, but it was a bark of pure excitement. He circled around toward Mark's open window, and I thought he was just going to bark some more. Instead, he took about four fast steps and jumped up, almost coming in the window. Mark yelped and elbowed him back and the dog disappeared from sight. He came back up and put both paws against the door and jumped again, trying to get in the cab.

The next thing I knew, I was squished over against Mr. Tom and making a noise that surprised both of us. For some reason that dog scared the pee-waddlin' out of me, and there was no reason for it.

"Get down!" Mark pushed him away again before a woman opened her screen door and came outside.

Being suddenly scared sometimes caused my lungs to close up. My puffer was in my pocket, and I had to take a deep breath full of medicine to get my asthma under control.

"Blue! Behave yourself and get down from there!" She came down the wooden steps, followed by a boy about our age I knew from school. Sam Walls.

The tired-looking woman pulled a loose strand of dishwater-blond hair behind one ear and shrugged a dingy, threadbare sweater around her shoulders. It fell right back down. "I swear, that dog's tried to get in every car or truck since Butch left. I guess he just wants to go, too. Probably wants to find him."

Mr. Tom nodded, talking across us through the open window. "Mrs. Walls. I have a couple of bags back there for you, if you'd take 'em."

Crow's-feet at the corners of her eyes deepened when she smiled. I liked the way it made her face look younger. "You didn't have to do that, Mr. Tom."

"I know I didn't, but I wanted to."

"We'll pay you back as soon as we can."

"That'll be fine." He spoke to Sam. "Son, would you get those two sacks out of the back? One has some of that Mrs. Baird's pull-apart bread in the top, and the other one has one of those jumbo packages of little cereals in it."

No one wanted those tiny boxes of cereal except for adults who didn't know better. There were eighteen of them in a Kellogg's Jumbo Pack, but most of 'em weren't cereals a kid wanted to eat. Miss Becky bought them a couple of times. At first the little packages lined with wax paper were fun. You poured milk directly into the boxes that served as bowls, but by the time we got through with the Froot Loops and Sugar Pops, there wasn't anything left but Raisin Bran and Rice Krispies.

The look in Sam's eyes, though, made me reconsider those little snack cereals. All of a sudden I realized I was spoiled rotten. My spirits sank as he looked into the sacks as soon as he was on the porch.

Mr. Tom called through window "There's a carton of cold drinks there that're yours, too. I'd have Mark help you, but I figure that hound dog of yours'd squeeze in here with us if he opened the door."

The dog outside screwed up his back end and barked in excitement, making me jump again. We were all used to Hootie and his manners, and that hound was acting crazy, likely from excitement, but big, rangy dogs always scared me, because I knew what they could be capable of. Mark didn't like it one little bit, neither.

Sam almost skipped around to the tailgate for the Dr Peppers, kicking the excited dog out of the way. He came around and reached into the cab to hug Mr. Tom's neck. Mr. Tom laughed loud and long, and I'd never seen him throw his head back like that. "Hang in there, kid. It won't get no worse than it is now."

Sam stepped back and nodded at us but didn't say anything to me or Mark. I believe he was embarrassed at how excited he'd become, or maybe it was because Mr. Tom brought them the groceries.

Mrs. Walls came to the window after Sam left and gave Mr. Tom a soft pat on his arm. "We sure do appreciate you." She looked at me then. "Are you Ned Parker's grandson?"

"Yessum."

"I thought so. It was me on the phone."

I put two and two together and remembered her call.

"I'll see you again soon, Mrs. Walls." She waved, and Mr. Tom shifted into reverse. Once we were back on the gravel road, he flicked a finger back over his shoulder. "Poor thing. Her old man's disappeared, and they don't have two nickels to rub together."

We drove on down to the turnoff and Mr. Tom stopped. His shoulders started shaking and for one shocking moment, I thought he was crying. There was no way a tough old Texas Ranger like Mr. Tom would cry. Lordy. He'd been shot and left for dead in Mexico, so in my mind, nothing could get to him.

He dug a handkerchief from the back pocket of his jeans and wiped his eyes, and that's when I saw he wasn't crying. He was laughing. Before we knew it, he had both of us grinning like possums, but we didn't know why. It seemed like five minutes before he finally stopped.

Mark leaned over to look past me. "What's so funny?"

"I've been thinking about that dog." Hot from laughing so hard, Mr. Tom took off his hat and fanned his face. He rolled down his own window to battle the heater and laughed again, then broke down coughing. He finally got control of himself. "You boys should have seen yourselves when he jumped up at the window. Top, you almost crawled in my back pocket, and Mark there leaned so far back in the seat I might have to replace the springs."

My face burned from embarrassment. "That dog scared me to death. What was so funny about that?"

"It reminded me of something that happened down in the Valley when I wasn't much older'n you two. I was working a ranch as a full hand when we were in the middle of a drought, one that came before the Great Depression.

"Anyways, it was bad and on top of that, there was a rabies outbreak. We killed a few skunks that weren't acting right and several coyotes. It got so bad that Billy Roy Johnson had a calf come down with it. He'd been keeping it in a pen by the house and had to take the rabies shot himself."

We shivered in the truck with both windows wide open to admit the chilly air.

"Rabies is the disease that scares me to death. I had a friend get treed on top of his house by a mad dog that kept him up there for two days before somebody came by and shot it."

Mark hung his arm back out the window. "I remembered them up at the store telling about somebody a few years earlier was bit by a rabid coon. They say Grandpa shot it with his pistol, but the man had to take them shots in his stomach for weeks."

Mr. Tom nodded and blew his nose. "It's a bad disease, all right, and they say those shots hurt like the dickens."

I couldn't imagine the pain from shots directly in my stomach muscles and was about to say so when I sensed more than saw a shape rushing toward the truck. Before I could register what it was, a large varmint flew through the open window and into Mark's lap, throwing melting snow all over us and the dash.

Someone shouted in fear. "Rabies!"

I think it was me.

Mark shrieked and swung at the animal like an elementary school girl in a slap fight. His headband came off and long hair flew as he battled the varmint the size of a Hereford calf. A huge wet mouth full of white teeth seemed everywhere before a large black hat slapped it away.

A sharp pain erupted in my leg. Something slashed my arm. I was bitten by a rabid animal!

I shrieked like a little girl as Mr. Tom hollered and flailed even harder with his hat. I tried to curl up in the floorboard, but the big hairy creature's paw dug in my shirt pocket for a better hold. In an effort to save myself, I shoved my elbow into Mark's ear.

In turn, he did his best to crawl underneath me amid a cacophony of bellows, yells, and a few hollers that turned into an outright din when the muddy, hairy monster the size of Bigfoot dug its back claws into my lap and went completely over my head.

Warm liquid flowed. Blood!

Mark yanked at the door handle that refused to cooperate. When that didn't work, he hung halfway out the window like a limp dishrag.

More shrieks.

Slaps.

In a shockingly calm voice, Mr. Tom gained our attention. "Stop! Y'all hold it!"

Surprised at the order, I stopped fighting and the monster in my lap turned back from a rabid beast into Sam Walls's young hound dog that did its best to shove his nose into my shirt pocket where I had a half a leftover biscuit from breakfast. I pushed him away and dabbed at what I thought was blood on my face, and found it was dog drool.

Mark pulled himself back in and opened the door and shoved the dog out. "Git on outta here!"

The hound finally jumped out of the cab. I pitched the crumbling biscuit out the window and the hungry dog wolfed it down. Throwing us a sad look back over his shoulder, he walked slowly back down the road.

"I bet you boys just got religion!" Mr. Tom threw his head back again and laughed until he got the hiccups. He wiped his eyes still again. "Oh, my Lord! You two were something else. I thought y'all were gonna run around inside this cab for a while. Poor thing's starving to death for food and attention."

Embarrassed and relieved, I sank back in the seat, wiping dog slobber off my face. We finally started laughing, too, as Mr. Tom drove us out of the bottoms to Pepper's house.

———

She was wrapped in a quilt on the porch swing with Jett McClellan when we pulled up. Mr. Tom nodded. "Y'all think before you act or talk."

I frowned at those words as Mark pulled on the door handle. "Thanks for the ride, Mr. Tom."

Pepper unwrapped herself from the quilt and came out to the truck. "Mr. Tom."

"Hi, hon."

"Howdy. Grandpa called and said ask you if you'd come to the courthouse with him and Uncle Cody."

"Sure will. Would you boys carry these bags in the house?"

We got out and he motioned for Jett to come out. "I'd appreciate it if you'd help with these groceries."

Jett nodded. "Sure will." He grabbed a heavy wooden case of Dr Peppers and carried them inside like they didn't weigh more'n a roll of toilet paper.

"Did your grandpa say why he needed me?"

"Sure did. They found Butch Walls's body this morning down in the Sulphur River bottoms."

Chapter Thirty-Nine

Ned looked up from the paper-covered jury room table when Tom Bell walked in. Judge O. C. Rains peered over the tops of his readers. "Tom. Take a seat."

This time there was a hat rack. Tom added his black Bailey to the bloom of others belonging to Judge Rains, Deputies John Washington and Anna Sloan, and Sheriff Cody Parker. He settled into the nearest empty chair. "Got word you wanted to see me."

"Yessir." Ned leaned his elbows on the table. "They tell you somebody found Butch Walls."

"Yep."

"Thought you'd be interested, since you've sent a couple of bills of groceries over to his house since he's been gone."

"Took some more to Mrs. Walls a little bit ago. The grapevine works pretty good around here, don't it?" Cody raised an eyebrow and Tom shook his head. "It ain't like that. I saw that boy of his up at Neal's store, asking for a few canned goods on the tab. Neal gave 'em to him but said to tell his daddy it was tallying up. I asked and Neal said they were way behind on the tab. About two days later, I heard somebody say the boy's daddy'd run off, and I can't stand to see anybody go hungry."

O. C. nodded. "Well, he won't be paying that tab off hisself. John?"

"Yessir." Big John shifted his bulk in the chair with a creak. "Couple of my people went out to shoot a few ducks or geese early this mornin' and found Walls's body in a thicket of cedars on the north side of the river."

"I'd assume that's the Lamar County line?"

John nodded at Tom. "Yessir. About twenty feet from the bank, so that's our case, for sure. Couldn't tell how long he's been dead, though, and I 'magine the cold's gonna mess up they autopsy, though, so's we'll never know how long he'd been there."

"Cause of death?"

Cody shrugged. "No telling. No holes in him of any kind."

"Strangled?"

"Don't know. Still waiting on the coroner."

Tom studied the men around the table. "So why'm I here?"

The judge stepped in. "You have a lot of investigative experience. We were thinking maybe you saw something like this down in the valley."

"We had a lot of killin's down there, all right. Knives. Gunshot wounds. The like. But nothing like this string of deaths here."

Ned wiped at the smooth table, as if invisible crumbs needed to be cleared away. "Well, we figure you can move around and maybe see what you can scare up."

"Y'all know I'm retired. You know as well as I do there's a Ranger assigned to this division. Company B. Why don't you holler at Jeb Henry?"

"I've talked to him already. He's gonna look into it." Judge O. C. adjusted the papers in front of him. "But a Ranger's hands are tied in many ways. All this has to do with that Starlite Lounge, and I need somebody who can poke around without permission. I've seen you scare up a rabbit every now and then."

"Well, to tell the truth, I kind of like having something to do." Tom Bell glanced around the table. "I was in there the other day."

Cody grinned. "Told y'all he was already poking around. What'd you see?"

"I saw an empty joint, for one thing. But those old boys running things didn't like me being in there, and we had some words."

"You're talking about the day I dropped by?"

Cody looked surprised at Ned's question. "You were there?"

"Sure was. The day John got shot."

Clouds built in Judge O. C.'s eyes as he leaned forward. "Wait a minute. Ned, you went in there after I told you not to?"

"That's why me'n John didn't say nothing, O. C. I've been behind this badge almost as long as you've been a judge, so I do what I want. You want to fire me over it, give 'em a call down to Austin and have 'em run me off."

Anna's voice cut through the tension. "I went back before the storm hit."

O. C.'s face reddened. "Well, goddamn it! Have *all* y'all been over there after I told you to stay out?"

Big John didn't make eye contact. "Nossir, I was shot on good ol' Texas dirt, for sure."

The room exploded in laughter, letting the air out of O. C.'s anger. He rubbed his hooked nosed in thought and ran fingers through his white hair. "What'd you find out, Anna?"

She turned toward the judge. "Not much. Mostly a lot of people he-ing and she-ing, having a good time, but there's something going on over the counter. I told Cody and…"

"You know something I don't." Judge O. C. pointed a finger at Ned but included everyone around the table. "Y'all are gettin' on thin ice here…"

"Judge, you know as well as I do it's called plausible deniability." Cody's voice was sharp. "I haven't been there. And in the second place, I need to run my investigations free, without having to sign in or get permission." His voice softened. "O. C., we're partners in upholding the law. I don't work for you, nor you for me. The sheriff is required to work *with* a judge, but not *for* a judge. If a judge tells a sheriff to go arrest somebody, the sheriff investigates it and decides what to do. Times are changing."

Judge Rains thought about arguing further, then leaned back in his chair. "All right. I'll talk to y'all later about this. Now, what do we know?"

Ned snorted. "People are still dying, and I can't find out why."

"You gave me a list of names."

"I did."

"Who's left?"

"Warren Christie, Vaughn Cunningham, and Silas Cornsilk."

"Where they from?"

"Cunningham is out of Roxton. Christie grew up in that rough mountain country near Pickens, Oklahoma."

Judge Rains laced his fingers. "He kin to Ned Christie, that Cherokee that was killed by the marshals back in the 1800s?"

"He is."

"I bet he's a tough son of a bitch, then."

Anna spoke up. "Who was that?"

Judge Rains leaned into the table. "A Cherokee statesman who got crossways with Judge Isaac Parker. It was a damn mess that hasn't been unraveled to this day. He was accused of murder and made his house a fort. The whole thing turned into a war before a whole gaggle of U.S. Marshals killed him. If Warren Christie is anything like his kin, he's likely still alive.

"Find 'em and get those boys somewhere safe until you get a handle on this, Cody."

"Yessir, but I'm way ahead of you."

"Have you considered Cunningham or Christie could be your man who's thinning this herd? Hell, it could even be Cornsilk."

"Of course we have…them and some young man we can't yet identify."

Anna jerked. "Oh, no."

"What?"

"Last night they brought in a body. Car wreck, but since it was a common accident, I didn't think anything about it."

Cody tapped a finger on the tabletop. "Let's check that out. Get a name."

"Will do."

"So, we're down to two living people, if that's our missing dice shooter." Judge O. C. scribbled on a sheet of paper. "Any thoughts that they could be the killer?"

"Could be more than one," Tom Bell said.

"Could be. But why would they want to eliminate everyone at the game?"

"Because they lost." Tom Bell made a gun with his thumb and forefinger and shot an invisible target.

Judge Rains pursed his lips. "What do we know about Christie and Cunningham?"

"Perfectly clean records, as far as we know." Ned rubbed his head in thought.

Cody drew a deep breath. "Neither one has ever had a ticket."

Ned grunted. "That don't mean nothin'."

"No, but they're family men."

"Didn't Cunningham have an ex-wife somewhere?"

"What about it, Ned?"

"Well, just saying he has a past."

"Everyone has a past." Cody chewed his lip. "Judge, anything from Austin on who that piece of land belongs to?"

"Not yet." The judge rocked back and forth, not willing to get sidetracked into another subject at that moment. "Get those men somewhere safe, and let's find out what's going on. Put them under arrest."

Cody was surprised. "Why?"

"No one can get to them in a jail."

"Arrest 'em on what charge?"

"Suspicion of murder. We can hold them for a good long while with that."

"Until one of 'em starts squawking they want a lawyer."

The judge almost grinned. "We'll play it that way until then."

Cody rocked back in his chair. "Fine then. Anna…"

"I know. Find them."

"You're the best I know at that kind of paper investigation. Why don't you go pick up Cunningham, too?"

"It doesn't pay to be good at your job."

Cody shook his head. "You're right about that…on occasion."

Chapter Forty

Since she didn't have an office, Deputy Anna Sloan went straight to Sheriff Parker's office and checked the phone book. Vaughn Cunningham was listed in Roxton, so she dialed and it rang twenty times before she hung up. Making a note of his address, she called information.

"I need a number for Warren Christie, around Pickens, Oklahoma."

"Hold, please."

Anna felt a draft. Holding her hand up, she followed the stream of cold air to the old wooden casement window.

"I have a number in Pickens, but it also shows an address in Cloudy."

"That figures." Anna picked up a pencil. "Shoot."

The operator read off the numbers and Anna hung up. She next called the sheriff of McCurtain County.

"Sheriff's office."

"This is deputy Anna Sloan in Lamar County, Texas."

"Howdy, Anna. This is Sheriff Anson Sweeny. How's Cody?"

Taken aback, she paused. "Does everybody know him?"

"Well, I know Ned Parker, and Cody had a little trouble up

here a couple of years ago… Hey, I wasn't supposed to talk about that. He and I, and Ned, agreed that we wouldn't let that little cat out of the bag, so I'd appreciate it if you didn't say nothin.'"

"Sure." Surprised at the interesting information she couldn't ask about, Anna had to switch gears. "Look, I'm calling for the sheriff's office here. We're looking for a Warren Christie."

"I know that guy."

"Any idea how I can get in touch with him?"

"Sure. Drive on up here, and you can talk to him today. I have him in a cell right now."

"On what charge?"

"Drunk. Domestic abuse."

"How long do you think you can keep him there?"

"In McCurtain County? If you say so, he might need a wheel-chair when he gets out."

She laughed. "Likely not that long." She explained what they were working on, the Starlite, the dice game, and the string of murders. "If he's locked up, he'll be safe."

Sheriff Sweeny chuckled into her ear. "I'll keep him here until you say so. You want to come up and talk to him?"

"Maybe you can ask him a couple of questions for me."

"Shoot."

"Who was at the dice game?" She gave him the date. "Did he see anything suspicious? Did he win any money? We just want to know what happened that night. I'd drive up, but this weather's been a booger, and I figure it'll be worse up your way there in the mountains."

Fortunately, the McCurtain County Courthouse was in the fair to middlin' size town of Idabel in the Ouachita Mountains, sixty miles southeast of where she expected Christie lived, and the roads into town would be better than those pig trails up in the mountains.

Sweeny grunted. "Sounds like a rough game. I've heard about that place, even over here. Picked up a guy the other day that was bragging that no one would touch it. Believe you me, if I was the sheriff of either county, I'd shut the place down."

"That's what Cody wants to do, but we're having some political issues."

"I bet. You want me to call you back?"

"How long will it take you to talk to him?"

"I can lay the phone down and do it now."

"That'll work."

Cody still hadn't returned to his office, so Anna rounded the desk and settled in his creaking wooden chair, taking care to adjust her gun belt and holster so they wouldn't catch on the arms.

Tom Bell stuck his head in the door seconds later. "Hey, gal. I thought Cody was back."

She rested the receiver on her shoulder so she could hear when Sheriff Sweeny came back on. "He hasn't been in, Tom."

"Look, I know you can take care of yourself, but if you have to go back to the Starlite, I'm going with you."

She started to open her mouth and he lowered his chin. "I know what you're going to say, but listen to me. I'm an old man, and I know things. You either tell me and let me come with you, or I'll follow you out and be in your hair that way."

Grinning, she relented, but he wasn't through. "There's a lot more going on here than any of us knows, and I think it's getting dangerous even for lawmen…and women."

"You got it, Mr. Man. Hang on a second, then."

Tom Bell lowered himself into a chair and a moment later Sheriff Sweeny came back on the line. "Deputy Sloan? You're in luck. Christie say he was at that game, just like you thought. There was one man who was winning a lot of money, cleaned out everybody and the house. It looks like the other players in the game saw at least three men roll him in the parking lot. Your victim fought back, and one of them choked him down. "The players were all threatened not to talk. Christie says he cleared out the next day and hasn't been back, though. So that's all he knows. Now, if you ask me, those guys come up here looking for Christie, all we'll have are three bodies to deal with, if they don't vanish somewhere out there in Weyerhaeuser land. He's tough as boot leather and takes after his great granddaddy, Ned Christie."

"I've heard of him. Did he have names on the killer?"

"No, but there's a description." Sheriff Sweeny gave her the details, which Anna wrote down on a pad.

"Sounds like half the men who come in and out of that club."

"That's what I figured. Christie says he's content to sit in here as long as you want. Three hots and a cot for that guy is all he needs, except for an occasional whiskey."

"And a dice game. Thanks, Sheriff." She hung up and looked across the office at Tom Bell. The old Ranger had been taking it all in, smoothing his mustache with one finger. Ned Parker walked in, and Anna gave him the news. "Let's go to Roxton."

Ned looked from Anna to Tom Bell. "What're we going to Roxton for?"

She held up a notepad. "I have a description of the man who killed R. B."

"No name?"

"Not yet, but we might get that from Vaughn Cunningham. He and Silas Cornsilk are our last hope, and Cornsilk hasn't been seen since the night of the dice game."

"If either one of 'em's still alive." Ned smoothed his bald head and set his hat just right. "Let's go."

Chapter Forty-One

It was crowded in my cousin Curtis Parker's blue Comet on Saturday night. He'd called to see if we wanted to go to the show again with him and Sheila, but this time we had to add Jett and Blu McClellan.

The smell of Aqua Net hairspray was strong when he picked me and Mark up. Miss Becky embarrassed us to no end when she went out on the porch. "Curtis Parker, you keep both hands on the wheel when you're driving these kids."

His arm had been around Sheila, and he yanked it back real quick when we got in the back seat. She wasn't done. "You get 'em home before midnight, and watch the road. It'll freeze again and there's gonna be ice patches that you can't see."

"Yes, ma'am."

"You drive slow, too, you hear?"

"Yes, ma'am." He backed us out of there pretty fast. The heat was so high we had to come out of our coats. Neither Curtis or Sheila were wearing theirs, and I couldn't figure out how she wouldn't freeze to death when we walked from the car to the show. This time she was dressed in jeans, but her blouse looked like it was thin enough to read through.

We picked up Pepper next, and it was an awkward moment when she started to get in the car. Mark's face fell when she didn't get in the back with us. Instead, she climbed in the front next to Sheila.

Our next stop was to pick up the twins. That's when things went south…for me. Pepper hopped right out as soon as the car stopped in front of the house. Blu and Jett came out together, two of the prettiest people I'd ever seen.

Jett slipped his arm around Pepper when he got to the car and leaned in, but she wouldn't let him kiss her. I was glad of that, because I saw their mama standing in the door, watching. She had a glass in her hand and took a sip of what looked to me like lemonade.

Pepper stuck her head in the car. "Top, why don't you ride up there with them in the front seat and the four of us can fit back there."

Ears burning and realizing this time I was the seventh wheel, I slid out without arguing, leaving the two couples in the back. I knew then I had no chance to even sit next to Blu, because Mark moved over, and she wiggled across to snuggle up to him. Curtis turned up the radio, and there was a lot of giggling and laughing under "Born to be Wild" as we pulled out onto the highway.

Curtis was just driving with his right hand on Sheila's thigh, and I didn't want to watch all that. I twisted around to look over the back seat. Mark's face wasn't what I'd expect from him sitting beside Blu. She had something in her hand, and he looked mad.

Jett had his arm around Pepper's shoulders, his nose in her hair. I realized he was whispering in her ear. She grinned and nodded. The next thing I knew he pulled a joint from his shirt pocket and lit up.

Curtis glanced in the rearview mirror and grinned. "Pass that up this way!"

Jett and Blu whooped, and the joint came to the front seat. Curtis took a deep drag, then passed it to Sheila. She did the same and handed it to me. I was tired of being left out, and tired of being a good boy. I took the joint and sucked in a deep breath.

The next think I knew, I was coughing my lungs out and everyone in the car was laughing. Tears welling from the smoke and even more embarrassment, I took another deep drag, this time managing to keep it inside for a few seconds before hacking again. I held it out and someone plucked it from my fingers.

Blu leaned forward and put her hand on the back of my neck. I shivered at the contact and she leaned even further, whispering in my ear. "I don't like grass, either." She was almost hanging over the back seat. "I think you're cute. Turn around."

I did, and she tilted her head, and the next thing I knew, she kissed me. It was my first real kiss, and my heart almost exploded. She drew back and studied me for a second. She did it again. This time she stuck her tongue in my mouth for just a quick flash. I knew about French kissing but didn't expect it.

She pulled back and I stared at her, mouth open like a fish, not paying any attention to the others who were watching us with wide eyes. Instead of kissing me again, she raised one finger and pulled down my bottom lip. "Wider."

Mind reeling and giving up to a torrent of teenage hormones, I opened my lips and was shocked when I felt her finger slip in and out of my mouth. I'd never heard of anything like that and shivered. Closing my mouth, I waited to see what she had in mind next and felt a tiny piece of paper on my tongue.

She dropped back in the seat, laughing and, good Lord, she was beautiful. There was a lot of quick talking back there while I picked a tiny piece of soggy, bitter paper off my tongue. There was more, but I accidentally swallowed it. Holding the shred on the end of my finger, I looked over to Pepper or Mark for an explanation.

The expression on Pepper's face told me whatever had just happened was bad. "What the hell!"

I twisted around to see what she was talking about. Blu had a piece of orange paper in her hand. "What's that?"

"It wasn't much, see?" She held it up. "Don't make a federal case out of it. I just wanted to bring you into the real world. It's blotter acid, but I tore just a piece of it off. You probably won't feel a thing, but at least you can say you're a man now."

"Oh, shit!" Pepper shouted. "You idiot!"

"What?"

"Spit, Top! Spit it out the window!"

I held the piece of paper on my finger that looked like a tiny spitball. "It's right here."

"No. Spit it out. Spit! That's LSD!"

Curtis pulled over on the shoulder. "I can't believe you did that."

Blu seemed disinterested. "It wasn't much. It probably doesn't even have any acid on it. Jett, this is another of your dumb ideas. I told you they'd freak out."

Pepper and Mark knew what could happen. We'd talked about drugs in the barn when we were away from the adults. It was those conversations that kids have, about the wonders of adulthood, sex, and the drug culture that was on television and the news almost every night.

Their concern, and suddenly mine, was what acid would do to my Poisoned Gift, or worse, what it would do *with* my Poisoned Gift.

Chapter Forty-Two

Melvin LaFleur slipped back under the wheel of his Plymouth Roadrunner parked in front of Frenchie's Café. Jess Plemens and Ricky Toscani were waiting.

"Two of 'em are in there with that gal that came in alone and asking all those questions." LaFleur slammed the door. "She's a goddamned deputy sheriff. Buster was right."

"Rawlins is always right." In the back seat, Plemens glanced out the frosted side window.

"Well, he didn't know that fat old man was a constable."

"How do you know that?"

"Saw the badge as he was putting on his coat." LaFleur pulled onto the street, following the deputy's cruiser. "And the funny thing is, that other old man in the club, the one who was in black, he's with 'em."

"That explains the gun belt." Toscani barked a laugh. "I thought Rawlins was gonna shit when he saw that pistol on the old man's hip. I knew the old fart looked dangerous as hell, but you have to be some kind of tough, or crazy, to wear one in a bar. If I was a bettin' man, I'd say he's law, too."

"You *are* a betting man." In the shotgun seat, Toscani adjusted the heat. "How about we make a bet right now? It's getting colder and now they say it'll start snowing again tonight. Weatherman thinks we're gonna be down in the teens for another week. I say it'll be this way for a full seven days."

"You're on. Hundred bucks. There's no way it'll stay below freezing for that long."

"Yeah, but you bet me I wouldn't shoot that damned nigger deputy, neither."

The two old men came out with the female deputy and slid into the back seat of the deputy's car. She dropped into the driver's seat and started the engine.

LaFleur took his eyes off the sedan turning off the town square and heading west. He accelerated slowly to maintain a safe distance. "You shot, but you didn't kill him. I expected you to wear him out."

"Hey, he moved fast for a big guy and he ducked. If I'd known he'd do something like that, I'd a used double-ought buck."

"Well, he won't be back sniffing around for any cocaine, that's for sure. And now they're after those two Okies for it, and Rawlins believes it was them."

They laughed at hanging the story on the two innocent men.

Toscani picked at something between his teeth. "You reckon that's why he was sitting out there? The drugs?"

"It all makes sense, now." LaFleur nodded. "That woman deputy came in asking all those questions, and before you know it, we have two more lawmen inside and a deputy watching the place. What else would you think?"

"I think that we need to finish this."

LaFleur followed the car west on Highway 82. "That's the truth. Roth called and told Rawlins the law was out at the coroner's office. He wanted to keep us in the loop."

"Sounds like he's doing his job," Plemens said from the back seat.

LaFleur looked over his shoulder at Plemens. "He said something about another one of those guys who was in the game got stomped to death by a bull."

Plemens laughed and pulled his blond cowlick out of his eyes. "Helluva way to go."

"Ain't it, though?"

Chapter Forty-Three

The two old lawmen let Deputy Anna Sloan drive to Roxton. Her cruiser was newer, and her reactions much faster on icy, potentially dangerous roads. They sat in the back seat, and looking in from the rear glass, it would have been impossible to tell they weren't criminals in custody.

In fact, they were a couple of rough old cobs, throwback lawmen to those days when Western justice was swift and true, and sometimes handled on the side of the road, or in the woods, or on a street corner.

As the car sliced through the icy evening, Anna made eye contact in the rearview mirror. "I bet you guys have made hundreds of trips like this in the past."

Ned glanced through the windshield. "More than I can count."

"I was usually driving." Tom Bell ran a finger under his white mustache, chasing a rogue hair. "We never had this kind of weather down in the valley, though. Makes it all feel different. So tell me about this Vaughn Cunningham character."

On Highway 82, Anna stayed in the tracks where the ice had burned off under the constant passage of tires. "Nothing on him. I'm considering this more of a welfare check. He hasn't answered the phone, and when I called the community store, they said they haven't seen him. With all that's happening, we need to lay eyes on him or at least the house."

Ned adjusted himself in the seat, pulling his holster around so the pistol butt wouldn't poke him in the kidney, the constant irritation of those who always wore a gun belt. "When we get finished here, I want to go out to Neal Box's house, too. We need to talk him and Clarice into going away somewhere until we find out who's doing all this meanness."

"Will he go?"

"Well, Tom, he'll do what he wants, but I want to give him a little nudge. This thing's worrying me to death. Maybe if we scare Clarice, she'll talk him into going for a while."

Anna turned off Highway 82 down a farm-to-market road that was still relatively clear, but when they turned once again onto a county road, rutted ice and snow covered the ground. The pastures tracked by cattle and deer looked as fresh as when the snow first fell.

"Think we'll find Cunningham off in here?" Ned asked.

"I know where he lives, but whether he'll be here is another story." Anna's eyes flicked to the mirror. "When I called the store up here, they said he lives in a fairly nice house. No matter, I'd rather be looking for him than going up to McCurtain County to talk with that other guy in this weather."

Tom Bell watched the fence posts go by. "Either one can be dangerous."

Chapter Forty-Four

The cold winter sun was long gone behind thick, heavy clouds full of snow when Big John Washington pushed through the door and into the darkness that was Sugar Bear's. The all-black juke joint in an unincorporated part of the county was a great place to gather information, and John had been there more than once when facts were elusive.

Squatting in a sea of cedars, the brightly colored building was once a knocked-together carriage house that converted to a drinking establishment right after Prohibition. Off by itself, the bar seldom drew attention from local officials. Even the constable of the precinct turned a blind eye most times, and only dropped by when a rare explosion of trouble brought him in.

Deputy Washington was the only official in the county who made it a point to be seen in the backwoods bar. He knew they served beer and setups, and that most customers brought their liquor in brown paper bags. Most of the time they didn't even try to hide their drinks.

Tables hammered together from scrap wood and mismatched chairs huddled at one end of the building in preparation for the night's crowd. The only new additions were red glass candleholders covered with netting that glowed like jewels in the dim light.

A jukebox blazed near the dance floor, and beside that, a low, empty stage full of music stands and chairs waited for the performers who were surely on their way. Warmth enveloped him and John shivered.

Still wearing his uniform, and with his right arm in a sling, John waved his left hand at Sugar Bear standing behind the bar. The short, stocky man responded with a wide smile. "Jay Dub!" Short for John's initials, it was a nickname the deputy'd worn on the south side of the tracks since he was a kid.

John reached out to shake with his left hand. "Shug, you doing all right?"

"About to starve to death if this weather don't break and warm up."

"Well, I hear there's another front on the way."

"Ain't that a bitch? How's that shoulder?"

"Still hurts, but it could have been worse."

Sugar Bear wiped at the bar. "You want a beer?"

"You know better'n that, with me in this uniform. You ain't moving any whiskey in here, are you?"

"I don't see no pop-skull around here." Not a liquor bottle rested among the glasses on the wooden shelves behind the bar and, though tubs of ice were ready and waiting, there was no beer in any of them. "I might be able to find a cold Jax if you've backslid."

They laughed, and a slender man came from the storeroom with two cases of beer in his hands. Seeing the uniform, he spun to duck back inside when he registered who it was. "Jay Dub!"

"Bobby Day!"

"What are you doing in here?"

John settled onto a stool. "Came by to see if y'all could help me."

Bobby Day put the cases on the bar and joined Sugar Bear's position leaning over the top. "You tryin' to find them that shot you? You have any idy who it was?"

"Not a one. We think it was somebody from across the river. They likely made a beeline for the Kiamichi, and if that's what happened, we'll never be able to dig 'em out of those woods."

The southeast part of Oklahoma was a vast, rugged area with ancient mountains reaching as high as 2,500 feet above sea level. Fractured with winding lakes, live-water streams and rivers, and hundreds of thousands of acres filled with pines and hardwoods, it was a place where generations of families dug in and lived as far away from civilization as possible.

"Maybe one day somebody'll talk." John's head snapped around when the front door opened. Two rangy men in fedoras and battered guitar cases came inside. Taking note of the deputy in uniform, they waved and headed for the low stage.

Bobby Day waved at two couples who came in right behind them. Heads turned from Washington, they followed the musicians who settled on empty stools in the corner and opened their cases, their guitars.

Resting his good elbow on the bar, John glanced around to make sure they were alone. The odor of fresh sawdust overpowered the spilled beer and whiskey. "I'm here for something else. Y'all know about what's been going on out near Center Springs?"

Folding the damp bar rag, Sugar Bear nodded. "I've heard about that crooked dice game. You don't think it's one of us killing white folks, do you?"

John raised an eyebrow at the comment. "No, I don't, and a couple of them were Indians. Anyway, me and Mr. Ned think it has to do with that or a dice game at that new joint, the Starlite. Sounds like we might be close to right."

Sugar Bear and Bobby Day nodded at each other. Sugar Bear hefted the bar rag. "We heard about that place. High end."

"And dangerous as hell." Bobby Day added.

"What do you mean?"

"Well, they sure as hell won't let people who look like us in there, but what I've heard tell, you better not win too much at them tables they got in the back."

John grinned. "Y'all already know as much as we do."

"Should have come here first." Sugar pointed at John's shoulder. "If you had, you wouldn't be wearing that sling."

"That's liable to be the only truth I hear tonight."

They laughed. Sugar Bear flicked a finger toward the heavens. "Too bad you can't ask Old Jules. He knew what was happening on both sides of the track."

Bobby Day set his jaw. "Well, Mr. Ned killed him, so now you're sniffin' up different trails."

Both John's eyebrows and tone lowered to dangerous levels. "You better not say that around me again, Bobby Day. You know as well as I do that Mr. Ned didn't kill Old Jules, he just helped that old man cross, when he couldn't get loose of the chains holding him here."

"Easy, John. I'm just repeating what I heard."

"You hear it again, you tell me who's spreading those kind of lies and I'll handle it, and you tell them I said that, too."

Old Jules, the elevator man, had worked in the courthouse for decades before he had a massive stroke and fell out in the middle of the lobby. Ned was there, and drew on his own, long-buried Poisoned Gift to help the centenarian pass by simply holding him and completing an unknown cosmic circuit.

An old hand at calming barroom disputes, Sugar Bear stepped in to cut off any further argument. "John, you shoulda come in here when y'all first started working on Mr. R. B.'s death. From what I hear, it all points back to that Starlite Club. You know none of y'all have done anything to shut the place down. I guess white joints get treated different."

"Well, it's complicated, and no one knows what state it's in, but that's not why I'm here. Besides, how long y'all been runnin' this place? Those two cases of beer settin' there ain't exactly legal. This county's dry, and you don't have a license."

"'Course not. We're grandfathered in."

"Umm-humm." Lowering his voice, John twisted around to keep an eye on the musicians. "So tell me what you know about the Starlite."

"They let Indians in." Bobby Day laughed. "Guess they have more money than us colored folks, because they sho' won't let us even in the back door."

"Damn the back door." Sugar Bear unfolded the rag and refolded it, thinking. "There ain't much to know. It's run by a chinless Coonass from Louisiana that you don't want to tangle with. Better let Mr. Ned or the sheriff do the hard work."

"I can't do a lot with this bad wing, anyways."

"You're more man than most folks walking this earth." Bobby Day pointed at John's huge bicep. "I doubt that'll slow you down."

"I'm trying to get a handle on what's been happening after that dice game." John adjusted his arm in the sling.

Neither man's expression gave anything away. Sugar Bear raised an eyebrow. "Who's left?"

"Well, let's just say I need to talk to a couple of old boys who might know more'n me. One's Vaughn Cunningham. Lives over in Roxton. The other's Warren Christie."

"Don't know 'em." Sugar Bear worried with his bar rag and Big John's eyes narrowed. "Anybody else?"

"Silas Cornsilk."

There was a slight hesitation in Sugar Bear's folding that would have been unnoticeable if they'd been anywhere else. As it was, John's radar perked up. "You know that name, don't you?"

Bobby Day hadn't seen Sugar Bear's reaction. "Sure do. He's in here regular."

"So you've seen him recently."

"Couple of days ago. Came in alone and stayed most of the night, listening to Leroy and Gerrard over there make music. We had a saxophone that night, too. That's why I remember it so well, because we don't usually have a sax, and that Indian was having a ball."

John tilted his hat back. "With who?"

"Whoever'd dance with him. He was snugglin' up to Flea Pickett's gal for a while, at least until Flea got that look on his face. Cornsilk was smart enough to back off then."

John knew what he meant. Flea Pickett was a little five-foot-two piece of rawhide-wrapped wire who always had a knife on him and usually a .38. Everyone knew it, and it was said that Flea'd shoot in a New York minute if he took a notion.

Sugar Bear went back to wiping the already clean counter. "We didn't have no trouble, though. After a while, Cornsilk sat down over there with his back to the door, and that's where he stayed until a white man came in looking for him."

Bobby Day took up the narrative. "Sheeit, man. You should have seen this place when that white dude come strolling in like he was *somebody*. He was looking for Cornsilk, because he stopped right there in the door for a second and looked around until he saw him. Folks made a hole for him, and he strolled over there easy as you please and talked to Cornsilk for a minute or two, then he just up and left."

Sugar Bear grinned. "That was one tough white man. He didn't care who was lookin' at him or what they thought." He reached down and picked up a chair leg from under the bar. "I had this little persuader in my hand, just in case somebody acted the fool, but I didn't need it." He put the club back. "He left and that was that."

Another customer came in. "Dayum! It's snowing to beat the band." The man's smile faded when he took one look at the uniform and headed as far away as possible.

John chewed his lip "What'd he look like?"

"A weasel." Sugar Bear shrugged. "A skinny weasel in jeans and a T-shirt with a pack of cigarettes rolled up in the sleeve. Hair down over his collar and the sides slicked back."

"Sounds like the description I have of Vaughn Cunningham. You ain't seen Cornsilk since?"

"Nope. But it wouldn't surprise me none if he came walkin' in that door tonight. There ain't too many places an Indian can go, and I doubt he'll be back at the Starlite."

The other joints in Juarez tolerated Indians, but most avoided those places and the trouble they'd see if they went. Indian clubs were unheard of because, according to Oklahoma law, they weren't allowed to drink anyway, and the only beer they had across the river had a lower alcohol content that came to be known as 3.2.

"So you expect to see him in here?"

"I never know what to expect, John." Sugar Bear grinned. "That's why I love running this place."

"I need to talk to him, Sugar Bear."

The man's face smoothed. "You think I know where he is."

"I think that if I sit here all evenin' waiting on him, your kitty behind the bar there's gonna get real hungry. You said yourself that business has been slow."

Sugar Bear glanced down at the cash box out of sight from most customers. "You wouldn't sit there all night?"

"Might. Shoulder's hurting and this is as good a place as any to rest it."

Sugar Bear and Bobby Day passed a look. Sugar Bear nodded and Bobby Day walked the length of the bar and into the store-room. Setting a hat on his head, he came back out a second later in his coat, a set of keys in his hand. "I'll see what I can do."

"I'd appreciate it." John rapped his fingers on the bar in a soft beat. "How about a co-cola while I wait?"

"You're killin' me, brother. You and that damn snow out there's gonna cost me money tonight." Sugar Bear pulled the cap off a bottle of Coke and sat it in front of John. "You want a glass with that?"

"Naw. Folks might think I have something besides Coke in my Coke." He tilted the bottle and waited for Bobby Day's return while the musicians finished tuning and played for the three people in the audience...four, if you counted Big John.

Chapter Forty-Five

Melvin LaFleur stayed way back once the deputy's car turned onto the farm-to-market road. It was easy to keep sight of the cruiser on the highway, but the small FM road made it more difficult to stay hidden.

"I wish we'd brought your old truck, Tuscani. I'm afraid one of 'em's gonna notice us back here."

He pointed through the windshield. "They'll be watching those snowflakes, not looking behind them. What's to be afraid of out in here, this time of the day?"

Heavy clouds giving way to nighttime dropped large, heavy flakes in front of them. The Roadrunner's speed was enough they streaked up and over the windshield.

The sedan's brake lights flickered and the turn indicator told them she was taking a county road. Plemens leaned forward over the seatback. "Dammit. We're gonna have to back off even more."

"No worries." LaFleur took his foot off the gas and drifted past the T intersection. He coasted until the marked car was almost out of sight in the falling snow, then shifted into reverse and backed up. "Look."

Toscani grinned. "No need to stay close. We just follow those black tracks right up to where they're going."

"Buster's gonna ask us where we been. What are we going to tell him?"

"Why, Mr. Plemens," Toscani laughed, smiling at his suddenly self-induced formality and the ease in which they could follow the car, "we'll tell Mr. Buster Rawlins that we were ensuring that no one will be interfering with the next shipment to the Williams Funeral home."

Chapter Forty-Six

Instead of driving us on into town, Curtis turned right toward Lake Crook, a little eight-hundred-acre man-made lake about five miles north of Chisum. Lined with hardwoods, it opened in the early 1920s and was the lake for recreation before they built Lake Lamar. Now it was all but forgotten except by older folks, kids wanting to watch the submarine races, and migrating geese.

In the back seat of the sedan, Pepper and Mark were in a panic, while Blu and Jett sat beside them wondering what all the fuss was about. For once, Sheila was quiet, probably thinking about how she could get in trouble and working on a good excuse to get herself out. She turned the music up to drown out the arguments behind us and crossed both arms under her large blessings, glaring at the glowing radio.

"Where are we going?" Pepper was so mad her words were slurred.

Curtis steered left, following the skinny asphalt road. Ice patches glittered in the headlights. "Away from everybody." We wound through the bare hardwoods down a narrow road that eventually took us to a dark playground. "You sure as hell don't want to go to the show now, do you?"

A rush of thoughts filled my head. I'd been looking forward

to seeing Dean Martin in *Bandolero!*, but that wasn't happening now. I left the house a good kid. Now I was a druggie, an acid head. Any other time my asthma would have kicked in, but it seemed like my head and lungs were suddenly opened wide. There was no way to tell if it was from adrenaline or the LSD.

LSD! Acid! The Mighty Quinn!

I was doing acid!

Bile rose, but there was no way I was going to puke in the car. I choked it down as Curtis hit the brakes and we slid to a stop about twenty feet from the lake. Snow was falling again, big fat flakes that came down so hard we could almost hear them hit the windshield.

He shifted into park and leaned forward to see my face on the other side of Sheila's pouting figure. Flakes flashed in the headlights. Had it been warm, the air would have been filled with the night sounds that were always a powerful cacophony of trills, chirps, croaks, and whistles, most coming from frogs and insects. Instead, the only sounds came from us.

Despite the cold, both back doors opened and everyone spilled out, arguing. Pepper jabbed her finger in Blu's face. "That was the stupidest thing I've ever seen!"

Blu slapped her hand away. "Get your finger out of my face, bitch!"

Mark lunged forward and grabbed Pepper at the same time she launched herself at Blu, who stumbled back against the car, leaving a dark streak where she brushed off a thin coat of fresh snow. "Don't you ever call me that..."

"Hey, back off my sister." Jett stepped between them and pushed at Pepper.

Mark whirled her over his hip and held her back with one hand. "This is between the girls, dude."

Curtis stepped out from under the wheel. As the oldest of the group, he must have felt he was in charge. "That's enough!"

The only person who didn't have anything to say was Sheila, who was watching me. "Are you all right?"

"I think so." I shivered. "Can we turn the heat up?"

"Sure." She slid a lever and blessed heat blew from the vents as "Crimson and Clover" came on the radio.

I swallowed. My mouth was bitter from fear. "Maybe she's right. Maybe there wasn't anything on that piece of paper."

Curtis looked back inside. "Don't bet on it."

"Well, you don't have to be so confident," Sheila said.

"Hey, don't freak out. I might be the only right-thinking person in this car right now."

Sheila frowned. "Present company excluded, for sure."

"Oh, yeah." Curtis hedged his bets. "I was talking about those other idiots arguing over there."

Feeling better than I expected, I turned to see what was going on outside the car, and my head moved with startling ease, like someone had oiled my neck. They'd divided off into two couples, Jett and Blu, and Mark and Pepper. Both of the guys were pointing fingers, and I could see waves of heat coming off them, like something just out of the oven.

"Man, they're mad."

"They sure are." Sheila twisted around and yelled through the open doors. "Would you guys cut it out and get back in the car? It's too damn cold to be standing out there."

"Yeah, with all the heat pouring off y'all, we could close the doors and be warm and toasty." A shooting star flared across the horizon and I watched the trail grow brighter and wider. "Man, that's the biggest meteorite I've ever seen."

Dropping back behind the wheel, Curtis looked through the windshield. "Uh, it's cloudy and snowing. You can't see anything up in the sky."

"No, it was huge. See, the tail is still up there."

"Uh oh." Curtis twisted around and yelled over the back seat. "Y'all need to get in here now."

The tone of his voice made me sad. "Hey, relax, all right?"

"What's the matter?" Mark was at my door. "Top. You all right?"

I grinned at him, and my mouth got wider and wider. I was suddenly afraid it would be so wide Mark would shut the right side of my face in the door. Reaching up with one hand. I squeezed that side back into place, feeling my teeth lock into the socket of my cheek. "You can close the door now."

His eyes grew to the size of dinner plates. They grew even larger, pushing his eyebrow up into his hairline. He closed the door and pushed against it until the latch snapped. "Pepper. Get in the car."

For once she didn't argue with him, but it wasn't like he wanted. She flashed around the car and opened Curtis's door. "Get out. Sheila, slide out on this side."

"Why?"

An incredibly long arm reached in and grabbed Sheila's collar and pulled.

"Hey!"

"He's tripping."

"No way. It doesn't hit you that fast."

"I bet it does when you have Second Sight. Now get out of the way. I need to be there with him."

Sheila shook her head that moved so fast it was a blur to me. "Well, I'm not getting out in the cold. Y'all get him in the back seat."

"Good idea," I said. Seeing how her fingers stretched, like Reed Richards's in the Fantastic Four comics, I raised my arms and flowed into the back seat like a snake.

Chapter Forty-Seven

Anna saw a flicker of lights in her rearview mirror and then nothing as snow drew a lace curtain closed behind them. "We turn up right here at an old tin barn, and then it's about another mile."

Tom Bell rested one hand on a bony knee. "I know it's colder'n sin right now, but I do love the snow."

Ned shook his head. "We had enough of that in Washington a couple of months ago."

"I know it, but most of that was dirty snow. Look how pretty and clean all this is. Snow hides the ugliness of the world."

"It just makes me cold. My blood's thin, I guess."

Anna laughed. "You two sound like my daddy and granddaddy when I was little. If one of 'em said the sky was up and ground down, the other one would argue."

"Ned, I believe this little gal up there just said we were old."

"I was old when she was still in *diapers*."

The barn she was looking for was easy to see, and Anna made the turn down a frozen gravel road. At the end of it was a dark, out-of-place brick house with a yard unmarked by tracks.

Ned settled deeper into the back seat. "Well, this was a water haul."

"I was hoping he'd be home." Anna watched the wipers sweep

melting snow off the windshield. "The man up at the store said Cunningham would likely be here."

"Well, he ain't."

Headlights glowed in the background and Anna grinned. "There he is."

"Well, I be." Ned almost smiled. "We just beat him here."

Tom Bell turned to look out the back glass. The car seemed to hesitate, then crawled forward. "You know what Cunningham drives?"

"A sedan of some kind."

"Well, that's a car, all right."

Arm across the back of the seat, Ned squinted at the headlights that continued to grow larger. He glanced back through the windshield, studying the dark house. "Tom, there haven't been any cars here in a while."

Catching the constable's tone, Tom turned his attention back to the front. "Anna, hit your brights."

Using her foot, Anna tapped the dimmer switch. The bright headlights emphasized the big flakes even more and lit the house in greater detail. "Snow's piled against the door."

Ned unsnapped the strap holding his .38 snug in its holster. "He's been gone two or three days and we get here the minute he comes home?"

"Could be coincidence." Tom Bell shifted and drew his own pistol. "Better safe than sorry."

The driver behind them switched his headlights to high beams, making it bright as day in the cruiser. Ned squinted against the glare. "Anna, I saw a shotgun muzzle up there beside you in the front seat floorboard."

"It is."

"Don't bend over, but slide up and get ready to use that street sweeper if we need it."

The driver opened his door. The dome light illuminated a second figure. The passenger door opened. Neither man said anything, nor shouted orders or questions.

Something was terribly wrong. Ned's voice was sharp as the crack of a pistol shot. "Drive us out of here, gal!"

She accelerated and hit her blue and red bubble lights at the same time, but knowing the ground was slick, it wasn't as fast as any of them wanted. The flashing lights were enough to illuminate the driver with a pistol in his hand. It rose level with the moving cruiser. Anna shouted. "Gun!"

Tom Bell's Colt .45 rose at the same time he rolled the window down with his left. "Don't shoot my ear off, Ned."

The constable leaned across the seat, his own pistol coming up level with Tom's automatic. "All I see's shapes now."

A flash of light and the simultaneous crack of a firearm told them it likely wasn't Vaughn Cunningham and a friend.

Then the world was full of pops, flashes, and blowing snow.

Chapter Forty-Eight

Two hours after John took a seat at Sugar Bear's bar, the joint wasn't half full. The bar owner came back from delivering two Cokes to a table. "John, you're killin' my business tonight."

"Probably my cruiser parked out front."

"Why'n't you go home, and I'll send somebody for you if Cornsilk shows up?"

"Well, that'd cost money for me to drive out there and back and for you to send somebody. I'druther sit right here and wait."

Sugar Bear picked up John's second Coke bottle and wiped the wet ring the same way he'd done a dozen times earlier. Any other Saturday night, the joint would have been hopping, but John's presence had put a damper on the customers. Where bottles in brown paper bags would have been common, not one table held anything but soft drinks.

More than one customer stepped outside with a half-drank Coke or Seven-Up and returned with it full to the neck. Not a one made eye contact with the deputy as they passed, shaking snow off their shoulders, bare heads, or hats.

The room wasn't tense, though. A number of men and women dropped by to visit with John as he sat at the bar. A tiny woman with a huge Afro stopped by to hug John's neck. "Jay Dub!"

"Howdy, Peanut."

"What're you doing here, killin' Sugar Bear's business?"

"Just workin'"

"This far down in south county?"

"Gotta earn my paycheck. Who you here with tonight?"

"Nobody. I don't need no man to have fun."

"I know that's right."

She gently rubbed the back of his wounded shoulder with her small hand. "I heard you got shot. They say it was a white man."

"Don't know for sure. I believe the guy driving was white, but I can't say about who was in the back seat. Could have been any color, but the color of a man's finger on the trigger don't make no difference."

"You don't never come around here. Who you looking for?"

"Who said I was looking for anyone?"

"Shoot, man. We all know you're sittin' there waitin' on somebody. Tell me who it is, and I'll have one of these sorry outfits go drag 'em in here so we can get to havin' some fun."

John laughed. "You won't do it yourself?"

"Well, I could, but I'd have to do it a different way."

"You behave yourself, Little Bit. I'm looking for Silas Cornsilk."

"I know who that is. Big Indian. Square jaw. Eyes like lightning."

"You know him, for sure."

"What you want him for?"

"That's my business. You seen him anywhere else?"

She shrugged.

"Hiding out, huh?"

"Could be. What you want with him?"

"You're too nosy."

Her face lit up in a smile. "That's what my mama always said."

"That's why you're standing right here, ain't it?"

She nodded. "He's back there in the storeroom, waitin' on you."

John shot a look across the bar. Sugar Bear was at the other end with Bobby Day, and they were both looking his way. "You and Cornsilk been hanging out?"

"Maybe."

He thought back. "I didn't see you come in the front door."

"We came in the back after Bobby Day say you wanted to see him."

"You could have told me, Peanut, without all this."

"I know it, but Silas is afraid. You know he was in that dice game at the Starlite."

John stood. "Why didn't he come see me earlier?"

"Like I said. He's afraid and he ain't thinking clear."

"Let's go talk to him, then."

They walked the length of the bar and John stopped beside Sugar Bear and Bobby Day. "You two should have told me the minute he got here."

"It's Peanut's idea, John. She wanted to make sure why you needed him."

"I reckon you told her already."

"I did, but not everybody trusts the law like I do."

Shaking his head, John followed Peanut through the door and froze at the sound of her shriek. It came from deep inside the little woman, who screamed again. Using his good hand, John grabbed her collar and yanked her tiny frame back.

Silas Cornsilk's sightless eyes were turned toward the open door leading outside as a pool of blood from a dozen stab wounds crept toward cases of beer stacked against one wall. Melting snow from fresh footsteps led out the back door.

Chapter Forty-Nine

"Jesus!" Pepper yelled. "He almost broke his back sliding over the seat like that!"

"Far out!" Jett laughed. "He looked like a damn snake."

"You must be looking in a mirror." Pepper's voice snapped like a whip.

The car shook like it was in an earthquake and all of a sudden four loud bangs made me jerk upright. "Someone's shooting at us!"

Mark's voice was calm beside me. "We just got in and closed the doors. You all right, buddy?"

"Far out. He said far out. That's right." My eyes filled with tears. "That music is beautiful."

Someone laughed loud and long, and voices rose, almost drowning out "Crimson and Clover."

"Blu, if you say anything else to him, I'm gonna beat the shit out of you!"

Jett's voice snapped sharp. "You aren't touching anyone, Pepper."

"Whose voices are those?" I patted the air with two oversize Mickey Mouse hands. "Y'all be quiet so I can hear this music. Psychedelic!"

The tremolo effect of Tommy James's voice vibrated in time with the music, amping up the effects of the drug in my system. I tried to sing the same way, but the results were so disappointing that I plugged my ears with giant index fingers.

"Change the station." Mark's voice was peaceful and calm. "You couldn't be playing a worse song right now."

My voice sounded like Tommy James. "How, chief."

More laughter and the sound of a slap.

I sensed the action around me as colorful blurs. "Hey, the record's stuck."

"That's part of the song." Mark's voice was back. "Sheila, change the damn *station*."

My big, floppy face turned toward my best friend. "You didn't say heap big part of the song."

"You're right."

Another loud laugh. It was Blu and she sure seemed happy. I figured it was because of the bright stars overhead and the silvery lake that looked like mercury. "Put some of that in my hand. I like the feeling."

Pepper whispered in my ear. "What's that, Top?"

"That mercury water."

Someone punched me on the shoulder, hard, like a pile driver. Jett's amplified voice was in my ear. "Ride it out, dude. That's what I got it for."

"Yep. My name is Top. I'm on top of the world." I took a deep breath. "Look, my asthma's all gone. I can breathe." I drew in another breath that pulled in a long line of colors from the radio lights. I kept inhaling, and a few stars flowed in as well.

I started coughing and someone was pounding me on the back. "You all right?"

"Yeah, just inhaled a star."

I leaned my head back against the seat and stared upward

through the back glass. Stars moved around, and spaceships passed by. The constellations swirled and all of a sudden angels started singing. "It's the rapture."

Mark's voice cut through like a hot knife and I felt the heat. "It's gonna be for these two freaks in a few minutes."

Pepper's tone made me sad. "Who are you talking about, Mark?"

"The Bobbsey Twins here. You two are nothing but pushers."

Stars lined up and spun in circles and then formed themselves into an arrow. I followed its curve as it arced northward. Two sets of arms circled me and I had to blink a couple of times to focus on Mark and Pepper. "Hey guys." I smiled again and my cheeks hit the windows on both sides.

"You're lucky he's happy."

"It wasn't much, man." Blu's face appeared in my field of vision and Pepper shoved it away.

"Doesn't matter. He has this…gift."

"My Poisoned Gift!" My head fell off and rested on one shoulder so I could see Pepper. "Don't tell anyone about it."

I wanted to say something else, but I was lying in such a way that I could see a huge star rise in the north. Using both hands, I put my head back on my neck and leaned over to see past Pepper. "Look!"

"What do you see?"

"That star rising over there. It's made out of neon. It's beautiful."

Mark's voice was low in my ear. "Is it the star you saw from the smokehouse roof the other day?"

"Yeah, but the colors are brighter. It's *intense*." My breath caught. A group of men argued between our car and the lake. Other cars appeared, lights flickering off their chrome and windshields.

One man in the middle tried to push through the group, but someone shoved him back. He slung another out of the way and backed against a pickup so no one could get behind him. A man with Johnny Cash hair hit him in the stomach, and the blow caused a flash of light bright enough for me to see his face.

"R. B.!"

Mark was still talking into my ear. "What do you see?"

"It's R. B. and he's fighting some men. They're hitting him in the stomach and side."

Dark figures on each side hammered at his body, and R. B. busted one of them in the jaw. He reeled back and stumbled into Gus Davis. Something flew off R. B.'s wrist and I saw Gus pick up a watch and put it in his pocket.

The next thing I knew, the big neon star was brighter, and all the cars around us were clear as day. R. B. was giving as good as he got until a man wrapped his arm around R. B.'s neck from behind. In seconds, R. B.'s eyes glowed bright, looking right at me, and then they went dull and cloudy. He went limp, and I saw his soul float up into the air like smoke.

The man followed R. B. to the ground and kept squeezing as the pages of a calendar hanging in the sky flipped off and flew through the air, counting down days, then weeks, then months. He finally turned loose and stood up while another man dug through R. B.'s pants pockets.

Tears ran down my cheeks as they shoved his body into the cab of his truck. One man slipped behind the wheel and drove away while a line of about a hundred cars followed him into the sky like Santa and his reindeer. Colors streamed by and the next thing I saw was a big explosion and the bottom of a pickup. A huge sadness fell over me and I sobbed.

"Bad trip," Jett and Blu said in unison.

"What do you see, Top?" Mark's voice was smooth as honey,

but I didn't turn my head because I didn't want him to see me cry. Pepper took my chin and pulled my face toward her. My chin made it first, then the rest of my skull caught up. She had the softest eyes I've ever seen. They looked like the eyes of a doe, and her lashes were so long they tickled my nose.

"Top. What's happening?"

My mind tore in two. That's a helluva thing to feel, because it crackled at first as the tissue separated, then made a soft, dry sound that came from down deep in my spine. The cars outside vanished with firecracker pops and the men looked into our back seat one at a time before they were yanked into the ground.

The last man was younger than the rest and he had blond hair. His soul was tiny and dried up, even for his thin frame. He smiled and dropped into flames that licked out of the ground as it closed up, and then we were back beside the cold lake with shores frosted by drifts.

My mind lay in the floorboard, and I reached down to gather the pieces up, but Mark and Pepper held me upright. Tears poured from my eyes because I'd never be right again. Great rivers of mercury flowed from the lake and into my empty skull, and I grew heavier and heavier as the liquid metal seeped down through my circulation system like embalming fluid fills dead veins and arteries. In seconds, I couldn't move. My heavy head fell back, and I sank into the seat and was gone.

"Embalming fluid," someone said.

A voice laughed.

A voice cried.

Tuneless music played.

I heard someone say, "I'm dying."

And I did.

Chapter Fifty

Instinct kicked in at the sight of the man with a gun. Anna punched the accelerator too hard. A bullet starred the driver's window, piercing the glass and missing her nose by only inches before shattering the opposite window.

Street tires hissed on the frozen ground and the back end broke for a second. What sounded like cannonade behind her head momentarily disoriented the deputy. Steering into the skid, she let off the gas and the back tires caught up. More cannonade came from Ned and Tom Bell's pistols as she aimed for the darker tracks, knowing the packed snow would give her better traction.

The back windshield exploded. A distinctive slap only two feet away told her a bullet had punched through the dash. The car radio flared, awoke with the scream of a rock and roll song, then sparked and went silent.

Her rearview mirror showed Ned twisted around in the seat, firing slow and steady through the empty frame. Tom Bell leaned out the passenger window pulling the trigger of the big .45 automatic that roared over and over with sharp bursts of light.

The cruiser had recovered and was rolling straight and true when a muzzle flash from beside a nearby cedar told them someone had been dropped off to cover the rear.

Chapter Fifty-One

"Out the way!" Big John whirled and pushed past Peanut, who stumbled backward, falling into a group of men crowding around to look into the storeroom. The people between him and the front door parted to make room, lest the giant deputy barrel over them.

Slamming the door open with the hand holding the snub-nosed .38, John rushed out into the parking lot. Two couples walking up to the club reeled out of the way as he exploded into the open. Pistol extended, he swept the parking lot and saw nothing. No cars were leaving in a snow-covered rush.

Wheeling left, he charged around the side, fully expecting to run into the killer holding a bloody knife. Maybe he beat him into the parking lot. If so, the guy'd be coming around the side. Planting his left foot in the fresh snow to make the turn, it went out from under him in a vicious slide. Landing hard on his wounded side, hot pain shot down John's shoulder and into his right arm.

Gasping in agony, he rolled over, the pistol ready for defense. Nothing. Only snow-drifted cedars with rabbit trails winding through the trees. Groaning, he struggled to one knee and swept the area again, this time seeing a single set of footprints circling around the opposite side.

Nearly crying from the pain, John followed them around the building, but when he reached the parking lot a second time, the only thing he found was a sparse crowd of customers milling around the front door. Several pointed down the highway.

Breathing hard and wincing from the sharp ache in his shoulder, he slipped the little revolver back into his pocket. "What?"

Bobby Day pointed down the drive. "A car just pulled out while you were around back. It was a white man driving."

"You recognize who it was?"

"Naw. I didn't. Snowing too hard and it's damned dark out here. Sugar Bear?"

"Nope. Just saw he was white."

John rushed to his car and slid to a stop at the sight of four flat tires. He dropped into the seat and grabbed the microphone off the dash. "What kind of car was it?"

"Couldn't tell for sure." Sugar Bear shrugged. "Might have been a Pontiac."

"What color?"

"It's too dark. Coulda been anything under all that mud and dirt."

Every truck and car in the lot was covered with a layer of snow and ice-deposited mud that robbed all color from the paint.

"Dammit!" John keyed the microphone. "Dispatch! This is John Washington."

"Go ahead, John."

"I'm out here at Sugar Bear's club and there's been a murder. The suspect just left in what might be a Pontiac. Color undetermined. Suspect is likely a white male." He threw a question at the crowd. "Anyone have any idea how old he was?"

No one knew, and his frustration rose even higher.

The radio squawked again with a familiar female voice. "John."

"Go ahead."

"It's Cody. I'm out on the south loop. I'll head your way. We'll catch him between us."

"Can't. He cut all four of my tires."

———

Standing in the doorway of Sugar Bear's storeroom, Sheriff Cody Parker slid both hands into his pockets and studied Cornsilk's body lying on the floor, and ragged letters written in blood on the floor. Big John Washington sat on a stool just outside the door, recovering from his fall.

The deputy shook his head. "I'm sorry, Mr. Cody. I shouldn't have let 'em get away."

"It's not your fault, John. It's just one of those things." Cody tilted his head, studying the scene. "The only way I could have missed him would have been if he used one of the back roads. John, what do y'all make of that? Him writing letters as he died."

Fingers covered in his own blood, Cornsilk died trying to send a message. Four letters spelling CORN were distinct, and the next smeared as the man finally succumbed to the wounds.

"He bled to death, that's for sure. It looks like he was writing his name for whoever found him."

"That some kind of Indian tradition, Sheriff?" Sugar Bear and Bobby Day leaned inside the door. Behind them, the club was empty after Cody had ordered everyone outside until they could remove the body. "Maybe they write their name when they're dying like that."

"A dying man might do strange things." John shook his head. "Maybe he was just making his mark."

Cody considered his Choctaw ancestry. "I bet he was just letting people know who he was."

Beside the bar, Sugar Bear shook his head. "We all know Cornsilk. Hell, I saw him at least once a week for years. There weren't no need to make his mark."

A voice behind them caused Sugar Bear and Bobby Day to turn. They separated to let Buck Johnson squeeze through. "You guys are wearing me out."

"It's a crop we don't want." Big John shook hands with his left as Buck went by.

The justice of the peace studied the room for a moment. "All right if I go in?"

Cody nodded. "We've done all we can do."

Buck knelt beside the body. "He's dead, all right."

"What do you make of those letters beside his hand?"

"Not sure. What was his name?"

"Silas Cornsilk."

"Choctaw?"

"As far as we know. Maybe Cherokee."

"Know who killed him?"

"That's what we're working on."

"This guy's more traditional than what we're used to around here."

"What do you mean?"

"Look here. He has a vest on under his coat. It's a Levi, but he's decorated it up some. Headband, though his hair isn't that long."

Cody shrugged. "That doesn't mean much. Our boy Mark Lightfoot wears a headband, like about half of the hippies in the world these days."

"Yeah, but I think there's more." He pointed to Cornsilk's neck. "You want to come here?"

Cody moved closer to the body lying on its back. Buck pointed to a leather thong. "That could be a necklace, but I bet it's more. You mind if I open his shirt?"

"Go ahead on. We've already checked his pockets, but I didn't think anything of a necklace."

Buck unbuttoned the multicolored cotton shirt down to his belt and spread it apart to show Cornsilk's nearly hairless bare chest. A blue design was tattooed on the left side of his chest. "What does that look like to you?"

"An arrowhead with a head of corn off one side and a hawk's head on the other."

Buck slipped his finger under the leather thong and pulled upward. A small leather bag that had dropped down under the body's left arm rose into view. "You want to cut this off?"

"I don't see why not." Cody took a folding knife from the pocket of his jeans and cut the leather strip.

"Open it up and see what's inside."

The leather decorated bag about the size of Cody's palm was closed and tied. He worked the loose knot free and shook the contents out into his hand. A small bone fell out first and Cody grinned, despite the grisly scene. "That's a coon-dick toothpick."

John's deep voice rumbled. "I bet it meant more to him."

"Half the boys I grew up with carried those," Cody said. He shook again, emptying the contents. A glass marble, a lock of hair tied with yellow thread, two more smaller, unidentifiable bones, a tiny bird-point arrowhead, a crystal shard, a bundle of leaves tied with red thread, a Bronze Star without the ribbon, and several grains of corn made up the contents.

Buck pointed. "I've seen this before, in some of the old-timers' medicine bags. That's cornsilk tied in there with those leaves. His medicine was corn, though I haven't seen anyone his age in the last few years who carried them."

"He was in Vietnam. Got that Bronze Star there."

"So, it looks to me like he was writing the word *corn* to make his medicine stronger, maybe to help fight those wounds."

The club's doors opened behind them, and two snow-sprinkled men came in carrying a stretcher. John shook his head and watched them get ready to carry Cornsilk to the funeral home ambulance. "That doesn't make any sense."

"None of this does." Cody stood and dropped the contents back in the bag.

Chapter Fifty-Two

"My lands. Po' little thing. How long has this baby been like this?"

It was dark, probably because I had my eyes closed tight. If they weren't, my soul would leak out on the floor. Instead, I just laid on a soft mattress and listened to what was going on around me. *Howdy, Miss Sweet.*

"What time is it?" That was Pepper's voice.

"Eleven o'clock."

"He took it about dark."

Hello, Curtis.

"Say he took it."

"No, ma'am." Mark's voice. "This girl out there in the car gave it to him without him knowing it."

"Some of that LSD."

"Yes, ma'am. We didn't know what else to do. If we'd taken him to the hospital, they would have run all these tests and called Grandpa and Miss Becky and told them he was dying." Mark was talking fast, and I wished he would slow down so I could follow. "But you know about his Poisoned Gift, and those drugs kicked it in and made it worse. They didn't need to see that at a hospital."

"You know I got to call Miss Becky and Mr. Ned and tell 'em you's all here."

"Yes ma'am, but that's better than going to the hospital."

"One of y'all's likely to need a hospital when they find out."

"Yes, ma'am." Curtis's voice was soft, like you use in a funeral home.

Am I dead and in a casket? I died, so maybe that's where we are.

Curtis wouldn't shut up, though, so I could rest. "He's better now, but he started wheezing and we didn't have his puffer, so we thought you might have some more of those leaves you used on him that night a few years ago, and if you did, the kids said it would help."

I wanted to tell Curtis to use shorter sentences, but my tongue was stuck to the roof of my mouth. I was breathing just fine by then and didn't need any of Miss Sweet's medicine. She's Mr. John Washington's old aunt, a twin and a healer for the black community in and around Chisum.

Wait a minute. You can't be dead and breathe.

Her old voice was strong and steady. "Say it was those twins out there who did this to him?"

"Yes, ma'am." Pepper's voice was as just the opposite, weak and trembling, and that was unusual for her. "They're demons, as far as I'm concerned now. A couple of preacher's kids who need the hell beat out of them."

The sound of a familiar slap reached my ears. Muffled by thick hair, I knew Miss Sweet had whacked Pepper on the back of the head with her big old gnarly hand.

"Ow!"

"You watch yo' mouth in this house, Missy. Miss Becky don't take to that kind of talk, and neither do I."

My grin wasn't nearly as wide as it had been in the car. I guess they weren't paying any attention to me as they talked.

Now I could tell I was in a bed that had to be in Miss Sweet's house. It was soft under my back, and I recalled the creak of old bedsprings at some point, likely when they laid me down. I felt really good and rested, like I'd been asleep for a month. The only problem was that nothing wanted to work when I needed it, like my fingers and toes. I'd tell them to do something, and it would be a couple of minutes before they listened to me.

A deep, rich voice came through the darkness. "Here I am. He all right?"

"Howdy, John. He's fine now. Layin' in there on my bed. They tell me some devil child put some of that LSD stuff on his tongue."

"Good Lord. Who was it?"

"A color. Blue or something or other."

Pepper cleared her throat. "It was Blu McClellan."

"The Baptist preacher's kid." Mr. John's voice took on that deep tone that meant he wasn't happy.

"Yessir. She thought it would be a good joke."

"Where are they?"

Miss Sweet stepped in. "I made 'em all stay out there in the car. I knowed these two, but not them others."

"You think I need to get him to a doctor?"

Mark's voice came through again at the same time my toes started wiggling on their own. "Mr. John, they'll ask a lot of questions and he might tell them what he saw."

"And what was that?"

"Visions. It was his Poisoned Gift that woke up, we think. It teamed up with the LSD and it was the worst I've ever seen with him. He mumbled a few things we understood, but if they hear about it at the hospital, some of those doctors might want to commit him to Terrell or somewhere worse."

The mental hospital in the small town of Terrell, about a

hundred miles south and not far out of Dallas, was the only facility we knew about. It was where my mama spent several months before she and dad were killed in a car crash.

"He's right, John. They was some talk about Mr. Ned helping Old Jules pass on here 'while back." Miss Sweet popped her lips and I figured she didn't have her teeth in. "If his gift, and Top's get on their minds, those crazy doctors might want 'em both to go there. I think it's best we keep them out of it."

"He's all right, you think?"

Well, I was kinda all right. My toes had settled down, but my arms and legs were heavy as lead. With that thought, my right arm rose like a helium balloon, my Mickey Mouse hand floating in the air. I opened one eye to see it hanging up there, limp, like it was asleep.

"Well, all right then. I'm going up to the drugstore and call Mr. Ned on the pay phone. I don't need to use the radio for this."

Pepper came through loud and strong. "That's probably not a good idea, Mr. John. Phone rings this time of night, Mrs. Whiteside'll sure as shootin' pick up on the party line and hear everything you say."

My other hand was floating beside the first. One after the other, my fingers stretched out. Those on the right became snakes that curled and undulated in all different directions. The ones on my left turned into happy little fat worms, like Mr. Peppermint's Mr. Wiggly Worm, with ink-dot eyes and a fixed smile. They watched the snakes, in case the right-hand serpents were hungry.

"The child's right. Why don't you go on up to Mr. Ned's house and leave these two here with me? They'll be up directly and y'all can take 'em all home when they're satisfied he's all right. You can scat them others on, though. I don't want 'em around my house."

"I'll be back directly, Miss Sweet." Mr. John went outside, letting the screen door slap.

"No hurry, hon. I'm gonna feed these babies and let the boy sleep."

Like she'd hypnotized me with those words, my hands returned to normal and fell at my sides and I drifted down a dark hole and into a deep sleep.

Chapter Fifty-Three

Deputy Anna Sloan gave an involuntary squawk when a second shot shattered the windshield into frosted glass. She instinctively ducked, giving the wheel a jerk. The right front fender crumpled against a blackjack tree that snapped off at the ground. She was off the gravel drive.

Another blast took out the windshield, turning it opaque.

The only thing that could do that was a shotgun.

Shotgun! Her Remington pump lay across her lap.

More explosions of gunfire came from the back seat.

She steered away from the last muzzle flash, then swung the car back to the dark tracks in the snow. Another blast took out the radiator and steam boiled out, blinding her. She slammed the brakes and clicked off the shotgun's safety.

"Anna! The shotgun's yours!" Tom Bell's voice was loud and surprisingly calm in light of the gunfight going on around them. "We have the rear." Tom's door opened, the dome light casting the scene in harsh light. She sensed him stepping out in an easy, fluid motion.

The opposite door opened, and Ned rolled out, thumbing his Colt's cylinder aside and slapping his palm against the injector pin. Empty shell casings flickered then disappeared at his feet.

She barely had time to process what was going on toward the rear of the car before the shotgun was at her shoulder and she stepped around the cloud of steam. There he was, lit like a deer in the one remaining headlight, the shooter frantically stuffing fresh shells into his upside-down shotgun. He looked up, saw her, and flipped the weapon around.

It came up.

As did her own shotgun.

He got off another round. The load hissed past. Flashbulb pops from the exchange registered in her peripheral vision. Her first shot took the man full in the chest. He went backward, arms outstretched. The shotgun disappeared into the darkness.

She shot him again for good measure, even as he sprawled in the snow, before swinging around and joining the fight behind her.

Chapter Fifty-Four

Furious that his Colt .38 revolver was out of bullets, Ned scrambled to get behind his open car door for shelter. He knelt and thumbed rounds from his pocket into the cylinder. A bullet punched through the sheet metal, burning a streak across the crown of his hat.

Behind him, the thunder of a shotgun battle told him Anna was still in the fight. Tom Bell's big .45 hammered away. Knowing the old Ranger was keeping their assailants down, Ned dropped in the last round and snapped it shut.

Raising up, he saw Tom Bell stand upright beside the back bumper and thumb the empty magazine from the Colt. It slid out easily and he slapped in a fresh one. Then he did something that stunned Ned, who thought he'd seen everything. "Dammit!"

Tom Bell advanced on the car behind them, shooting at the muzzle flashes that momentarily froze the action in brief strobes. Ned couldn't let Tom take the brunt of the exchange. He stepped out from behind the door and moved toward the two hiding behind their car, dividing their attention and fire.

Bullets snapped past through the snowflakes. One ricocheted

off a hard surface, whining into the woods. Falling snow made it hard to see anything other than the flashes of gunfire.

A female voice came from several feet back. "Behind you, Ned."

The sound of a fresh shell shucking into a shotgun's magazine told him Anna had come out on top.

He registered snow coming over the tops of his dress shoes, melting and running inside. A flake landed just below his left eye, startling him for a moment when his brain momentarily registered it as a bullet wound.

A muzzle flash to the left. Using one hand, Ned aimed in that odd, old-school technique he'd learned as a kid. Elbow bent and down, the pistol leveled barely eighteen inches from his face, he thumb-cocked the Colt and fired. Flame licked out around the cylinder and a long streak of fire stretched toward the shooter.

The heavy thump of the 12-gauge sounded at the same time Tom Bell squeezed the trigger on his .45, firing slow and steady. The tough lawman continued to advance, inexorable as moving lava.

Someone shouted "No," but the sound was cut off by the thunder of Tom's pistol and a simultaneous blast from Anna's shotgun. Ned's target shot at them again, but three feet from where the first shots came from, and lower, as if the man were kneeling.

Ned fired, and fired again, while Anna's shotgun boomed until it ran dry.

There was a beat of silence, then Tom Bell's .45 barked one more time. "They're all down now, y'all."

Ned and Anna approached a dark body lying in the snow. He kicked a half-buried pistol away. "Well, looky here. I believe I recognize what's left of this feller. I saw him in that Starlite joint. Were you aiming at his face?"

Anna barked a hysterical laugh, barely in control. "At the muzzle flash."

Ned took her arm and held it tight for a moment. "Take a deep breath. It's over."

She giggled again, softly, and got hold of herself.

Tom Bell joined them, breathing hard. "Anybody hurt?"

Startled that he or Anna might be wounded, Ned stopped to check himself. He reached out to run his hands over Anna's torso and jerked back as if she were covered with flame. The look on his face lit by the light coming from inside the car made her laugh, this time with relief at his embarrassment.

They were alive.

Chapter Fifty-Five

Deputy Anna Sloan settled behind the wheel of her destroyed cruiser. Glass crunched under her feet and frigid air flowed through open doors and shot-out windows. Snow dusted the dash and part of the seat. Hand still shaking, she took the Motorola's handset off the bracket and turned the key.

"Please work." The dash lights flickered for a moment, then sparked out as the radio died. "Dammit!"

"That's all right." Ned called from beside the bad guy's Roadrunner. "We'll use the phone in the house."

She walked back to the two old lawmen standing beside the still-running car's open driver's door. Heat flowed from the open doors but did little to battle the arctic air and falling snow.

Shivering both from the cold and residual adrenaline, she tucked both hands into her coat pockets. "It's locked, I bet."

"It won't be in a minute." Ned kicked through the snow and up onto the porch. Turning the knob, he nodded. "You're right." Bracing himself, he slammed his shoulder against the door and rebounded.

"It was easier when we were younger." Tom Bell joined him. "Let me try."

Rubbing his arm, Ned stepped back. "Don't break nothin'."

Anna called from the edge of the porch. "Guys, that could be called breaking and entering."

"Naw, you said we were here for a welfare check, and besides…" Tom Bell pointed at a fresh pockmark in the brick near a window only two feet away. "That's a bullet hole and we need to check inside to make sure nobody's hurt."

Holding onto Ned's shoulder for stabilization, Tom Bell slammed his boot into the door beside the knob. The frame gave and the door swung inward. "Frames are always the weak point."

It was dark inside, and Ned felt around for the switch. A porch light came on, and he flicked the one beside it. The living room exploded in light. "Here we go."

The house was warm and heat flowed from ceiling vents. Tom Bell held the door open for Anna. "Come on in here and out of that weather. We'll deal with this when the time comes, but there's no reason for us to stand around out there and freeze."

Ned pointed toward a phone on the wall just outside of the dark kitchen. "There it is."

Anna passed him. "I'll call it in." Lifting the receiver off the hanger, she dialed a five-digit number. "Dispatch? This is Anna. Calling because my radio's out. I'm in Roxton, and there's been an officer-involved shooting here at Vaughn Cunningham's house. Constable Parker and Mr. Tom Bell are here as well. I need to talk to Cody."

Listening to Bobby Lee's response, she watched Ned open a door and stick his head inside. "This is what I was looking for," he said. Flicking on a light, she saw it was a bathroom. He disappeared inside and closed the door.

Tom Bell remained beside the door, staring down a short hallway. She noted that he tilted his head like a dog watching something unusual.

Dispatch's voice came through the avocado-green receiver. "Anna, I put out a call to Cody, but he hasn't answered. He and John Washington are out at Sugar Bear's club. There's been a killing out there tonight, and they're likely inside with the witnesses."

Frowning now and still staring straight ahead, Tom Bell walked past the closed bathroom and disappeared from sight.

"Fine then. Get me another deputy out here. My car's shot up." Emotion rose up in her throat and she paused to choke it down.

"My God. Are you hurt?"

"No. We're fine, but there are three dead suspects, so we're gonna need an ambulance. I don't know who the constable of this precinct is, so you'll want to reach out to him too, and we're gonna need someone to drive the three of us back into town."

"Four." Tom Bell stepped around the corner at the same time Ned opened the bathroom door.

"Four what?"

"Four dead people." Tom Bell jerked a thumb back over his shoulder. "A man's body is back there in the bedroom. I figure it's Vaughn Cunningham."

Chapter Fifty-Six

Howard Taft, Channel 5 weatherman, pointed at a paper map of the United States. Thick blue chalk lines described another strong push of Canadian air that intersected a huge slug of moisture coming from a slow-traveling front from California to North Texas.

"This one is a significant weather event. With all the cold air still in place here, and the ground barely above freezing, all this snow will accumulate, and right now I don't see an end to it until midweek."

Mark rose from reading the Sunday comics in front of the Dearborn heater and turned up the TV's volume. Even though the picture was usually full of static, that particular morning was worse.

Snowy, just like outside, he thought. That morning the snow fell thick and heavy. At that moment, it had slacked off enough to see all the way across the pasture to the little church two hundred yards away. The cold, white world looked like what he imagined Minnesota to be in the winter.

The motorized VTG Alliance Tenna Rotor on top of the television growled as he twisted the knob to adjust the antenna towering over the house. The screen cleared some, enough for him to get a better look at the weather map.

Mr. Taft looked into the Parkers' living room. "Even when the snow stops, I'm looking at least another week of cold temperatures and up to eight inches and possibly more of accumulation in our northern tier of counties up along the Red River."

Mark watched Miss Becky come in from checking on Top, who was still in bed. She passed through the living room and into her warm kitchen full of the smells of baking, where Norma Faye was stirring up a second batch of tea cakes. From his position in front of the heater they generically referred to as the stove, it was easy to watch Miss Becky open the oven to check on the cakes inside. Cody brought Norma Faye by not long after daylight so she wouldn't have to stay at their house alone through another snowy day.

Miss Becky told him at daylight she would have preferred to attend the little church across the pasture, but after Top's rough night, and consequently, the rough night for the rest of them, she stayed home.

Stirring the dough, Norma Faye blew a strand of red hair from her eyes. Realizing Mark was watching, she grinned at him and blew the strand again, just for fun. "How's Top this morning?"

"Well, he's better." Miss Becky cleared the dishes from the table and peeked into a bubbling saucepan on the stove. Once again inside moisture ran down the windows to pool on the wooden sills. "I swanny. It's a wonder that boy's mind is right after that drug."

Mark's mouth watered at the thought of those soft, lightly sweet cookies, but he kept still so they'd forget he was there. More than once that morning he'd made up his mind to go into the kitchen and tell the ladies what he knew and suspected about the Starlite Lounge.

It would be easier than explaining it to Grandpa or Uncle Cody. Men tended to listen different, and always offered solutions for everything, whereas women simply absorbed what anyone had to say and often asked more and more questions to draw the subject out into the open.

That's what Mark and Top both needed right then. They'd been quiet way too long, and the weight of what they knew about the club and Top's vision rested heavy on his shoulders. It was about to break the young man's back.

Norma Faye placed a blue Pyrex mixing bowl on the counter. "Cody picked Jett and Blu up, and took them in to see the judge this morning. Both of the McClellans threw a fit, but he explained how serious LSD was, and they cooled off. He has the twins for possession, but since they're minors, he figures Mr. O. C.'ll just remand them to their parents and have the kids do some community service. They're lucky. If this was Dallas, they'd be in juvie until they turn eighteen."

"How can a preacher's kids be that way?" Using a folded dish towel, Miss Becky took the baking sheet full of fresh tea cakes from the oven and rested it on an orange and green crocheted trivet. "Sometimes I don't understand how the good Lord works."

"I heard they were wild back in De Soto, and before that, Mount Pleasant. It's their mama who's the worst."

"I heard tell she goes across the river to drink."

Norma Faye raised an eyebrow. "Where'd you hear that?"

"Why, a little birdie told me."

"How's Ned after what happened out in Roxton?" Norma Faye changed the subject and sat at the table.

"He tossed and turned all night, what there was left of it when he finally got in. You know how he is, and I 'magine Cody's the same. They hold it in and won't talk about it until it almost eats a hole through their soul."

Mark kept his eyes on the television but wasn't registering what was coming across on the news. He was more interested in the conversation in the kitchen. The women quit talking when the kitchen door opened and Ned came inside, stomping snow off his boots.

"That pool's froze as hard as a rock. Like to have never broke it up enough for the cows to get a drink."

Miss Becky took a Melmac cup from the cabinet and set it on the counter. "It didn't take you long to get to town and back."

"That's because I went early. I'm fixin' to put chains on the back tires. James'll be here in a few minutes to help me, and Cody and John's coming too. There's no way John can handle them chains with just one good arm. It's gonna get pretty bad out there before it gets better."

He poured a cup of coffee from the percolator. "How's Top this mornin'?"

"He's fine. Dozing in and out. Mark's in there, watching the news."

Sipping the coffee, Ned passed the chrome and Formica table, picking up two warm tea cakes on the way. In the living room, he handed one to Mark who looked up with sad eyes. Ned took a bite. "You know I ain't mad at either one of y'all."

Mark took a bite of the vanilla cookie that was suddenly tasteless in his dry mouth. "I know, but I feel bad about the whole thing. We were just going to the show."

"So the truth is he didn't take that stuff on purpose."

"Nossir. Blu stuck it in his mouth after she kissed him..."

Ned smiled with his eyes and sipped again. He bit into the tea cake to keep from chuckling. "You didn't tell Miss Becky that part?"

"Nossir." Mark peeked through the door and saw Norma

Faye wink as she spooned dough onto a much-used cookie sheet. It looked like eavesdropping worked both ways.

"Well, that goes to show you how a person can get into trouble in a heartbeat. Like I've told y'all before, if you ain't where trouble starts, you won't get in trouble."

"Grandpa, that's what I need to talk to you about."

A commercial for Shell came on, urging consumers to buy their gas with Platformate for better mileage. The commercial had been shot in Yellowstone and the Grand Teton National Parks, and Mark was drawn to the snow, white and crisp, like they had outside.

The sign and snow.

Top had talked about the Starlite sign in his acid-cum-vision trip, and Mark struggled deep inside with the need to tell Ned everything he knew. He'd never been good at keeping secrets, and when in doubt, the youngster always plowed ahead until whatever situation he was struggling with played itself out.

He couldn't come clean at that moment, though, because he'd promised Top that if it came to the point they had to confess everything they knew, they'd do it together, and maybe even with Pepper there, too.

After waiting through the commercial and not hearing anything else, Ned finished his tea cake and washed it down with the cooling coffee. "I'm listening."

Mark wished for coffee to help soften the treat. Swallowing with an effort, he couldn't take it any longer. "Grandpa, is Pepper coming with Uncle James?"

"I don't know. Why?"

"Well, because we need to tell you something, and it's gonna take all three of us."

"About what?"

"I'd rather not say until everyone's here."

Mark's heart fell when Ned studied him with those ice-blue eyes. "Are y'all in trouble?"

"We might be."

Ned glanced outside at the darkening skies. "I'll call James and make sure she's with him."

Chapter Fifty-Seven

All three of us kids sat on the couch like the little monkeys who saw, heard, and spoke no evil, except there was nothing happy about anything around us. Mark looked like he wanted to hide his eyes like one of the monkeys, and I think it was because he's the one who started the ball rolling.

I was as nervous as all get-out and almost shook. Mark told me he couldn't keep our secret any longer, and I agreed with him, especially after what I'd seen the night before. We heard what had happened with both of last night's killings and what we knew had needed to come out right then, but we were terrified at our punishment.

Pepper sulled up and sat on the couch like it was an island in the middle of the ocean. We had to wait until the men went outside and put chains on all the cars. That took longer than I figured, and by the time they were finished, it was almost dinnertime.

They probably figured that if they let us stew a while, we'd be worried enough that we'd spill our guts, but the truth was that me and Mark needed to get it over with, and to heck with Pepper.

All the while Norma Faye, Miss Becky, and Aunt Ida Bell kept cooking. Miss Becky came in the living room and turned the television off and the radio on. A Sunday-morning preacher shouted at us through the one speaker, saying that the end was coming.

My long-dead daddy materialized in front of the Dearborn, backed up to the flames and warming his hands. He grinned just like he always did. *They been saying the end was here since I was a kid. Every time Mama took us to church, I'd come home convinced I'd wake up in Heaven the next morning, but it was always that same dirt floor shack with a hungry stove I had to feed.*

My mouth must have fallen open, because Mark gave me a puzzled look. "You all right?"

"Daddy's standing there."

He looked where I pointed, then at Pepper. She raised an eyebrow and spun a finger beside one ear, saying I was crazy. "That LSD's probably still in his system."

"No it's not." I shook my head. "I think it's a light version of my Poisoned Gift, but he's right there…"

And he was gone and everything was back to normal in the house. All three of the women buzzed around that kitchen, working around one another and chattering up a storm. They tried to get Pepper to come in and help, maybe to talk, but she sat on that old blue-and-black couch, listening to the preacher shouting through the speaker and telling us we were all sinners.

I already knew that.

We were about worried out by the time the men streamed up on the porch, stomping snow off their feet. Grandpa came in, pitched his hat on top of the metal TV cabinet, and settled down into his rocker by the stove while Uncle James leaned against the door.

Uncle Cody snapped the radio off and rested one butt cheek on the arm of the couch.

Miss Becky, Norma Faye, and Aunt Ida Belle came in with them, and I'm not sure if it was moral support for us kids, or to keep those three serious-looking men in check. Miss Becky sat down at the telephone table. Arms crossed, Norma Faye backed against the hall door.

Aunt Ida Belle couldn't be still. She went back into the kitchen, returned with a damp cup towel, then went back to wipe the table down. It was all nerves, and I wished I could have done the same, instead of sitting on that couch while all the adults looked at us.

Pepper shot Mark a look that could kill, but her jaw was set, and I wasn't sure she was going to say anything at all.

It was Uncle Cody's big old grin that lightened the mood. "Top, how was your *trip*?"

"Aw, Uncle Cody, you know I didn't intend to take that stuff."

"We all know it. You were just lucky Curtis used his head."

"Yeah, after that stuff kicked in…" Grandpa rocked once and stopped. "He could have brought you kids home when he knew."

"Daddy, I don't think that's what the kids want to talk about right now." Miss Becky sat straight, like she does when she's trying to make a point.

"Well, I'm not sure taking him to Miss Sweet's house was the right thing to do."

"That's where the good Lord needed him to be, Ned." Miss Becky spoke quietly, like she did when she needed Grandpa to listen.

Someone stomped up on the porch and we paused. Miss Becky called into the kitchen. "Come on in!"

The door opened and she grinned. "Why, Tom. Come on in this house. Coffee's in the percolator."

"Yes, ma'am, I believe I will." We sat there as Mr. Tom Bell filled a cup and came into the living room, black hat in one hand

and coffee in the other. He paused, scanning the room and I saw his eyes go flat. "Do I need to come back?"

Grandpa shook his head. "No. You got here just in time."

Uncle James crossed his thin arms. He looked like the hardware store owner he was, and that's the best way I know to explain him. He showed he was tougher than I'd ever thought when Pepper ran off a couple of years earlier and he went out to bring her back. Him and Grandpa and an Indian named Crow had some dealings with a few bad men out there in Arizona, and when he got back, I heard Grandpa tell the men up at the store that Uncle James was tougher'n boot leather.

"Pepper, the boys look worried." Uncle James leaned back against the wall and almost put his foot up against it before realizing where he was. "I suggest you follow their lead and fall into line. Whatever they have to say, I 'magine you're part of it."

"Dad, why did I have to…"

"Pepper!" His voice cracked like a whip and both Mark and I jumped. We'd never heard that mild-mannered man speak above a normal tone of voice. Apparently, Pepper hadn't either, because her face turned white and for once I felt sorry for her.

"We need to tell y'all something, and I wish we'd done it earlier." To take the attention off her, Mark started. "I know I'm not blood family…"

It was Miss Becky's turn to snap, and that was worse than hearing Uncle James step out of character. "Mark! You're ours. Blood's important, but it ain't everything. You know we all love you as much as those other two sitting there, and I don't want to hear that no more."

Mr. Tom raised an eyebrow, and my heart sank that he was having to be part of all that was going on in our little farmhouse.

"Yes ma'am." Mark stopped and gathered his thoughts. "Like

I said, we just need to tell you something we should have when all this started."

"That's the second time you've said that." That was Grandpa, who leaned forward, elbows on his knees and laced his fingers. That was his best listening habit. "All what?"

"Oh, hell!"

"Pepper!"

"Well, you can wash my mouth out later, but we're already gonna be in trouble, so I don't care. The truth is that the night R. B. died, we were all out there at the Starlite Lounge."

You could have heard a pin drop in that living room and most of the air sucked out when all three of the women inhaled at once.

I figured I'd better get us out of the doghouse pretty quick. "We weren't *in* the club. What she means is that we were in Curtis's car that night. He wanted to get some beer after the movie, so we went out there and he went in and got a six-pack."

"And I was talking good about him just a minute ago."

"Ned, the boy's old enough to go in the army and get shot at." Uncle Cody saved all of us with that statement. "He's old enough to die for his country. That's old enough to drink a beer."

"But he didn't have to take these kids…"

"Let's chew on that part later. Go ahead, Top, with what you were saying."

I told them about getting out of the car that night and sneaking around the parking lot to see into the club's back room. The three of us took turns describing what we'd seen, and how it made us feel.

When we were finished, Aunt Ida Belle pinched her mouth and frowned. "What'd you want to do that for?"

I wanted to shrug but knew that kind of response wouldn't tell them anything. I wasn't going to get Pepper in trouble, either. She could do enough of that on her own. "I guess it looked interesting."

"Let's just hear him out before we pick this boy apart." Uncle Cody's voice was soft, but firm.

I told them about Gus on the back porch, drinking beer with his friends. When I said that, Uncle Cody and Grandpa exchanged glances that spoke volumes. Grandpa's cold blue eyes bored a hole in me. "You knew all that while we were at that boy's house and didn't say anything."

"Yessir." Embarrassed and guilty, I couldn't meet his gaze.

Mark helped shoulder part of that load, and I wanted to hug him. "Grandpa, we didn't think seeing him was important right then."

"And you didn't want to confess your sins." Aunt Ida Bell's mouth was tight as a cat's butt.

Instead of going down *that* rabbit hole, I told them about Jett McClellan being there and what I saw around the dice table, and with that, everything else spilled out.

When I ran out of breath, Mark put in his two cents, and then Pepper surprised us all.

"We got out at the club because of me. I wanted to see inside that room, but we really didn't do anything wrong. If anybody's going to get in trouble, it should be me." She reached out and rested one hand on Mark's knee.

It was the only way she knew to apologize for everything that had happened.

She finished, and my lungs were about to burst. They'd given me time to gather my thoughts, and I launched into what I'd seen on the LSD trip, the lights, the men, the murder, and the faces that were as real as those in the living room with me.

After what seemed like an hour, I ran out of steam and felt like a limp dishrag. Miss Becky was wiping tears with a cup towel, and all the men were staring at the floor, thinking. If it hadn't been for the hissing of the heater, we could have heard the snow piling up outside.

Grandpa finally drew a deep, sorrowful breath. "So now we think we know what happened at the Starlite. This one was clearer than most. I believe them three we tangled with last night might be the ones you saw, but that may not be right, neither."

Uncle Cody stood and hooked his thumbs in the gun belt hanging on his hips. "Well, it's part of it, anyway, but none of that is admissible in court, other than what the kids saw in the back room. They'd laugh us out of town if we brought up Top's vision."

I felt about a hundred pounds lighter and it seemed as if I could float to the ceiling. Startled that I might actually rise up, I glanced down at my hands, expecting to see them transform again. I'd heard about acid flashbacks and wondered if that would happen so soon after the first time.

Good Lord. I could still be suffering the effects of the drugs. I looked at my hands again and realized everyone was looking at me. I was the center of attention, and that's not what I wanted right then.

What I wanted less was the colored flashes of light in my peripheral vision. When I turned my head to find the source, they quit.

Uncle Cody grinned. "You all right, hoss?"

"Uh, yeah." I decided not to mention the oily, flowing colors that oozed out of the corners near the ceiling and danced along the edges above everyone's head. They were kinda pretty, and not at all frightening, like I'd expect if I was having another one of my visions. As quick as a finger snap, I felt good. No, I felt wonderful, like I'd taken a three-week nap and was about to fill up on Miss Becky's fried chicken.

Chest swelling, I wanted to smile, to stand up and spin around and watch the colors swirl, or maybe crystallize and flip around like one of those cardboard kaleidoscopes they had at Woolworth's. Instead, I concentrated on Uncle Cody's face, and the colors faded back to the beige walls.

"You have anything else, hoss?"

"Yessir." I pulled myself back into the room. "I forgot to tell you about the guy I saw last night in my vision that was directing the others. I could pick him out of a crowd in about half a second."

"How?"

"The way he looks. He don't have much of a chin, and his big ol' nose almost comes down over his mouth."

Grandpa and Mr. Tom exchanged glances. Mr. Tom smoothed his big white mustache and Grandpa nodded. "We know exactly who that is. Top, think hard, son. Was he the one who killed R. B.?"

"Nossir. But he figures in somehow. He's meaner'n a snake."

Uncle Cody frowned at Grandpa. "How do you know who it is?"

"It's the man who runs the Starlite. We both saw him in there ourselves."

Studying on Grandpa's comment, Uncle Cody came back around to 'em. "Did any names come to mind?"

"Nossir. But there was a blond-haired man carrying a ladder, if that means anything to y'all."

Grandpa had enough and was running a hand over his bald head. "A ladder? That don't make no sense, but one of them fellers we shot last night was blond." He studied the linoleum at his feet. "Anything about corn? Any Indian stuff?"

"I don't recall anything like that."

"Figures."

Aunt Ida Belle couldn't stay out of it. "Why'd you ask that, Ned?"

"Because Cody said Cornsilk wrote the first four letters on the floor in his own blood before he died. He wrote the word *corn.*"

Aunt Ida Belle went white at the news. "Dear God."

"He probably should have written *them* two words instead." Grandpa said. "Starting a letter like that might have helped him get through the gates of Heaven."

Chapter Fifty-Eight

Buster Rawlins hung up the phone and studied the neon-lit interior of the Starlite through the open door of his office. He was on the phone with Tony Roth. The coroner called to tell him he had three familiar-looking bodies in his cooler, men named LaFleur, Toscani, and Plemens.

Roth was matter-of fact and curt. "LaFleur took a load of number four buck in the face."

"Why'd you tell me that?"

"I wanted you to know what we're dealing with here. I hear it was the sheriff, that woman deputy who was in your club the other night, and Ned Parker, the constable of your precinct."

"I'm not *in* any precinct."

"That's the only reason they aren't in there with you right now, and I doubt that'll hold them for long. We had a deal here, that all of this was supposed to go away if I kept quiet about everything I know. I've held up my end."

Rawlins was silent, staring at a neon Hamm's sign high on the wall.

"Everything."

"I heard what you said. I told you it was all taken care of."

"Well, you know what this means. Folks could find out who was there that night your people lost their minds and beat that man to death."

"I heard it was just my boys." Rawlins thought about slamming the receiver down. "But they paid for it all yesterday."

"But we don't know why. I have them under John Does right now, because none of them had licenses on them, but once they start digging, and maybe asking me to compare dental records, then everything's likely to lead right to you. I'll do what I can, but I know what kind of man you are. You'll start talking and take me down with you."

Rawlins scratched the three-day growth of beard on his inward sloping chin. "You don't think much of me, do you?"

"Look. We had a good thing going here and we all made a lot of money, but now we can't move those drugs anymore. That's off the table and I'm washing my hands of it. That one we can get out of free and clean. You've made your money, I've made the call, and the supply has stopped. Now I expect you to keep your word about that other thing and make sure no one else talks."

"You don't have any right to shut this pipeline down."

"It was coming through my funeral home. That's all I needed."

"We'll talk about that later. You keep saying *that other thing*."

"I'm not going to speak it on a phone. Who knows who's listening? You're doing a good job at tying up all the loose ends, though, and I thank you for that."

"I *am*?"

"Don't screw with me, Roth."

"The same goes from me to you." Rawlins grinned, stretching the skin tight over his cheekbones and revealing bad teeth. He tried not to smile too much, because a woman once told him that it made his chin look even smaller. "Your boy was here that night. Because of that, you'll work for me until I say we're done."

Roth was silent on the other end of the line, but heavy breathing told Rawlins the man was still listening.

"So you understand. I own both of you. Say I do."

A beat. "Yes."

"No. Say it."

"All right. You own both of us."

"Good. As long as you remember that, we'll be just fine. And by the way, your boy still owes me over a grand from a while back. I've been patient, what with the weather and all, but I'm losing business over it, so I'll take delivery in cash tonight."

"Come on, Rawlins. It's snowing like hell out there. I doubt I can get in and out on that crappy road of yours. How about when the weather breaks?"

"You." Rawlins snorted. "You're bailing that boy of yours out again, huh?"

Instead of answering, Roth grew silent. Since he was in the office alone, Rawlins laughed, revealing even more bad teeth. He didn't care. There were no men, women, or mirrors around him. "You get out here *tonight*."

Rawlins loved having power over people, and this one made him the happiest. Even though he'd lost three good men, and one who was closer to him than anyone since he'd left home when he was a kid, he felt good. All the loose ends were almost tied up with the deaths of those three. Though he couldn't figure out why his men had tangled with the law in the first place, he could bring up three new replacements who might prove more valuable because they were hungry to please their boss.

"You better be here by dark, or I'm gonna send my new boys over to visit with your son, and frankly, I don't know what kind of men they are yet, or what they might do. You probably don't want that, do you?"

"God, no! I'll do it. I'll be there after I get off work."

"You call cutting up my dead boys work?"

"They aren't the only ones in here, and because of them, I suppose, I'm backlogged with former dice players."

"I heard about that." Rawlins chuckled. "It's a good game when you win, and a dirty little world when you lose. I'll be waiting for that money."

He hung up and left the office, crossing the nearly empty bar to his usual table beside the Starlite's front door. The jukebox was loud and Hank Williams music filled the smoky air. Where LaFleur, Toscani, and Rawlins once sat were three others who'd just that morning been promoted after he heard the news from a customer who couldn't wait to tell him about the Roxton shooting.

It didn't bother Roth too much to lose those three. They were employees, not family, and there were certain dangers in what they did. Everyone in his world knew what the cost would be if they were caught, and most didn't care. They'd served time in county jails and penitentiaries, usually more than once. That's the kind of men they were, rough and morally bankrupt.

Those were the best kind.

Rawlins took his usual chair. "There better be a cold beer right here the next time I sit down, Johnny B. Since you tended bar, I guess it'll be your job now."

The weasel-faced former bartender rose and went for that beer.

The other two were heavies he'd used in the past as bouncers and gofers. With slits for eyes, Wilburn Sorrels, a two-time loser who was fresh out of the Huntsville penitentiary, was a psycho who would just as soon shoot a man as look at him.

The other mountain of a man had thick hands and a lantern jaw full of scars from fighting. "What do you want us to do now, boss?"

"Well, Butcher, we just sit here and enjoy ourselves while we wait for a thousand dollars to walk in that door after 'while."

Levon Butcher licked his lips and tilted his head at the only woman in the club. She was drinking by herself at the end of the bar and had been there since early that morning, alternately weeping and soaking up one gin after the other. "Mind if I go talk to that lady, since we ain't hardly got any customers?"

"Why sure. That's what I meant by enjoying ourselves. We play hard and work hard. Go play while you can."

All six-foot-six of the big man who weighed nearly three hundred pounds stood and sauntered across the bar to settle onto the stool by the woman. He flicked a finger toward the new bartender for him to serve her another drink. The records on the jukebox switched just in time for Rawlins and Wilburn Sorrels to hear their exchange. "Drinks are on me today."

"Thank you."

"What's your name?"

"Mildred."

Merle Haggard came on, drowning out the remaining conversation, but it was enough to make Rawlins chuckle. He waved a finger in their direction as Johnny B. came back with a cold Pabst. "You boys know who that is?"

Johnny B. and Sorrels shook their heads. Sorrells's eyes narrowed even more, and Rawlins wondered how he could even see.

Rawlins licked his lips, leaving his tongue out way too long. "Why, that's a Baptist preacher's wife from over in Center Springs, and I bet by the time she leaves here tonight, we're gonna have a good use for her." He took a swallow of cold beer and studied how much money he could blackmail out of her husband. He was getting pretty good at that, as the coroner could avow.

Chapter Fifty-Nine

"Here's the God's honest truth," In Judge O. C. Rains's office, Ned spoke to Cody, John, and Anna Sloan. "We know good and well who's been behind all this."

Judge Rains leaned back in his chair, barricaded behind stacks of files and papers. "But you don't have *proof.*"

"Not legal proof." Ned pursed his lips. "But with them trying to kill us last night, I'd think you can get warrants by now."

"I'm leaning that way. There's been a lot of coincidental killings since that place opened, and the state district attorney agrees with me, so I'm gonna risk closing it down like you want. Now, tell me why Neal Box and his wife are living in the Holiday Inn and eating on the county's dime."

Cody reached out to adjust his hat perched precariously on a stack of papers. "Well, since he listed everyone who was at that dice game and is the only one alive that we know of, except for that feller in jail up in Oklahoma, I wanted to keep it that way."

"One of y'all could have taken them home with you."

"Wasn't gonna risk it. It don't make any sense to bring trouble to your own house. We all have families that we need to take care of. Nobody but you, us, and them know they're there, and that's where they need to stay until we catch whoever's killing these folks."

"That could be weeks."

Ned was getting frustrated. "It'll be faster if you let me get over to that damned club and arrest those people."

"All based on Top's dream."

"You know as well as I do that most of what he sees comes through in the end."

"But you usually don't know the truth until after everything's over."

"You know it's real, though." Cody spoke up to take some of the heat off Ned. "As real as Ned's own Gift…" He hadn't meant for those words to come out and drifted off. "Sometimes we have to believe in other things, O. C., and not just laws and papers."

"Listen, that boy described the sorry son of a bitch running the Starlite down to a T, and even one of them men who tried to kill us last night." Ned tapped his index finger on the desk to punctuate his words. "Top said that man killing folks was a blond and one of 'em we laid out was a towhead, and he was right."

"That doesn't mean anything, Ned. Hell, there's blond people everywhere. Now, if one of them had a Mohawk haircut, then I might be more convinced."

"I'll give *you* a Mohawk, if you don't give us a warrant."

That broke the tension and they all settled back. O. C. rocked in his chair for a moment, absently reaching for the flyswatter on his desk. Realizing he didn't need it, he nodded as if some profound statement was whispered in his ear.

"All right. I'm gonna sign a search warrant for drugs, but it ain't a license to shoot. You got that?"

"You get us that paper, and I'll have 'em all in jail, then we'll find out who's doing all this killing."

"I doubt it. Y'all get out of here until I can get it drafted. Go get something to eat over at Frenchie's and be back in an hour."

Chapter Sixty

"Well, that didn't go bad at all." All the adults were out of the living room, and Pepper was snuggled up close to Mark just like nothing had ever happened. Grandpa and Uncle Cody headed up to the courthouse where Mr. O. C. was waiting for them.

The TV was back on and it was snowing to beat the band outside. I really wanted a bowl of snow ice cream and was about to go get a pan to go outside when the walls shimmered around me like lace curtains.

I plopped back onto the couch. "Ohhhhh."

Mark was beside me in a flash. "What is it?"

Primary colors like melted crayons ran down the walls, then it all washed away, and those shimmering curtains were back. The kitchen was gone and so was Miss Becky and everyone else.

I was staring at a man leaning over a naked body laid out on a chrome table. He was arguing with someone standing with his back to me.

"Top, get your skinny little ass back here." Pepper's voice cut through my head like a sharp knife.

I turned inside my mind to see her, but there was nothing but deep snow behind me, snow that was soon covered with strawberry red. The drifts were capped with a light-tan color that I knew was Eagle Brand Milk. It looked like a strawberry snow cone, but the red was blood, and then I disappeared down inside a tornado of vibrant colors and soft music while a loud preacher told me I was going straight to Hell.

Chapter Sixty-One

Toting a signed Texas search warrant, Sheriff Cody Parker led the way through the heavy snowfall toward the Starlite Lounge. There was no wind, and the soft flakes fell straight down, quickly building on what had already accumulated.

Behind him was a line of cars. John Washington insisted on going and rode with Deputy Anna Sloan in a borrowed cruiser. Constable Ned Parker followed them, with Tom Bell riding shotgun. Only he didn't have a shotgun. He'd somehow gotten his hands on a Browning automatic rifle, just like the one he'd lost across the river in Mexico a few years earlier.

Ned raised an eyebrow at the fully automatic 30.06. "You never fail to surprise me."

"Well, I hated to lose old Doris. I used her down in the Valley more than once. The Mexicans named her Alejandra, meaning defender of mankind. I used that BAR against criminals and bad people to defend myself and those in Company D for years. She was kinda famous."

Concentrating on staying in the ruts made by the other cars, Ned grunted. "So you gonna name that rifle?"

"I didn't name the other one, but Erizelda comes to mind."

"That have some kind of meaning, or do you just like the name?"

"It means a battle maiden."

Ned's eyes flicked to the rifle riding muzzle-down against the floorboard. "That suits it."

———

In front of them, Anna was working to keep her heart from racing. It aggravated her to feel that way when John Washington sat there as calm as if he were in church. "You don't think anything will happen, do you?"

"You never know." John adjusted his right arm in the sling. "This is Sunday, so I doubt there'll be too many people around, especially with this storm. I declare, I do love to watch it snow. I'd rather be settin' by the fire with Rachel and the kids eatin' snow-cream."

"What's that?"

"Nothin' much. I gather snow in a dishpan and we mix it in bowls with sugar, cream, and a little vanilla. The kids love it, and to tell the truth, I like it too."

"I'll have to try it."

"Well, come on over to the house after all this and we'll mix us up some."

She couldn't get it off her mind that there were so many of them going out to the Starlite. "You think we'll be all right?"

"I don't know why not. It's just a search warrant."

"Does Cody usually take so many people for a search warrant?"

John's eyes flicked to the sheriff's car ahead, then to the snow-covered side mirror and Ned's red Plymouth. "Not usually. He wants Mr. Ned in on this, though, because of Mr. R. B. This place has been worryin' him to death, and these days, where Mr. Ned goes, so does Mr. Tom Bell. I swear, that old man is vengeance under a hat."

"You know what's worrying me the most, don't you?"

"No ma'am, I don't."

"That Judge O. C.'s up there, riding with Cody."

"That was a surprise to me, too. That and the Oklahoma sheriff who's supposed to be here any minute."

"Cody waited as long as he could stand it."

"Probably didn't need to wait. Oklahoma law don't want nothin' to do with this side of the river. To tell you the truth, I doubt that sheriff'll show up at all."

———

Sheriff Cody Parker was drawn tight as a fiddle string. "I know we need to do this, but I got a bad feeling about it."

"That's why I'm along, son."

"Judge, I don't like putting you in harm's way."

"I'm out of practice, but I'm not afraid of any kind of fight. You know I was in the war, don't you?"

"Yessir. They tell me you laid out a lot of Germans."

"Them that needed it."

"How'd you know which ones were which?"

"I just shot the ones speaking German. They were the ones that needed it."

Chapter Sixty-Two

Mildred McClellan cried in the warm, smoky darkness of the Starlite Lounge. "Those aren't even my kids."

Levon Butcher took another sip of his beer, wondering if this woman weeping into her gin and tonic would be worth the time he'd wasted sitting there with her. "What kids?"

"The twins I told you about. Jett and Blu."

"Oh." The acne-pocked thug had only been half-listening, mostly staring at the tops of her breasts when she talked. "What about them?"

"They aren't mine. He had them when we met. They were mean little shits even then, and now they're passing out drugs. Colt took them to the courthouse this morning, but I wouldn't go with them. I couldn't take it. I can't bear to go home and look at those two. I hate them both."

"How'd you wind up with 'em in the first place?"

"Colt's brother got killed in a car wreck."

"What about his wife? She wouldn't keep the kids?"

"She died from cancer about a month before he died. All that was too much for Colt. He got religion and started preaching. I met him right afterward. They were cute little kids, but the older they got, the crazier they've acted. We've been raising those two little demons ever since."

"Leave him."

"I'd love to, but then I wouldn't have any money. I don't have any skills, and everything's in Colt's name. Here's the funny part. He already had money. Family money, and a lot of it. But he wouldn't use any of it. Millions are in a bank in our name, but he won't let me touch it. He says we have to make it God's way, or not at all."

Butcher snorted. "Hell, lady. Preachers don't have any money."

"This one does. His parents made their money in oil down in Houston. That's why it doesn't make any difference where they send us…him…to preach, he has more money'n the government. He won't let me use much of it, though. He has us on a monthly allowance." Mildred's laugh was harsh. "He's rich, and all I get is a few bucks a week, barely enough to keep me in Bombay."

She drank half her gin and tonic in several long swallows.

"You said millions."

She threw her head back and laughed, switching moods like many professional drunks. "Honey, his daddy was one of the richest men in Texas and all of it belongs to Colt." She finished the drink. "And it keeps coming in, because those wells pump around the clock. Think of it. My husband is a Baptist preacher in this little one-horse town and we could be living in luxury in New York City, but he won't touch but just a little bit of it each year."

She thought for a moment, her eyes heavy from the alcohol. "That's the other reason I drink. You know, if something ever happened to him and those bastard kids of his, I could own half of Houston and not be sitting in this stinking bar in the middle of a snowstorm." Mildred drifted off for a moment, then squinted at Butcher. "Well, aren't *you* handsome?"

"I'll be right back." Butcher waved a finger at the bartender. "She's on the house from now on." While the bartender mixed another drink, Butcher made his way over to the jukebox and dropped in a handful of change before going over to Rawlins's table. "Hey boss, do I have some great news for you. We're gonna be rich."

While Rawlins listened, Butcher gave him the information they needed to make up for the now-defunct funeral home/drug-running business.

Chapter Sixty-Three

Ned thought the good thing about honky-tonks was the lack of windows. Not worried about being seen, they pulled into the snow-covered parking lot.

Setting his hat against the still-falling snow, he stepped out as Tom Bell moved with fluid ease belying his age. The old Ranger cradled the BAR in his left arm and waited for instructions. Far down behind and below the Starlite, the Red River gurgled over brush and logs washed up against the bank.

Cody slipped out from behind the wheel at the same time Judge O. C. Rains quietly closed his door on the other side. "Judge, you stay back."

"I will, but you don't worry about me. I'll just be right here until one of y'all comes to get me."

"Good. Anna, you know how to get around the outside and into the back room?"

She pointed at the covered walkway on the side. The snow in that direction was trackless. "It's down around there."

"Good. You and John come in through the back."

"What if the door's locked?"

Cody thought. "If it is, John can open it with his foot."

The big man's voice rumbled. "Be glad to."

Turning toward Ned, Cody's eyes widened at the sight of Tom Bell's BAR. "I thought you lost that thing in Mexico."

"Did. This one's new."

"I don't want to know where you got it, or if it's fully automatic."

"Wouldn't be worth anything if it was a single shot." Tom Bell's mustache twitched in a grin, and Cody had the strangest feeling that he'd been transported back to 1910, and a much more dangerous Lamar County.

"All right. We're just walking in like regular customers. Ned, you say this Rawlins guy sits right here at the table to the left of the door." Cody pointed to that corner of the building at the same time John and Anna disappeared around the side.

"He does, or did when I was in there."

"Fine. I'll step inside and cover them. You two follow me and make sure everyone else in there behaves themselves."

"I count seven cars." Tom Bell inclined his head toward the snow-covered vehicles.

"Let's expect at least seven people, then." Cody opened the padded red door and disappeared into the darkness as Ned and Tom Bell followed.

Chapter Sixty-Four

Rawlins was already planning a way to put Colt McClellan in a shallow grave and keep all his money by the time Butcher was back over there with her, sitting shoulder to shoulder like two lovebirds. Buck Owens sang "Your Tender Loving Care," the perfect song for a distraught woman in a beer hall.

Butcher slipped an arm around her shoulders and she leaned in. The record ended and Tammy Wynette sang "I Don't Wanna Play House."

The woman in the crook of Butcher's arm wailed and he pulled her close.

Rawlins chuckled and spoke to Johnny B. "I love this job."

The front door opened, allowing a sliver of light to illuminate the tables nearest the entrance. Arctic air rushed inside, along with a man in a silverbelly cowboy hat and thick jacket. Rawlins watched him pause for a moment like most people to let his eyes adjust to the dim light. Two more customers entered, and Rawlins felt a little better. Business was picking up.

But then they spread out, facing the wide, dim room.

The door closed behind the trio and the first man stepped up to Rawlins's table, stopping at Butcher's empty chair. He pulled his unbuttoned jacket back to reveal a badge. "You must be Buster Rawlins. I'm Sheriff Cody Parker, and this is a search warrant." He dropped a folded piece of paper onto the table. "You men keep your hands on the table where I can see them."

Rawlins started at the sight of a big rifle in one man's hands. What the hell was this? Black hat. Black coat. It was that ancient cowboy who'd warned him not to cross the fat old man who'd been disrespectful to him a few days earlier.

They were all lawmen.

The cowboy with the rifle moved across the bar like a black cat and knelt to reach behind the jukebox. He unplugged it and Tammy Wynette's voice warbled and went silent.

Annoyed, Butcher turned. "Hey!"

The fat old man held out his left hand. "Constable Ned Parker. The sheriff there has a search warrant for this place. Everybody just stay right where you are."

Butcher pushed away from the woman and rose to face the two men. "You two're a little long in the tooth for this, ain't you?"

"Don't make no difference." Constable Parker rested one hand on the butt of a pistol on his hip. "I said stay where you are. Sit down."

"Make me."

The slender old man in black raised an enormous rifle and pointed it waist-high at Butcher. "Texas Ranger. You heard him. You might be big, but this thing right here's bigger."

Hand resting on the butt of his holstered .45, the sheriff held out a hand when Johnny B. slid his chair back and planted his feet. The sheriff pointed a finger at him. "Don't. We're just here on a search warrant. Just sit right where you are with both hands on the table."

Rawlins kept his hands where they were. "Your paper don't work here. This is Oklahoma."

"Paper says it's not. It's under Texas jurisdiction here in Precinct Three."

"You're not searching a damned thing here." A muscular man stepped into the office doorway, leveling a sawed-off double-barrel shotgun at the two old men. "Hands up!"

No one moved. Rawlins was thankful that his croupier had sense enough not to point that scattergun at the sheriff. He'd soak up part of that load if Wynn Puckett needed to shoot.

Rawlins grinned at the sheriff. "Looks like we have a little impasse here, Sheriff. Wynn, steady on that trigger until we all come to an understanding."

"Sure thing. I'll keep it on that fat old man right where he is until you guys settle this thing."

But his smile disappeared at the same time an unseen force yanked Wynn Puckett back into the office and out of sight.

Chapter Sixty-Five

Cody's blood iced up as cold as the outside air at the sight of the twin muzzles pointed across the club at Ned. There was no way the man standing in the office door could miss with a shotgun at that range, and depending on the pattern spread, he could take out Tom Bell, too.

Tom already had his hands full with the huge man with slicked-back hair. And good Lord, the crying woman who'd been in the giant's arms only moments before turned her head to reveal it was Mildred McClellan, the Baptist preacher's wife.

Across the table, Buster Rawlins was as disgusting as he'd heard. The man's breath reeked so badly Cody wanted to back away. Unshaven and with a startling receding chin that almost blended into his neck, he looked as evil as Top had described.

But the intelligence in the man's flashing eyes told Cody he shouldn't underestimate him. Mouth dry as cotton, he absorbed Rawlins's comment. They were at more than an impasse.

Life changes in an instant, and it did when the man holding the shotgun disappeared as if he hadn't been there at all. Noises of a scuffle came through the open door as Cody drew his .45 as smooth as silk and leveled it at Buster Rawlins.

"Don't you move." He knew without turning around that Ned had done the same with his Colt, and he hoped it was aimed at the men still seated at the table. Somehow the one with slitted eyes had moved his hands below the edge, and now he could be holding a pistol, a knife, or a hand grenade, for all the sheriff knew. "Ned?"

"I'm watching that table."

"Good. Mr. Rawlins. That Texas Ranger back there in the black hat won't hesitate to kill the big fella standing at the bar. Call him off, and both of you get your hands on top of your heads."

Anna's soft voice came from the office door. "This guy's cuffed up."

Still seated, Rawlins slowly laced his fingers across the top of his head. "There's more of us in here. Y'all aren't through."

"Where are they?"

"That's for me to know and you to find out."

"We're not playing kid games, Rawlins. Stand up and turn around. You other two. Hands on your heads *now*."

"I don't believe my buddy here wants to." Rawlins smiled, revealing horribly rotten teeth. "So now what are you gonna do, friend?"

Cody opened his mouth, but before he could speak, the top of the table in front of Slit Eyes exploded in a mass of splinters. A hot bullet whizzed an inch away from his neck and he instinctively pulled the trigger on his .45 at the same time the Starlite Lounge erupted in gunfire. Muzzle flashes cut through the smoky air like lightning in a storm cloud.

Chapter Sixty-Six

The old man holding the BAR on Butcher was in great shape for his age, but his reactions were a hair too slow. The big bouncer carried a Walther PPK .380 in the small of his back, and when Johnny B. shot at the sheriff from under the table, Butcher's big hand grabbed the pistol grip and brought it to bear as fast as any old west gunslinger.

The little automatic was up and firing before the Ranger could pull the trigger on the big rifle, but pull it he did, and the detonations hammered the room. Butcher saw the muzzle flash and the smoky air actually dimple in water-like rings from the 30.06's pressure wave.

———

Startled by the gunshot coming over his left shoulder, Tom Bell was a hair off his game. In that world of fast, violent action, he was disgusted with himself for being so slow. He was once fast as lightning, but the accumulated years weathered his reactions just enough to put him a microsecond behind the thug's response.

The big man's hand disappeared in a flash and reappeared with a James Bond pistol that was firing from the time it materialized. The problem lay in his speed, and not accuracy. Hot lead whizzed past the old Ranger. The safety was already off the BAR, and Tom Bell squeezed the trigger, anticipating the recoil. The big rifle opened up with a deafening roar.

Three rounds hit the monster with little effect. Bullets that could take down any large animal on the North American continent did nothing to stop the giant from shooting and advancing like a furious grizzly bear.

In response, Tom Bell held the trigger down.

———

Ned was a pace behind the others. One minute they were talking, then all of a damned sudden, people were shooting.

Because of a *search* warrant.

People didn't shoot over search warrants that were as common as traffic tickets.

Slit Eyes fired at Cody and shoved back in his chair, raising his pistol to shoot again, this time without the table in the way. The second round might have hit Cody in the face, but he reeled backward. The bullet cut a channel through his hair between his ear and brim.

Ned's first round caught Slit Eyes in the side of the chest. He folded sideways with a groan at the same time Cody cut down on Rawlins, who produced his own .45 automatic from midair.

———

A stunned Tom Bell and Anna Sloan turned the charging man into Swiss cheese before he fell. No one had ever absorbed that many 30.06 rounds from an M1918, not to mention three more from Anna's .38 before succumbing, and the wiry Ranger couldn't help but admire the big bear of a man for sheer determination.

Dead on his feet, the shooter finally dropped to reveal the bartender standing there with a pistol pointed at Tom Bell. He shifted the muzzle only a fraction of an inch and cut down on the assailant at the same time John nailed the would-be shooter from the side. His limp body disappeared behind the bar, and they shifted their attention to the remainder of the room, fully expecting more people to pop up like gophers.

———

The dim bar was filled with rolling thunder as guns opened up all around him. Ned killed the Sitting Man with one shot through the chest, the bullet plowing through both of the shooter's lungs. Gasping and kicking backward with his feet, Sitting Man didn't know the slug had already wrecked his engine room. Graveyard dead, he still tried to raise the gun to shoot a third time, this one at Ned, but the arm dropped. Ned fired again, and still in his chair, Sitting Man's chin dropped to his chest.

———

The drunk woman beside the bar kept screaming until Anna crossed the room and grabbed her by the arm. "Shut up! It's over and nobody was shooting at *you*."

The woman's screams morphed into tears, and she dropped back down on the stool to lay her head on both arms and dissolve into deep sobs. Disgusted with her reactions, Anna emptied the clutch purse on the bar to be sure there were no

weapons, then turned to help everyone check the bodies lying
still in the sawdust.

———

Sheriff Cody Parker knelt and propped Rawlins against the
wall. Blood poured from the dying man's grievous wounds as he
struggled for breath. The sheriff had seen many people die, but
none who fought so hard to live.

"Rawlins, right?"

He nodded.

"You're a damn fool."

"I believe you." His voice was soggy.

"Don't die yet, you son of a bitch." Ned pushed the table out of
the way and sat in one of the chairs, still warm from men dead or
dying. "You need to tell me what happened the night R. B. died."

"Who?"

"My nephew. R. B. Parker."

"Don't recognize the name." Rawlins coughed and holding
both hands over the two small entry wounds, struggled for air.
"Get me to a doctor."

"It's too late." Tom Bell cradled his BAR, keeping an eye on
the door. "Tell him what you know."

Afraid Rawlins would die before he could get the information he needed, Ned leaned forward. "A week ago, Friday night
after a dice game. Somebody killed him."

"Oh, him." Another cough. "It wasn't none of my people."

"Had to have been."

The front door opened behind them admitting cold, light,
and Judge O. C. Rains.

Ned gripped the back of the chair, his knuckled turning
white. "I know all about that dice game going on back there.

R. B. died because of it, and maybe those drugs y'all sold through here. Who killed him, if it wasn't you?"

Drowning in his own blood, Rawlins coughed softly and deep. "That's why you killed us, because you thought *we* killed that hayseed?"

"We killed y'all because you tried to shoot us." Knowing the man wasn't much longer for the world, Cody glanced up and met Judge Rains's eyes. He shook his head and the judge seemed to shrink in on himself. "It was only a search warrant and you lost your minds."

"Those new boys of mine weren't too smart, were they?"

"Neither were you."

"Never was." Rawlins coughed and died.

Two hours later, Buck Johnson pronounced him and the others as officially dead. The bodies were loaded into two ambulances and delivered to Tony Roth, the coroner, and the Starlite was empty.

———

The snow-covered lot was crisscrossed with tire tracks, and a light scattering of flakes still drifted downward. High overhead, the neon Starlite sign glowed through the low clouds. Ned, Anna, Cody, and John gathered beside Cody's car, finally dealing with the leftover reactions of the shoot-out.

Pulled down low into her thick jacket like a turtle in its shell, Anna had her back to the lounge. "That was insane. You should have seen big John grab that guy with one arm. He yanked him completely off his feet. That feller was so scared he would have told us his bank account number, if he had one."

"What did you find out when you questioned him?" Ned seemed impervious to the unusual cold.

Cody shrugged. He was pulled down just as deep into his own heavy jacket. "He remembered the dice game. Said R. B. was winning big that night and it was making everybody mad. Then he quit while he was ahead."

"That's what Neal told us. Did something happen in the back?"

"No. Guy says he walked out with a pocket full of money. Somebody rolled him in the parking lot."

"Was it Rawlins' people?"

"Yeah. He says they worked him over and took his money, but it wasn't them who killed him."

"So who, and when did they kill my nephew?"

John finally spoke up. "The sixty-four-thousand-dollar question is *why*. They got his money, so there was no reason to kill Mr. R. B."

Tom Bell came from around the side of the club, hands in the pockets of his coat. Ned stomped his feet to get the blood flowing. "You feel better, Tom?"

"What do you mean?"

"Well, I figured you went around back there to pee."

They all chuckled, and Tom shook his head. "Nope. Just making sure the place was really empty."

"There's no sense in standing out here freezing to death." Cody opened his door. "Let's go to the house and get in out of this cold."

Anna inclined her head. "Which house?"

"Ned's."

They climbed back into their cars and slowly rolled down the snowy lane to the highway. Turning eastward, they drove away from the Starlite. Ten minutes later a glow rose behind the Starlite where Tom Bell had been only moments before. An hour later it had burned to the ground.

Chapter Sixty-Seven

An even deeper cold settled down over Northeast Texas the night Grandpa and everyone got back to the house from the shoot-out at the Starlite Lounge. Miss Becky, Norma Faye, and Miss Anna heated up everything in the icebox and the comforting smells of fried foods filled the air. All the adults gathered around the kitchen table.

It was still like that in southern homes back in 1969. Food came out at any sign of trouble. Little bitty kids ate first, then the men, and if there was room at the table, kids our age, then the women finished up. It wasn't fair. They were the ones who cooked everything, but Miss Becky once told me she was already full by the time everyone sat down, because she'd been taking bites here and there all the way through.

She once told someone on the phone that she didn't understand why women those days didn't take care of their husbands like they were supposed to. I think it meant times were changing and that women's lib thing I'd been seeing on television where hard-looking women burned their bras in streets was on her mind.

Our farmhouse had little in the way of insulation in the walls.

On those cold winter nights we slept under layers of colorful patchwork quilts sometimes so heavy I felt I couldn't turn over. There were only two warm places, one in the kitchen and the other in front of the Dearborn in the living room. That's where Mark, Pepper, and I ate that evening while the adults talked.

Sitting on the floor in front of the fire, Pepper waved a cold chicken leg like a wand. "I heard them say that Mildred McClellan was in that joint today."

"She should have been home with her crazy kids." Mark absently pulled his hair behind one ear. "She's no mama."

Pepper's eyes dropped to the plate, and I saw sadness pass through that distant gaze. "They're all crazy, even Colt. He's not who we think he is."

"How do you know that?" Mark scooted, closer to her. "Did you see something?"

She sighed. "I know more than I can tell, and please don't ask me anything about him or them. Heard it from Jett, and that's the last time I'll ever say that son of a bitch's name."

We both watched her. She glanced up. "It was Jett gave Blu the LSD they slipped you, Top. He talked her into giving it to you. He's all fake, and he hates you because you're the smartest of all of us. He wanted her to get a hit into you too, Mark. They both just like to stir things up and then sit back to watch."

Mark's hand came up and went down her back just once and their knees touched. He gave Pepper's leg a pat, and I wondered how those two could have made up so fast after her and Jett did what they did.

He was mean as a snake, and I wondered if he had something to do with those murders. He was just a kid, a little older than me, but he'd been at that dice game behind the store, and he was blond, and I saw a blond figure in my vision out by the lake.

Meanness wasn't just for boys. Blu had her mean streak,

too. Or maybe it was a combination of the two. I'd heard said that twins were sometimes the same person. The world shrank around me in front of that Dearborn stove and lights flashed in my head and the world spun for just a second.

Two people stood next to each other in my mind. One was a little bigger than the other, but they were indistinct, like I was looking at them through muddy water. I'd heard tell that twins were split forms of a single person. Blu and Jett together. That would explain some things. The two images came together and then separated again. All of a sudden, I snapped back into our living room. It wasn't a real vision, not like the others with color and light. It just popped into my mind and then went away.

It wasn't Blu and Jett, but two other people who were just alike.

Pepper and Mark were still looking into each other's eyes and she held her drumstick up for him to take a bite. They hadn't noticed me and everything was normal. We didn't have the radio or TV on, so the adult voices came through loud and clear over the rattle of dishes and utensils. I glanced up from the plate on the floor in front of me and swallowed. Blinking my eyes clear, I looked into the kitchen.

Grandpa sat at the head of the table facing the living room, Uncle Cody was on his right, and Mr. John on the left in Miss Becky's usual seat. Mr. Tom Bell sat with his back to us. Judge O. C. Rains was out of my sight.

Grandpa Ned dipped green beans from a small bowl and dropped them on his plate with leftover fried steak, chicken, red beans, warmed-over mashed potatoes. Then he covered everything with gravy saved from the day before.

Not wanting to watch Pepper and Mark with their goo-goo eyes, I absently took a bite of chicken and listened to Grandpa.

"We've had three people tell us nothing happened to R. B. inside the club, so it was likely in the parking lot, but I tend to believe Rawlins and that guy John cuffed up...what do they call him?"

"A croupier." Miss Anna sipped at a glass of sweet tea.

"I can't say that word." Grandpa cut a bite of steak. "Did he have a name?"

"Wynn something or other." Uncle Cody had food on his plate, but he wasn't eating much of it.

"Yeah, but he says it wasn't them men at the club, neither, and I believe him."

Judge O. C.'s voice floated across the table. "So who was it?"

Uncle Cody put down his fork. "We didn't ask him if anyone else was winning that night. Or losing. Neal Box didn't tell us that, so I'm wondering if somebody else lost so much to R. B. they couldn't stand it."

The phone rang and none of the adults in the kitchen made a move to stand up, so I answered. "Hello?"

"Who's this?"

"Top. Top Parker."

"I need to talk to the sheriff. I hear he might be there."

I remembered my manners. "Who is this?"

"The coroner here in Chisum, Tony Roth."

"Just a minute." I put the phone down on top of the telephone table and went into the kitchen. I was still a little groggy from that little flashback a few moments before and had trouble forming that word. "Uncle Cody, the cor...corner Mr. Roth wants to talk to you."

They all laughed as Uncle Cody stood. "That's the *coroner*..." His face went blank and everyone looked up at him. "Corner. Coroner."

"What's wrong?" Norma Faye's voice broke him out of his

thinking trance. He pointed a finger in my general direction. "Top. Tell Roth I'll call him back in a few minutes."

"Okay." I went back and spoke into the receiver. "He'll call you back in a little bit."

"Thanks, kid. Tell him not to take too long."

Uncle Cody sat down and looked around the table. They were all waiting for him to explain. "Coroner. If you can't spell it, or you're in shock, or you don't have time, a dying man might write the word *corner*."

Miss Anna frowned. "I don't get it."

"Cornsilk wasn't writing his name as he died. He was trying to tell us who killed him. He was trying to spell coroner, his killer, and died before he finished. That what the message *corn* meant. Coroner."

"Tony Roth?" Grandpa paused. "It's him?"

"It all makes sense. The man handles all the bodies that come through the coroner's office and has part ownership in the funeral home. He's in the perfect position to cover up every death we've been dealing with."

"But all you have are four letters wrote in blood." Mr. John took a giant bite from a homemade biscuit and chewed.

"It's enough, isn't it, O. C.?" Uncle Cody looked wound up as a spring.

"We don't know why." Miss Anna shook her head. "What's his motive?"

Uncle Cody shook his head. "I don't know." He sighed. "Maybe I'm wrong."

"There's enough to bring him in for probable cause." I heard a chair scrape on the linoleum as Judge O. C. stood.

"We'll pick him up, then."

More chairs scraped as they all rose, but Miss Becky put a stop to it. "Well, y'all can go, but right now we're going to say a prayer for those men who died this morning and then bless this food for the rest of y'all. Now, bow your heads, and you kids in there, put down your forks and bow yours too."

"Well, shit." Pepper took a huge bite of her chicken, closed her eyes, and chewed through Miss Becky's long prayer.

Chapter Sixty-Eight

Neal and Clarice Box were sitting in the Holiday Inn's coffee shop. His wavy white hair wasn't combed back as neatly as usual, and dark circles under her eyes told of long, sleepless nights.

The air outside was the kind of cold that cuts to the bone in a matter of seconds, despite thick coats and gloves. Warm and toasty, Neal sipped on a cup of steaming black coffee. "This weather reminds me of when we were kids. I haven't seen it this cold in years."

"I swear, I think the world's freezing over. Maybe this is the way we're all punished. God said he wouldn't flood the world again, and some folks think it'll end in fire, but I think he's just gonna freeze us all to death." Clarice patted at her frosted hair that needed touching up. "It'd be better if we could be home in front of our fire. I hate sitting in that little room. I'm ready to go."

"We can't. Not until Cody gets a handle on all this."

"I told you we needed to stay out of that place."

He glanced around at the same time his big white hand patted the air. Diners occupied almost half of the tables, and four men lined up at the counter, two hunched over coffee and the others digging into greasy hamburgers. Neal lowered his voice. "Not here."

Her mouth tightened. "I can't sit here much longer. I need to get out."

He adjusted the pistol's bulge in his coat pocket. "Let's go to Dallas. We can do what we want there."

"Can we?"

"We're not under arrest. If no one sees us leave, then they can't find us."

"You're leaving Oak Peterson all the business."

"He carries enough stock that nobody'll get in trouble."

The door opened and a well-dressed young man came inside. Wearing a cowboy hat and long overcoat that was more common in Dallas instead of Chisum, he glanced around and saw a much older man sitting alone in a booth. Recognizing each other, they shook hands and the young man slipped into the other seat, smiling.

Neal nodded. "That older guy right there's the mayor."

"I've seen the other one somewhere, but I can't place him." Clarice held her coffee cup with two hands and sipped. "He sure is dressed nice."

The gum-chewing waitress with "Gail" written on her badge appeared with the coffeepot and overheard the last part of their conversation. "That'un who just came in is always around glad-handing people. He's the coroner's son, running for city council. Name's Ray Roth."

Neal frowned. The mayor faced him, giving him a clear view of the man, but Roth sat half-turned, so all they could see was the side of his face not hidden by the hat. "You're right. The young guy looks familiar."

"Somebody needs to educate him on his manners." Gail pursed her mouth. "I declare, these young folks don't know you're supposed to take your hat off at the table. That one should know better. He's liable to lose votes for acting like that. They say he's so good and personable that he'll be governor someday. I heard the mayor say Roth even has plans to run for the senate."

"That's not something I'd ever want." Neal smoothed his hair.

"He probably won't get it. They say he has a little problem."

Clarice added cream from a tiny glass container to her coffee. "Drinking?"

"Naw, hon. They say he gambles across the river, but I don't know if that's true or not. He always has a wad of money when he comes in here, though." Gail popped her gum.

Clarice put down her cup. "He needs to take that hat off. I might just march right over there and snatch it off his head."

"You'll do no such of a thing." Neal studied the two in the booth. "Order you some pie or something."

At that moment the man removed his hat and laid it flat on the table and not upside down. Grinning at something the mayor said, he turned to survey the customers and his gaze fell on Neal Box.

The hair rose on the store owner's neck when he recognized the man whose eyes widened slightly before he turned back to the mayor. He leaned into the center of the table and they spoke softly.

Unconsciously angling himself away from the booth, Neal leaned toward the waitress. "You say his name's Roth?"

"Yessir. Ray Roth. He sure is cute, ain't he?"

She left to pick up an order. Neal spoke softly. "Now I know where we've seen him. Shooting dice with R. B. that night in the Starlite."

Chapter Sixty-Nine

"I'm tired of all this cold." Ned told Cody as the sheriff steered into the icy parking lot of the sanitorium on West Walnut Street, where the coroner's office was located. "Weatherman says it'll start warming up soon."

"Won't be soon enough."

Anna pulled into the lot beside Cody's cruiser. Seconds later, John Washington came around the corner in his personal car and parked nearby, sliding an inch or two at the last. He gingerly stepped out, made sure the leather soles of his boots wouldn't slip on the crust, and adjusted his arm in the sling.

Anna wore a new pair of hunting boots that gave her better purchase on the crunchy surface. She came around to meet John at the same time Ned and Cody joined the two deputies.

Cody patted his pocket. "All right. Let's go in easy and pick him up. Ned, you stay out here with John."

"Why're you leaving us outside?"

"Because it's sheriff's office business here in town and we don't need all four of us in there taking up room. I'll just tell him what we're doing and I imagine he'll come along."

Ned and John exchanged glances. Ned adjusted his glasses. "He could come up shooting, too."

"I doubt it."

Frowning, Ned toed the snow. "Fine, then."

Cody opened the door and they stepped into the warm reception area. There was no one in sight, but the sounds of an argument came through the door. Cody held up a hand to stop Anna. "Shhh."

———

Tony Roth sat behind his desk, aiming a finger at his sullen son, Ray, who stood there with both hands in the pockets of his bulky overcoat. "I'm done with this, boy! You're throwing it all away!"

"I can't help what happened."

"Bullshit!" The man Cody identified by his voice as Tony Roth was mad. "You didn't have to be over there throwing those dice. You've lost everything you made in the last two years and you've almost driven me into bankruptcy. If word of your gambling gets out, it'll ruin you."

"It won't."

"You're always so sure of yourself, and that's the reason I'm in this mess, because you aren't as smart as you think you are. Your attitude is the reason I got tangled up with those people overseas in the first place."

"Nobody told you to start moving drugs."

"You've made me a part of this with that damned white powder and coming to get you at that club. You killed that man while you were there. Choked him to death because he was on a hot streak and you lost, and then the others so they couldn't talk. Son, you've ruined everything."

———

Cody leaned into Anna. "Can you understand them? My ears ring all the time from too many gunshots, and I can't make out what they're saying."

"One of them in there is Roth, but I don't recognize that other voice. They're mad, but I can't understand them."

"This damn door's too thick."

Cody leaned closer, hoping to get a handle on the players before he went inside.

———

Standing around in the snow made Ned mad. "I need to be in there. It was my nephew who was killed. I should be picking him up."

John flexed his wounded arm. "Mr. Ned. He's the sheriff. I can't speak against him."

"Well, I'm going inside."

"I'll wait here, then, like I was told."

———

"I started with those damned drugs to pay off your debts, boy. I didn't spend all these years trying to get you into the senate to throw it all away. Don't you realize what you can do for us if you get elected?"

"I'm doing just fine." Ray shrugged his shoulders, settling the coat. "I just saw the mayor and he thinks I'll be a shoo-in."

"The mayor in a hayseed town like this doesn't know a damn thing about real politics. We're in the middle of a swarm and need to get out of it. You listen to me, boy. You know what I have in there on those slabs?"

Ray smirked. "Like I said. I was just with the mayor. Bodies, and the place burned down this morning. Nearly everyone who was there is dead. We're almost free and clear." The coroner's son smiled as he took off his hat and ran fingers through a thick mop of blond hair.

———

Cody couldn't stand it any longer. "Let's go."

He turned the knob and stepped inside the office. A red-faced Tony Roth sat behind his wooden desk. Standing before him with his back to the door, a young man with a hat in one hand turned to see who'd come inside. The man took a step backward against the desk. Anna stopped beside an oak file cabinet as Cody hooked his thumbs into the gun belt around his waist. "Tony, I need you to come with me."

Lightning flashed through the coroner's eyes. "Why?"

"We have some questions for you."

"Ask them here."

Anna nodded toward Ray. "We'd rather you go where we can talk in private."

Tony Roth pursed his mouth, as if studying on the request. "No. He can hear anything you or I have to say."

"Everything all right, Dad?" Ray Roth settled the Bailey on his head and slid one hand into his coat pocket.

Tony Roth picked up his pipe. "I don't know. Sheriff, say what you have to say."

"Fine, then." Cody took a pair of handcuffs from the holder on his belt. "Stand up, Mr. Roth. We're taking you in for questioning in the murders of several individuals."

"Murders? Of who?"

"Silas Cornsilk, and Vaughn Cunningham, and others by the name of Rainwater, Kettle, Jones, Christie, and Walls."

The pipe was halfway to Roth's mouth when Cody made the

charges. It paused, then he clamped the stem between his teeth. "You're wrong. *I* haven't killed anyone."

Cody's face was expressionless. "I don't want to have to tell you again. Stand up."

The coroner's eyes went to his son and narrowed. A tiny shake of his head caused Deputy Anna Sloan to straighten in alarm. Her hand went to the butt of her pistol at the same time a pistol came out of Ray Roth's coat pocket.

His daddy shouted. "No!"

———

With no time to draw her own weapon, Anna swept her left hand out, knocking the young man's pistol aside. The .38 revolver went off with a sharp report, the slug ricocheting off the tile floor and burying itself in the file cabinet behind her.

Cody swung to face the threat as Anna slammed her shoulder into Ray Roth. He grabbed for Ray's left arm, jerking him off balance. Ray's revolver fired again at the same time Anna drove her forearm under his chin, forcing his head back. The man's bulky coat defied their efforts to get a solid hold on his arm. Twisting away like a coon within its skin, Ray squirmed out of their grip at the same time his .38 went off a third time. The round took his father in the chest.

Jerking upright and grabbing at the tiny hole in his shirt, Tony Roth collapsed where he stood, disappearing behind the desk. They lost their grip on his coat as Ray threw himself backward, falling through the side door leading into the exam room. He fired again and slammed the door shut with his foot.

Three rounds punched through the wood as Roth squirmed past the autopsy table. Gaining his feet, he rushed past two gurneys and lunged for the side door where he'd parked his car.

———

Anna gained her feet, cursing. "You hit?"

Cody shook his head and rushed around the desk to find the coroner laying in a pool of blood. Voices in the hallway turned him around. Big John Washington's deep voice reached their ears ringing from the gunshots. "Cody! It's me. Don't shoot!"

The office door slammed open and Washington bulled through, followed by Ned. Both held pistols that swept the room.

Her own revolver aimed at the examination room door, Anna pointed with her head. "He went through there."

Surprised, Ned kept an eye on the closed door as Big John disappeared back outside to circle around. "Tony do the shooting?"

"No, his son, Ray."

"What'n hell?"

"We don't have no idea. He shot his daddy, too."

"On purpose?"

"No. It was while we were trying to get hold of him." Ned reached for the doorknob, but Cody held out a hand. "Ned, Anna. Hold here." He rushed outside to assist John.

Ned covered the bullet-pocked door to the autopsy room and knelt beside Roth. He put his palm over the wound. "Hang on. We'll get an ambulance here in a minute."

Roth partially opened his eyes. "Don't shoot my boy."

"He shot *you*."

"It was an accident." Roth coughed bloody foam. "He's sick. He don't have any control of himself."

"Sick? What with?"

"Gambling. He's addicted to gambling and cocaine."

"That stuff from the casket."

Roth's eyes closed. "Don't hurt my boy. It was his sickness that made him do those things."

"What things?"

"Killed all those men."

Ned went cold. "What men?"

"From the dice game...to keep them quiet about his gambling. He didn't mean to kill your nephew...just wanted the money back..." Bloody foam ran from Roth's mouth and chest as he took one last breath and died.

Chapter Seventy

Neal Box lived in a sixty-year-old farmhouse at the end of a hundred-and-fifty-year-old wagon road cut through the hardwoods at the far edge of Center Springs. The approach through the trees was shady in the summertime and thick with understory brush. In the winter, bare limbs intertwined against the dark gray skies while down below, thorny vines tangled into almost impenetrable thickets.

The heavily wooded dirt road cut by generations of wagons through chest-high banks crossed a narrow plank bridge over a deep draw drifted with snow before emerging into a wide-open space that backed up to Panther Creek. Under the drift, a stream of water chuckled its way toward the Red River. It was isolated and peaceful most of the time.

Stomping his cold feet in the snow, Ned Parker was far from peaceful. The .30-caliber Remington Model 8 rifle cradled in his arms spoke of coming violence, as did the 30.06 BAR hanging in the crook of Tom Bell's arm. On the opposite side of the ice-and-snow-covered road, Deputies John Washington and Anna Sloan waited behind a leafless tangle of blackberry vines.

From their positions of cover, they watched the narrow

road leading to Neal Box's house. They'd been there since before dawn, waiting under the heavy gray skies on Ray Roth, who they figured was on his way to finish his string of witness eliminations.

"I'm about froze to death." Ned shifted his weight, eyes on the road tracked with only two sets of tires.

"He'll be here." Tom Bell leaned against the wide trunk of an enormous red oak.

"You said that half an hour ago."

"And I'll say it again half an hour from now. Cody knows what he's doing."

"I know that, but Roth got away from them at the coroner's office. He just walked out the back door and disappeared." Ned glanced eight feet down from his high point and to his left, where Cody was standing behind a yaupon bush with a pump shotgun. "I don't intend to let him get away again."

"I reckon this is the only way, if he shows."

"He will." Ned breathed deep to settle his nerves. "This is the last murder to tie up his loose ends. In his mind, it'll all be over and he can get on about his business."

Cody's APB on Ray Roth had produced zero results. The sheriff's department, highway patrol, and Chisum's police force had all come up empty in their search for the killer. Together, the lawmen came up with one last idea, to wait for Roth to come after the last person who could testify against him for the murder of those in the Starlite's dice game.

They stopped Neal and Clarice Box at the hotel, only minutes before they left for Dallas. Ned and Cody talked them to coming back to their house, guaranteeing their safety. Once they agreed, word got out that the Boxes were back home.

Ned chewed the inside of his lip. "Killing Neal won't do him any good. This is just a killing to make himself feel better."

"People delude themselves into thinking what they're doing is right. He'll be along directly," Tom Bell said. "Years ago I was after someone else who thought the same way."

"When was that?"

"Back in '34, when I joined up with Frank Hamer to chase down those mad dogs Barrow and Parker."

Ned's eyes widened in surprise. "You were with him on that? You helped chase down Bonnie and Clyde."

"Yep, it was a helluva lot warmer that morning, but we stopped 'em, all right."

"I never saw your name on anything about them or that day."

"No, you didn't." Tiny flakes drifted down to land on Tom Bell's black hat.

Feeling the hair rise on the back of his neck, Ned glanced over his shoulder to see the Boxes's house. A crow called from high overhead. "Well, some folks just need killin.'"

Despite their friendship, Tom Bell was still a mystery, and Ned realized he knew very little about the old Ranger. Smoke rose from the chimney and Neal Box stepped outside to look up his drive. Ned shook his head. "He needs to get his ass back inside."

"He's been cooped up in there too long. I'd be getting stir-crazy myself."

"They were gonna go hide out in Dallas, but Cody talked him into staying. Told him to spread the word that he was closing the store until this storm passed. I swear, I never heard of using a man as bait." Ned grunted. "Cody has some funny ideas. He figures Roth can't turn down the chance to finish cleaning up his mess. You think Roth'll give himself up, if he takes a notion to come up here this morning?"

"He'd better. Cody'll stop him down there. This is a natural enfilade."

Ned frowned. "What does that mean?"

"It's a perfect trap."

They stopped at the sound of a car engine approaching through the woods. Ned saw John and Anna crouch as Cody faded behind an oak. An old Dodge pickup crept forward at walking speed.

"Is that him?" Ned squinted. "Your eyes are better than mine."

Tom Bell waited several seconds, peering through the gray light. "I see one person in there. Male, behind the wheel."

"That don't mean nothin.'"

"Cody'll recognize him. Besides, who else would be coming down here this time of the morning in such weather?"

"If it ain't, that feller'll have to change pants when he sees all of us."

Chapter Seventy-One

Snowflakes drifted down as Sheriff Cody Parker stiffened at the sound of an approaching vehicle. He slipped behind an oak that was old a hundred years earlier. Peering around the side, he saw a faded truck coming in his direction. It looked to be a 1959 Dodge Sweptside. Cody knew that yellow-and-white pickup. There was only one like it in the county as far as he knew, and it was owned by a farmer south of Center Springs.

In the dim morning light, he couldn't tell for sure who was driving, but he was sure it wasn't the owner, who'd have no reason to be up on the Red River at that time of the day. From his cautious approach, Cody figured it was Roth in a stolen truck. He waited until the vehicle was twenty yards away, then stepped out into the open.

The pickup coasted to a stop, waiting.

Holding a Remington 12-gauge across his chest, Cody called out to the driver. "Kill the engine and get out!"

The engine idled and the shape behind the glass didn't shift an inch. The snow increased, falling through the bare limbs.

"I know it's you, Roth!" Cody adjusted his position to better see the driver's-side window. "I said get out!"

The shape moved as he cranked down the window. An elbow came out, along with half a face. It was Roth. The driver checked behind him and shifted gears. The back wheels spun in the snow as he hit the foot-feed.

"Roth!" Cody shouldered his shotgun. "Get out of the car now! I have laws on both side of you!"

Because he couldn't escape backward and was blocked by the steep banks, Roth changed tactics. He shifted again and this time hit the gas with a little less force. The truck jerked forward at the same time his arm emerged from the open window, holding a pistol.

He fired, the bullet hissing over Cody's shoulder. He shot again but missed.

Cody squeezed the trigger on the 12-gauge at the same time guns opened up from both sides of the road. The pickup caught traction as a hail of bullets punched holes in the sheet metal. The windshield and side windows shattered.

Cody stepped aside and his feet went out from under him. He slammed to the ground hard enough to knock his hat off as the truck passed with only inches to spare. Cody shucked another shell into the chamber and fired upward before throwing it aside. He struggled to reach the .45 in the holster under his coat.

Bullets punched through sheet metal and glass. Reports echoed through the bare limbs around them.

Roth fired at Cody one last time but missed when a line of 30.06 slugs raked his door. An eerie howl rose from Roth's throat as more bullets stitched through sheet metal from the high vantage opposite side of the road. Accelerating, the truck's light rear end skidded, slamming against one high bank before swinging back around.

The bare woods echoed with reports as the lawmen

continued to pour lead into the vehicle that passed Cody without stopping. Bullets plucked at Ray Roth's clothing. His hair flew from the impact of heavy slugs as the dead man slumped over the steering wheel.

Tires still spinning on the icy road, the Dodge drifted to the right. Only the left front tire met the plank bridge twenty yards away, and the pickup rolled off and nosed into the deep branch. The front end dropped off the steep edge and the truck flipped upside down, coming to rest at the bottom of the draw with the cab buried into the snow.

A trickle of icy water passing through the cab rose against the new dam, circling around Ray's slack face, before continuing downstream to ultimately flow into the Red River.

Chapter Seventy-Two

I met Grandpa and Mr. Tom Bell when they pulled up in the yard. Heavy snow fell, drawing a lace curtain around our old farmhouse. Pepper and Mark were there, and they followed me outside.

Mr. Tom got out and went to his truck parked beside the propane tank. He carried a big rifle in one hand and ruffed my hair with the other. Grandpa shut his door and shook his hand. Without a word, Mr. Tom got in his pickup and left.

Grandpa waved bye to the old Ranger and gave each one of us a big hug.

Pepper saw something in his face. "You all right, Grandpa?"

He nodded. "I am now that I've laid the bones." He went inside, leaving us standing in the snow.

Pepper took Mark's hand. "What'n hell did *that* mean?"

Mark shrugged at the same time a flash of light split the clouds overhead. I thought it was my Poisoned Gift again, but then saw the looks on Mark and Pepper's faces, and realized they'd seen it too. A low rumble reached us, and another flash fractured the dark clouds and falling snow.

It was lightning. I'd heard of thunder snow but had never

seen anything like it. We stood there for several minutes, waiting for it to happen again and it came. No one else saw that one but me.

It was a blue and yellow bolt that rose from the ground far to the east and plunged into the clouds, likely from the exact spot where the Starlite burned down. As it faded, another, softer glow of warm red rose from the creek bridge where R. B. had gone over, and I knew the thing was done for sure and understood what Grandpa meant when he said he was done laying the bones.

ACKNOWLEDGMENTS

My sincere appreciation goes to my publishers at Poisoned Pen Press, and now Sourcebooks, for their faith in this series. And as always, my exemplary agent, Anne Hawkins of John Hawkins Literary Agency, keeps me on the straight and narrow.

I appreciate the support of my good friend and bestselling *New York Times* bestselling author John Gilstrap, who has become family. Thanks also to my buddy Steve Knagg, who is also family and has been there for me since we met way back in 1981. To C. J. Box, Jeffery Deaver, Craig Johnson, and another writer/adopted brother from deep East Texas, Joe R. Lansdale, much obliged. Many other author friends have been supportive of my work and have offered friendship (and, on occasion, advice), and to them I say many thanks.

Without fail, the love of my life, Shana, is always by my side. Her editing skills clean up my work to levels I can never achieve on my own. A trained journalist, she has a skilled eye that catches the dozens of issues I overlook. Any mistakes after she is finished with the manuscript are my own. Without her, this novel would not be possible.

ABOUT THE AUTHOR

Shana Wortham

Spur Award–winning author Reavis Z. Wortham pens the Red River historical mystery series and the high-octane Sonny Hawke contemporary Western thrillers. The Texas Red River novels are set in rural Northeast Texas in the 1960s. In a Starred Review, *Kirkus Reviews* listed his first novel, *The Rock Hole*, as one of the "Top 12 Mysteries of 2011." *The Rock Hole* was reissued in 2020 by Poisoned Pen Press with new material added, including an introduction by Joe R. Lansdale.

Wortham has been a newspaper columnist and magazine writer since 1988, penning nearly two thousand columns and articles, and has been the humor editor for *Texas Fish & Game Magazine* for the past twenty-two years. He and his wife, Shana, live in Northeast Texas.

Check out his website at reaviszwortham.com.